KANA
the
STRAY

C.C. Luckey

First paperback edition December 2020

Front cover art by C.C. Luckey

ISBN 978-1-7341281-2-3 (paperback)
ISBN 978-1-7341281-3-0 (ebook)

Published by Patient Corgi

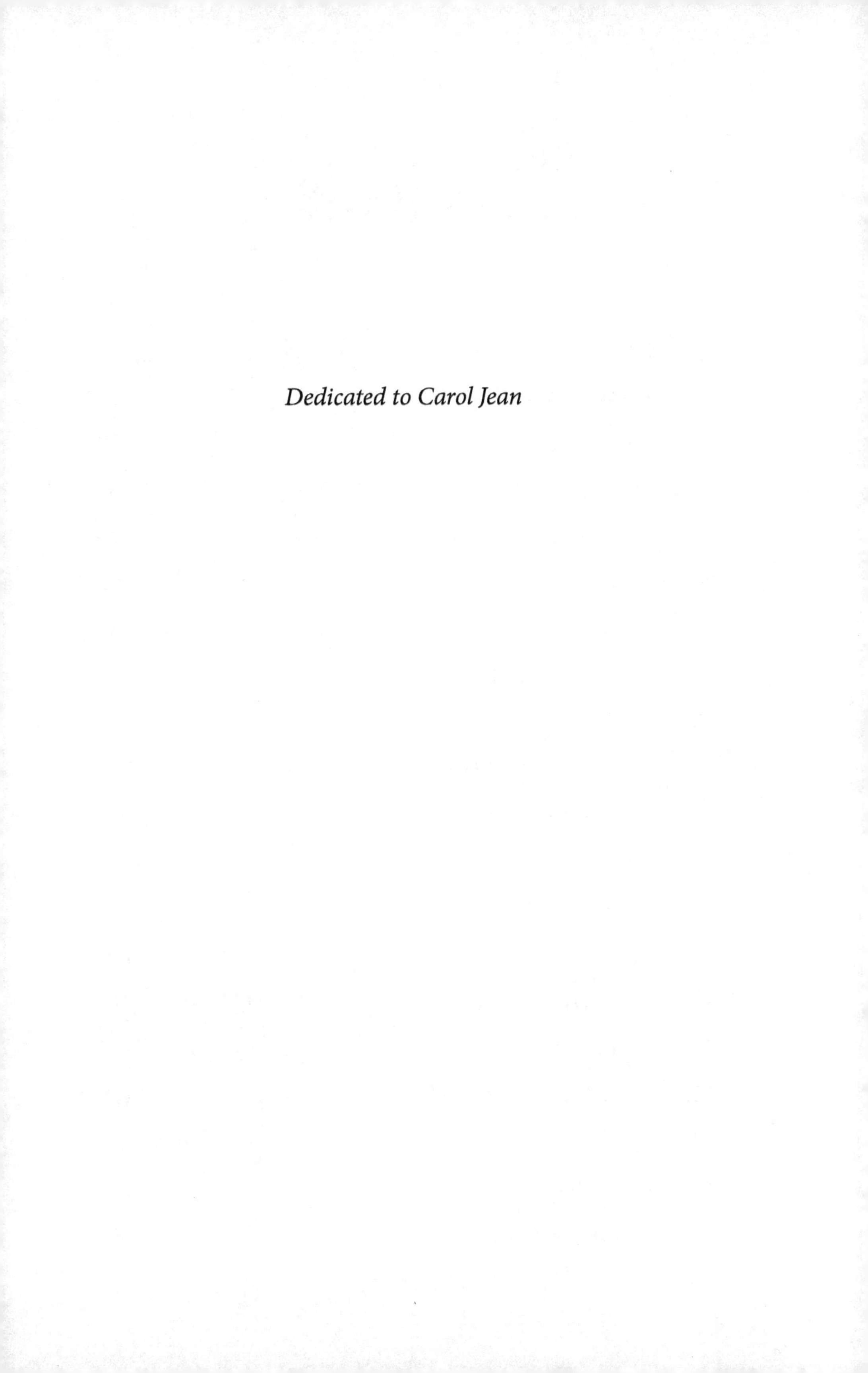

Dedicated to Carol Jean

Contents

1.

Under the 'Pass

Kana pulled her jacket up over her shoulders, wiped at her nose with a three-fingered glove, and shivered against a concrete wall as she watched the police interrogate Billy Banger.

Banger wasn't cooperating, and the cop's posture on the mud-slicked sidewalk showed her patience was waning. But Banger wouldn't talk, not if the questions were about anyone who lived under the 'pass. The cop pointed at a thin cut on Banger's forehead as her voice rose over the whistle of the autumn wind whipping through the concrete pillars until she was loud enough for Kana to catch a few words like "investigation" and "your real name."

Nah, he wouldn't state his old name. No way. Even his friends under the 'pass didn't have that info. The cop, weary with the cold, shrugged and trudged back toward her idling cruiser. Banger wasn't worth her time, and they both knew it. Burglary investigations were never solved anyway. They were only shuffled, shifted, and filed away.

Kana felt old. The streets had aged her, not time. And not drugs, like some other rough sleepers turned to. But no one living on the street stays young for long. She should have had a tent, but City Services had pulled up to the overpass in one of their white-paneled box trucks and torn it down last night, just minutes before the season's first dusting of snow settled on the bank beside the overpass. Men in dark blue uniforms tumbled from the truck like infantry as their foreman shouted something about "clearing the area." They didn't clear the whole 'pass though, not even close. Instead they half-heartedly knocked over one cardboard lean-to and confiscated a radio from another before zeroing in on Kana's tent, snapping the poles until it looked like a crumpled spider. Ignoring her protestations, they tossed it in the back of their truck without even an apology. They just handed her a card with a phone number and "Women's and Children's Shelter of Chicago" printed in bold, bail-bond font. She wondered which they thought she was; woman or child?

Banger, grumbling under his breath, marched off toward his tent in Southside. The show was over. Kana slid down the wall until her butt sat on her ankles, and wrapped her arms around her knees. Pegged next to her own empty campsite was a filthy blue tent which shuddered as the man inside grunted and rolled over, waking up from his evening nap. Jesse was his given name, but he had asked her to call him 8-Ball. He was an old dude with wrinkled skin and grey fluffy sideburns. They'd met last week—he had moved in on the same day she had. He'd arrived pushing a grocery cart loaded heavy with an assortment of broken chairs, tattered clothing, and plastic boxes. As she'd expected, Kana found him sullen and defensive but not dangerous. Still, she knew to keep her distance, even if he seemed like one of the good guys. Theft was a constant problem under the 'pass, and anything you didn't sleep on top of could be gone by morning. Best to keep people at an arm's length.

8-Ball poked his head out of his tent flap. "You're still here? It's getting pretty late in the season, little snowbird. I thought you were gonna head west last night. What you still doing here under the 'pass?"

"They took my tent," Kana said.

"All right, but if you're going west for the winter you won't need it anyhow. Didn't your mama give you a train ticket to Cali? Scooter told me."

"Yeah, she did."

"So?"

"Don't need her help." Kana turned her head aside, watching tiny white flakes of snow powder the branches of the trees on the embankment. "Don't need anyone's help. Mind your own business and go back to sleep, *Jesse*."

8-Ball laughed. "You best leave while you can, girl. Chicago winters get mighty cold."

"I know that. I've lived here my whole life."

"Sure, but have you lived outdoors your whole life? Don't look like it to me. You might think you're ready, but-"

"I lived in Uptown last winter."

"Uptown's gone, honey." 8-Ball's voice softened. A frown creased his forehead, making his lower eyelids droop like an old dog's. Fine blood vessels turned the whites of his eyes hazy-pink, shot through with tiny red lines, dry in the cold wind. "Uptown's been destroyed, and it's never coming back. Everyone's moved on."

"I know."

"I know you know. So go west, like your mama said. Get warm while you can, and come back next year if you have to."

"No. This is my home. I don't have to go anywhere."

8-Ball snorted, then flapped his hand at her. "Little idiot! All right, freeze to death out there if that's what you want. Can't save stupid." He continued to mutter to himself as he zipped his tent flap shut. "*Kids*. Hah! Don't know what they have, when they have it. Don't care, neither..." The tent leaned and rocked as he clanged a soup pot on a camping stove and lit a match.

"I'm not a kid," Kana called out, but he didn't respond.

The train ticket was still in her pocket, folded inside a Post-It Note with a California address written on it. The address was for a rehab clinic. Kana had told her mother she didn't take hard drugs, but the old witch refused to believe her; Mother thought all homeless people took drugs. Why would they be homeless, otherwise? And she reasoned that even if Kana was clean, the center might be a nice place for a vacation. Like a resort.

Kana had walked all the way to the train station, but at the last minute she'd balked. Taking advantage of her mother's charity felt like giving up. Using the ticket would be a betrayal of herself, brushing aside decades of traumatic abuse. Mother needed to know she had hurt her daughter, and that she was not forgiven. Not now, not ever.

Kana had struggled so much to stay alive and independent over the last year, but if she left now, it would be like none of it had ever happened. What was it all for if she turned tail and ran from the winter cold? She wished she hadn't even taken the ticket from her mother's hand, but the gift had surprised her, and she had accepted it without thinking. Kana shouldn't even have agreed to meet with her in the first place. Too late now.

It would be harder this year, though. Uptown had protected her, given her a new home, a place to live in peace for a while. The people she'd camped near weren't friends, exactly, but they had formed a fairly civilized community. And they never got moved along by City Services, or reprimanded for simply trying to exist. She'd even found a lover there for a while, until he moved along without her. Life had felt almost normal—but then the police routed them one afternoon without warning. The cops came armed with batons, driving trucks with metal grates attached to the grilles. The entire community had been herded like cattle. No one was given any time to grab their belongings, or even drag their tents out behind them as they ran.

After the community had been cleared, the city built a dog park in their place; a lush greenway hidden behind spiked fences and shrubbery. Just like that, Uptown was gone, as if it had never been.

Kana's mother had sent her a voice message after that, the first one in months. She had heard about the cleansing of Uptown, she said, expressing careful sympathy couched in a tone of *"perhaps it's all for the best, anyway."* She said she needed to talk. It was urgent, please call right away. When Kana returned her call, she begged Kana to come home. It would be like she'd never run off. Her old room was the same as she left it. Mother had kept it ready for her return. When Kana refused, the woman predictably resorted to vitriol. Kana was a spoiled little girl, she was playing games with her mother's heart, she was acting like a child. Kana hung up.

A strong gust of wind whipped under the overpass, rattling the tents huddled together in the dirt. Tiny slips of air found the gaps in her jacket and touched her skin, making goosebumps pop up like football fans doing the wave at Soldier Field. Without a tent, she was in danger. The prospect of building a shelter before dark seemed unlikely. The 'pass was a popular place, and most loose objects in the vicinity had already been claimed. She might be able to borrow a few pieces of cardboard from someone tomorrow, but the rough sleepers had grown stingy since the abrupt closing of Uptown, and she didn't have anything to trade anyway.

"Jesse," she said to the tent. "8-Ball. You awake? I need a cardboard box or something. Please. Anything."

The last sliver of the setting sun disappeared behind a building as the air chilled and hardened until the cold permeated her boots. Her small toe, the one without a nail on it, already felt numb.

Would it be worth the risk to steal a tarp from the heap near the big orange tent? The site was inhabited by a cruel shrew of a woman who hoarded everything she found. She even picked the stones from the smooth soil surrounding her doormat, gathering them in little piles like gold doubloons. If the woman noticed a whole tarp missing, she would raise hell.

Kana steeled her nerves to try.

"Hey."

A blonde woman leaned around the edge of the wall. She gripped it with a gloved hand and swung playfully in a transparent attempt to appear carefree, but Kana could tell she had something to say. Her fine hair was clean and airy, floating in wisps around a polished smile as white as the flecks of snow sticking to her red hood. The oversized jacket she wore was one of the most luxurious Kana had ever seen; it was lined with a gorgeous fluff of genuine fur that peeked out at the collar and cuffs.

The woman smiled. "I remember you. You're still here? City Services said they visited last night, to help some of you people out. They didn't give you a card?"

"Yeah, they did," Kana said.

"So why didn't you go?" The woman moved closer to Kana, slipping through a pile of damp trash. She nearly fell, but caught herself on the cement wall before she could tumble into the frozen mud and spoil her jacket.

"Don't know. Those places…" Kana shook her head.

"What about them?"

"They're full of bitches. I don't fit in there."

"No, no! Our girls would absolutely *adore* you! And we can

help you, I promise. I work there. Well, actually, I own the whole center. And we'd love to welcome you. We have food and blankets, and I can even help you find a job."

"Got a job already."

"Really? I didn't know that. Where is it?"

Kana shrugged. She pulled a tattered brochure from her pocket.

The woman read the paper. "It says 'Medical Research.' You're volunteering at a medical research lab? Do you really think that's a good idea?"

"None of your business. They give me a pill to take, give me some money, and that's it. So I don't need your help, okay? You can leave now."

"Kana, that's not a real job. That's not even-"

"How do you know my name?"

The woman winced, and threw her head back in frustration. She had made a mistake. "Look, I…"

"Did my mother send you?"

"Kana, she only wants to help."

"Not interested. Leave. Now."

"But-"

"Go!"

"Fine. But I'll be back tomorrow, if you're still here." The woman wobbled back through the slimy trash toward a van parked with its hazard lights flashing. "I hope we see you at the shelter tonight. We'd love to have you. So just think about it, okay?"

Kana stood expressionless as the van pulled away from the curb. When the sound of the engine had faded, she crept toward 8-Ball's tent. It was quiet inside; the old man had gone to bed for the night.

She gently lifted the edge of the tent until it was high enough to slip underneath. Cocooned between the plastic and the earth, she shivered in the dirt until she fell asleep.

2.

Sphere

As the morning sun peeked through the row of buildings across the street from the 'pass, Kana stood on the sidewalk and wiggled her toes inside her boots, trying to get the blood flowing. With her lips pursed she exhaled, watching her foggy breath waft away on the chill breeze. She was awake, but her pinky toe was still asleep. She should have taken off her boot and looked at it, but she was scared. What if it had turned blue? And even worse—what if it never woke up again?

In her left hand she gripped the brochure for the medical research lab. She had been there once before. Last week the soup kitchen on 32nd had been closed. A notice on the door said something about a rat infestation. She hadn't eaten in more than a day and was desperate when she found the brochure stuck to a streetlight pole. The place was a short walk from the 'pass, and she had only been in the lab for about an hour before she walked out with a twenty-dollar bill stapled to a receipt that bore her personal information, a 24-digit patient number, and the name of a pill she couldn't pronounce. If she went back again, the receptionist told her, she'd start racking up loyalty points that could result in an increase in pay.

Kana brought her other hand up to her nose and squinted at the business card given to her by City Services. It had become soggy, and the print was starting to fade. "Women's and Children's Shelter of Chicago," she read. "WCSC: Making Lives Whole Again."

The shelter was a three-mile walk. The medical lab was only one.

"Sorry, lady," Kana said, letting the business card flutter away in the wind. It smacked into a sodden tree for a moment as if holding on for its life before slipping off and tumbling into the gutter.

By the time Kana turned the corner at Ashland Avenue, her stomach was growling. She had eighty cents in her pocket, not quite enough for any real food. There was a truck on Polk that sold tacos for a dollar. Maybe she'd buy twenty of them after she was done at the lab, and give a few to 8-Ball. As she trudged down the street the passing cars splattered her legs with small chunks of brown ice, but she didn't notice. The only thing that really mattered was the prospect of a hot meal—and a friend to share it with.

The medical building was beautiful, in a way. The windows were like sheer panes of crystal, always sparkling, even in midwinter when the city streets were piled with dirty slush. Inside, everything was white. The counters, the walls, and even the floors were immaculate.

After you left the lobby, the first office on the left was the generically-named "Research Resource Lab." In the waiting room, Kana sat on a metal chair with soft vinyl padding and wondered what it would be like to come to work every day in a place so meticulously kept. It was stark and sterile, but there was a simplicity to it that she found soothing. None of the chaos of the streets in here. None of the mud or the trash or the blood.

"For Kobayashi," the receptionist called through a sliding window set into the low wall which separated the office from the lobby.

"Here," Kana replied, startled. She had expected a longer wait. As she rose from her chair, the seat of her pants left behind crusty streaks of dried mud. Wet sand and small pebbles grated under her boots on the white floor. All eyes turned toward her, judging her grimy clothes and discolored hair and the loud jewelry hanging off her tiny frame. At the sliding window, a frumpy woman peered at her over a pair of rectangular glasses. A badge pinned under the lapel of her white coat read "Mrs. Marcy German, Receptionist."

"Kobayashi?" she asked.

"Yes."

"You're…" The woman frowned at a clipboard. "Twenty-seven? Really? You don't look that old."

"And you don't look German," Kana snapped.

The woman glared at her, snorted, and tossed the clipboard onto the window sill. Kana caught it before it could clatter to the floor.

"Sit down. Fill this out, if you know how to write. Do you know how to write?"

"Yes."

"If you don't know the answer to a question, don't try to answer it. Just leave it blank. Don't come back to my window until you've answered all the questions you can. Don't talk to anyone else. Don't leave before the form has been completed."

"I don't have a pen," Kana said.

Mrs. German pointed, exasperated, at a cup full of blue ballpoints. "Or do you prefer purple ink?" she sneered.

Kana took a pen and returned to her dusty chair. She wondered if it mattered how honest she was with the information she gave. Her pen lingered over "Race" for a moment, hovering between "White" and "Asian" before she settled on *Decline To State*. Her age and weight had already been filled out. For "Allergies" she wrote "*None*." Most of the rest she left blank. If they wanted to know her any better than that, they'd have to pay her more.

"For Russell."

A balding man dressed in a red plaid jacket buttoned tight over his protruding belly stood and nodded. He was escorted through a swinging door by a male nurse in a lab coat and sharp white slacks. Before the door swung shut, the nurse glanced around the waiting room, counting heads. His eyes lingered on Kana for a moment. She glared back.

"Kobayashi?" the nurse said. "You can come too."

As Kana stood, the backs of her knees pushed against the chair, making it squeal on the linoleum. The heavy clump of her boots accompanied her through the room and past the nurse, who stopped her with a plastic tray in his hand.

"Leave your phone, your keys, anything else in your pockets."

Kana dropped her cell phone and eighty cents into the tray. "I don't have any keys."

"First room on the right. Have a seat on the table, and I'll be in soon."

The cool sterility of the examination room was an even greater shock than the waiting room had been. The black vinyl cushions on the examination table were wrapped in a layer of paper which crinkled as she sat on it. It was hard to believe only an hour ago she was shivering in the mud under the 'pass. But as nice as this place was, it had no heart. Excessively clean places weren't really much better than slums, she decided; just uncomfortable in a different way.

The nurse hadn't quite closed the door, so Kana clicked it shut. Privacy in a quiet room was something she did not often get the opportunity to enjoy. Sitting again—this time in the doctor's rolling chair instead of on the crinkly-paper table—she unlaced her boot. Might as well take a look at that toe. When she pulled off her sock, she was relieved to see the skin color looked mostly normal. The tip had turned a little purple, but there was yellow too, and that meant it would probably heal just fine.

The counters in the room were topped with little glass jars full of cotton swabs, cotton balls, rubber gloves, and hard candies. When she tried the drawers they were locked. Must be where all the fun stuff was. She fished a hard candy from the jar; green. Gross. After trading it for a red one, she sat in the chair and rolled it across the room, then back again. So boring.

From down the hall, she heard a short scream. It wasn't shrill like a woman's scream, but short and shocked like a man's. Someone must be afraid of getting their shot. Hopefully, they'd give her a pill again. She didn't like shots either.

There was another shout, this one in the hallway right outside. She rolled over to the door and pressed down on the handle, but it didn't move. It was locked from the outside.

"Hey!" she shouted. "*Hey!* I didn't consent to this! Let me out! You can't lock me up!" She kicked the door with her steel-toed boot, leaving a wide streak of black rubber.

No one outside took notice. There was the sound of running feet in the hall, and a woman screamed. The lights in the examination room dimmed as a voice alarm sounded: "*Stage 4 emergency. Stage 4 emergency. Evacuate structure immediately. Critical failure in all systems.*"

Kana beat the door with her fists in a blind panic. She felt tears squeezing from the corners of her eyes, and it infuriated her. She hated crying. Taking her rage and fear out on the door, she hit harder, punching until it was streaked with blood from her busted knuckles. The repeating robotic alarm persisted, but the screams outside ceased. The abrupt absence of people was ominous.

Had she been forgotten?

As she leaned on the door handle again, the entire room filled with white light. It was brighter than anything she had ever seen, compounding the glaring effect of the stark walls and shining metal fixtures. She fell to her knees on the floor and hid her face in her hands but the flash penetrated through her eyelids, sending a searing clap of pain through her head. Snaps of electricity like firecrackers penetrated the walls, buzzing so loud her eardrums flexed and ballooned, threatening to pop. When she screamed the sound of her voice was lost in the storm, whisked away under rolling waves of roaring thunder.

Then it was over.

She looked up, blinking hard, trying to squeeze the pain out from behind her eyes. The counter with the jars was unchanged, but a new kind of light now reflected in the glass. The fluorescent ceiling lamps were gone; instead, the room was radiant with bright, natural sunlight. Overhead, an open blue sky was framed by a ring of green-leaf canopies that rustled in a warm breeze. A single leaf broke away from the branches and fluttered down to land in the center of the crisp white pillow at the head of the examination table. Its healthy, vibrant color laid in sharp contrast to the starchy cloth.

The examination table had been sheared cleanly in half, a curving cut made with laser-fine precision. The door to the hall was missing, too. One entire side of the room ended in a sharp, arcing slice, like the inside of an enormous sphere that curved up from the floor to the ceiling. Half of the room was still intact; the rest of the room was gone. Where the linoleum ended, it met neatly with mossy forest floor—a mix of peat and mud from which a roly-poly pill bug tumbled, bringing with it a tiny shower of sand that speckled the white plastic tiles. It unrolled, stuck its legs out, and toddled back toward the dirt.

Kana blinked, but the scene did not change. She dug her fingernails into her left arm and bit her knuckles, but the pain did not bring her out of the dream. As she watched the tooth marks fade from her finger she realized she was really here, wherever here was. It certainly wasn't Chicago. It wasn't even winter.

The forest could have been a hallucination brought on by experimental pills from the lab, but she didn't remember taking anything. First she was in the waiting room, then she was locked in the examination room. Then the shouting started.

A wild, exotic cry rang out through the forest. She whipped her head around looking for the source until she caught sight of a yellow bird with a piercing, black eye, staring down at her from a high branch. It watched her, and she watched back.

The bird seemed real enough, until it spoke.

"Primate," the bird said.

Now Kana knew she was dreaming. She breathed deep, begging herself to wake up. Bringing her hand up to her cheek, she first tapped her face lightly, then struck it hard enough to leave a hot handprint.

The bird persisted. "Primate?"

"Leave me alone!" Kana screamed, either at the bird or at the dream, or at whoever was listening in the real world she could no longer see. Shaking her head, she sat down and hugged her knees, pressing her back against the remaining half of the examination table. Its normalcy, and the feeling of a metal drawer handle pressing uncomfortably on her spine, allowed her to believe nothing had really happened. It was just experimental drugs, probably, or a bad stress-dream. She squeezed her eyes shut and shoved her fingers in her ears.

For a long time, she sat still. She concentrated on reality: the cold examination room, the woman who had visited her last night, her conversations with 8-Ball, her mother. Normal things.

Real things. But in the end, it didn't make any difference. The lush scent of the forest was relentless, filling her nostrils, distracting her from her thoughts. Thunder cracked in the distance, and wind blew through the trees carrying the scent of petrichor. When she finally opened her eyes, it with was with resignation.

Whatever had happened, it couldn't be imagined away.

Her heart pounded as she stood and peered out from the chunk of modern office-building. For the first time, she looked closely at the trees. They were pretty, healthy, and in full summer bloom. They seemed normal enough. To her enormous relief, the bird appeared to have flown away. A fat black fly zoomed through the examination room, buzzed around her head, and left through the gaping hole where the ceiling had been.

Kana took a step forward, and felt the dirt the pill bug had tracked in grind under her boot. Real, undeniable dirt.

Another step took her a few inches into the forest. She turned and looked back into the room, half expecting it to disappear the moment she lost contact with it—but it remained unchanged.

On trembling legs she took another step away from the room, and turned to peek around the edges of the abbreviated walls.

There was more building past the examination room. It looked like a half-dome of the structure had been cut out—but no, it was more than that; a sphere, partially lodged in the earth. It appeared to have been carved out from the medical lab like a scoop of ice cream, about thirty feet in diameter. Another examination room that shared its rear wall with her own was nearly intact. A doctor's office full of papers had lost only a single corner, creating a triangular window to the inside. At first it appeared that no other people had been caught up in the strange event, but then she noticed a section from a higher story which had been sheared, along with the bottom half of a nurse. The legs and pelvis were severed as neatly as the examination table had been. Blood that must have gushed out with the initial laceration was now thickening and slowing, forming a gelatinous pool where it trickled into the doctor's office below.

Kana turned away quickly. She knew she should call out, should try to find other survivors. Maybe someone else was alive and stuck in the middle of the sphere, someone who needed help. But she couldn't do it; she could barely take care of herself. What if they needed medical attention? She was no nurse. She was no one. Just a street rat.

So she froze, standing on a thick mat of damp green moss, unable to make a decision about what to do next. The forest wasn't a hallucination—or if it was, it wasn't one she could break free of on her own. The round chunk of medical building was no place to shelter, but she didn't know anything about how to survive in a forest. Her own indecisiveness frustrated and frightened her. On the streets she had adapted to a difficult way of life by becoming confident and savvy, and had come to rely on her intuition. But this was different. Unable to move, she was trapped between a broken chunk of the familiar and a vast unknown.

"Excuse me," someone said.

Before Kana could turn to see who had spoken, her imagination raced through a rush of different possibilities; a nurse bringing her antitoxin for an accidental dosage of hallucinogenic medication, an injured and bloodied patient who needed help, or maybe a forest-dweller who wanted to know who had parked a medical lab in their front yard. But as far as she could tell when she saw the speaker, they were none of those things.

A figured enrobed in a massive grey cloak stood at the edge of the clearing. Its arms hung loosely at its sides, and its head was concealed by a dark, draping hood. Nothing of the person inside was visible except the folds of its clothing, as if it were made entirely of fabric.

"Do you need assistance?" it asked.

"I, uh, guess so," Kana stammered. "Who are you?"

"My name is Struthio. I am an ambassador of Falcoformia, sent by the Paragon to greet you. Welcome to our territories. May I be of assistance?"

"What kind of assistance? I mean…" Kana glanced back at the examination room. "Do you know how this happened? Where am I?"

"My apologies, but I am merely an ambassador. News of

your arrival has reached the ears of our esteemed Paragon, and her majesty is interested in meeting with you. Will you deign to follow me?"

"Why won't you show me your face?" Kana asked. "Why are you hiding?"

"It was thought that my appearance might prove disconcerting to you. If you believe you are prepared, I will remove my cloak."

"What the hell is that supposed to mean?"

"I will show you." As the figure raised its head its neck unfolded, continuing far past the normal range of movement for a human. When the hood fell back, a small pointed face at the top of an impossibly slender neck peered down at Kana from a height of eleven feet.

"You're a *bird?* Another…another talking bird…" Kana felt dizzy.

"I am Struthio. And yes, in common vernacular, I am a bird. Although the term is something of an insult among my kind."

Kana's legs buckled and she fell to her knees in the mud. She blinked hard as the damp from the cool earth penetrated the knees of her pants, making her tired bones ache.

"I knew it. I knew they gave me some bad drugs. I don't remember taking anything, but that's probably why they locked me up. This must be part of the test. They better pay me extra for this. A *lot* extra…"

The ostrich waited with an air of diplomatic patience. A single flip of its vestigial wings sloughed the cloak from its back, letting it tumble into a heap on the ground.

"Hello? Can anyone hear me?" Kana cried out. "I want to leave! Bring me a downer, or whatever it is you sick people do! I just want to wake up!"

There was no answer.

"Wake up, Kana. Wake up!" she said, pinching her arm. But nothing worked. No one shook her shoulder, handed her a pill, or gave her a shot.

She glared up at the ambassador. Now that it had shed its cloak, its entire body was visible. It was the closest she had ever

been to an ostrich. The bird's head was cocked at an inquisitive angle at the top of a ridiculous neck that stuck out from a plump body
covered in dull black feathers. Wings that were massive yet useless
for flight were tucked in neatly at its sides. Its thighs were bare and
pink, and disturbingly humanoid. The feet gave her pause; nails like
knives dug into the soft earth. This was a creature that appeared
goofy and unassuming, yet it was undeniably powerful in its own
right, and ready to hold its own in a fight; a perfect ambassador.

"I will not harm you," Struthio said.

"Maybe so and maybe not." If she was really here—and it did
seem that she really was—she had no food, no water, and precious
little shelter. Before long, the severed body parts lodged in the
building would begin to rot and stink. And what would she do
then?

She stood. "I'll come with you, but you walk in front. Like, *far*
in front. Don't get near me."

"That will be fine," Struthio said. "But please do not lose sight
of me. You are not entirely safe here."

The statement filled Kana with dread. Of course she wasn't
safe. She knew that. But to hear it out loud was something else. It
validated her fears, made everything feel more real. She followed
Struthio a little closer than she had planned to.

As he walked, his tail feathers flounced back and forth like a
burlesque dancer on a parade float. The sphere of medical building
dropped away behind them as they wound through the forest, and
once it was completely out of sight Kana became more apprecia-
tive of the bird's obvious power. He was now her only ally, for what
it was worth. Her hard-won survival skills—her practical street
smarts, knowledge of available government resources, and quick
wit—were of no use to her here. All she had now was the clothes
on her back, and a big ball of concrete and plastic that was rapidly
being left behind.

"The forest ends in approximately one kilometer, just before
the hills begin," Struthio called behind as he walked, turning his
head around nearly backwards without slowing his pace.

"That's like, about a mile, right?"

She had the distinct impression that her question had caused a sneer to flicker on the bird's face, although she could not have explained how she knew. Its beak was the same as that of any bird, hard and unmoving, but something about the eyes showed a certain disdain.

"Yes, in the common vernacular. A little less than a mile."

The forest ended at the edge of a field filled with waving golden grains. The ground here was dry, and covered with tiny slippery pods that had fallen from the grasses. Kana looked out for gopher holes, mindful of putting her heel in one, but the dirt was consistent and even. Other than Struthio and the bright yellow bird she had seen after her arrival, she had found no evidence of any animals living in this otherwise verdant land.

"You will be expected to treat the Paragon with respect," Struthio said, again craning his neck backwards to speak. "You will avert your eyes until given permission to view her gloriousness, and you will address her using only her complete and proper title, Paragon Exemplar Falca. Do you understand?"

"Sure. I guess. What does 'avert' mean, exactly?"

Struthio stopped in his tracks and turned to face her. His giant beak swung near her face, and she reflexively flinched. "You will stare down at your ungainly primate feet until she grants you permission to do otherwise. Do you understand?"

Kana nodded. Struthio lingered a moment, examining her from head to toes. His breath whistled from holes in the top of his beak which was almost close enough to touch her cheek. "It is a tremendous honor for you to meet our Paragon. Do not squander this opportunity. Do not offend."

"I'll try not to," Kana sputtered.

"We will soon approach the Great Castle. I will be leading you on a less populated route than the one which leads directly to the main entrance, but nevertheless you will still be stared at. You will be examined. Please be prepared for this and keep your eyes averted…starting *now*." Struthio resumed his march, moving more swiftly than he had before. Kana trotted to keep up.

They emerged from the golden field and turned onto a narrow trail that meandered through patches of stunted trees. The path was overgrown and rarely used, but they passed several larger trees that supported lumpy woven structures made from ropes crafted out of the golden grass. Despite the materials, they did not look primitive. The treehouses were intricate and beautiful, designed as much for beauty as practicality. Swags made of reed matting were draped between platforms which were dotted with planters bursting with bright flowers and ferns. Complicated ladder systems connected round-roofed huts in a gridded system of tightropes interspersed with elaborate gazebos. Glass windows of various shapes and sizes were laced into the weave with strategic symmetry.

"Amazing," Kana whispered.

"These humble villages house our lowest caste, the Passeri. They insist on remaining bound to the natural trees outside the Great Castle, despite having been repeatedly invited to live behind our protective walls. A primitive life, but suitable enough for those who desire freedom above civility," Struthio said with his cryptic sneer.

The path curved uphill, a change in terrain which Struthio managed better than Kana did. By the time she reached the top he was waiting for her, observing her gasping breaths with an air of aristocratic judgement.

"Observe our Great Castle."

A behemoth villa the size of a small mountain rose from the bottom of a deep valley. The hill on which Kana stood was hundreds of feet tall, yet the highest windows in the central castle were still above her line of sight. Stone turrets with steepled roofs jutted at regular intervals from the structure, topped by precariously perched rooms that could only have been reached either with long ladders or else via the open sky above. At the topmost levels, platforms like planks on pirate ships jutted into the clouds. Massive birds took turns landing and alighting from the openings. At the foot of the castle a river forked into a moat that ran around the perimeter and under a bridge adorned by huge statues of birds with wide-spread wings.

From behind Kana's back, the setting sun poured warm

orange light into the valley, illuminating the huge walls of the castle against a backdrop of grey thunderheads rolling in over a distant snow-capped mountain range.

"We will arrive before the rain does," Struthio said, turning his head toward the clouds. A cool mist was rolling in ahead of the storm. Droplets stuck to the fine feathers on Struthio's face, and chilled Kana's forehead. "That is good. We will descend now. And remember to keep your head down inside the castle walls. Many will not be pleased with your presence here. They will not harm you while you are my charge, but it will be in your best interest not to invite unnecessary attention."

Struthio resumed his march and Kana followed, stumbling down the hill toward the towering outer walls of the Falcoformia Great Castle.

3.

Kana Meets a Queen

usk fell on the Great Castle of the birds. The hill's black shadow crept up the towering castle walls, eating away at the evening's light as it grew. The booming thunderheads looming behind the castle chased the sun away as they closed in on the topmost turrets and odd runways sticking out from the roof peaks. Fat raindrops streaked and dampened Kana's hair before Struthio crossed through the first metal gate in the outer walls.

The largest eagle Kana had ever seen roosted on a sturdy perch adorned with crisp-creased flags and banners. On its head it wore a small leather cap similar to the blinders falconers put on their birds, but this one protected instead of inhibited the senses. It turned its head to one side and focused on Struthio with a beady eye.

"You've returned," it said. "And with a maggot in tow."

"At the queen's request. Do you recognize its species?" Struthio asked.

"No. But I am not familiar with all the depraved offspring of every Great Castle. Will you be at the Perch House tonight, Struthio? We will be celebrating a nesting. You should join us."

Struthio nodded toward Kana. "I have other duties to attend to first, but perhaps I will see you there later. Now, I must visit with the queen so she can inspect this new arrival."

"Hey, can I have a cloak?" Kana asked. "Like the one you were wearing when you found me. I don't want everyone staring at me in there. Especially if they're all birds."

"Birds!" the eagle squawked.

"Ignore her," Struthio said. "She is ignorant." Turning to Kana, he lowered his head to her level. "You will wear no cloak, no disguise. Every citizen has a right to view you. You are in their lands, and the truth will not be hidden from them."

"What about *my* rights?" Kana asked.

"We do not yet know what your rights are, as we do not know your species."

"I'm a human."

"That species is unknown to us. The status of your rights is therefore unknown. We will ask the queen," Struthio said. "Her word is the only word."

"Good luck," the eagle said. "And may the queen have mercy on you, ugly thing."

The road passed through a tidy courtyard, then widened and curved away from the outer walls. On each side, it was flanked by rustic shelters made of clay and wood. Like the treehouses outside the castle walls, these homes were beautiful, symmetrical, and intricately styled. The exterior walls were doorless and smooth, decorated with windows of multicolored glass framed with assorted pebbles pressed into the dried mud. Mosaics of colored river-rock adorned the connecting walls and pathways, creating muted rainbow arches and borders in every curve and corner. The roof of each house was topped with a unique assortment of bright plants, banners, and other markers to welcome home its flying denizens and usher them into hinged hatches set into the rooftops.

The overall effect was gorgeous but overwhelming. Kana looked down at the road passing under her feet to find a patchwork of timeworn fragments of smooth glass, worked together in a dizzying montage of color. She returned her eyes to the sky above, focusing on the clouds, and discovered a legion of flying birds vying for position in the air currents.

"Keep up," Struthio said. "Chin down."

The first citizen to take notice of Kana was an enormous peacock with a fanning tail ten feet wide. When he whipped his head aside to examine her, a fine chain attached to his beak swayed and bounced with the movement. A crest of blue feathers behind his forehead, already naturally brilliant, was additionally dusted with glitter. Polished jewels glued to the tops of his toes flashed as he strutted forth with affronted purpose, his beak parted just enough to reveal his pink tongue in an expression of distaste.

"Ambassador Struthio! What have you got there? Who is-"

"For the Paragon," Struthio interjected.

"For the Paragon," the peacock replied, apparently accepting the retort as answer enough to whatever question he had wanted to ask. Yet there was a twinkle of distrust in his eye.

Kana trotted behind Struthio, trying to stay close to his bouncing tail feathers—but the peacock followed as well. He trailed at a distance until Struthio turned a corner, then rushed forward and nipped at her elbow with his sharp beak, tearing away a tiny piece of skin.

Hearing Kana scream, Struthio doubled back and charged at the peacock, lunging with his long neck extended until he was close enough to tear an iridescent feather from the other bird's tail.

"I told you it is meant for the Paragon!" Struthio screeched, tossing the feather to the ground. He stamped his claw upon the feather, tearing it to shreds on the mosaic path.

The peacock, unfazed, showed his rear with contempt and walked away toward the gates. As he strutted he kept his head turned to the side, never taking his eye off Kana's bleeding elbow.

"Why did he do that?" Kana cried.

"To see how you bleed. What you taste like. What you are. Your species is unknown to us. He has a right to seek information—to a limit. He exceeded the limit. Stay close to me now, until we reach the castle."

As they neared the city center, the dwellings became ever more elaborate. Passages between the bulbous homes were trimmed with strips of precious metals and gemstones. Few birds walked the streets, but the sky overhead was a busy flurry of wings and wind as citizens arrived and departed from buildings in never-ending spirals. Kana understood why Struthio did not bother to conceal her presence; the ground-dwellers were flightless birds who seemed calmer and less aggressive than their skyward cousins. Their low homes at the street level were less flashy than those on the heights, perhaps representative of a lower caste. A family of penguins toddled past, hardly sparing her a glance. Kana saw another ostrich like Struthio strutting through a back alley, but its scrutiny of her became perfunctory as soon as it recognized her escort. A plump kiwi sat in a gold-gilded pot on a balcony and stared at her down its long, curving bill. When it spoke to her, it offered only a single word in a voice loaded with disdain: "*Hominid.*"

The rows of houses came to an abrupt end some distance before Struthio and Kana reached the center of the Great Castle. Before them, a long, sloping hill ended in a bank at the split river Kana had seen from the hilltop. In the wide open space between the residences and the river, any intruder would be visible from the guard towers overhead. A wide bridge paved with plates of cobalt and bronze spanned the river. Two pedestals flanking the bridge were topped with statues of birds with their wings and beaks open wide, a design clearly intended to welcome avian visitors and deter enemies of the Paragon.

"Try to stay on the path," Struthio said. "This place was not meant for mammals."

The road dissipated on the hillside, becoming indistinct and difficult to navigate. Kana rolled her ankle on a rock and fell to the ground gasping in pain, but Struthio did not slow to wait for her. He seemed anxious in the open field, walking faster than she could keep up. He arrived first at the bridge and quickly ducked behind it, lingering under an awning while he watched Kana slip toward him through the mud on the bank.

"This is the Bridge of Accipiter. It is very old, at least a thousand years. You are honored to cross it."

"Okay," Kana said.

She didn't feel honored. She felt cold, angry, and frightened. Her ankle ached and her elbow was still trickling blood. Worse still, her grip on the fading hope that this horrible place was a drug-induced hallucination was slipping. If she had been drugged at the medical lab, it would have worn off by now. Her strongest feeling wasn't of honor, but rather a sinking sensation in the pit of her stomach that told her she was stuck here, maybe for good. That the mud in her shoes, the bloody bite on her elbow, and the rain in her hair was all as real as it could be.

"Follow." Struthio climbed the gentle slope of the bridge, pushing with his powerful legs. Kana followed, dragging her boots along the tiles.

"Welcome to the Great Castle," Struthio said, approaching a blue gate set into a thick wall of stone.

"You called the city back there a castle, too. So I thought we were already at the castle."

"You are not incorrect. All Falcoformia domiciles are considered part of the castle villa. But before you is the Great Castle itself, home of our beloved Paragon Exemplar Falca. Now I must return to my other duties. The elite guards will escort you from here."

Two birds covered in shaggy hairlike feathers emerged from a guard's nook in the wall. They were not as tall as Struthio, but their stance and manner implied dangerous power and fighting readiness. Atop their heads jutted magnificent crests, and hanging from their necks were soft folds of bright blue and red skin. Their steps were slow and precise on feet strapped with shining metal claws like curved daggers.

"This is General Cass. She will take you to the Paragon's court. Her daughter, Wara, will also accompany you. I recommend that you do not provoke them."

General Cass moved close to Kana and ran her beak through her hair, parting it, smelling her skin. Kana endured the examination, wishing Struthio would not pass her off to these two but knowing better than to implore him to stay.

When General Cass spoke, her voice reverberated through her powerful torso. "Wara, bring the pinion."

The younger bird brought a rope with a loop at each end.

"Put your wings—I mean, your arms—behind your back, creature," General Cass said.

"No. Why should I?"

The younger bird dropped the rope to the floor and struck the nape of Kana's neck with its beak faster than she could react. It tore away a thin strip of skin and hair and swallowed it, tipping its head toward the ceiling and working its neck up and down until the scrap of flesh disappeared down its gullet.

"Put your arms behind your back," General Cass repeated.

Kana obeyed. The loops on the rope were brought up high on her arms, with the straight section spanning the distance between her shoulder blades. She was effectively shackled. A tiny trickle of blood ran down her spine under the pinion, mingling with the rainwater in her shirt. She put her head down, as Struthio had recommended, and tried not to cry.

"The Paragon awaits," General Cass said. "Follow us now, mammal. Quickly."

Kana followed the general through a maze of passages and halls. They climbed several flights of stairs, a task Kana found difficult with her arms secured behind her back. As they neared the throne room, tables loaded with opulent fabrics and vases lined the path. The higher they climbed in the Great Castle, the gaudier the decorations became. At the top of a carpeted stairway, General Cass squawked shrill orders to two guards who threw open a double-sided door, and Kana glimpsed the regal Paragon Exemplar Falca.

The monarch was engaged in a lively debate with another creature who stood before her throne. With each word she spat at her visitor, a fine crest of grey feathers twitched with agitation atop her head. She was the same species as the eagle at the gate, but larger still than he had been, and her body was draped in elegant velvet swags. A golden crown, identical in shape to the natural feather crest behind it, rested on her head above piercing eyes that pointed daggers at her argumentative guest.

"You have no right to the creature," the Paragon spat.

"I have more right than you do, Falca. She has hair, not feathers. That means she's one of us."

"She—*it*—was found in our territories. It is therefore our property."

The guest sighed. "What do you want, Falca? Stop this dance, and say it out loud."

"You know what I want."

"Tell me. Say the words."

"We want gems, we want precious metals…and we want the east fields."

"The *fields?* No way. That's too much."

General Cass nudged Kana toward a small alcove in the wall, and Wara stood guard in front of it. Kana craned her neck, trying to see the face of the Paragon's exasperated guest. He wore a ridiculously magnificent hat with two small holes cut in it, through which protruded a pair of fuzzy orange ears.

"You've heard my offer. Take it or leave it," the Paragon said. "If you wish to inspect the creature, my general is holding it in the sidebar. But do not linger. Make your decision and go. I have other royal duties to attend to besides you, foolish king."

The Paragon turned her attention to a meal at her side; a silver platter loaded with a lump of meat which most closely resembled a carved Thanksgiving turkey.

As the Paragon's guest approached the alcove, Kana shrank away from the opening, pressing her back to the wall. She had nowhere to run to, but she'd had her fill of being bit and bled.

"Move over," the guest said to the general's daughter. "I need to see."

General Cass scowled, but Wara sidestepped from the doorway, revealing the guest to Kana in full.

He was a giant house-cat, simply put. Not counting the hat, he was six feet tall standing on his hind legs. Soft black leathers fit tightly over his frame, matching a pair of wide boots and an elaborately scrolled scabbard at his hip. His hat was crooked, tilted at a haphazard angle that must have been intentional, for the holes cut for his ears were positioned with careful precision. His soft orange fur contrasted strangely with his battle armor. Kana froze under the cat's examination, as his sharp green eyes assessed her with the attitude of a housewife choosing which fish to buy at the market.

"She's a little worse for the wear, Falca," the cat said, noticing the bloody spots at Kana's neck and arm.

"A scratch here and there makes no difference. It's healthy enough, so don't try to haggle. My price is set," the Paragon said around a beakful of roast bird.

"Fine. It's a deal. But I want delivery. I can't take her now; I don't have enough guards with me. She's a lot bigger than I thought."

"No deal. If I'm not keeping it, I don't want the care of it. Take the thing and go. We are finished."

The cat hissed, and turned his attention back to Kana. The left side of his mouth twitched into a curling smile.

"Well, I guess you're with me," he said. "Ready to go?"

4.

The King of Cats

Despite the sound of metal chains clanging against the bars—and despite the fact that she was behind bars in the first place—Kana fell asleep. The gentle swaying of the prison coach and her knowledge that although she could not escape the cell, neither could any other creature take her by surprise, gave her a feeling of calm she had not felt since before she had left the sphere. She slept sitting upright, situating her spine so it would rest between the cold steel bars instead of grinding against them. As she rested her head on her arms a flickering headache threatened to turn into a migraine, but she was asleep before it could fully evolve. Instead, it generated a short series of uneasy dreams; her mother screaming at her, 8-Ball and Scooter trying to steal her train ticket from her pocket, and a giant bird hovering over her head, casting a dark shadow across her path.

She was startled from her nap when the coach came to an abrupt stop.

"Paragon!" one of the guards said near the cell door. "How may I serve you?"

"At ease. I've come to have a chat with the primate."

"Sir."

Kana raised her aching head with reluctance. Closing her eyes had felt so good, like a hot bath on a cold day. But the cat from Falca's court had its whiskers pressed up against the bars, and was examining her with intense curiosity.

"Hello again," he said.

"What do you want?" Kana asked.

"Such rude manners, coming from someone who was just rescued from a cruel captor. I could have left you there, you know."

"Rescued? I'm in a cell now. At least she didn't lock me up."

"It's for your own protection," the cat said, frowning.

"Yeah, right."

The cat sat back on his haunches and put his front paws on the ground. Each was five inches across, the size of a lion's, yet the creature resembled nothing so much as an overgrown alley cat. Even while sitting, he was over five feet tall.

"Ah, that's better," the cat sighed. "The birds reserve their respect for those who walk on two legs, but however much I practice, I find it an exhausting method of getting about." He tilted his head to the side and brought a hind paw up to scratch behind his ear. "I don't know how you manage."

"I'm a *person*, that's how I manage. A human. And you're just an oversized pet in a silly pirate costume."

At these words the cat sat erect and opened his eyes fully, the white flashing bright as winter moons. His mouth twitched, revealing a two-inch-long fang. "Careful, my dear. You want to be very careful with that kind of language. Perhaps introductions are in order. That should clear the air."

Kana said nothing. The cat seemed friendly, but she had an idea it was all an act.

"My name is Paragon Exemplar Fel. I am also known as the king of cats."

"And my name is Tinkerbell, princess of the sewers of Chicago. Go to hell."

Fel narrowed his eyes, examining her face. "I sense from your tone that your statement is false."

"Brilliant," Kana replied.

"I'll return when you're in a better mood," Fel said.

"I'll be in a better mood when I'm not in a cage."

"Noted." Fel strode away, lashing his tail with a wounded attitude. "Enjoy your stay, Tinkerbell," he called back.

Kana wondered if she should have been nicer, then dismissed the idea. She was locked in a portable cell, with poles sticking out the ends that were attached to saddles worn by four lions, each one even larger than the king. Three were golden in color, and the fourth was black with a grey mane. The traveling carriage was flanked by two tigers draped in flags emblazoned with coats of arms featuring the silhouette of the cat Paragon. She would be friendly when she was free, she decided. Until then, the king could go choke on a hairball.

The moving cage rocked her back into her dreams, but this time she had a vivid nightmare; she was locked inside a soap bubble, and whenever she tried to pierce it to escape she slid back down to the bottom. From somewhere outside the bubble, her mother was calling her name.

Kana was roused from sleep by a tiger guard calling out "Halt!" Her nap had been much longer this time; no clouds remained in the sky, which was now pitch black and studded with more stars that she had ever imagined possible. The terrain had changed entirely. High, rocky cliffs rose on either side of the path they traveled, and a cold wind whipped through the narrow channel.

The lions carrying the carriage crouched, lowering her cage to the ground. The lion with the grey mane came near the gate to stand guard. Would she be eaten now? Kana didn't think so; the king seemed to have paid a hefty fee to obtain her from Paragon Falca. If she was to be served for dinner, it would probably be a more special occasion than a roadside rest stop.

"Hello, Tinkerbell," the king said. He had walked up to the bars opposite the gate, behind her. "Have a nice nap?"

"Not really. When are you going to let me out?"

"Now."

The lion guarding the gate pulled a hollow metal stick from a pocket stitched into his tabard, and held it between his teeth so it protruded from his mouth. When he inserted the tube into the gate's locking mechanism, it popped open.

"Listen," the cat king said, "do us all a favor and don't run. Understand? You can't outrun us. I promise you that."

Kana sat idly at the edge of the cage in the doorway, pretending she did not much care that she was set free.

"There's some food here, and fresh water. Will you join us for dinner?" The king purred, but showed his teeth. He sat on a blanket spread at the side of the road as the lions unpacked an assortment of boxes and buckets, from which arose a flurry of small flies and a rich, gamey smell.

"And…I'm not the food, right?" Kana asked.

The cat king threw his head back, pointed his nose at the stars, and laughed with a high, mewling howl. After regaining his composure, he grinned at Kana. "Certainly not. We will be having antelope." He gestured with his paw at a plate piled high with raw, bloody hunks of meat. "And this, over here, is turtle. It might not look appetizing, but you really should try it. It's a delicacy, in case you were not aware."

"It's not cooked," Kana said. "I can't eat raw meat."

"Cooked?"

"Cooked! Like, in an oven. With heat."

Fel bared four sharp claws and scooped a dripping chunk of antelope to his mouth. As he ate he watched Kana, studying her tattered clothing, her motley hair, her beaten boots. "I can see we have much to learn from each other. Where are you from?"

"Chicago."

"Ah yes, as you said before. I've heard of it."

"*What?*" Kana said, shocked. "Are you serious?"

"It's a word that is written in one of our old books, describing an enormous city of primates from a time when they still dominated the world. The place no longer exists. I am not sure how you learned that word, but what you say is impossible and I'm no fool. You must stop lying to me, creature. I would prefer we were friends." The cat scooped another dripping morsel of meat into his mouth and licked his paw clean.

"I'm not lying."

"Really…Tinkerbell?" the cat said.

"Oh okay, fine! My real name is Kana. I don't have a home. I got here by accident. I really am from Chicago. I don't know why I'm here, but where I'm from cats act like cats, not spoiled kings, and it's better that way. And people are in charge, not animals. Humans, like me. Okay?"

"It's nice to finally meet you, Kana," Fel said. "Was that so hard?" He smiled, displaying his blood-streaked teeth. "My name, as you know, is Paragon Exemplar Fel, the king of cats. I am the ruler of the Felidae Great Castle."

"You have a castle too? Like that bird one?"

"Yes, but I like to think mine is far grander. At the very least, it is much more comfortable. In addition to Felidae and Falco-formia, the Kingdom has two more Great Castles; the marshland called Squamor, where the scaled ones live under Paragon Chel, and the oceans of Aequor, where Paragon Mobula rules. Have you truly never heard of the Great Castles of the Kingdom where you come from?"

"In Chicago, only humans can speak. We keep animals only as pets, or as food. And they never talk back."

The cat glowered at her in disbelief, trying to find a hint of deceit in her face but finding none. "Indeed. Well, never mind. It is time to rest for the night. We will talk again tomorrow." He rose to his feet and arched his back, stretching and digging his sticky talons into the picnic blanket.

"Where do I sleep?"

"The cell—with the door unlocked, of course—is the safest place for you. You can sleep there, or on the ground if you prefer. It does not matter to me, but the ground is cold. I won't lock you up again, if you're worried about that." The king walked away on all fours with his tail flicking behind. "It really was for your own protection, you know."

Having no better alternative, Kana made a bed of grass inside the cell. She dreamed again of her mother, yelling at her for getting herself into this situation. This time her sister was there too, sneering and disapproving. In the middle of the argument Kana noticed an orange cat sitting on a tall shelf. He wore a floppy hat, and bore identical markings to the king. The cat wore no black leather, but his back was black and his eyes were green. His white teeth flashed a smile in the darkness of the shadows before he leapt from his perch to sink his fangs deep into her mother's neck.

Her mother's shrill screams woke her, but she soon understood the sound was coming not from her mother but from a green bird roosting on top of a guard station outside the gate of her cell. She had slept so deeply the lions had resumed their journey without waking her; the rocky cliffs had been replaced by rolling hills. It was morning, and they were stopped at a border crossing. The king was arguing with a snide-looking parrot about their right to passage.

"But I'm a Paragon, you foul creature!" The cat hissed. "No, I don't have a written note…well, of *course* I don't! You damn birds and your bureaucracy!"

At the epithet the parrot screeched and raised an offended crest of spiky feathers at the back of his neck. "*Bird*, you say! Very good! Very well!" it squawked. "Then I'll just need to see your proof of passage in triplicate! I am more than happy to delay you indefinitely here at Avian Gate North if you will not respect the castle of Falcoformia. I don't care who you are!"

The king hissed and showed his teeth, which set the bird back for a moment. But in its devotion to its post, it remained undeterred. "Proof of passage! Triplicate!" it repeated.

"Damn it!" the king shouted.

Kana didn't much like the cat king, but she liked the birds even less. "Hey," she called out to the parrot. "Hey, you."

"The prisoner speaks?" the bird said. "What manner of creature do you have there, cat? Undeclared prisoners must be immediately taken into custody."

Kana rose to her feet and pushed the cell door open. The parrot was startled, and flapped its wings with surprise, sending small tufts of down floating on the air. It had not expected the cell door to be unlocked.

Kana slid to the ground and crouched, facing the bird with her hands plunged deep into the dirt.

"Do you know what I am?" she asked the parrot.

"Why, no, I just…"

"I'm a human."

"All right, well, that's…"

"You really don't know anything about us humans, do you?" Kana said, grinning. She let a thin stream of drool spill over her lower lip. "Our bite is the worst in the whole world. Our mouths are so filled with bacteria, you'll be poisoned in seconds after I bite through your skin. Our flesh tastes like ashes, and our urine burns like acid. We may be small, but poison runs in our blood, and our favorite food…is barbecued wings!" Kana lurched toward the parrot, growling and showing her teeth.

The act was unconvincing, but the parrot had had enough. The guard hopped to the top of his post and chirped in affronted shock, waving them by with an outstretched wing. "Get out of my sight, disgusting things! I'll let you go for now, but next time I'll be needing to see some real credentials, you mark my words. Don't try it again!"

As the carriage traveled through the gate, Kana again bared her teeth at the bird, who looked away toward the horizon and pretended not to notice. After passing the border, she looked back and saw him swinging his tail back and forth in violent, irritated motions. The guard whipped his head toward the carriage, then back in the direction of the Falcoformia Great Castle, as though wondering how much trouble he would be in when Paragon Falca heard of the king's quick and easy passage. Kana laughed.

The sound caught the cat king's attention. "What's so funny?"

He was again walking on his hind legs, his eyes nearly at the same height as Kana's as she sat in the cage. "Are you laughing at the way I walk?"

"No, at that green bird," Kana said. "Although the way you walk is funny, too."

The cat dropped to all fours, pacing the cell with his head down. "I'm not very good at it. And I agree, it does look silly. But it's just easier, you know, when negotiating with the birdbrains."

"When in Rome," Kana said.

"What?"

"Nothing. How much further is it to your castle?"

"Another two days of walking, I'm afraid. I hope we don't run out of antelope, because then we'll have little left but snacks to get by on. Nothing except bees."

"Bees? You eat *bees?*"

"Certainly. On the road, anyway. Insects keep quite well, you know."

"Ugh."

"Well, the only other meat we're likely to find out here is talking animals, and of course we can't eat the citizenry. It would be uncouth." The king cast a wicked, sideways smile.

"So, not all animals talk?"

The skin on the cat's shoulders twitched, as if the subject were an uncomfortable one. "No, not all animals. Most people don't eat meat regularly like I do, you know. Palatable flesh is very rare, quite hard to come by. Only non-talking animals should be eaten, and they must be hunted down in the wild. It's a lot of effort."

"So why don't those ones talk?"

"Let's save that for another day, shall we? Here, try a bee." The king nipped a sack hanging from a corner of the cell and tossed it through the cage opening before he bounded on ahead of the carriage in big, playful leaps. Kana peeked into the sack and found heaps of dry, crisped insects. The smell was horrendous.

That evening, they camped in a small grove of swaying willow trees. The cat king was clearly eager to get home; he climbed to the end of the sturdiest branch he could find, and stared into the eastern horizon. He sat for hours, surveying his lands and licking his paws. Kana fell asleep with him in her sight, watching his twitching ears and whiskers silhouetted against the backdrop of a million stars in the misty night sky.

5.

On the Hilltop

In the morning, dripping wet heat bore down on the traveling caravan even before the sun had risen above the low hills. Grey chirping beetles with red spots scuttled out of the path of the carriage wheels, then fell silent as the procession made its way through a field of rippling stalks of grain. The lions were protected from the heat by their coats, but Kana's skin was scorched red by midday despite her efforts to hide in any scrap of shade she could find. For an hour she tried walking alongside the carriage in its shadow, but eventually she surrendered to the convenience of riding inside, huddled under a thin blanket.

The king seemed distracted. He walked far ahead on all four paws, flicking the tip of his long tail back and forth, and when he glanced back at Kana the look in his eyes spoke of fresh distrust and uncertainty. It was a change from the previous day which Kana had no explanation for.

When the tiger attendants cried out the order to halt for lunch, the lions came to a stop near a crumbling stone cottage from which tumbled an energetic family of lynx. Their patriarch observed the king's entourage with upturned black-tipped ears and a flaring nose.

"Esteemed Paragon Fel, please allow my humble family to provide comfort to you and your guard before you continue along your journey," the lynx purred. His young kits sat in an untidy line, watching with awe as Kana descended from the carriage. As soon as their curiosity was sated, they began to growl and cuff each other in a playful fight.

The cat king nodded.

"We accept your offer, with gratitude," one of the tiger attendants said.

"Let's set up a tent for you on the hilltop, then, just to the east," the lynx said. "Give us a few minutes to prepare, and we will meet you there."

Within half an hour, the family had set up a small canopy shading a table loaded with bowls of fruit and a wooden platter of raw meat. Kana watched with fascination as the lions and lynxes used their mouths and claws to pull the tent ropes into place. Their actions were ungainly but well-practiced, bringing to mind the awkward movement of circus animals which had been taught unnatural tricks from a young age.

"Kana, join me immediately," the cat king said.

She didn't like being bossed around, but the temptation of the cool shade and the hilltop breeze was more than she could resist. The king sat at the table and lapped blood from the lip of the meat platter.

Kana refused the raw flesh—the lynx, disappointed, claimed it was a supreme cut of "dim elk," a phrase she could make no sense of—but she found a bowl of grasses and walnuts she could swallow after chewing them long enough. Her hunger was so intense, the weeds almost tasted good.

The king nosed at his meal, listless, then turned toward her and sighed in a calculated, dramatic manner. "Kana, I have a question I must ask you, and I find it disturbing to admit that both your life and, in fact, the safety of my entire castle may depend on your answer."

Kana looked up from her bowl of grass to see the cat's nose hovered mere inches from her face. A congealing dollop of blood was daubed on the end. His mouth hung open just enough to show a hint of his sharp teeth as he awaited her response.

"What do you need to know?" The king's suddenly formal attitude put butterflies in her stomach, but she was careful to keep her face neutral.

"I'm sure you have wondered why I was so eager to free you from Falca's castle. The truth is, I collect oddities. You know—strange artifacts dug out from the mud, old statues carved by mad people, occult items bearing cultural or magical significance.

Things of that nature. Most of my collection consists of ancient human books. And you, my dear, are an exceptionally unique oddity which I had simply desired to add to my collection. But early this morning, a runner arrived with word of a strange event that has occurred on my vast castle grounds, and I have heard rumors which lead me to believe the event is related to your recent arrival in the bird territories."

"What event?" Kana asked, picking a string of dry grass from her teeth.

"It gives me heart that you claim ignorance of the current situation," the king said. "But unfortunately I am not yet ready to accept a clear distinction between your arrival and our unfolding disaster. In my lands, far to the western border, the earth has been desecrated. There was a farm—a lovely, beautiful farm!—that grew grains to feed our dim creatures, and it is now missing. Or, rather, half of it is," the king said. Over his bright green eyes, his brow furrowed in confusion. "My understanding is weak, as I have not seen it personally, but I am told that a section of the farm has been replaced with an altogether different structure. The damage was spontaneous and without warning. To my immense grief, the event seems to have taken several young leopards with it. They are… missing."

Kana swallowed a mouthful of weeds and looked at the king very carefully. "Was it—was the new building in the shape of a sphere?"

"What is a 'feer?'"

"A sphere. Like a ball," Kana said. "Like the shape of an eyeball."

The king hissed. "So, you *do* know of these events! Please, tell me you are not the orchestrator of this foul attack."

"I'm not. I didn't do anything. Look, Fel, I did show up in one of those things, but it wasn't my fault. It just happened."

"Ah, so you are a victim of this wretched tragedy, too? I am relieved to hear this, Kana. Otherwise, I may have been forced to command my guards to tear you to shreds."

Kana chuckled before noticing the grave look on the cat

king's face. He was not joking.

"What happened to the leopards?" she asked. "Did anyone actually see?"

"No one knows. They were standing in the place where the ball appeared, and after it showed up, they were gone. While no one has yet ventured inside the strange structure in an attempt to find them, it seems unlikely they have survived the disaster."

"My condolences, Fel. I can't prove it to you, but I promise I'm not the one making this stuff happen."

Fel smiled, but his face looked sad. "I didn't really think so, you know. But it's a very serious matter. And I…"

At that moment, a small brown bear broke from a cluster of trees near the edge of the field. It staggered and nearly fell, but with a mighty effort it caught its feet enough to continue up the hillside toward the canopy. When it arrived, it gasped with the last of its breath, "Fel, my Paragon."

"What is it?" the king asked. "What's wrong?"

Too exhausted to speak again, the bear turned on its side, showing its hind flank. There, above its back leg, was carved a shallow gash. The laser-sharp cut was caked with mud, from which beads of blood seeped. He had rolled in dirt to slow the flow, but his strength was quickly fading away.

"It must have happened again!" Kana said. "It looks like he was caught right at the edge of a new sphere."

"We must go, now!" the king said. "Without delay, we must return to my Great Castle."

The rest of the afternoon and evening were spent in a prolonged forced march that nearly killed the lion guards and the tiger attendants. Kana rode inside the cell, leaving only once to eat a hurried dinner and use the bushes. Long before the outer walls of the cat's castle appeared, the lions were leaving behind a trail of red-spotted footprints from their shredded paws. The injured young bear laid for a while on Kana's grass bed in the cell, but he died in the merciless heat of the afternoon, and was laid to rest under a pile of branches off the side of the road. The guards then abandoned the cell, forcing Kana to trot behind on foot until they finally approached the Felidae Great Castle.

"Oh, thank the sun and moon, it's all still there," the king said of his home when it came into view through the rolling hills. The bulky structure was similar in size to the birds' Great Castle, but the shape was entirely different. No gangplanks jutted from the top spires. Instead, narrow catwalks connected every peak and tower. Vines covered many walls, allowing feline residents to bare their claws and ascend directly into wide-open windows. The lower housing outside the castle walls was round and cavelike. Among those humble hovels lumbered families of bears, massive and jovial. Their necks were adorned with strings of intricate jewelry which were fashioned from wire-strung birds' beaks and threaded scales.

"Our summer army," the king said, surveying the camp with pride. "The most powerful military force in the Kingdom, and our closest allies."

"Summer? Do you have a different army in the winter?"

"The bears hibernate in the winter, of course, during which we must fend for ourselves. But birds don't fly well in rain and snow, and the reptiles become somewhat torpid in the cold, so we are able to defend our castle well enough during those dark months without outside help."

"So you are always at war with the other animals?"

"Not always," the king said. "But you know, everyone takes what they can get. We must remain vigilant." The king flicked his ears forward in recognition. "Ah, Major Ursa!"

The largest animal Kana had ever seen—even on nature shows—lifted its head up from behind the crowd of bear warriors. She was the size of a garbage truck, and her neck was draped with so many beaded chains the fur there was no longer visible. The cluster of jewelry resembled a massive lion's mane and must have weighed a hundred pounds, although the bear carried it with little effort.

"Paragon Exemplar," Major Ursa called. "We are readying for battle!"

"Against whom?" the king asked. "As of yet, we don't know

who our enemy is."

"Against anyone at all, my Paragon!" the bear roared.

"Good enough," the cat king grinned. "Come along, Kana. We will continue alone from here, and let my lion guard rest."

Kana followed the cat king in much the same way she had followed Struthio through the outer castle walls at Falcoformia. Fewer of the mammals stopped to examine her, though; they were busy with problems of their own. Panic was spreading through the city as news of the mysterious spheres traveled from mouth to ear. Worried, gossiping crowds parted for the Paragon and Kana, but none spoke to him directly. They only bowed in reverence until he had passed, then resumed their hushed conversations.

Feline heads with pointy, attentive ears poked out from fur-lined portholes set into the walls of each home they passed, then darted inside again to gossip about the king and his new companion. The inner city housing was designed for practical comfort, unlike the gaudy bird homes. Soft feather-pillows were affixed to every window sill, where cats could sit and watch the crowds pass by on the roads below. Cats climbed and sharpened their claws on thick ropes dangling from treelike constructs that bowed high over the rooftops, painted in a splashy array of bold colors.

"Cute," Kana said.

"I beg your pardon?" the king snapped.

"Nothing. But are all the residents inside the castle cats? What about the bears, where do they live?"

"There are many mammals in the Felidae territories, but felines are the ruling class. We do not disparage against any mammal, of course. Everyone has their place."

"So the bears aren't allowed to live in the nicest houses?"

"They prefer the comforts of the woods."

"Hmm. How much further is it?"

"To the Great Castle? It is no further," the king replied. "We enter my courtyards here."

Before the Great Castle arose a sturdy wall. It was studded with round bumps fashioned from balls of woven reeds. The king crouched, his hind muscles bunching before he leapt nearly all the way to the top. He used the jutting knobs to gain the last few feet, then looked down at Kana with a soft smirk as he perched atop the wall.

"But I can't do that," Kana said. "I don't have claws like you do."

"So I noticed, my dear. But you'll have to try. You can't stay out there, can you? Where else would you go?"

"You don't have a gate I can just walk through?"

"There is a gate. But you won't find it without my help, and I cannot guarantee your safety if you wander off without me."

After several attempts—during which the king laughed with an open mouth, showing off his many teeth—Kana finally threw her leg over the top of the wall. She straddled it, fifteen feet above the ground, and scowled.

"That wasn't fair," she said. "Why did you make me do that?"

"I was just curious. It was not built for primates," the king said. "I wanted to see if you could do it."

"But how do I get down?"

"Same way you got up, obviously."

The king extended his long, furry forearms and descended several feet down the other side of the wall before jumping the rest of the way to land neatly on all four paws. Kana descended rather more quickly, but was lucky to land with no greater injury than a twisted ankle. Once inside the walls she felt safer, but she knew this was probably an inappropriate reaction. She had no reason to feel safe here.

"All right," the king said, looking around. "Well, there's no one here to greet me. I see it will be heavy work to bring this place into order. I should not have left for so long. It's amazing how much can go wrong in only two months."

"You left your subjects and your castle alone for two whole months?"

"Yes. I like to wander, you know. Castle life is so dull."

"Okay, but still…you're the *king!* You can't just…"

The king bared his teeth. "Oh, so the clawless young primate thinks she can tell the king of cats what his responsibilities are?

Who are you to pass such judgement on royalty?"

"Royalty, bull! You're a spoiled brat prince, nothing more! A real leader doesn't take month-long vacations, and he doesn't keep all the best stuff for his personal friends! Why don't you let the bears live in the nice houses? Tell me the truth!"

The king sat back and stood on his hind legs, snarling. Kana had almost forgotten how tall he was. He raised a massive forepaw over his head and held it the air with the talons extended, fighting an urge to strike her.

"Do not forget your place, primate," the king hissed at her. "We are not peers. We are not friends. Where you come from, felines may only be pets—but here you are mine! *Guard!*"

A white lion wearing an ornate tabard strode toward Kana. "Welcome home, Paragon," he rumbled. "Do you need my assistance with this small creature?"

"Find it a cell. Give it some nuts to eat. And give it a pillow," the king sneered. "To pad its soft, infantile skin, as it has no fur of its own to keep it warm."

As the guard led Kana away from the courtyard, she glanced back to see the king staring out through a barred window over the rows of homesteads below. His face softened as he gazed into the distance, searching the fields for any sign of the appearance of more spheres. His expression was both shocked and grave, mocking no longer but filled instead with worry for his people. Kana was furious at his sudden cruel behavior, but her heart knew Paragon Fel was distraught with grief and fear for his citizens. Yet she could not forgive him, and he did not trust her. It seemed likely he never would.

6.

Running From, Running To

Kana's new cell was smaller than her last one, but more graciously appointed. She was supplied with a soft feather-stuffed cushion which was somewhat sullied by cat hair, and a chipped saucer filled with watery milk. In the corner of her room sat a shallow tray holding an inch of clean sand, awaiting her eventual need.

A large brown bear passed by every twenty minutes, chewing a thick wad of beeswax and humming softly under his breath. He would pause, frown at Kana's blunt nose and long legs, then sniff at her cell, drawing deep breaths with his snout jammed between the bars.

"Hey," she whispered. "Bear."

"Mmm?"

"Let me talk to Paragon Fel. Tell him I want to talk to him, okay?"

The bear rubbed its nose on the bars, wiping snot on the metal. "You've affronted him, you know. Ought not to have done that."

"Yeah, I can see that now. But really, I think if he would just talk to me and let me apologize…"

"Nuh," the bear huffed. "If he sends for you, then we go. 'Til then, you stay."

Kana sighed, watching the bear's stubby tail retreat as he continued his vigilant march down the hall.

No longer in fear for her safety, intense boredom set in. She picked a long purple thread from the hairy pillow, and wove it into a braid in her hair. With her thumbnail she plucked sand and tiny rocks from the tread of her boots, a collection gathered over the three days since her arrival in this strange land. Humming, she tried to sort out her thoughts in the silence of her forced rest.

Had it really only been three days? She had spent two nights in the cat territories, so it could not have been more than three days since she had checked into the medical lab. Her journey with Struthio had taken several hours, but the cat king had removed her from the birds' Great Castle before night fell.

Her argument with Paragon Fel made her sad. Even now, locked in his jail, she did not exactly feel like a prisoner. She did not believe he would give an order to hurt her. But he was selfish and petty and frightened for his people all at once. He was not a friend, but not truly an enemy, either. With reluctance, she realized she was fond of him despite his poor treatment of her.

Nevertheless, she would need to escape. But the bars were steel, and the cell walls were built with solid bricks of stone. The bear who guarded her did not seem the gullible type; he was curious and slow, but not stupid enough to be tricked.

After the bear's next round, the Great Castle fell silent. Visitors left for the day, and much of the staff retired for the night. When she pressed up against one of the cell walls, she could see a glow from torches mounted on the walls near the entrance to the hallway. A shadow moving across the light was fair warning for when the bear guard was making his way through.

When all was still, she reached around the lock on the door and explored it with her fingertips. It was like the one on the prison cell, but she didn't have a metal tube like the lion guard carried. There was a keyhole and a latch, as well as small metal nubs situated at the top and bottom of the square device. She pressed one, and it slid in easily until it was flush with the lock. Under the palm of her hand, she felt something shift inside.

Could it be that easy?

She opened her hand wide and pressed the top and bottom nubs at the same time, pinching the device between her thumb and first finger. The contraption clicked, and the door swung wide.

Kana laughed aloud, dumbfounded. The lock was as simple as that of a child's diary. But what cat could have operated the device? They probably didn't even know the latch could be opened in that way. Without separated thumbs and fingers, the maneuver would have been impossible.

Who, then, could have manufactured such a cat-unfriendly lock in the land of Felidae?

No matter. She could escape now. As she stepped out into the hallway, she clicked the cell shut behind her. The careless guard was less likely to notice the breakout if the door was closed.

The torches at the end of the hall were visible now. They danced in a breeze, the flames moving together at the same time; someone was coming.

She went the other way.

The prison-block hall intercepted with another hall that ended at a window on Kana's right, and wound away toward a room to her left that sounded like a kitchen. Pans clanged, water trickled, and meat was being chopped. The cats may not cook their food, but it was clear they still took great care in preparing high quality meals for the upper class.

She walked straight forward, continuing down the hall from the prison until she exited through a wide open doorway. Here she found a stack of crates with a packing form stating the goods inside were recently imported from the Squamor territories to the Felidae Great Castle. An itemized invoice, written on thick parchment in sloppy scrawling letters, was stuck under a rope which bound the boxes together into a single bundle.

In the largest box was a stack of neatly folded grey cloaks, similar to the woolen shroud Struthio had worn when he greeted her. She pulled the top cloak from the stack and threw it over her shoulders. Its large hood was designed to rise up in two tall points, to allow room for a cat's ears. As she had none, the points fell limp to each side of her head. But due to the slack, the hood covered her entire face and her hair, with room to spare. The cloak was huge, nearly long enough to touch the ground and wide enough to wrap around her body three times, should she ever need to. At least now her strange appearance might be more vague to onlookers. Perhaps she could be mistaken for a skinny feline, if she kept her head down.

Only a hundred feet away, an arched doorway led beyond the castle walls to a sewer canal rimmed with green mold and black algae. She followed a narrow path along the canal until a break in the outer wall granted her access to the fields beyond, and freedom.

Kana knew how to move inconspicuously. The main thing was to look confident, like you were exactly where you were supposed to be. She took long strides, ignoring a sentry who watched her progress through the field and a small kit at the corner of the road who looked up briefly before returning to his job of plucking the tender tops from the grains. Dry leaves and sticks from the grasses clung to the bottom of her cloak, for which she was grateful; it was all the better that she look like a road-worn traveler, one who had wandered in the wilds for days or weeks, a stranger of no particular interest.

As the Great Castle retreated behind her, she took a turn toward the west. She knew the bird castle was to the east, and she had no desire to return there. The chunk of medical lab that had traveled here with her would not help her, but perhaps if she could find a different piece of her world—another sphere—she could learn more about what had happened to her.

Late in the day, Kana took shelter in an abandoned hut which was barely visible from the road. It was made of the same wood as the trees it hid behind, and looked hundreds of years old. Inside its single room, she found items which looked newer; a moth-eaten blanket and a pot full of decaying grubs which still had some moisture trapped under their taut skin. When she lifted the blanket, she discovered why the place seemed so recently abandoned; the resident was still there, in his bed, two or three weeks deceased.

She turned to leave, not wanting to share the room with a corpse, but then she hesitated. A horrible, awful idea had come into her head, and she knew immediately that it might also be a *good* idea—perhaps even a lifesaving one.

Turning back to the body in the bed, she whispered, "Sorry about this."

Using a bread knife from the table, she scored a fine line across the corpse's skull and cut away the fuzzy cap, including the ears. Holding the scalp in her left hand, she scraped at it with her right, using the blade to remove caked blood and extra tags of skin. When she was done, she had a peculiar hat; one that, when worn, would give her the tall pointed ears of a cat.

By then, the sun had set and darkness was falling on the fields. Having already desecrated the corpse, she decided the worst was over anyway and slept on the floor for several hours until morning sunlight brightened the room. When the day had become bright enough that she could see the outline of the body in the bed, she pressed the cat scalp onto her head and flipped the hood of her cloak up over the ears. Now the hood's points stood upright, supported by her disguise. She tucked her hair under the cap, and darkened her nose and cheeks with dirt from the hut's floor. It certainly would not stand up to scrutiny, but she hoped at a distance it would at least be convincing enough to make her ignorable.

She momentarily considered taking the body's tail, too, but dismissed the idea. She'd had enough of slicing up corpses. The cloak would hide enough of her body to keep her form indistinct.

For a day and a night she walked, with her head bowed, across the countryside. She wandered, exploring with her ears open for news of another sphere. She passed through three villages, creeping behind barrels and huts, eavesdropping for information on any anomalies like the one which had brought her here.

She heard nothing. Perhaps she had picked the wrong direction.

After a cold night spent behind a tavern, Kana began to despair. There was little choice but to move on, to keep searching. Memories of her cell in the king's castle returned to her with a faint nostalgia; fresh water, and a pillow. Perhaps she had been ungrateful.

For another day, and then another, she walked. On the sixth day, she was almost ready to risk asking someone about the spheres directly. If she didn't hear anything by that night, she decided, she would try it. But through the afternoon she marched on, south and east through endless winding woods.

Then, as she emerged from a dense cluster of trees that flanked a worn, dusty path, she saw a building ahead that brought her to an abrupt halt.

It was shaped like a circus pavilion, but enormous—as big as a football stadium, with a pointed roof that ended in something like an antenna. It was the most man-made looking building she had seen since she had left the sphere of medical lab. While its design was modern, it appeared to be ancient; time had worn cracks in the side panels, and draping ivy festooned decorative spires that jutted from window sills which must have once held flags. The place reminded her of pictures she had seen of the Coliseum, but most of this building was intact, and in fact looked still in use. The ground where the doors swung open was clear of brush, and fresh tracks in the dirt showed they had been opened recently. A panel near the doors had a tiny blinking light, the first sign of electricity she had seen since her arrival in the Kingdom.

While she ached with relief at seeing evidence of civilization, she was dismayed at the sense of dread she felt when she looked at the structure. It wasn't right; it wasn't even familiar, not really. Under the layers of grime it was smooth and shiny, like a city building, but it felt intensely alien as well. It was not built by people like her.

But it definitely was not built by animals, either.

She stood still, hesitant at the edge of the wood, unsure of how to continue. She had no reason to believe the building held anything that would help her, yet she had no other leads.

"Lost?"

The voice made Kana jump. Hidden in a bush near the edge of the wood, a furry animal sat back on its haunches and wiggled its nose at her; it was a large hare.

"No, I…" Kana started. "Well, yeah, I guess I am. But I don't think you can help me."

"Don't be so sure," the hare said. "I've been living in these parts for half my life. Three whole years, you know. I've learned just about everything there is to know about these woods."

"Great," Kana said. "But really, I'm fine. Actually…" Kana reconsidered. "Can you tell me what that building is for?"

"Sure can," the hare said. It looked smug. "It's a reproduction center. I suppose you've never seen one before? Quite striking, isn't it?"

"Uh, I guess. What's a reproduction center?"

"Your mother didn't tell you about reproduction?"

The question caught Kana off guard. "Well, yeah, I guess she did. I mean, we had sex-ed at school. What does that have to do with anything?"

"Well, *everything*, of course. Pregnant people go in; non-pregnant people come out, usually holding a baby. Right?" The hare smirked.

"So it's like a hospital?"

"What's a hospital?"

There was movement at a side door of the building. It cracked open, and from the gap slipped a leopard, biting a pair of wet kittens by their scruff. She hid the kittens in the brush before returning to the building to nose the door shut, then sat and licked afterbirth from her matted fur. Kana could hear the kittens mewling in the grass.

"So there, you see? The miracle of life!" The hare grinned, pooching out its cheeks until its whiskers pointed nearly straight up like river reeds.

"What's it for, though? Are there doctors in there?"

"Well, how should I know!" The hare said, laughing. "I'm male, of course. Never set foot inside. Thank the sun and moon for that! But of course those who are not born inside the reproduction center come out dim. Out of their mothers, you know," the hare said, wiggling his nose. "Not out of the center. As I said."

Kana shook her head, confused as much by his words as by his phrasing. "Dim?"

"Dim-witted, although that's not a nice term. Dumb, dull, stupid. Can't talk."

Kana remembered the king saying something about the meat he ate coming from a dim creature.

"Do they get eaten? These dim babies?"

"Sometimes," the hare said, before losing interest in the conversation. "Do you want to meet my wife? She's over there, by the oaks."

"No, thank you. I have to get going."

"Suit yourself," the hare said. "Be careful, though. Night comes." He leapt toward the oak trees, flashing the white underside of his tail before pausing to turn back.

"By the way," he said, "Not to be rude, but you smell bad. And I mean terrible—really *terrible!* Is there something wrong with your ears? You don't look well at all."

She reached for her cat ears and pretended to rub them in discomfort. "Uh, maybe. But I'm fine. Really."

The hare sniffed, flaring his nostrils. "Well, you'd better bathe soon. Stinking like that, you'll draw predators from miles around."

As soon as the hare dashed into the tall shrubs and disappeared into the shadows, Kana tossed away the ears, relieved to be rid of them. So much for that clever idea. She'd just have to keep her hood up and her feet moving.

7.

Foxtail

From a distance the length of a fallen tree, an old fox heard the tiny scratches of rodent nails balancing on a dead twig. A young opossum, most likely—unfortunate, that. A mouse or shrew would be easier prey. But the fox was hungry, and skipping the opportunity for a fresh meal was not an option.

Of course, it was likely that the opossum was intelligent. In this part of the Felidae castle lands few dim creatures still roamed, a result of the cat king's voracious appetite for meat and his finicky morality regarding the origins of his meals. It was nothing but the hubris of the entitled. If his dinners were not always carried to him on silver platters, his ethics would be more easily compromised.

Panicum the fox did not have the luxury of such philosophical dilemmas. He was not yet elderly, but no longer young, and must take his food when he could get it. He could not afford to allow the relative intelligence of his prey to figure into his own fight for survival.

The little opossum shifted its weight on its branch, but did not take a step. Panicum had been detected, yet the game was not lost if he was careful. He froze, slowing his breath until he was as still as a rock on a riverbank, willing even his heartbeat to calm beyond detection. Minutes passed.

From the direction of the opossum, he heard a sharp crunch. The creature had finally dismissed the danger, and was chewing seeds.

Panicum took a step forward, aiming his paws for places where the forest floor was clear of leaves and sticks. His thick brush stuck straight out behind him, keeping well clear of interference from the undergrowth. He weaved through the shrubs under the damp pine trees, each step measured and slow, until the opossum was close enough to grab in a single bound.

He leapt. Straight into the air, almost, but angled forward just enough to close the final distance in his descent. He landed on the opossum and swept it into his jaws in a single swift motion. A swarm of tiny flies arose and flew around the clearing, startled by the sudden attack.

The opossum screamed. "No, monster! You cannot! I have…I have a pregnant mate…I have…"

Panicum did not reply. Regardless of whether the opossum told the truth, the fox's life depended on eating today. But he also recognized the opossum's trick for what it was. He would have to open his mouth to speak to the rodent, risking its escape. In silence, he clamped his jaw, snapping the opossum's back. It spoke no more.

The fox was not cruel. The injury he inflicted on his fellow creatures for the sake of his survival did not please him. His meals often brought with them a faint sensation of wrongness and despair, a feeling which he had never understood. Why would attending to his natural needs—using the innate survival skills that were his by birthright—generate aching grief that accompanied every necessary bite?

His confused regret did not prevent him from enjoying his food. He tore long strips of flesh from the opossum's body, swallowing each chunk with guilty appetite. When he had finished, he licked every drop of blood from his paws and rubbed his fur in the pine needles on the forest floor until his golden-red coat shined like wet autumn leaves.

With his belly full, he curled into a ball under his long brush to rest. He slept for longer hours, these days. Age and cynicism had stolen the peacefulness of sleep from him, and he needed increasing periods of nighttime rest to make up for the disturbing dreams that tormented his afternoon naps. Sunrise was still an hour away, yet he did not wait for the forest to brighten before drifting into a fitful slumber.

Dreams invaded instantly. A reproduction center. A blinking light, like a star but much brighter, and green like the cat king's eye. From a hidden alcove, an animal made of metal rolled forward on squealing wheels that sounded like the cries of the wounded opossum he had eaten for dinner. The metal creature looked at Panicum, and then he knew for certain that he was dreaming. He tried to wake himself; he chewed his arm, scratched his ear, and tried to cry out, all without taking his eyes from the metal animal. But it approached, relentless, with a long slender item held out in front; a sharp metal thorn, dripping liquid from the end that smelled as sour as rotten mushrooms. The dripping point came closer, closer to Panicum's nose—but the moment before it could pierce the skin, someone stepped on his tail.

He woke with a yelp that echoed through the forest. It was answered by a short scream that sounded like a frightened bird's call. Something crashed into a bush and struggled in the branches, kicking and cursing.

Panicum's instincts carried his paws a short distance away before he could stop to turn around and face his attacker, but what he saw only confused him further. Protruding from the brush were two long feet wrapped in black animal skins unlike any he had seen before. The legs of the stranded creature were covered in thick fabric, which was tattered and torn at the knees. The top half of the creature was not visible but for long pale appendages which flailed and grabbed for a hold on the surrounding shrubs.

He sat back on his haunches and waited to see. Curiosity was one of his great weaknesses; this monster had nothing to offer him, he was sure of it. But what else did he have to do today, other than find and eat another weeping opossum? So, he waited.

After a great deal of ungainly struggling and thrashing, the leggy creature's torso came into view. It was adorned with gaudy chains, and its head-hair was unevenly streaked with bright unnatural colors like those the birds were fond of. But it was not a bird, unless it had been badly damaged. Its skin was humorously naked; other than the ugly thatch on its head, no fur or feathers were visible at all.

It noticed Panicum and paused, looking uncomfortable. "Uh, sorry. Er…you can speak, right?"

"Certainly," Panicum said.

The creature sighed. "Of course you can."

"You stepped on my tail."

"Oh! I'm sorry. I was avoiding someone on the road. I tried to cut through the trees, but I think I'm lost now. Do you know which way is west?"

"Are you serious?"

"Yeah, I'm serious. Don't make fun. I'm not much of a hiker."

"What's a hiker?"

"Never mind. Forget it." The pale creature looked at the sun, eyed the distant mountains, and frowned. She picked a direction, and started to walk.

"That's not it."

The creature spun around and snarled. "If you aren't going to help me, keep your mouth shut!"

Panicum grinned. "Where are you trying to get to?"

"I don't know. West. I was going east, but I guess that was wrong. I'm looking for a sphere. You know what I'm talking about? A place where the land has been transformed."

"I have no idea. But that's not west. West is this way; toward me."

"Yeah, right. Keep your teeth to yourself, dog."

"If you are trying to insult me, you have failed. I'm not as sensitive as those you've met in the castle."

"How do you know I was in a castle?"

"You reek of cat. Also, bird. You've really gotten around, haven't you?"

"Not by choice. I'm not from around here."

"No kidding."

"Sarcasm. Nice. Okay, well, I'm going now." The creature made her way around Panicum in a wide arc, trying to move west without coming close to the fox. At least she knew her own limitations.

"You don't need to fear me," the fox said. "You're far too big to be my prey."

"All the same, I'll keep my distance."

The fox laughed. "Smart. But wait a moment."

"No. Well…why? What do you want?"

"Perhaps we can help each other."

"Doubt it. What could a talking fox need from me?"

"A name, first. I am Panicum. Does your species use formal names?"

"I guess my formal name would be Kana Kobayashi. But regular people just call me Kana."

"Excellent. Now, I want something you might be able to get for me. Do you know what an acorn is?"

"Sure. I mean, I'm not sure I'd recognize one if I saw it, but it's like a nut, right?"

"Good enough. I will accompany you for a while, if you'll allow it."

"Um. I guess," Kana said. "But no funny business."

The fox grinned. "Your distrust is commendable."

They left the forest behind and entered a region of grassy foothills. Avoiding the slopes, they stayed low in the valleys, walking between hills. Crickets chirped in the creases between rises, hiding in the reeds that lined cold streams trickling through the culverts. The water was icy and devoid of fish, but clear enough to see a kaleidoscope of tiny colored pebbles at the bottom.

For hours they walked without speaking. Kana often glanced back to check on the fox, either out of concern or fear. After an hour of this he caught up and walked by her side. He found her relentless determination to keep moving to be impressive. She rarely stopped to rest, and ate almost nothing. Whatever she was looking for, it was clear she would not stop until she found it. When she tripped and fell near sundown, Panicum convinced her to sleep for a few hours under his watch.

The next day, they left the foothills and arrived in a region of vast green plains. The walking was easier, but the sun was baking hot while the wind carried a hint of ice. The combination made Kana's skin turn red and pop out little bumps with every gust. They walked on, ever westward. Panicum wanted to ask what she sought so intently, but decided to wait until she was ready to speak to him of her own accord. He flanked her in silence. At midday, she stopped and put her hands on her knees.

"Pan, I…" Kana gasped, her voice faint.

"Yes, Kana?"

"I'm starving. Really. Aren't you?"

"I am hungry, yes, but I ate right before you found me."

"What did you eat? Can you find me some food?"

The fox hesitated. "I don't think you'd like it."

"I'm sure I'd like it better than starving to death. Which is what I'm doing right now, in case you couldn't tell."

"Let's go a little further. There is a town up ahead. I've been there before. It's filled with raccoons, unfortunately, but they may be able to help you. The raccoons are filthy creatures, but they're occasionally useful. And the town might have food, if you have anything to trade."

They could smell the town long before it became visible. Odors of rotting fruit and stale musk were picked up and carried by the plains breeze. The reek stung Panicum's sensitive nose, making his nostrils flare involuntarily.

While the town's mud huts and stick fences were still distant, they were greeted on the road by a scruffy raccoon who demanded to know their business on the grass plains. After some haggling and frustration, an agreement was struck; no access would be granted to the town, but in return for one of Kana's necklaces—the raccoon favored a chain made of purple plastic—she would give the travelers a sack of dried beetles and ten apple cores.

Panicum agreed readily. He would not have to hunt tonight. Kana said nothing, but removed her chain and passed it into the raccoon's tiny black hand. She tucked it away in a pouch slung over her shoulder, and dragged a cloth sack out from the hedge.

For the next hour, Kana and Panicum sat on a hilltop, munching beetles. Kana preferred the apple cores, but they were not as filling. She nearly gagged as she swallowed, and holding her nose didn't help at all; the taste and smell of the bugs weren't what bothered her, but the texture. Crispy on the outside, gummy in the middle, and if she didn't chew carefully they popped between her teeth.

"Do you have any idea where we are?" Kana asked. "I mean, in relation to all the different castles."

"We are reaching the boundary of my knowledge of this area," Panicum said. "Perhaps I can help you choose a destination if you let me know exactly what you're looking for."

"Why are you following me? Let's start with that," Kana said.

Panicum licked a beetle shell from his paw. "Fine. The truth is that I'm not a very good hunter. Or, rather, I excel at hunting, but do not enjoy it like I should. I have heard rumors that it is possible to subsist instead on the meats of the trees: acorns, walnuts, and such. But I am no climber, and the ones I have found on the forest floors are often molded in their shells, and as hard as rocks. You, however, look like you can climb."

"Wait. You're a fox…who won't eat meat?"

"I didn't say I wouldn't. I do eat meat, almost every day since I was a pup. But it has always made me feel…"

"Sad?"

"Yes. I am not a very good fox."

"What about other foxes? What do they do?"

"They eat without remorse."

"Then it sounds to me like you're the good fox, and they're the bad ones."

"They are simply following their nature. My instincts are not natural. I am not proud of it. I've tried living off of bugs in the past, but I am not built to capture such tiny prey. I nearly starved to death. One time, years ago, I found a beehive and swallowed many of the insects whole, but they stung my tongue until it swelled up as big as a pinecone. And then, once again, I nearly died. The honey kept me alive until I healed, but I never again braved a hive. I am a born killer, and without killing, I will die."

Panicum laid down and put his chin on his paws in embarrassment, now that his truth was spoken aloud. He found Kana easy to talk to, and the words spilled from his mouth more quickly than they had with any other creature before. Why was he so eager to bare his soul to this strange being? Perhaps because she was so clearly from another world, altogether outside his own. This human, as she called herself, brought none of the judgement he had experienced in the company of his own species, but neither was she his prey. She merely listened.

"You shouldn't have to be ashamed of who you are," Kana said.

At these words, tears welled in Panicum's eyes. "No one has ever said those words to me before. At least, not all of them, and not in that order." He curled instinctively, hiding his face under his bushy tail. Shame pierced his heart; he was crying like a pup, in front of this human—and why? Perhaps he was becoming old and senile. Had he lost track of his years? Or were his consecutive nights of disturbed sleep finally catching up to him?

He felt a soft, fleshy hand stroke his head. He recoiled, twitching his skin, but did not snap at the hand or pull away. After his initial shock, a sweet comfort spread throughout his body, from his pointed nose to his rough toes. It was an instinct he had never experienced before; perhaps it was similar to the connection felt between vixen and pup, or brother and sister on cold winter nights. The strange fingers smoothed the fur on his head, warmed his ears, and spoke wordlessly of an acceptance and forgiveness that he had never before felt in his long life.

Under Kana's watch he fell asleep, and for the first time in weeks, he did not dream.

8.

Double Back

anicum listened to Kana's description of the spheres with restrained terror. His tail was whipping back and forth with anxiety long before she finished speaking. At least he did not seem to doubt her story, even when she told him about her world; the dominance of her species, the animals that could not talk, and the machines they used to make every aspect of their lives more convenient.

"You must miss your home very much," he said.

"I guess I do. I'd do anything to get back there, just because it's what I know. But actually this world is nicer in a lot of ways. I was stuck outside without food a lot of the time in Chicago too, so that hasn't changed much. But it is my home, so I should try to find a way back."

"So you want to find more of these sp…sh…I'm sorry, I can't pronounce the word you use. Spears?"

"Spheres. That's okay. But yeah, maybe if I can find more chunks of my world, I'll figure out a way to get back."

"I'll help you, but you know my price."

Kana laughed. "Nuts and seeds. I dunno, that's pretty steep."

Panicum looked hurt.

"Oh I'm only kidding, Pan. I know it's important and I'll help you, I promise. But there aren't any trees here. I'm no expert, but if you want nuts I'm pretty sure we need to find another forest."

The road they sat near was well worn, but they had not passed a single animal all day. One time, far overhead, an eagle soared, but it took no notice of the travelers. The lands were lonely and vast. Kana would have to hunt for insects in the weeds before long, or her hunger would weaken her beyond the point of no return.

"Shh," Panicum said.

"I didn't say any…"

"*Shh!*"

Kana listened. She heard nothing but the wind whistling in the grass, and in the far distance, a small creature digging in the dirt. She wondered what it would say to her if she found it. What do mice talk about?

Panicum rested a paw on her shoulder and pressed her to the ground until she lay flat under the cover of grass. He crouch-walked toward the road and squinted through the cover.

"Halt!" a lion guard shouted from the middle of the open path.

"Wait!" Kana cried, sitting up in the grass. "Don't hurt him!"

"Human, you are who we have come for, not this canine. Are you Kana?"

"Yes. Who's asking?"

"Paragon Exemplar Fel has sent for you. You will accompany us to the king. Do not attempt to flee; you do not need both of your legs to attend an audience with the Paragon. Do you understand?"

Kana nodded. She walked to the road and glanced back at Panicum, who still crouched in the bushes. "I guess I'll see you later, Pan."

Panicum didn't reply, but he stared at the lion guard, snarling. The guard glared back until the fox turned his head away.

No carriage cell was provided for Kana this time; the walk back was a brisk march in a direct line across open fields. The lion guard were less kind than they had been before, and Kana neared exhaustion long before the Felidae Great Castle came into view. But each time they stopped to rest, Kana could look back and find a thin trail winding through the grasses that paced the lion guards' route. Panicum followed close behind.

On the group's arrival at the castle, Kana was again locked into a cell, but this time her hands were bound. A bowl of water sat in the corner; she had to stoop forward to drink from it, like a cat lapping from a saucer. They left her alone and hungry for a day and a night before the king called for her. She felt sure this was his way of making a statement. He wanted to remind her that he was in charge; it was one of his favorite things to do, it seemed.

On the morning of her second day in the cell, she was collected by the lion guard and guided to the king's private chamber. The room was excessively posh; velvet blankets padded every surface, and the high ceilings were draped with swags of silk. On a table sat a tray loaded with smelly fish. The king sat in the center of the room with an affronted look on his face, picking food from his teeth with a slender claw.

"Why did you run from me, Kana?" the king asked. "Why did you betray me?"

"*Betray* you! Betray *you?*" Kana sputtered. "You locked me up. Of course I ran away!"

"It was for your own protection."

"I'm tired of hearing that, Fel."

The king gave her a miserable look which was both remorseful and genuine. "I admit, I am not good at keeping friends. You angered me, and I acted rashly. The truth is that I enjoy your company. So, I had you brought back."

"See, that right there…that's not something friends do. You can't order me to be nice to you. That's not how it works."

"I know that, of course. But would you have come if I had simply sent you a formal summons, written on parchment, along with a nice sack of dried bees?"

"No."

"See?"

Kana sat on a feather-stuffed pillow and hugged her knees. "So, now what? Are you going to lock me up again?"

In reply, the king stood on his hind legs and kicked one rear paw forward. He bent low in front of Kana, with one forepaw on his chest and the other stretched out in front. "Dearest Kana, I beg your forgiveness. My actions were unwarranted. Can a kindhearted human forgive an idiotically pompous cat king?"

Kana knew he did not use the epithet lightly, and his gesture was sincere enough. She smiled.

"Stop bowing like that. It looks silly. And yes, I forgive you. But no more prison cells, okay?"

"Of course," the king purred. He sat back and licked a paw, already forgetting his shame. "Never again."

"I have a favor to ask, though," Kana said. "If you really want my forgiveness."

"Oh?"

"When your guards brought me into the castle, we were being followed by a friend of mine. A fox."

"Oh, I see. We captured him. He's currently locked up."

"In a cell. Of course."

"I'll let him out. Guards!"

Five minutes later, Panicum was crouching behind Kana in the king's chamber. He leered at the king, both fearful and mocking, despising the monarch's proud mannerisms yet envious of his privileges. The wild alpha predator felt scruffy and weak within the walls of the Great Castle, and his vulnerability made him snippy.

"Nice to meet you, Sir Panicum," the king said. "Would you like a bee?"

Panicum sneered, but the temptation was too great. He approached a silver platter and licked up a single insect, then sat in a corner, crunching blissfully with his eyes half shut.

"Very good!" the king said. "That's settled. Now, Kana. There is another reason I sent for you. I am sure you can deduce what it was."

"Another sphere showed up, I assume? I hope no one else was hurt."

"Yes, another sphere, and unfortunately I have lost several more subjects. And these ones were…" the king coughed. "Severed."

"Oh, yeah, that happened to a human, too. At the sphere I arrived in. It was pretty bad."

"There is another problem. Someone arrived intact, along with the sphere. Someone like you."

"What! A human?"

"Yes. A male, I believe. At least, he smells male. Unfortunately, he arrived somewhat the worse for wear. He was battered in his journey. We have patched him up, licked him clean, and sealed his open wounds with wax. But he is quite unconscious. Breathing still, last I checked, but we do not think he will last the night. Would you speak to him? Try to wake him? You may have methods we do not know, when treating your own kind. I must question him."

"I'll try. But I'm not sure what I can do. I'm not a doctor."

The king led Kana and Panicum to the Great Castle's infirmary. A young man lay on a stone slab padded with woven reed mats which were soaked through with blood. His breathing was slow and unsteady.

Kana noticed his uniform, and her mind spun with a sensation of surreal disconnect. He wore a blue polo shirt, and his tan pants were smeared with a thick red liquid that was not blood. It smelled more like tomato sauce. A patch ironed onto the shirt pocket said "*Domino's.*"

"He's a pizza delivery guy. Pizza's a food we have where I come from. Oh man, what I wouldn't do for one right now." Kana's stomach growled loudly, despite the gruesome scene.

"We've tried to wake him several times, but nothing works. Will you try?"

Kana leaned over the man. He looked to be about twenty-five years old, and had a thin, wiry mustache on his upper lip. His head wound had caused purple bruising to spread across across half his face, swelling his eyes shut.

"Hey. Domino's guy. Can you hear me?" Kana said. She grabbed the man's wrist and felt his pulse. "Hey!"

The man started breathing more heavily, but he he did not wake up. His chest started to lurch and hitch, and Kana could see his eyeballs rolling under the lids. His heels struck the soaked mats as spit bubbled from his mouth. A leopard nurse ran to the man's side with a wet towel gripped in his teeth, but paused, unsure of what to do with it. He settled for draping it across the man's sweating forehead.

When the man stopped shaking, his breathing also ceased. His arms fell to either side, hanging loosely off the pallet. Kana gently lifted them, and placed them on his stomach.

"I think he's dead, Fel. He had a seizure. I'm sorry."

"Damn it!" The king said, hissing. "I need answers!"

"What is the custom of your people?" the leopard nurse asked Kana. "Bury? Burn? Stuff?"

"Bury. We usually bury our dead, and leave a marker over the mound. Will you do that for him?"

"Certainly."

Kana searched the pockets of the man's pants, and found a name tag. "His name was Alejandro. Can you label his grave with that name?"

The leopard nurse agreed, and left to make arrangements.

"Kana," the king said, "Will you go with me to examine the new sphere? Will you help me?"

Kana nodded. "I'm ready whenever you are."

"Rest, for tonight. You and your friend have been assigned an ambassador suite. Tomorrow we will go to the site where we found this human, and perhaps you can enlighten me."

The lion guard showed Kana and Panicum to a luxurious room at the northwest corner of the Great Castle. It was beautiful; nothing less than a smaller version of the king's own chambers. To Panicum's great joy, a servant soon arrived bearing a tray with an assortment of nuts: walnuts, pecans, acorns, and piles of meaty seeds. The fox frolicked like a pup.

"You see this, Kana? I've always wanted to try these!" He nipped a walnut delicately between his front teeth then chomped it, tossing pieces of the nut back into his molars before swallowing with glee. "It's even better than I ever thought! I was only thinking of not killing others…but these are *delicious!* Amazing! Oh, you must try them!"

"I've had walnuts before. They're okay," Kana said. What she really wanted was pizza, especially now that she had been reminded of it. Or tacos. Or steak—especially if the steak had never been able to talk before, or plead to the butcher for its life. Homesickness swelled and overwhelmed her.

"I'm going to sleep, Pan. I'm more tired than hungry right now. You can have the walnuts."

"*All* of them?" Panicum's eyes were wide. "You sure?"

"All of them." Kana climbed onto an oversized pillow and

curled up like a fox, except she had no brushy tail to warm her. Instead, she pulled her grey cloak over her head and squeezed her eyes shut, thinking of home.

9.

Diamond in the Dust

When Kana and Fel arrived at the sphere, the lion guards had already set up a perimeter of dead brush to deter curious animals from approaching the disrupted site. Concerned feline citizens stalked and gossiped past the circle of guards, while their disinterested kittens and cubs played together in the dirt, pretending to be invaders from another world. Occasionally a citizen would break from the huddled circles to direct questions at the stoic lions, who shook their heads and refused to address the rabble.

Sighs of relief rose from the tense crowd as the king arrived in the company of a small entourage. The presence of his authority had a palpable effect on the citizenry; now there would be some answers, surely. Their gossip faded into silence as Kana and Panicum followed Fel in a single line, bypassed the brush barriers and the circle of lions, and walked right up to the sphere. Fel hung back with his guard, looking over the anomaly with an expression of puzzlement, but Kana rested her hand on the curved outer wall of an apartment building. The concrete was warm in the sun.

The quiet crowd gasped with awe at her courage. Someone growled, someone coughed, and then they went silent again. Kana leaned in through a hole to examine the interior. As she peered into the dim room, she felt the strange sensation of momentarily crossing a border between worlds, glimpsing a modern setting that now felt alien to her. It was like poking her head into a television and looking at a show from the inside.

"It's just someone's bedroom," she said. "It's nothing special." A pile of dirty clothes in the corner of the room consisted mainly of blue polo shirts and sauce-smeared work pants. "This is a normal apartment. Actually, I think it belonged to that pizza delivery guy."

Kana crawled through the gap in the wall, a simple action

made difficult as soon as her body blocked the sunlight coming through the hole. After she squeezed through and stood on the slanted floor, light once again washed the room, and she spotted what she was looking for: On a dirty nightstand next to the man's bed was a cell phone, still plugged into the wall. She rushed to pick it up, but when she tapped the screen it was slow to respond. The battery wasn't dead, yet the screen was dim, and the touch-response was sluggish. After insistent pressing, a home menu with several apps showed up, flickering on and off. It wouldn't last long.

Could she actually make a phone call? If so, who would she call? Not her mother. Not the police, either; what on earth would she tell them? And they were never really helpful anyway, even under normal circumstances. She didn't have the number for the Women's Center memorized. She actually only had three numbers committed to memory: her sister, the soup kitchen's open-hours hotline, and her old friend Spike from Uptown—but he had passed away from a heroin overdose last year. No good.

She hesitated, her thumb hovering over the "Phone" app icon. So, maybe she had a line to the real world, but what difference did that make when there was no one to call? She tapped the icon for the web browser, but there was no data connection. Did that mean the phone wouldn't work, either?

She dialed her sister's number, and to her surprise, it rang. The voice that answered on the other end of the call was faint and irritated.

"Hello? Who is this?"

"Hina, it's Kana. I'm…I'm lost. Can you hear me?"

"Kana? Whose number is this? Did you steal someone's phone again? Mom's really pissed off at you. She…"

A burst of static interrupted the call, loud enough to hurt Kana's ear.

"*Hina!* Listen for a minute, I don't have much time. Have you heard anything about a whole apartment building disappearing? Or anything else in the news that sounded really weird?"

"How stupid do you think I am? You're the one who has al-ways insisted on being out of touch. At least I watch the news every morning like a normal person, and don't just put my head in the sand whenever something horrible happens. In fact, I did a charity walk just last weekend. I…" another burst of static interrupted the call.

"Hina! Please, just tell me if-"

"…headed north. They're actually forcing people. Mom thought you were caught in the…" Static broke through again, now lingering as a persistent low hiss. The phone's battery was dying. The last words that came through sounded like "social worker wants you…" before the line went quiet.

So much for that.

Kana set the phone back on the nightstand, feeling more alone than she ever had in her entire life. Before trying to decide who she would call in her own world, she had not realized how alone she had been there. Her friends, while mostly nice people, were transient and unreliable. Her family was distant; in the case of her mother, intentionally so.

Why was she always in the wrong place, no matter where she was?

"Kana? Everything okay?" Panicum had crept up behind her and poked his nose through the hole in the wall. "What is this place?"

"It's nowhere," Kana said. "It's just a little chunk of the world that used to be my home. This was someone's apartment. Their home. Not mine."

When she climbed back through the hole, she took with her only two items; a flip-open pocket knife from the nightstand drawer, and a picture postcard of the Chicago skyline at night.

"Sorry, Alejandro the pizza delivery guy," Kana said as she cast a final glance back into the room. "I…I hope what happened to you wasn't somehow my fault."

"Well?" Fel said when Kana arrived back at his guarded entourage. The king had kept a safe distance from the sphere while she was inside, but his sharp ears pointed forward in eager anticipation of her report.

"I can't see any reason why this sphere appeared, specifically.

It's just a piece of an apartment building. People's beds and stuff. There might be some computers and phones and maybe some other technology that might interest you, but nothing that would make your life a lot better. The power is going out, so most of it will be dead soon anyway. It's pretty boring, to be honest."

"There has to be something. Some clue why this happened. Evidence of an invading force, or…"

"Nothing, Fel. I'm sorry. This whole thing is starting to feel like some kind of random accident."

Fel flashed anger again, as he tended to do when he felt helpless and confused. He kept his verbal retorts in check, but he scowled at Kana and paced around the exterior of the sphere, peeking with nervous caution into the broken gaps that had created windows to the inside. The lion guards watched his progress, ready to pounce on any threat that might emerge from the structure. Kana followed at a short distance, hoping he did not take long to satisfy his curiosity. She wanted to leave this place.

The air was suddenly heavy with the scent of something familiar as they rounded the other side of the sphere. It was a foul odor, nostalgic and threatening. Something from long ago, some-thing from childhood. Cooking in the kitchen when Mother wasn't home, frying a frozen hamburger in a pan, barely able to reach the knobs on the oven. For a few seconds, she couldn't place the smell, but then her mind clicked.

It was a gas leak.

"Fel! Wait! Stand back!" She ran to catch up to the cat king, but from the corner of her eye she saw a cub batting its paws at a jumble of loose wires hanging from the side of the sphere. The young bear must have sneaked past the guards while they were focused on Fel's exploration. The king turned toward Kana the mo-ment before a spark flew from the cub's toy and lit an explosion that burst outward from the hole in the curved wall.

Fel was tossed clear of the blast, and Kana was thrown onto her back in the dirt. Panicum, who had followed behind at a dis-tance, ran to her side.

Kana's ears rang with a high buzz; she was half-deafened

by the explosion. Panicum was talking to her, his voice low and muddled, his words indistinct. Then a thin, desperate howl pierced through the haze and noise. It was the sorrowful wail of the cub's mother. Ignoring the flaming brush and the smoke, the mama-bear ran to the place where her cub had been playing, but she found nothing in that dark spot except ash and blackened scraps of fur. The baby had been disintegrated. A splash of burnt blood seeped into the dust. The cub's father joined its mother and roared with rage, throwing his head back to howl at the sky.

Fel spun around in a fury and marched toward Kana and Panicum as the cub's parents cried over the scant remains.

"Treachery! Mutiny!" Fel shouted as he approached on his hind legs. He towered over Kana. "You said this thing was no threat to us!" He rose up as tall as he could and arched his back, his fur sticking out in his anger. No longer did he resemble a house cat; he looked now more like a jungle tiger, ready to claw her skin from her body.

"I never said that, Fel!" Kana yelled back. "I said there was no technology that would help you! There aren't any weapons in the sphere, nothing useful." Kana struggled with her words, finding no simple way to explain an electrical fire and a natural gas explosion to the cat. "It's something we used for power, to cook food. But it's all broken. That doesn't mean it's a weapon. It was just an accident!"

Fel nodded to his lion guard. A soldier moved close, holding a pair of shackles. "You have one minute to explain, primate. Explain to me why a citizen of mine—a *child*, even!—is dead."

"Fel, listen to me. In my world we have figured out how to trap lightning and make it work for us. The reproduction centers your people use to give birth run on the same power, so I know you can understand what I mean. And you know me well enough by now to know I'm not your enemy. Please, I know you're angry, but think this through. Why would I lie to you?" Kana made herself stop talking. She held her breath, waiting to see if she would once again be locked up at his command.

"Paragon?" the lion guard said. "Should we bite off her hands?"

"Wait," Fel said. His face was still pinched and frightened, but even through his rage he had heard Kana's voice. "No. I…we must choose to believe her. Leave her alone."

"Thank you, Paragon," Kana said.

"Don't speak to me right now, primate. Not yet." Fel's eyes still flashed with fury, but he fell again to all fours and turned away from her. He strutted toward the grieving parents and said soft words to them that Kana couldn't hear.

Panicum wrapped his sinuous body around her shaking legs, and his bushy tail warmed her thigh.

"It's ok, he'll come around. He knows you aren't really responsible. But Fel cares deeply about his people, despite his carefree attitude. You are his only hope to solve to the mystery of the spheres, so you bear the brunt of his frustration. His rage is not truly directed at you, yet you are from the same world as the spheres, so his trust can not be complete. He will require time, and you must be patient."

Fel called out for more guards as he escorted the sobbing parents away from the sphere.

"This entire area is now off-limits to visitors without my personal permission," he cried out. "Set up additional fences and barriers immediately. Use local materials, tree branches, anything you can find nearby; but do it quickly." His voice sounded strong and commanding, yet under its strength it trembled with sorrow and regret. His eyes darted and avoided Kana as he shouted his instructions for the building of taller walls, and the installment of a rotating contingent of guards.

"Let's leave this place now, and never come back. It makes me nervous," Panicum said.

"I couldn't agree more."

Kana and Panicum made their way back toward the castle without waiting for the rest of the entourage. When they arrived in their suite, she curled up on the large feather-stuffed pillow and thought again about Alejandro, the young pizza delivery man. He had done nothing to deserve such a strange death. Were the spheres the result of a natural phenomenon? Or perhaps a government experiment gone wrong? It was pointless to speculate, yet Kana could not stop her mind from picking at the problem. Round and round her thoughts chased one another, racing for answers and finding none.

The next morning, she awoke with a sense of resolve. Her exploration of the sphere had been hurried and careless. She realized now the only goal she'd really had in mind was finding a phone. Looking for answers had been secondary, and that was selfish. Had she given up even before she started? If so, she had failed the Paragon and the entire Kingdom. Perhaps she had deserved a small portion of the wrath he had directed at her.

Despite Panicum's protestations, she approached the king in his throne room and announced that she would return to the sphere.

"You're kidding," Fel said. "No. It's too dangerous." He looked guilty. "Look, I apologize for my accusations yesterday, they were unfair. But I can't let you return. I don't want anyone else to get hurt."

"I'll be fine," Kana said. "I know what caused the explosion, and I know what to watch out for this time. We both need answers, and cowardice will get us nowhere. I need to take a closer look."

Fel frowned. "Are you sure?"

"I'll go without your permission if I have to."

"You'd never get past my guards," Fel said. "But that doesn't matter; I'll grant you permission. Be careful, Kana," he said, flattening his ears. "It may very well be a piece of your own world, but all is in chaos now. The spheres are gateways, and we don't know for sure whether they are open or shut. Anything may come through them, maybe even those who would harm you despite your origins."

"Maybe. But I don't think so."

"There's something else, Kana. Several of my runners returned this morning with dire news. More spheres have appeared. I don't know how many."

"Where?"

"Scattered across the land, with no pattern or method. I await further news of casualties but…Kana, if this does not stop, our very existence will be threatened. Please, beg the spheres to return to wherever they came from. You must reason with them, plead for our lives, do whatever you can. Will you go forth and do this on my behalf?"

"Fel, I can only promise to try."

Kana permitted Fel to assign a lion guard to accompany her to the sphere, but she asked Panicum to stay behind in the Great Castle. He was hurt and frustrated by the request, but she insisted. The honest truth was that she was not as sure of her own safety as she had implied to Fel. Her intent was to find her way to the exact middle of the sphere. Her science knowledge was shaky, but she thought that if the transported matter was perfectly round, the force must have come from either outside it or inside it, and applied evenly in all directions. A sphere was nature's simplest task, yet one of the hardest for humans to emulate. She had no way to learn about any exterior phenomena that had occurred in her own world when the spheres were created, but maybe she could explore the center that existed in this one. The longer she thought about it, the more she suspected the core of the structure would hold some answers.

After leaving the lion guard outside the perimeter walls, she started her exploration over from the beginning, entering once again through the gap in Alejandro's room. This time, she ventured into the dark hallway beyond the bedroom. Across the hall she found a a tiny, filthy bathroom. She made her way down the hall and around a corner into a small kitchen filled with the overwhelming odor of rotting food. It was a dead end.

Backtracking to the living room, she found a wall with stress fractures, and a door that opened onto a common room. Metal double-doors with an "EXIT" sign overhead led her to a wide hallway that proceeded straight toward the center of the sphere.

Kana pulled the flip knife from her pocket and held it out in front, although what she expected to use it on, she had no idea. Fel was so sure of an invasion or alien force he had almost convinced her of the possibility.

In the quiet darkness, her own breathing was loud in her ears. Framed generic photographs of wildlife hung crooked on the walls. A large picture of the previous owners of the apartment building was mounted over a faux-bronze plaque. Paper banners taped high on the walls were covered with photos of middle-aged men and women, and a golden-glittered poster read *"Thursday Night Poker Pals, Spring Tournament Champions, Pine Bluff Apartments."* The hall ended with doors on the left and the right. The right door, unit 92, was locked. The left door was ajar, but one of the numbers had flipped upside down, turning the "91" into a crooked "61." Kana judged it was the apartment closest to the dead center of the sphere.

She pushed the door open using the tip of her knife. The lights were out, and the apartment was far enough from the sphere's exterior that no sunlight could penetrate the room. But a few feet ahead, near a wall with a dead television screen mounted on it, flickered an artificial light.

It was a luminescent ball, floating five feet above the carpeted floor, glimmering like a solar eclipse through a pinhole projector. The furniture in the room was illuminated with a cool turquoise glow.

The light didn't respond to her approach, but it emitted a muted cacophony of indecipherable noise; a mixture of humming machinery, scraping metal, and low animal cries. The loudest sounds turned the star briefly pink, with waves of color splashing across its surface. Between soft bursts of static, she heard a few words she understood; "Contain it…Mother commands…don't care…"

"Mother?" Kana whispered.

The orb dimmed, as if someone had stepped near it, blocking the light. A voice said, "What was that? Shut it down!"

The core flashed, then blinked into darkness. It was gone.

10.

A Distant Rumble

W eeks passed, and no more spheres appeared. The existing structures blinked and darkened as their sources of stored electricity died. They settled in place, sinking into the earth where they had landed. Paragon Fel sent runners to every known sphere location to arrange for the construction of barricades and to organize searches for injured animals or human invaders. No living humans were found, although some runners reported the odor of rotting bodies. Several spheres had not transported buildings, but had instead brought chunks of desert or ocean, which had disintegrated and collapsed upon their abrupt entry into the Kingdom.

As the appearances stopped, Kana rose considerably in Fel's esteem. He trusted her more, allowed her free movement in the castle, and frequently requested her company at breakfast. Kana didn't understand what she had done to deserve his favor, but she was grateful for his friendship.

The memory of what had happened during her second trip to the sphere was hazy. She had talked to someone, of that she was sure. But what had they said? Had she convinced the spheres halt their intrusions, as Fel had asked her to? There had been a bright light and strange voices, but more than that she could not remember. What little she could recall, she had related to Fel, but his interest in the matter faded as soon as the spheres stopped invading his lands.

Paragon Fel and Paragon Falca exchanged information on their discoveries via their ambassadors. When the final numbers were tallied, the count totaled thirty-one spheres recorded across both territories, and an additional unknown number in the reptile lands. Fel sent this information on to the reptile Paragon Exemplar Chel by way of a lion ambassador and entourage carrying a generous assortment of gifted foods and goods, in a bid to bribe his cooperation. Fel's hopes were high that recent events might entice the reptile Paragon to open up new lines of communication with his neighbors.

Peace settled over the villages of the Felidae lands.

One bright morning three weeks later, Kana was sitting in the Great Castle kitchen chewing on walnuts and sipping black tea with honey when the king stormed past the door, spitting and hissing with rage. A small collection of nobles trotted behind him, uttering placations and pleas for his patience, but the king was undeterred. He howled for the fastest runner in the land, and for a scribe to write down his reply to a message received from the "stink-scaled despot Chel." Clearly there were no takers; at the first sound of his caterwauling, any creatures capable of putting pen to paper had scattered to the winds. None wanted to volunteer for the task until the king had calmed, for fear of becoming a target of misdirected rage.

Kana decided she would risk an audience with him. He was more patient with her than he was with his other subjects; she often brought an outside perspective that he found enlightening.

She found him, as she had expected to, in his throne room, pacing and lashing his tail. His whiskers stood straight out and his ears laid flat. Stuffing was caught in his right front claw; he had been taking his anger out on the furniture.

"Fel, what is it?" Kana asked. "Tell me what's wrong."

He didn't answer her. Instead, he muttered under his breath, and turned his wild gaze upon the sputtering dignitaries and lion guards that had followed him into the room.

"Scat!" he cried. "Get out, useless things!"

The entourage dispersed, with great relief.

Fel leapt atop his pillowed throne and rested his chin on his paws. He feigned calm, but Kana could see his fur twitching with deep agitation. She waited for him to speak first.

"Kana, I just don't know what to do," he sighed.

"What happened?"

"The ambassador I sent to the reptiles has finally returned. I thought her delay was due to bad weather"—Fel hissed and smacked his lips, as cats sometimes do when they smell something putrid—"but I have now heard that it was due to interference from Paragon Chel himself. Fiend! Monster!"

"Did he imprison her?"

"No! She is…" the king bared his teeth again. "She has been declawed."

"What! But, why?"

"I cannot accept the action as anything less than a declaration of war. Our gifts were returned to us—moldy and rotten now, from the prolonged trip—and one member of the entourage did not return at all. The ambassador will survive, but she is forever disgraced. Chel will pay for this! I swear it, on my life!"

"Maybe there is another explanation. Are you sure this reptile king commanded it himself?"

"I trust my ambassador at her word."

Kana sat on a small cushion before the throne. "So, Chel won't help with the documentation of the spheres, that's clear. What happens next?"

"Retaliation."

"No, Fel. There has to be another way. Your citizens will suffer if this incident turns into a war, and I know you don't want that. You're angry, and I understand why, but…"

The king sat erect on his throne, flashing his green eyes in beams of sunlight that penetrated the windows high on the stone walls.

"Yes, Kana. Violence is not my desired solution, yet neither can I ignore the torture of a valued diplomat. But first, I must know *why*."

The king had not long to wait before the reason for the rejection of the ambassador and her offerings became apparent. Messengers arrived with rumors of bands of roving reptiles pouring in from the territory to the east, sweeping the countryside and prying every scrap of wire and metal from the spheres in the cat king's land. They gutted the structures of furniture, electronics, and appliances they had no hope of understanding. Spheres which were composed of building materials were stripped bare, down to their twisted metal beams. The spheres that contained only natural matter were ignored; the reptiles sought only human-made items. Fel's royal bear army repelled some of the reptiles, but Chel's strategic troops moved through the land in small strike forces, spaced far enough apart from each other that it was impossible to contain them in the wide open fields of the Felidae territories.

"But why? Why do they ransack my territory for what they cannot use? What could they have to gain from this collection of junk?" The king asked the most intelligent members of his court, again and again. He tasked them with researching the parts they pulled from the spheres. But they had no answers for him; the unpowered devices they had picked out and carried back to the Great Castle for examination were dark and still. Some, like the cell phone Kana had found, briefly emitted light or sound, but none were useful and all died quickly under the animals' desperate experimentation.

A messenger arrived from the Squamor Great Castle, harried and frightened. He was a python, streaked with black and yellow, and in the middle of a terrible molt. He sloughed bits of skin as his belly scraped across the floor of Fel's throne room. Kana sat near the king, having been summoned by him as soon as the reptile approached the gates.

"Speak immediately!" Fel shouted at the tattered snake. "Tell me what right the reptile Paragon thinks he has to my lands and the bounty upon them?"

"Sssimple. You weren't using it," the snake replied. "Paragon Chel wants it. Paragon Chel is stronger, so the reptiles will take what they want."

"I have no wish for our castles to be at war."

"Then let us take what we want, and call your silly bears off our noble soldiers. Paragon Chel demands this: Leave his represssentatives alone, and your citizens will be spared."

"Never. This land is mine, and all that exists on it is mine. If your people stay, they will die. Take that back to Chel."

The snake exited the Great Castle, leaving pieces of himself behind as he went.

"Preposterous!" the king cried. "Two-faced, pompous, idiotic-"

"Paragon," a lion guard interrupted. "There is another visitor here to see you. A bird. Several of them, in fact."

Fel rolled his eyes and sighed through his whiskers. "Just what I need. Fine, then. Let them in."

A small cluster of flamingoes with pink, blue, and purple feathers bustled into the throne room. They bobbed their heads and whipped their beaks side to side, taking in the plush surroundings. Their wings glittered with glued-on rhinestones, but their sparkle was dulled by a layer of road dust.

"Paragon Exemplar Fel, most gracious of felines, our fondest neighbor and friend, shining example of regality and magnificence, limitless and fearless..."

"Please, do get on it with it," Fel said. "What do you want?"

"Paragon Exemplar Falca, our magnanimous leader and glorious matriarch most worthy of our worship and praise, would like to know your intentions."

"My intentions? Regarding what, exactly?"

"News of your plight has reached the incredibly sharp and flawless ears of our precious ruler. She knows all, always and forever, and yet her grace has a question for you, her beloved ally. And her question is this; will you go to war with the reptiles?"

"It is not my preference to do so. However, they are warring with me, it seems. And I would show nothing but weakness if I did not answer their actions with action of my own."

The lead flamingo, a purple bird with a tail like a spray of lavender flowers, cocked its head at the king. "An—excuse me, but this is the truth—intentionally vague answer, my liege. So, your answer, in short; it is yes?"

"Why does Falca need to know? This is not her business."

"I cannot guess as to our magnificent leader's whim."

"Then what use are you? A messenger with no information is nothing at all. Leave me until you can find a way to be more useful to your ruler and to your insignificant castle."

The flamingo's neck straightened, hoisting its affronted head high above its body. "The queen would know whether you are friend or foe; if you fight the reptiles you are friend, if you capitulate you are foe. For the reptiles also invade our castle, and tear the bounty from our lands, and we would join with you in solidarity against this threat to our sovereignty."

"That's more like it," the king said. "I understand now. Was that so hard?"

The flamingo arced its neck into an S and feigned indifference. "I am not authorized to share so much, but neither do I wish to fail my queen in this duty of securing an answer from you, feline king. Please supply me with your response quickly, as I must leave by tomorrow morning."

"My lion guards will assign you a suite. I will call for you at sunrise. You are dismissed."

The colorful group scuttled from the throne room, their tails waving like flags behind them.

Fel slumped on his throne. "Kana, tell me this: How can they say so much, yet communicate so little?"

Kana grinned. "I'm sure every word seems important enough to them, Fel."

"I'm sure. Well. It looks like I have a long night ahead of me." The king spoke in Kana's direction, but he was lost in his own thoughts. She said nothing, sitting on her pillow, wondering why she was there at all.

"What did you think of the snake?" he asked.

"I have no idea. He was a big talking snake. What else do you want me to say?"

The king turned his head toward her, surprised out of his reverie. "Something wrong? I was wondering what your impression of him was. Is that too much to ask?"

"Why am I here, Fel? I'm not one of your dignitaries or court members. Why are you asking me?"

"Because you will tell me the truth. My own people fear me, but you are wonderfully irreverent. Even aside from my delight at your blunt manner of speaking, I know that I can trust your judgement to be raw and honest, without regard for my possible reaction to your words. So, tell me; what did you think of the snake?"

"He should finish molting before meeting with a king. Also, he seemed honest to me. I don't think he was lying, anyway."

"Me neither."

The cat king licked his paw and rubbed it over the back of one ear. He repeated the motion on either side until the fur was smooth and straight.

"The birds will align with us, according to that gaudy flock. I can see the best way to proceed, but it comes with a great deal of risk, and I am not sure the necessary party will be interested in my plan."

Kana felt uneasy. This would surely involve her; she knew the king well enough now to understand when he was plotting around her.

"I believe there is still a chance for peace. So, here is my question for you; would you be my ambassador, to both Paragon Falca and to that terrible reptile Chel? Falca may not respect you, but she *will* recognize you, and showing that I have brought you into my inner circle may impress her. Your appearance before Chel, flanked by a large regiment of my best bears and lions, will give the old turtle a terrible shock. I promise you will be guarded by my most trusted people. I do remember and understand that you are not from our world, and I am not your king, so it is much for me to ask. But will you at least honor me by considering it?"

Kana thought. Life in the Felidae Great Castle was easy, but she had become bored enough to count the stone bricks in the walls of her suite two times over within the last week. Was boredom worth risking her life for? Probably not, but there was something else to consider; traveling and exploring the Kingdom may help her find a way back to her own world.

"You don't have to answer tonight," Fel said. "And I will understand if you must deny my request."

"No, I'll do it," Kana said. "On one condition."

"Anything, my dear."

"Panicum comes with me as my personal assistant. If he wants to."

"Very well. But do take your time and think about it until morning. This journey will be arduous and dangerous, and I want you to be sure."

"Ok, Fel. I'll keep thinking about it. But I'm already sure."

When Kana told Panicum about the king's idea, he was elated. Life in the Great Castle did not suit him at all. He had even been thinking of moving on by himself now that Kana seemed safe, but he dreaded the thought of leaving her behind. Their friendship had grown in the weeks since their arrival. He had been torn between returning to his beloved wilds or staying curled at her side.

The king assigned no less than eight bears and four lions to their protection. Skilled lynxes and minks assembled a luxurious velvet robe for Kana to wear during her appointments with the Paragons, although she planned to wear her grey hooded cloak on the road. To aid the journey, an ancient four-wheeled cart was brought out of storage from the bowels of the Great Castle dungeons. Panicum explained that the animals had knowledge of the function of wheels, but great difficulty creating new ones due to their physical and technological limitations, so the usage of this antique was considered an extreme honor. Two bears in harnesses pulled the carriage, which was decorated with sprays of river reeds and wildflowers. When the procession was ready to disembark, it resembled a festive parade—as perhaps it was, evoking a celebration of camaraderie with the bird castle and the prospect of reconciliation with the reptiles.

On the day of Kana's departure, the animals formed a procession, cheering and escorting the carriage as it made its way through the courtyards to the exterior castle gates. Onlookers tossed rose petals on the path in a symbolic gesture of love and gratitude. As Kana rode away with Panicum at her feet, she looked behind to see the cat king perched atop a high balcony. He stood alone, solemn and worried, as he watched Kana carry all his hopes to distant lands.

11.

Snakes and Adders

And then what happened?"

The mottled-brown snake tasted the air with his tongue, trying to get a measure of his master's mood. It wasn't looking good—but it remained to be seen whether the snake would spend the night in the dungeon.

"Sssir, that's all I know," he said. "The caravan was seen moving away west, toward the bird castle; three or four lions and a contingent of bear soldiers. The female primate is keeping the company of a mangy red fox, well past its prime. Their specific mission remains unclear."

Paragon Exemplar Chel chewed a wad of seaweed as he watched the snake sputter and twitch. It was a quick messenger, but not smart. It wouldn't do to send out more like him; they would gather little else of value. A slower but more competent spy must be enlisted to the mission. Someone with wit and deductive skill.

"Fine, serpent. You may go." Chel pushed his mountainous body up on his forelegs and stretched his neck for a bite of fresh cabbage. Greens were not his favorite food, but after a thousand years his tastebuds did not work as well as they used to. If it were not for his sedentary life, his 1500-pound frame would have been impossible to nourish. Tangy-sour cabbage, grown in the lows of the eastern swamps, was one of the last vegetables he could actually taste.

As he ruminated, the twitchy snake slithered out of the throne room and was replaced by an apologetic supplicant; a lanky iguana with grime under his scales and a furtive, glancing look. He stood on his hind legs, a power move designed to make him seem more important than he was. Obviously he wanted something he knew he did not deserve.

"Who admitted you?" Chel demanded.

"No one, sir. I sidestepped the guards, sir, to save time. But you will forgive me, because I bring the information you want."

Chel's eyes widened. Something of interest, at last! "Oh? And who are *you* to tell me what I want?"

The iguana smiled, tilting his head down to display the sly curve of his mouth. "I know what you want because I pay attention. You want pieces torn from the metal orbs."

"Your information is outdated. We already got them all."

"No, sir. I have found one more. And this one is, uh, speaking. It talks."

Chel had heard rumors of noises and voices coming from some of the orbs. The ones still making sound were generally the most well-preserved specimens. If the iguana spoke true, the orb was valuable, and should be secured immediately.

He narrowed his eyes at the iguana. "Where?"

The iguana shifted his weight back and forth on his hind legs. "First, a pledge from you, my liege. To my family."

"Where?" Chel shouted in a booming voice that made the loose floor tiles rattle. The iguana was shaken, but persisted.

"My family is starving. We require insects. Please, sir, have mercy and I will tell you."

"You would blackmail your Paragon?"

"Blackmail! Sir, never! But we must survive. We are on the brink, and after the heavy rains this year..."

Chel looked closely at the iguana's torso; his joints were sunken, the lines of his ribs visible through his scales. He told the truth about starving, so perhaps he told the truth about the orb as well. But if Chel began handing out food to whoever asked for it, he would have no peace.

"Guard, set aside a crate of insect paste. Let this subject take it when he leaves."

"Oh, thank you Paragon! The orb is..."

"Don't tell me. Tell my assistant outside. And be precise with your directions, or I will send guards to retrieve the crate of food from your family, and your head along with it. Understand?"

As the iguana trotted for the exit—an odd sight, as he contin-ued to balance on his hind legs—Chel called over another guard.

"After he leaves, catch up to him and take off his tail. Don't do it inside the Great Castle, wait until he is past the outer walls. But let him keep the food."

To Chel's deep regret, he was not able to personally attend to the ransacking of the orbs. These days he rarely moved from his throne room, as the effort to haul his enormous shell across the floor had become too excessive for his decrepit muscles to handle. Of all the reptiles in the Kingdom, he was the largest and the oldest. He could still remember the tales of the Great Calamity told by his grandmother, and to his knowledge he was the only animal still liv-ing to have received those tales second-hand rather than third- or fourth-. Everyone he had known as a young turtle had passed away long since. His grandmother had been eight hundred years old when she recited the stories to him, but she had died when he was barely fifty. He could still hear her words as clearly in his mind as he had in her home on those long-ago days, when he had sat near her bed to listen to her rasping voice tell tales of the ancients.

None of her stories had ever mentioned an appearance of orbs that displaced pieces of the Kingdom, although some of the technology found inside them made him think of the ruins his grandmother had described from her youth: screens that flick-ered strange light that was somehow also a kind of communica-tion, straight-lined structures made by machines, perfectly round wheels, and exotic foods and pleasurable entertainment beyond any known since before the Great Calamity. The fantastic fables of those riches had stayed with Chel for hundreds of years, stuck in his mind as an ideal. In his throne room at night after the day's busi-ness was done, he often dreamed of what it would have been like to live in an era of such decadence.

And now, after the appearance of the orbs, his only question was this; could these strange structures grant his people the knowl-edge to resurrect the glorious past?

The reptiles were, regrettably, not the most scientific of the four animal classes. The birds were all silly aesthetics and frilly colors, in no way a threat to his sovereignty no matter how many orbs they may have been blessed with on their land. If the aloof fish had received orbs in their waters, they had likely gone unnoticed. But the mammals were clever, and it would not do for them to get their ugly paws on the riches of the orbs first.

So, the race was on.

The female primate, now, that was something else. Chel had no doubt the creature was somehow related to the appearance of the orbs, but was it dangerous? News of the primate's arrival had rippled across the entire Kingdom. Humans were known only from pictures, having all died during the Great Calamity. But if there was one primate, there must be more. Ignoring the possibility sounded like a terrible risk—almost as much a threat as the mammals beating Chel in the race for the orb technologies. He could not fathom what an invasion of primates might look like, but the thought filled him with dread.

So, then, every last orb must be secured and the primate must be interrogated. Everything depended on it.

Chel shifted his weight, settling deeper into an enormous throne constructed from the intricately carved skull of a blue whale. This berth in which Chel spent all his time had been a gift from his dear friend Mobula, Paragon Exemplar of the Great Castle Aequor. She could be a powerful ally, but her realm's unique position—a vast territory of water that surrounded the Kingdom on all sides—made her apathetic toward most landbound advancements and politics. He had tried to entice her before, seeking a strong ally in case of a mammal or bird invasion of his lands, but the fish Paragon remained indifferent. Her fancy was in fortune-telling and mysticism, subjects for which Chel had no patience. A shame, but she was a beautiful creature; a ray resembling an enormous bird, yet with the intelligence of a hundred of them.

No, Mobula could not be counted on to help with Chel's current situation. The technology would mean little to her, and the possibility of war even less. The reptiles were on their own against an unfathomable threat; a mammal uprising in the north, backed by all the power of ancient human knowledge they could glean from the orbs.

"Assistants!" Chel belched. "All head advisors, aides, and ambassadors must assemble immediately!"

In minutes he was surrounded by an assortment of middle managers: a chief of military operations, an agricultural liaison, a land use engineer, a sallow diplomat who served as the castle's only foreign emissary, and a variety of generic civil servants. They gathered near, muttering, wondering why the rare meeting had been called.

This speech would be important. Chel breathed deep.

"Dignitaries, nobles, and those with whom I have entrusted the care of our sacred lands! Today I must make clear to you the terrible danger that we face. You are aware that we have been examining a number of mysterious structures that have appeared in our lands; from them, we have been blessed with an abundance of metal parts and technology that has been granted us by unknown sources. However, the full truth is deeper, and more sinister. For, along with these structures, there has appeared…a *primate!*"

Several in the crowd gasped, and a low rumbling of voices began.

"No, please stay calm. As of this day, the primate is moving away from us, toward the bird castle. But the danger is still very real, and we must be vigilant. The creature may bring with it disease, sedition, and violence. Worst of all, it appears to be allied with Fel, the devious king of cats."

Chel paused for effect, and received the expected response: anger, fear, pledges of action. He was proud of his people. They were fierce and determined, every one stout-hearted and loyal to his castle. Remaining quiet, he left the next move to them and was not disappointed.

"We must find this primate!" the sallow diplomat called out. "We must discover its plans, and determine its true motivation!"

The managers nodded to each other.

"Yes," Chel said. "I think that is an excellent idea. But if we send someone to spy, they may not return to us intact. Primates are quite dangerous. You may not know about this, but I have heard the stories. I have been educated about the ancient Age of the Primates, a time when reptiles were laid low and forced to live in dark, hidden places. This primate may be similarly empowered, or even armed with weapons beyond our understanding."

"I will go!" cried someone from the back. More hands shot up, volunteering; every attendant was willing to make the trip.

"Thank you, my brave subjects. Your enthusiasm honors your Paragon," Chel said. "I will deliberate, and send for one of you tomorrow. Please go now, and discuss this meeting only amongst yourselves. Gather your resources, but do it quietly. Do not alarm the populace. For they will know fear soon enough, if we do not stop the threat where it stands."

When the assembly had dispersed, Chel closed his eyes. In his mind he replayed the stories passed on to him in his youth; massive cities that rose high enough in the sky to touch the stars, shining carriages that transported animals wherever they wanted to go, bountiful varieties of food and medicine that appeared on demand without effort or exchange. His legacy must be the resurrection of that dead world, even if it meant working with a primate—or working against her.

He would stop at nothing to bring about the glorious new Age of the Reptiles.

12.

Kana the Ambassador

The parrot at Avian Gate North remembered Kana well. He was the same individual who had been on duty when she had passed through with the cat king. He eyed Kana from his perch, but waved the procession through with a casual flap of his wing.

"Welcome back Kana, ambassador of Paragon Exemplar Fel," the parrot said. "I have been instructed to allow your passage."

"Thanks," Kana said. "But how did Falca know we were coming?"

The bird ignored her, instead turning to focus instead on the distant horizon. He lifted his tail so Kana had a regrettable view of his rear as the carriage passed through the gate.

The journey was slow this time—far more leisurely than the panicked march they had led to the Felidae Great Castle in the wake of Fel's full realization of the danger presented by the spheres. More important than rushing to their destination was being seen by the populace. The king had told Kana her approach should be witnessed by the common folk on the road, so that rumors of their advance would spread ahead of their arrival at Falca's Great Castle. The lions kept the carriage shining clean and adorned with sprays of fresh flowers to impress the citizenry and get their tongues wagging. Long before they neared the castle's outer walls, their route was flanked by onlookers and tourists trying to catch a glimpse of the Felidae king's new primate friend. Kana realized the flowers were not just for appearance, but also a subtle tribute to the particular aesthetic of the bird folk she was to parley with. The king of cats knew what he was doing.

When the Great Castle came into view, Kana noticed for the first time the true scale of the tremendous mountain range behind it. During her previous approach, a storm had been tumbling in over the mountaintops, obscuring the peaks of the range. The Great Castle had looked huge then, but now it looked utterly dwarfed by the ridges beyond. Each point swept down onto the land in enormous curving slopes. White stone points at each apex gradated into charcoal grey at the base, spanning many thousands of feet from top to bottom. No living thing could survive on those sterile slopes: no trees, no shrubs, no birds.

"Pan? Do you know anything about that mountain range?"

Panicum was curled up on a round pillow, with his tail under his chin. When he talked, his jaw stayed flush with the cushion, making his ears flap forward and back with each word. "It's called the Gludair Chain. We're near the start of the range now, actually. It continues for several hundred miles until it meets the western ocean, and I've heard that where it ends the peaks continue into the water, creating a series of small islands. I've never been there, myself."

"The Gludair Chain," Kana said. "What's on the other side? I mean over the tops of the peaks, to the north."

The fox closed his eyes. "It's bad luck to talk about it."

"Oh come on, Pan. You don't believe in luck."

He lifted his head from his tail and gazed up at the jagged peaks. "The Badlands. You don't want to go there. And I don't want to talk about it."

"I'm the ambassador for Paragon Exemplar Fel. I need to know as much about the entire Kingdom as possible. Please, Pan, help me out. If there's something I should know, I need you to tell me."

Panicum wrinkled his nose. "The Badlands are…dangerous. More than dangerous; *poisonous*. Normal animals don't go there. Sometimes abnormal animals—not dim, but something else is wrong, something in their heads—they spill out, either through the mountains or across the plains near the deep ravine that flanks the northern edge of the reptile lands. They stumble when they walk, like they have a fever. Some bleed. That's all I know."

"It's not another animal castle, then. Not like the other three territories."

"There are four, actually. Cats, birds, reptiles, and fish—if you will pardon my crude terminology. You'll probably never meet a fish, though."

"Why?"

"Really?"

"Oh. You mean, because they're all underwater."

"Obviously."

Kana shielded her eyes from the sun with her hand and looked past the sharp peaks. She could not see anything beyond them but the wide blue sky, although it looked a little paler than the sky directly over her head. The air above the Badlands had a greenish tinge, like Chicago sometimes did on a smoggy summer day.

"It's air pollution, isn't it? There has to be a city over there or something. I wonder if…"

"Please, Kana. Drop it. I don't like talking about it. No one does."

"Sorry, Pan. I'll stop, if it's really that important to you."

The Gludair Chain stayed always to the right of the procession as they neared the outer castle walls in the bird territory. The mountain range's presence weighed on Kana, now that she had taken full notice of it. On her last visit to the bird castle she had been distracted by her guide Struthio, the inclement weather, and her eventual imprisonment. Now that she had returned at a more dignified pace the mountains loomed overhead, watching her every move. She could understand why Panicum didn't like talking about them.

The caravan's final approach to the Great Castle came near midnight, so they were shown directly to guest quarters. The meeting with Paragon Falca would have to wait until morning. Their rooms were not as comfortable as the suites in the Felidae Great Castle, but the decorations were stunning; corded beads of painted wood and glass dripped from each fixture. Strips of colored cloth were tied around everything that could support them. The flamboyance approached gaudiness.

"Ugly," Panicum muttered.

"I guess it is, kind of," Kana said. "It's different, anyway."

Panicum brought his own pillow from the carriage, gripped in his teeth. He nosed it into a dark corner and curled up on top of it, shunning the suite's lavish bedding.

Kana's bed was in the shape of a large circular nest, with two rough straw-stuffed pillows like blue robin eggs. It was the most uncomfortable bed she had ever experienced. After trying to sleep in it for an hour, she gathered up piles of silk strips and tore down a curtain to make a small mat beside Panicum, whose canine smile curled at the corners as she fell asleep by his pillow.

In the morning, they were awakened by a screaming stork. It strode into their room on long legs, holding a food satchel clamped in its beak. The bag dripped with sticky fruit juices.

"Eat first, then you will attend the Paragon! Throne room, one hour," the bird screeched.

"Where is the…" Kana started, but the bird turned and left before she could finish her question.

"Rude!" Panicum said, delicately selecting a kiwi fruit from the satchel with his front teeth. "*Birds!* Well, at least the food's good."

Kana sat on the edge of the uncomfortable nest, nibbling almonds. "I'm really nervous. Fel never told me exactly what to say to Falca. He said that I'd know what to say when I got there, which is the stupidest thing I've ever heard. I'm not really an ambassador."

"I don't think it matters. I'm sure Falca knows why you're here. She already knows about the spheres. Your highly visible approach to her lands has been performed carefully with reverence and respect for her traditions, and I have no doubt she is aware of the encroachment of the reptiles. A personal visit to request aid and alliance is a mere formality."

"I guess you're right. But I'm the furthest thing from a diplomat. I'm nothing but a street rat, with no home in this world or any other."

Panicum frowned. "You say that a lot, but I don't think that's true any more. *None* of those things are true. Life can change. Don't try to hang on to a past you didn't like anyway."

Kana smiled. "You're pretty smart, you know, for a dog. How old are you, anyway?"

"Forty-seven, last I counted."

"What! You're forty-seven years old? Are you serious?"

"Yes. Is that such a surprise?"

"Uh, no. I guess where I come from, canines don't live very long."

"From what you've told me of your world, I'm not surprised."

Kana was unsettled. Was her world so broken? The Kingdom felt like an alien planet to her, and yet there was so much about it that felt right, too. Wildlife was thriving all over the Kingdom, plants grew everywhere and flourished, and the oxygen in the air was so thick her head spun when she took a deep breath. But there was still war and disease in the Kingdom, and the business with the Badlands sounded especially disturbing. She decided that the worlds were different, but neither was better than the other, so she must be careful to always follow her own heart; she was still Kana Kobayashi, a little good and a little bad, and utterly unique. But Panicum was right; she was no longer Kana the stray. She was now Ambassador Kana, assistant to a king. The notion filled her with hope and unfamiliar pride.

"Pan, if you're done eating, let's go. I want to get there early. Let's show Falca how serious we are."

Panicum grinned. "Ready when you are, love."

When Kana entered the Paragon's throne room, Falca was in the middle of an animated discussion with a flamingo aide. The pink bird nodded her head at the top of her long neck, then shook it back and forth in between exchanging words with Falca in low, urgent tones. Kana waited for five minutes, then ten more, but the conversation continued on.

She took a deep breath, and cleared her throat.

Falca's head whipped around. Her sight settled on Kana, but she said nothing before returning to her conversation with the aide. Kana bristled.

"Ah-HEM!" Kana shouted. "Your *magnificent* excellency, Paragon Exemplar Falca! I am honored to be in your presence this morning! I humbly request your full attention to…to…"

"Go on," Panicum whispered behind her.

"To the urgent matter at hand regarding the invasion of the uh…detestable reptile forces!"

The Paragon twisted her head around to eye Kana, slow as an owl at daybreak. "You are making too much noise, primate. Your attendance is noted. All of your requests have already been approved. You may leave now."

"But I haven't said anything yet!"

"You don't need to. I knew what you wanted before you arrived. You may leave."

Kana felt deflated. Acting as an ambassador was the first job she had ever been proud of, but it seemed her services were not needed. She really was only a pawn, after all. As always, her presence was unwanted and pointless.

The Paragon's guard approached. General Cass was among them, ready to escort Kana back to her carriage.

"No. Wait," Kana said. "I'm not leaving until this is all… what's-it-called…formalized. Write it all down, all the things you said. Whatever you think Fel needs from you, write it down, and include your price for your help too. I know you have one."

"That won't be necessary," Falca said.

"No, I'm afraid it will be necessary," Kana said. "If you don't have a scribe of your own, I'm sure one among our procession is able to write. Panicum, could you run off to the carriage and ask the lions if…"

"No need to bring your brutes up here, Ambassador Kana." Falca sighed. "I have many scribes. Meet me at sundown in my private chambers, and we will get this nonsense over with," she said with a sneer. "But leave me for now."

"Good job," Panicum whispered. "She would have helped Fel only on her own terms, and probably changed them as she went. You did it! I knew you could."

Kana hid a smile as she followed General Cass back to the suite. Deeper confidence than she had ever felt before burned in her heart with an intensity she had never imagined was possible. She was now, officially, a king's ambassador.

13.

Fear on Both Fronts

Fel paced the room. He looked out a window, caught a gamey whiff of the bear soldiers' soiled training ground, and circled back around toward his throne.

Kana had been gone for three days. Swift spies had notified him that she had gained access to Falca's Great Castle, but had not yet re-emerged. He had anticipated that Falca would make Kana wait for an audience, and had included that extra time in his plans to allow for it. But three whole *days*…

"Update!" he called out.

A gangly lion youth entered the throne room with an apologetic expression. "Nothing new, Paragon. The carriage has not yet left the bird castle."

"What's going on?" Fel hissed. "What's taking so damn long?"

The lion pinched his lips shut; he didn't know. No one knew.

Foolishness! How was Fel to lead, if he had no information? And how was he to get information if his subjects were careless and lax? That was the problem, right there. Lazy cats. He had depended on them to keep track of Kana, but now…who knew *where* she was? Could be anywhere! And the bears! Oh, the ridiculous, bumbling bears! Those wretched bruins slept half the year, yet he was expected to take them at their word that they had tried everything; marched every mile, turned over every rock, peeked behind every tree. But Fel could not be everywhere at once. He had no choice but to trust his minions, addled as they were. The king of cats, the most unique of creatures, surrounded by—and reliant upon—utter fools!

He strutted back and forth between his throne and the double-doors at the entrance to the hall, unaware that with each breath he emitted a low hissing sound. How was he to rule without the tools to do so? It was on him—Fel, alone!—to care for his people, ensure their safety, cultivate their happiness. And for what, really? What was it all for, in the end? There was no glory to be won, not for the one who already ruled all he saw. No satisfaction to be had for a lonely Paragon whose enemies' ineptitude was outdone only by the fatuity of his own dependents!

Fel sulked to his throne pillows and curled up in the middle of them, closing his eyes. After several minutes of pretending to nap, he cracked one eyelid open and smacked his paw on the lip of a large bowl of bees, sending them flying onto his chair and tumbling to the floor. After sullenly licking up every bee, one at a time, he called again for an update.

Then—finally!—someone brought him something he could use.

"She's out, Paragon. She is headed east again, toward our northwest border." The messenger was a skittering fennec fox, tapping its delicate nails on the stone floor.

"Good! But she's not supposed to come here. Her next destination is Chel's domain. I expect her to pass north of the castle and continue on to the east. Send a runner out—not you, pointy-ears, you need a rest—to ask her what happened during her meeting with Paragon Falca. Quickly, now."

So, the girl still lived. And more, the carriage was released, not kept as a souvenir by the devious Falca. Not that he needed the carriage back specifically, but it was a good sign.

Fel left his throne room for the first time in days. He toured the training grounds, checked on the kittens in the nursery, and personally attended to the preparation of the royal dinner. The air was fresh, now that he knew what was going on. His servants were quick and smart, and the entire castle hummed with energy and forward progress—truly, a wonderful hub of civilization like no other in the Kingdom! Pride filled him, from the tip of his tail to the points of his ears; he was the proprietor of the largest gem in the crown of the world, a king not only of cats but of all mammals, the regal class of animals which most embodied civility and gentility.

He smiled at everyone he walked past. Life was beautiful.

On Fel's way back toward the kitchen for a pre-dinner snack, a blast threw him to the grass, sending him rolling nose-over-toes. By the time he leapt to his feet and dashed to safety behind a pillar, the noise of the concussion was already echoing away, fading into the distance. His ears buzzed; the explosion had been the loudest sound he had ever heard, louder than the thunderbolts that struck the parapet during spring storms. But from where had it come?

He jumped up to the first-story rooftops, then made his way in strong bounds to the upper ramparts. Without a pause, he climbed to the pinnacle of the library atop his private chambers, the highest point of the castle, before looking around.

The sky over the bird lands in the west was clear and still. Nothing but white clouds could be seen over the eastern reptile lands. Fel's territories to the south were peaceful as well, all the way to the remote ridges which blocked his view of the Unspoken Graves.

Fel looked north, and nearly fell from his perch.

A smooth round cloud the shape of an egg balanced on a thin line of smoke which rose up from the ground. Spires of dust a mile high swirled around a tree of smoke that grew from the western plains of the Badlands. It ascended slowly, drifting into the sky as heat-lines wavered at its edges.

Fel's tail was fuzzed out with alarm, a condition which he normally took considerable pains to hide when he was in public spaces. But now he trembled without a trace of self-consciousness as the ominous cloud looked down over his lands, an enormous signpost written in a foreign language. Winds in the upper stratosphere began to pick at the top of the cloud, sifting off hairlike tendrils and carrying them away on the currents.

Kittens mewled below. A nursemaid was sobbing. Major Ursa had stopped running drills in the yard, and called for the entire bear contingent to stand ready for orders.

Fel could not afford to stand stunned. There might be people wounded or even dead from the blast. And he had no explanation to give them for its cause.

Once again, after too brief a rest, Paragon Fel was plunged

into the darkness of the unknown.

"What was that?" Kana screamed. The lions flanking the carriage tumbled into the tall grasses, and the bears pulling in front lurched forward in fear. Panicum ran circles inside the carriage before coming to rest under a pile of pillows.

The blast had tugged at Kana's hair and vibrated her teeth. Her ears rang, but she could still hear the carriage's wheels on the gravel road. The sound had been massive, seeming too big to have come from a single direction. She scanned the horizon.

The mushroom cloud in the sky was, like the spheres, painfully out of place in the antiquated landscape of the animal Kingdom. The birds' Great Castle was still visible far off to her left, but it now could no longer be viewed without also taking into measure the horrifying cloud rising behind it, beyond the Gludair Chain in the distant region Panicum had called the Badlands. From her position, the mountains blocked the stem she knew attached the cap to the ground, but she had seen enough vintage pictures of nuclear blasts to recognize what she saw rising into the atmosphere.

"Panicum, have you ever seen a cloud like that before?"

"No."

"How do you know? You haven't even looked at it. Come out of the pillows."

"No need. Never seen it. Nothing like it."

"Pan?"

"Leave me alone."

She could hear the terror in his voice and decided to let him hide for now. But if this had happened before, she wanted to know what he knew. Many possibilities crossed her mind, but there was only one thing she was sure of; the animals of this world, even the most selfish of them, would not do this. Only humans could be responsible for such a blast.

"We have to keep going," she said. "Lion guards! We must press on."

The frightened guards looked back at her. "Where? Back to Felidae?"

"No. We must continue under the instructions we were given by Fel. I mean, Paragon Exemplar Fel. We will proceed to the reptile lands, as the king has requested."

"But…"

"Move out!" she commanded.

The lead lion guard hesitated, but growled instructions to the harnessed bears, who took up the carriage and continued on their slow course toward Paragon Chel's Great Castle in the eastern marshes.

Fel was frozen in the wake of an inconceivable crisis.

The kittens stopped mewling, but did not return to their playground. The bear soldiers in the yard were forced to back down when they realized they had nowhere in particular to go. Runners reported back to Fel that they had found no significant damage throughout the Great Castle except for some cracked panes of glass in the north-facing windows and one collapsed apiary.

In the absence of information, citizens started to gather in a throng outside the main castle walls. They gossiped and worried, preening nervously, hoping for an address from their king. He would have to speak to them, and what would he say? That all was well? He could not know if that was the truth, yet he had no choice but to state it. They could not hear from their king that he did not know if death was imminent. It was a good ruler's primary job to know when to lie, and how to do so artfully.

He readied a speech that spoke of duty and order; the explosion would be studied, looked into, understood. And when the understanding was complete, he would promise to pass that knowledge on to the populace. In the meantime, normalcy would rule the day; return to labor, prepare meals, care for the kits, and leave the big decisions to the people who knew how to handle them.

But that was just the problem. He *didn't* know, did he? All he could hope for was that another explosion wouldn't occur right in the middle of his speech. What would happen then? Chaos, probably. Public trust decimated. Panic in the streets. Disorder and disaster.

Fel wanted to know the cause of the cloud as much as any of them. He wished Kana was back already; he had a feeling she might be able to give him some of the answers he sought. But he had sent her away. A wise choice, it had seemed at the time. And perhaps it still was.

How was he to know?

As her carriage rolled along, Kana watched the cloud drift over the Badlands. The wind carried it north, away from the Felidae lands, and she sighed with relief. If the winds blew south, she felt sure sickness would follow. Clutching a pillow to her chest, she closed her eyes and tried to remember what she knew about nuclear bombs. The radiation was like poison on the wind. Even if you weren't caught in the blast, you could get sick. And the effects lingered for a long time at the site of the explosion, maybe even for thousands of years.

She had lived in Uptown for a year, long enough to call it home. The sprawling encampment had defended her against an especially harsh Chicago winter, and she had made friends there. Or, at least, some solid acquaintances. One of them had called himself Rad. He was obsessed with nuclear conspiracy theories and the "upcoming nucleo-pocalypse" which he would describe in detail to anyone who would listen. She could have found him cute, if he had ever shut his mouth about his doomsday predictions. Rad refused to use electricity of any kind, even to the point of avoiding the use of a cell phone or a flashlight. He could always be counted on to have a match.

When Rad was younger, his interest in nuclear science had earned him a scholarship at a university to study energy production, although he dropped out in his first semester. He had even visited Chernobyl, once. But something was wrong with his brain, he said, that made him hear nuclear energy within the environment. It rang like a high bell. Some of it was natural and some was man-made, each with its own distinctive timbre. Kana didn't really believe he could hear radiation, but what he had said about bombs came back to her now.

It wasn't easy to create a nuclear explosion. Someone had to have done it on purpose. So, that meant there were sentient people in the Badlands. And now some of them would be sick, and a lot might be dead. But whoever they were, they were probably human. And some of the animals in the four territories—such as Panicum—knew something, but they didn't speak about it openly. Was it out of fear, or merely a societal taboo?

"Pan," Kana whispered. "I need to know."

His nose poked out from under a purple pillow covered in cat hair. "I don't want to talk about it."

"I know."

Panicum crept to her side and sat next to her. When they both sat upright, he was a few inches taller than she was. She looked up at his bright eyes, his greying face.

"This stuff comes from my world, Pan. If anyone can help the Kingdom understand what's going on in the Badlands, it's probably me. I don't know much, but I probably know more about it than you do."

He closed his eyes. "Twenty-two years ago. That's when it happened. That was the last time I saw that kind of cloud. I didn't think it would ever happen again." He whined and turned to the north, eyeing the remnants of the explosion as it dissipated. "Last time, there was an invasion soon after the blast. Confused creatures…damaged animals…poured from the mountains. You couldn't talk to them. They died quickly, no danger to us. Or, at least, no danger from any deliberate act of violence. But many normal animals who interacted with them, touched them, tried to help…"

Panicum put his head down and whined.

"It's ok. Go on."

"They got sick. With sores. My sister…"

"I'm sorry."

"I was twenty-five years old. Old enough to stay, to help. But I didn't. I ran away. And by the time I went back, my family was gone."

"But you couldn't have helped. This kind of sickness, it's hard to fight. You would have died too."

"I don't care. I should have stayed."

Kana wrapped her arms around his scruffy neck and em-braced him. He trembled with grief and fear.

"It's ok, Pan. I have a feeling you're going to get a chance to help, this time. I don't know what's going on but it has to have something to do with the spheres, and that means it has something to do with me—or, at least, with my world. I'm going to do every-thing I can to find out what's behind all of this."

Panicum sniffled. "Okay."

"Will you help me?"

Panicum turned to her and licked her forehead.

"Yuck." She wiped the spit from her skin with her wrist.

"I'll help, Kana. But I'm still scared."

"Me too. But we can't let that matter."

Panicum put his ears forward and glared at the distant cloud, facing his fears.

In the corner of her eye, Kana noticed movement in the bushes; a rattling motion that was not caused by wind. As soon as she turned her head toward the bush it stopped moving, yet she felt sure someone was hiding there. They were being watched.

14.

The Hard Decisions

Chel pushed, and a small army pulled. Ropes were slung over his shell, looped around his hind legs, and even lashed to his tail. It had been too long since he had moved from his throne, and he had nearly forgotten how to do it. Hopefully he would be able to walk to the nearby vantage point on the balcony under his own strength, but in case his old bones would not support him, a sled had been arranged.

"Three, two, one, *pull!*" The group leader shouted, and with a massive thrust Chel pushed himself from the whale-skull crib. After a minute of rest he tried his legs, and found them still able to hold his weight—barely. He turned his back on the spiteful sled, pleased he would not have to humiliate himself further with the use of it, and made for the sunlight shining through the open doorway that faced north.

He set his face to a neutral expression. Neither shock nor surprise should be distinguishable by onlookers, however stunning the view might prove to be. The last time he saw a cloud blossom over the northern lands was more than twenty years ago. That incident had made him fully aware, for the first time, of the Badlands as a real place rather than an abstract idea from myth and lore that could be ignored unless one was telling scary stories to children. Despite the silence and stillness of the northern region, sentient things lived there—what kind of things, he did not know, but he often wondered about them in his deepest internal ponderings. Did those who resided there retain any of the old technology? At the very least, they had explosives. That was something.

Sunlight warmed the old turtle's leathery skin. Glorious! He pledged he would try to visit the balcony more often in the coming days. Good for the body, good for the soul.

He stretched out his long, bony neck and craned his head toward the north. No mountains blocked his view; the Gludair Chain ended at the central point of the animal Kingdom. Between Chel's territory and the Badlands was, instead, a tremendous chasm, the depth of which was beyond knowledge. Its ancient name was the Neath Gap, but its common nickname among the reptiles was the Vale of Death, in memory of the many foolish souls who attempted to conquer it. None had ever succeeded; each and every one inevitably plummeted to their demise in the name of exploration and glory. Rumors regarding the chasm abounded, the most popular being a tale about a supposedly vast store of artifacts and ancient treasures hidden behind a mystical door. A giant spider lived at the bottom, some whispered, larger than a mountain and the mother of a million spawn.

Past the Gap, a row of rotten rolling hills stood between the reptile territories and the center of the Badlands, yet Chel had a clear view of the mushroom cloud rising far beyond. Many among his advisors were too young to remember the previous blast, but Chel remembered it to every last detail. He had been in his throne room that day, as he was today. Very little had changed since then, actually.

"Sir, should we…"

"Shh," Chel said. "Wait, and watch."

He could feel no breeze. Either the winds were uncommonly calm, or they were pointed toward the north, blocked from his position by his own castle. He hoped for the latter. After staring at the cloud in silence for several minutes, he concluded his lands were safe, for now; the swirling mists were moving north by northeast, almost directly away from the Neath Gap.

"Attend!" he bellowed. Advisors, diplomats, and dignitaries scuttled forth, clustering around his shell. "There can be no doubt that there is a connection between the spheres and the cloud. Furthermore, there can be no doubt that there is a connection between the human girl and the spheres. The foul cat king protects this girl; therefore, we must logically assume a connection between him and the cloud."

His advisors muttered, whispering in each other's ears and twisting their tails worriedly in their bony fingers. It sounded reasonable enough. War now seemed inevitable. How could it not be? The cat king must be kept in check!

"Many of you may not remember the last time we saw a cloud like this. Hear and remember my words now; that kind of cloud is toxic, and some of that poison will likely spill into our lands. We must be ready in case this happens."

Chel looked around, swiveling his head but keeping it level. With his angular neck extended, he was taller than his assistants— an important manipulation. "But listen closely, as I tell you the most critical point. The primate, the cloud, the spheres, and Paragon Exemplar Fel are all clearly scheming together. And this cannot be permitted, or the age of the reptiles will falter and our bloodlines will be severed. Summon our armies, arm our warriors, gather food and supplies. Equip and train every single able-bodied citizen. We will not wait here for Fel to call one of his wretched clouds down upon our lands! Marching out to meet him is our only option, even if the fight must be brought to his own soil. His power may be immense, but waiting for him to invade will only grant him enough time to grow his influence ever greater. The king of cats must fall!"

He was exhausted but could not let his advisors notice, lest he risk losing face. After waiting as long as he could for them to mutter to each other and assent to his commands, he sent them away, calling for a new contingent of fresh assistants to help him back to his throne.

The speech had gone well. Bold, commanding, and brave without divulging the fear which stabbed at his own heart. The truth was that he did not believe Fel had been responsible for the blast, but he did think the cat king was somehow mixed up in all of these strange happenings. Fel's acceptance of the primate girl as his ambassador, the sheer number of spheres which had appeared in Fel's own lands, and the generally advanced state of the Felidae Great Castle occupying its central position in the cat territories presented a confusing variety of threats both physical and political. Fel was too powerful already, and if the cat king had somehow allied with the Badlands…well, it could not be left to stand.

As the assistants settled Chel neatly into his throne and brought out refreshments, he looked around at their strong faces. A fine group, young hopefuls chosen by Chel's top generals as promising military prospects. Bright white teeth, shiny soaped scales, foolish optimism around the eyes. They waited for his dismissal or reprimand, energetic and attentive. Chel smiled.

"War," he said. "*War!* Think about that word. Do any of you know what it means? What the whole idea really means?"

The stunned attendants opened their mouths, unsure of how to answer—or whether an answer was even expected of them. Paragon Exemplar Chel rarely addressed the lower rank-and-file directly. Their training had not prepared them for the possibility.

Chel continued. "Death, that's what it means. But less death for us than for them, I'd wager. And that's also what war means; a wager. A best guess, on the part of the leaders, about whether more of their own army will die or more of the enemy's army will die. A simple answer for a complex problem, isn't it?"

"Sir," one of the lizards squeaked.

Chel craned his neck toward the youth. "Yes? You have something to add?"

"Only that we trust you, sir. We believe in your judgement, and we are honored to serve. You would never lead us astray."

"Good," Chel rumbled. "The rest of you are dismissed. You, lad, what's your name?"

"Rhys, sir."

"Stay with me for a while, Rhys. I am in need of a new personal attendant, and I think you'll do just fine."

The young lizard bowed, nearly frightened enough to shed his tail. But he managed to speak again; "I'm honored, sir. Thank you, sir."

As Kana's carriage moved ever closer to the reptile lands of Squamor, the peaks of the Gludair Chain diminished until they smoothed into a wide plateau. The flats were clear of trees or boulders, providing a direct sightline to the middle of the Badlands. In the distance, the jagged skyline of a crumbling city loomed in grey-scale through the smoke. Hazy remnants of the mushroom cloud still lingered in the atmosphere, creating sickly-colored horsetails in the air currents above the ruined buildings.

The flats then inverted and descended, forming cliffs on the Felidae side before deepening into a massive ravine that stretched away toward the eastern ocean. After the carriage passed the flatlands, trees became more abundant along the route, as did large rocks that forced the bears to weave a narrow path between them.

"That's the Neath Gap," Panicum said, pointing his nose toward the chasm. "No one knows how deep it runs. It marks the northern border of eastern Felidae as well as the entire breadth of the Squamor territories, which we will enter soon. We can expect some resistance at the border, unless Paragon Chel has already noticed our progress and sent permission ahead of our arrival."

"What's that, near the ravine? It looks like a little town." Kana pointed to the east where, in the distance, small structures jutted into the sky atop a green pine forest.

"So it does. Honestly, I have no idea. I haven't been up this way in decades."

Kana considered. She was not eager to enter Chel's marshlands. The idea of a territory run by reptiles seemed all too strange to her, even more so than a land of birds. She needed time to think, and to prepare herself for whatever came next.

"It's nearly in the direction we need to go, anyway. Let's head there, just to see what kind of town it is. Maybe they can tell us more about the passage into the reptile lands."

"Do we really have time for that, Kana? It's along a more northerly route than we had planned. The cloud-"

"Well, it's my choice, not yours, Pan. I need to stop for a little while. We have to rest. Anyway, I'm the ambassador, not you."

Without another word, Panicum curled up behind a stack of pillows and rested his chin on his tail.

RUINS
THE BADLANDS
THE GLUDAIR CHAIN
THE NEATH GAP
AEQUOR
FELCOFORNIA
WILLOWS
GRASSLANDS
DUNES
WESTERN SHORE
LAKE PINION
DUNES
BAMBOO FOREST
PAOH RIVER
UNSPOKEN GRAVES
FELIDAE
VILLAGES
SOUTHERN VILLAGE
CACILIA SWAMP
SQUAMOR
N
THE KINGDOM

15.

The Trees Grow Tall

The town atop the pines was further away than it looked. The lead lion guard flared his nostrils in the wind, scenting a shift in the weather; encroaching humidity and unstable air. The atmosphere was heavy. With a rumbling growl, he called for the procession to halt and set up camp as a sharp wind picked up. It arrived in fitful gusts from the direction of the yawning Neath Gap, carrying the smell of pine, sulfur, smoke, and mold.

Kana regretted snapping at Panicum, but did not know how to apologize. She had never stayed in one place long enough to worry about developing complex adult friendships. Everyone she knew in Chicago had been as transient as she was. Conversations were limited to a joke, a commiseration, a shared cigarette torn in half by shivering hands in tattered gloves. Nicknames like Junkyard or Helix kept people at a comfortable distance. Relationships never lasted long, as the changing seasons drew in the snowbirds with summer warmth then washed them away again with winter storms, year after year. Squats could appear and disappear in a day, or less. Nothing stuck, and nothing ever got complicated.

Of course, nothing had ever seemed to stick before she ended up on the streets, either. She had nothing in common with her family. Conversations with her sister ended with a fight every time, and her mother was incapable of leaving her alone. Until the day she left home, Kana was accosted by her mother's relentless urging to get involved in pastimes they both knew she had no interest in; invitations to get her nails done, gossip over afternoon tea, find a new gym, attend a useless class. Her mother's list of uninteresting interests was endless, but the woman likely couldn't name a single one of Kana's favorite hobbies. She was self-absorbed and arrogant, despite her seemingly generous offers. So Kana had always felt alone; her mother wanted a pet, someone who would follow her around and keep her company. Not a daughter with a mind of her own.

She shivered, clutching a pillow to her chest. "Pan? Are you cold?"

The fox didn't answer.

"Pan!" Kana felt around under the pillows until her hand found his tail. She yanked on it.

"Hey!" he cried. "What are you doing?"

"Sorry," Kana said. "Are you awake?"

"I am now," Panicum growled. "What do you want, your majesty?"

Kana felt her face heat up and turn red. "I'm sorry about what I said last night. I'm not used to this kind of pressure, and I let it get to me."

Instead of accepting her apology, Panicum sat up and licked a forepaw. She could tell he was thinking. After thoroughly wetting his paw, he turned his head toward the distant town, smelling the breeze. It seemed the issue had been dropped.

"What do you think we'll find there?" Kana asked.

"A community of cats, most likely. We're not near the reptile lands yet. Could also be hooved creatures, though. That town is near the Steppe Cliffs. Some small antelope and goats like to brave the rocky ridges. Can't imagine why."

She considered. It occurred to her she had seen very few hooved animals since her arrival. Where were the horses? The deer? She had seen perhaps two or three as they passed through the outer Felidae villages, but not in numbers that approached the populations of the cats, bears, and birds.

"So the hooved animals live in the cat-ruled territories? Like the bears do?"

"Yes, the few that remain. I have heard that they were once much greater in number. Centuries ago, the world was full of an enormous variety of species, according to what I was taught as a young pup. Near my hometown, the bones of massive hooved animals have been found. They were called 'elk.' Very impressive horns."

"Where I come from, we still have elk. And cows, and horses…"

"Ah! I've met a horse or two over the years. Flighty creatures, but nice in their own way."

"What about donkeys? Or elephants…"

Panicum growled.

"What's wrong?"

"Sorry," he said. "That wasn't exactly directed at you."

"Then what…"

"We don't discuss the elephants. It's simply not done…just so you know."

"What do you mean? Why not?"

Panicum gazed off in the direction of the pine trees. "Look, Kana, our Kingdom is a sad place. Our numbers—and I mean all animals, not only mammals—are much reduced from what they were in prehistory. For the most part, we don't know why. But we do know it had something to do with primates and their greed. And then they all died. That's why your arrival here is so shocking."

"Yeah. No monkeys or apes here, huh? And no humans."

"But there were elephants, and not too long ago. They formed an exclusive commune in the south. And then they all died; totally decimated. And it wasn't done by primates. You understand? Animals killed them. *We* killed them. And the events surrounding that disaster are deeply shameful to the citizenry of the entire Kingdom. So we do not discuss the elephants. Ever."

"Oh. I'm…I'm sorry."

"You couldn't have known. But keep in mind that bringing up the subject to someone who isn't a friend could get you in trouble, or even hurt."

Hearing that one single word, Kana lost the flow of the conversation. Panicum had called her a friend! The word, casually used, filled her with warmth. She had a friend. Not a street buddy or a partner or a roommate, but a real friend. Someone who chose to be near her, talk to her, share their feelings. She felt giddy, but also terrified. Now she had so much more to lose.

They slept in the carriage, and awoke the next morning to

the sound of fat flies buzzing in the blue sky overhead. The bears had slept in a pile. Lion guards were stationed facing out in different directions from the carriage, watching for the approach of any stranger. Kana stretched, felt Panicum's fur under her hand, and smiled. He wasn't a pet, but he wasn't human, either. More like a testy pillow that talked back—but also a dear companion she couldn't survive without. He was shorter than she when he walked beside her, but taller when they sat together, and nearly twice her age. Wise, yet at times cowardly, the result of a wealth of experience combined with everyday trauma. Never had she imagined anyone could become so precious to her in so short a time.

Panicum growled. Kana raised her head in surprise and looked at his face; his eyes were still squeezed shut, but his nostrils were flaring. All four paws twitched. He was dreaming.

A lion guard turned her head and looked toward the carriage, noticing Kana was awake. Strutting forth on giant paws, she approached Kana with her head down.

"All is quiet, Ambassador. Shall we move on?"

"Yes, let's go. It's too cold to spend another night outside. We should try to find shelter in the town for a little while before crossing into the reptile lands."

"Yes, Ambassador."

Panicum lifted his head, blinking sleep from his eyes. He scratched behind an ear with a hind paw, and with both ears pressed flat he stretched his nose toward the sky, straightening his spine. "Gah, I'm old. Too old to be camping under the stars in the cold north."

"We'll reach that town today. Even if it's abandoned, we'll at least get to sleep under a roof for a change."

The bears found a wide road within the first hour of travel, speeding their progress through dense trees which increased in size as they moved along their route. Small spiky shrubs turned into medium-sized fir trees, which graduated to massive pines scratching at the underbelly of the blue sky. The tree branches spread until they touched each other, creating cool wet canopies overhead, blocking out the sunlight. As they followed the road further north, it drew nearer the gorge to within a half-mile of its gaping darkness before swerving east to flank the chasm, weaving through the thick forest. Loops of light- and dark-green mosses swung from the trees, connecting the branches in soft latticework like Christmas garlands. Beetles of every color studded the moss, flashing bright shells which concealed fine black filament wings. As the sky became obscured by tree limbs and an artificial twilight set in, chirping rose up on all sides.

"What's that sound? Are those frogs, Pan?"

Panicum lifted his nose from his tail, where his nostrils, dripping with forest dew, had left a wet spot. "No, the songs you are hearing are sung by crickets. I've heard old stories about frogs before, but there are no wet lizards now left in the Kingdom. What were they called…'fibians?'"

"Amphibians." Kana fell silent, listening to the insects call out. Each tiny chirp was nothing but a gentle chime, yet in excessive numbers the overwhelming chorus was disruptive to the peace of the forest. There were too many of them. The harmonies were too loud, too robust. The insects did not even quiet down as the carriage passed close by; they were granted unnatural bravery by their massive population, living without fear of any meaningful danger from predators. One time, long ago, perhaps there had been enough larger animals who fed on the insects, keeping their population low. Now, they ate the forest, the grass, and even each other with their population unchecked.

The path split. To the right, a wide road led uphill among clusters of thinning trees, wending its way out of the forest. To the left, a narrow road ran deeper into the thick pines, a tunnel almost as dark as night. At the fork where the road separated was planted a wooden sign carved in the shape of a cat, marked with an arrow that pointed north—toward the left path.

"Cats to the left," Panicum said. "But the right path is a more direct route to our destination."

"I still think we should check the town."

Panicum frowned, but said nothing. Kana tried not to resent his lack of support.

The lion guard, without questioning her decision, led the carriage down the northern path into the deep forest.

16.

Meeting the Ounce

The town was a disappointment. It was little more than a cluster of old treehouses built out of soggy boards, attached with clumsy braces to the pine trees' crooked branches. They were not well constructed. Several of the shelters had already collapsed, and many more seemed on the brink of tumbling to the forest floor. The few still intact were lined with dried moss and stale pine needles which crawled with beetles and crickets.

A tribe of snow leopards inhabited the little dens, although they were clearly not the ones who built them. The cats were lazy and disinterested, allowing the carriage to pass into the heart of their village without offering a word of either threat or welcome. Even in the dim light, their bright white pelts glowed like a congregation of full moons. They laid draped over the branches which supported their dens, gazing down at the carriage, tails flicking back and forth with amusement. To Kana's embarrassment, the lodgings were far too small for her or her guard to fit inside; the snow leopards themselves barely fit. Coming here had been a mistake.

A large male cat approached. His mouth wore a curled smile, and his eyes had a look of playful mischief and mockery.

"I am called Ounce. So, you may call me…*Ounce.*"

The leopards tittered, amused at their leader's apparent joke. Kana didn't understand the humor, and decided to take a diplomatic approach. Ounce grinned with sarcastic patience, leering as Kana climbed down from the carriage with Panicum following behind. She approached the cat and caught herself before holding out her hand; the gesture would surely not be greeted kindly by someone who walked on all four legs.

"I'm Kana, and this is my friend, Panicum. And these are…"

Kana glanced around at her guard and realized with dismay she did not know a single name. She hadn't taken the time to learn any. "Are my guard. We are pleased to meet you."

"Likewise, I'm sure. You are welcome to visit our villa, but I don't know what you expect to find here." Ounce strode toward the carriage, leaving massive paw prints in the mud. He circled the road-weary bear soldiers and dirty carriage with an air of faint disgust.

"We had hoped to ask for shelter for the night," Kana said, trailing behind. "But I see now that your village is not going to work for our purposes."

"Certainly not. Is that all?"

"Well, yes," Kana said. The question sounded loaded. Ounce wanted to ask something else. She sensed he expected more from her, but she had no idea what he might have in mind.

"Well. My apologies for your disappointment," Ounce said, "but your raiding party will find nothing of use to you here." His eye twitched, but Kana could not be sure whether it was another display of displeasure, or an unconscious tell.

"Raiding party? No, you misunderstand, Mr. Ounce. I'm an ambassador for Paragon Exemplar Fel. Your own king. I'm on my way to…"

"Lies!" Ounce said. He hissed, bristling his cheeks. "I know you have come to take our food, for we have already caught your spy!"

Two snow leopards walked toward the village center. Between them, they guided a human boy dressed in strung leaves and reeds. He was filthy and scratched, and the ridges of his ribs showed on his chest. His bare feet were covered in bloody cuts, and a fresh wound circled his left bicep like a red armband.

"A *human!*" Panicum cried, dashing back into the carriage. "Where in the world did you find that?"

"The shocked look on your face makes me feel hopeful this was all a misunderstanding," Ounce said, grinning at Kana. His eye twitched again.

"I…I am sorry, but I don't know who this is," Kana stammered. "I assure you, he does not belong to our group."

"Surely you must be able to imagine how difficult that is for me to believe," Ounce said, sitting down between the two humans. "Two primates, both on my land, at the same exact time. Lightning does not strike the same ground twice."

"No, really! I don't…" Kana turned to the boy. "Who are you? What's your name?"

He bowed his head and examined his bruised toes.

"We caught him stealing food from our meat storage," Ounce said. "We have little enough already, living this close to the barren ridges of the Neath Gap. Unchecked, his actions would have caused us all to starve."

"I promise, Mr. Ounce, I have never seen him before in my life," Kana said.

"Ah, a promise! My favorite kind of lie. Well, you do seem sincere. In that case, you will not mind if we eat him," Ounce said.

"No! Wait…"

"Ah, so he *is* yours!"

"I never said that! I don't know who he is. I just don't want you to eat him, okay?"

A look of satisfaction settled on Ounce's face, his whiskers flared from his cheeks. His eyes did not twitch again, but instead they narrowed with anticipation.

"A trade, then," Ounce said.

Now Kana felt sure this had been on his mind all along. "Well-"

"Let me call for my negotiator."

Ounce let out a low, screeching howl. An aged leopard with patchy fur leapt down from a tree branch. Around his neck he wore a string with a series of colored beads; a kind of simple abacus. He strode near the carriage, sniffing at its contents before sitting across from Ounce.

The negotiator spoke. "You want the human boy, but offer nothing in return. I have a counter-offer. We will accept nothing less than your ten finest pillows, five bags of dried bees, two honey-combs…"

"Hold on!" Kana said. "We don't have all of that!"

"Kana," Panicum whispered at her side. "Just listen to his proposal first, then make your own counter-offer. That's how it's done."

The old leopard continued, "One gold chain, a sack of fresh white feathers, three spools of decorative ribbon, and one of your strongest bears to stay behind as our personal guard."

Kana glanced back at the carriage. "Um…"

"Counter-offer!" the old leopard demanded. "You must counter immediately, unless you have decided to accept our terms!"

"No! I can't accept any of that! Here's my counter-offer."

"Careful. Keep your offer low, but respectful," Panicum muttered. "If they think you scorn them, we will fail the negotiation."

"Three pillows, one bag of dried fruits, uh…" Kana peered into the carriage and found four blankets, various grasses, and a stack of spare leather straps for the harnesses. "One blanket, a handful of really tasty grasses from a distant land, and three leather straps. Great for holding together soggy wooden beams."

"Five pillows, two bags of dried fruit, two blankets, and all of your grasses. Half of your leather. And we still want the bear!"

"Everything except the bear!" Kana said, grinning.

"Done!"

A snow leopard guard shoved the human boy forward with its broad nose, causing him to trip and spill into the mud. He knelt without moving, eyes shut, until one of the bear soldiers nudged him back to his feet. His eyes were the soft green of the plains grasses, red-rimmed from crying. Kana approached him with a blanket while the lion guards counted out the goods to pay for his release.

"What's your name? I'm Kana."

"Jack." The boy mumbled and would not look her in the eyes, but accepted the blanket she offered.

"I have a very important question for you, Jack. A question only you can answer."

"What? What question?"

Kana smiled. Good; she had his attention. "Are you from Chicago? How did you get here? Did you come in a sphere?"

The boy frowned. "A what?"

"We should go," Panicum said. "The deal is done, and I'm sensing that we're not really welcome here. Are you ready?"

Kana helped Jack into the carriage, and they sat shivering under the blankets as the caravan continued down the path. As soon as the snow leopard village disappeared behind the trees, the boy pulled a blanket over his head and fell asleep. He did not show his face until the pines started to thin and beams of sunlight once again flickered between the swags of hanging moss.

When Jack finally looked out from his blanket, Kana and Panicum were eating dinner. He stared at the dried fruit and beetles with a desperate, famished look.

"Want some?" Kana said, holding out a bag.

Without a word, Jack plunged both hands into the food and began to stuff it into his mouth.

"Now, Jack," Kana said. "Tell me how you ended up here."

Jack glanced up at Kana. Between bites he said, "I went through the gorge."

"Impossible," Panicum sniffed. "No one can cross the Neath Gap. It's far too wide, and much too deep. Monsters in there, too. Never been done. And anyway, that's not what she asked, is it? Exactly how did you get into the Kingdom? Did you come here from Chicago?"

Jack shook his head, but the question seemed to upset him. Kana shrugged at Panicum. She would have to try another approach.

"So, you don't know Chicago. All right. But don't you come from…uh, the normal world? Maybe even from the United States?"

None of the words sparked recognition in the boy's eyes. "Past the gorge, like I said. A long way. You would call it the Badlands. That's where I'm from."

"Hmm. He's not from your world at all, Kana," Panicum said. "He's a local, it seems. I had no idea there were still humans in the north."

"Are you from that big city?" Kana pointed toward the distant ruins which were starting to become visible again as the cloud cleared from the horizon.

Jack shook his head. "Further. We had a town, east of the city. There was a big explosion in the west. I ran away."

Panicum growled, showing his teeth, and leaped to his feet. "*No!* He might be sick, Kana. It sounds like he was pretty close to the blast. If he's contagious, he could kill us all!" His tail puffed up in terror as he backed away from Jack until his rump hit the carriage door.

"Calm down, Pan." Kana turned back to Jack and looked carefully at his smooth skin and tired eyes. "How do you feel?"

"Hungry still," Jack said. "But mostly just tired."

"No, I mean, do you feel sick? In your stomach, or in your head. Do you know what I'm talking about?"

"I know what you mean. But I'm not sick from the cloud. I ran upwind, and away. Others got sick, but I feel fine."

Panicum dashed under the pillows. The bedding vibrated with his trembling.

"Pan, come out of there. He's obviously not sick. It's okay."

"Even if you're right—even if he doesn't kill us all!—what are you going to do with him?" Panicum barked from under the mound of cushions. "He jeopardizes our entire diplomatic venture. This isn't what we're here for. And Chel won't like it at all, I can promise you that."

"I don't know yet, but we couldn't just leave him there. Can't you understand that?"

The pile of pillows fell still and quiet.

"Where are you from?" Jack asked. "Are you from the western villages, the ones near the Chain?"

What could she tell him? She had no wish to lie to the boy, but the truth would only confuse him, and she needed his trust if they were going to help each other.

"I'm from a village that's very far away. I'm lost, and I'm trying to find my way home. The place I'm from is called Chicago."

"That's a lie," Jack said.

"What?"

"Chicago is one of the ancient cities. It's gone now; they all are. Everyone who ever came from there is dead. Why are you lying to me?"

"I'm not, I promise! I really am from Chicago."

Jack again pulled his blanket over his head. Kana looked to Panicum, exasperated, but he still hid under his pillows.

Kana scowled. Fine, then! If they wanted to cower in fear and confusion, she would let them. She called for the carriage to halt, and jumped to the ground.

For the next several miles, Kana walked ahead, near the lead lion guard. She plucked twigs from the bushes by the side of the road, making a small bouquet of herbs and wildflowers. Crickets leapt around her feet when she strayed into the brush, clinging to her boot laces. The trees remained tall but the woods continued to thin as oaks and elms took over, the colors of their jagged leaves fading into warm, autumn tones. Broad-leaf trees became more common than the firs as they moved east, and eventually they left the last of the pine forest behind.

When they stopped for the night, Kana made an effort to learn more about the animals she traveled with. The bears were all related—brothers, she discovered, and they felt honored to pull the carriage together as a family. The dutiful lion guard did not speak much, but they offered their names as well as their opinions on the progress of the journey. The lead lion guard, Lieutenant Barbar, admitted the trip was his first excursion through densely wooded lands, but he was enjoying it tremendously. The bears wondered if the trees held any beehives, and whether those might have honey for the taking. The group talked late into the night around the light of the fire, until Jack emerged from his blanket and wordlessly took a seat at the perimeter of the conversation. The bears eyed him warily, but said nothing. At last, Panicum sneaked around the edge of the circle and sat on the opposite side from the human boy, watching him with a steady gaze.

"I am grateful to you all," Kana said, addressing the group. "I know your loyalty is primarily to Paragon Exemplar Fel, yet I still feel I am personally in your debt for your exemplary service, labor, and assistance. Thank you for protecting me and Panicum, and now our young friend Jack." At his name, the boy raised his head and looked at her with sad, tired eyes.

"Little primate," Barbar rumbled, examining the long cut on Jack's upper arm. "You need medical attention. Will you let me help you?"

Jack winced, but nodded. "Yes."

As Barbar cleaned Jack's wound, Kana beckoned to Panicum to join her at the door of the carriage. As they sat on its step, Panicum never took his eyes off Jack.

"Well? Are you over it yet, Pan?"

"He doesn't seem sick, I'll admit. But you don't understand the danger. You haven't seen it, what the poison does to people. I have." The fox grimaced, watching Barbar clean Jack's wound. "Even just *touching* the boy is dangerous. His blood could be…"

"It's true that I haven't seen what you've seen, but you're wrong about me not understanding it. I know what radiation sickness is. He doesn't have it."

"Even if that is true, I still don't know what you're going to do with him. Have we now adopted a puppy, to care for and nurture on a perilous journey through enemy territory?"

"We'll worry about that later. For now, he comes with us. I'm sorry Panicum, but I won't have it any other way."

By lunchtime the next day, the carriage had left the sparse forest and entered a rocky plain with clear views of the distant hills on the southern horizon. The road led gradually further from the Neath Gap, bending southward while staying within sight of the chasm. The soil was uneven and permeated with stones, but the air was warmer than it had been near the snow leopard village and Kana was grateful for the change in temperature.

"Where are we going?" Jack asked, crunching on a handful of spicy beetles. He was talking more now, but his appetite was unabated.

"I am an ambassador for the Felidae Paragon," Kana said. "I am on a mission of peace, to secure support for the king of cats and to attempt to talk the invading reptiles into a pact of reconciliation."

"Wow."

"Are you being sarcastic?"

"What does that mean?"

"It means…never mind."

"But aren't you human, though? You're like me. So why are you working for the cats?"

"Paragon Fel is my friend," Kana said, wondering at the truth of the statement even as she spoke it. Perhaps her flattery at being assigned such a vital mission had muddled her judgement. No one had ever trusted her with anything important before, and the surprise of Fel promoting her to a position of such worth had been a pleasant shock. She had mistaken manipulation for kindness before. Seeing through the deception of others was not one of her skills. Her suspicion of Ounce had been easy; the snow leopard wore his heart on his sleeve—or paw, or whatever. But Fel was a clever cat, and a king as well. Falca had not been particularly impressed by Kana's arrival, and Chel would be even less receptive. So why was Fel so interested in her wellbeing?

Was she being used?

17.

The Northern Gate

For two more days the caravan continued, in increasing discomfort, along the road parallel to the cavernous Neath Gap. Intense winds, no longer held back by a forest, roared up from its winding intestines to create a constant rumbling that could be felt underfoot as the ground shuddered with the pressure of the rising air. Sounds, especially raised voices, echoed easily in the chasm, which created an unsettling effect unless an effort was made to keep the volume of conversations low. Few animals lived on this desolate terrain which laid within view of the outer edge of the Badlands.

The difference between the territories on either side of the chasm was dramatic. The grass under Kana's feet, while pallid, was still green and healthy enough. But nothing seemed to thrive in the Badlands; the trees were twisted and dark, the grass was eternally dry, and the dirt was brick-red dust. The only movement on the other side of the Gap came from swarming clouds of gnats which arose in whirling spirals from crevices in the ground.

"How did you get across, Jack? Is there a bridge somewhere?"

"In the middle of the Kingdom there is a flat place. Between the Gludair Chain and the Neath Gap. Haven't you seen it?"

"Oh, yes, I have," Kana said, remembering. "So you simply ran across the plains, then?"

Jack flinched, then his expression went blank. "It's more complicated than that. I'll tell you later. Not now."

Panicum snapped at a fly hovering around his ears. "Can't wait to get away from this damned ravine. It stinks of tar and mold."

"It will be another day of travel at least," said Barbar, the lead lion guard. "Before the road breaks away from the gorge. Then the road should, I believe, curve toward Squamor and the reptile castle. But before we can leave the Gap, we must pass an inspection point at the border."

"Inspection? What are they looking for?"

"Whatever they want," Barbar sneered. "A lot will depend on whether Paragon Chel has sent word ahead of your arrival, granting permission for your passage. If he hasn't, we may lose even more of our supplies buying our way through the gate than we did with the purchase of your new friend."

Jack looked sullen. "Sorry you had to pay off those stupid cats."

"We didn't have to, Jack," Kana said. "We wanted to. And we'd do it again. Right, Pan?"

Panicum scratched behind an ear, pretending not to hear the question.

The following morning, Kana woke to discover Jack had run away during the night. Barbar bowed his head in shame.

"I should have noticed, Ambassador. I take full responsibility for the disappearance of your ward, and will organize a search party at once."

"A search party? Made up of whom? We need the lion guard and the bear soldiers here with the carriage, and we must continue on to the reptile lands without delay."

"But, your investment-"

"Investment! Jack was not an *investment*. He was not a slave, understand? I freed him because it was the right thing to do. You will not hunt him down like he's a…a…"

"Snack," Panicum muttered.

"A piece of property!"

"Yes, Ambassador," Barbar said, lowering his head so far his nose touched the dirt, dotting a tiny spot of slimy mud between his nostrils.

"Jack wanted to leave, so he left. I am sad about that, but we will not go after him. If he wants to leave us, he is free to do so. Understood?"

Barbar nodded, and left Kana and Panicum to their breakfast.

"Do you know where he went, Pan? Would you even tell me

if you did?"

"I'd tell you," Panicum said, looking hurt. "I was only joking. I have no idea where he went. He's probably just not used to spending time around other people, after all that he's been through."

Kana peered out across the grassy fields that ran up to the edge of the Gap, squinting in the crisp morning sunlight. "I guess so. But he seemed happy enough to be with us."

"You never know. People are good at hiding pain."

"You don't have to tell me that."

Panicum tilted his head to one side and assessed Kana with a glinting eye. "I have a treat for you. This seems as good a time as any." He fished under the pillows with a paw and hooked out a sack tied with a loop of braided grass.

"What's that?"

"Open it. Easier for you than it is for me, with your clever hands. I only hope the contents are what was promised me. I wasn't able to check."

Inside the sack, Kana found a delectable mix of nuts and dried fruits. When she popped a few into her mouth, her eyes flew open wide with joy and astonishment.

"*Salt!* Oh my god, it's salty!"

Panicum nodded. "Good, that's what I ordered. Salted foods are uncommon in the Kingdom, but I know they are plentiful where you come from. I thought you might like this."

Kana's eyes watered as the over-salted trail mix stung her tongue. She had almost forgotten what salt had tasted like. Her stomach rumbled happily as she chewed another handful.

"Here, try it!" she said, holding out a handful of fruit. Panicum gently selected a morsel from her hand. His face contorted as he chewed, twisting with disgust as his eyes watered.

"Agh! It's awful! How do you eat this?"

"It's wonderful," Kana said, with her eyes closed. "Reminds me of French fries, potato chips, hot ramen, pastrami. And pizza! And the winter broth stew they used to serve at the free kitchen during the week before Christmas."

"Can't be good for you," Panicum muttered.

"Want more?"

"No! No, please, you enjoy them."

"Makes me thirsty, though," Kana said, reaching for a water skin. "Oh! We're almost out of water!"

"It won't matter, soon," Barbar said, walking up to pace the carriage.

"What does that mean? Sounds ominous."

"I only mean we're getting close to the reptile marshlands. The gate is just up ahead. See it?"

In the hazy distance, two rusted metal spires reached into the sky. "Is that the entrance to Squamor?"

"Yes. We will arrive at the gate in less than an hour. I don't know how this will go, Ambassador. Ready yourself for anything."

"Couldn't we just go around? We don't have to actually use the gate, do we?"

"We could. But our caravan is conspicuous, and we would be quickly noticed. At that point, our advance would be considered an invasion. We must give the Squamor territories the courtesy of making a proper approach, and announce our intent in their lands."

"Yes, I understand. Thank you, Barbar."

Kana's stomach fluttered as it had before her meeting with Paragon Falca. She was only meeting with guards, not royalty, yet she sensed what happened here would affect all that came after. Whether they were permitted access to the reptile lands or not would set the tone for future negotiations between the castles, and her performance today might have far-reaching implications. Her apprehension caused a brief rebellion within her mind as she wondered again whether she had any right to be affecting this strange world in this way—a drifter from Chicago laying the foundation of a new relationship between two countries. But, as always, she found a way to push back the imposter feelings and focus on the matter at hand. Despite her lack of qualifications, her job meant everything to her now. Perhaps that alone lent her the legitimacy she needed, to wield the power to make positive change.

As the carriage neared the gate, two eight-foot-tall lizards watched its approach. They stood upright on their hind legs in front of the metal spires, overseeing the door to Squamor, which stood wide open. Their tabards were adorned with strips of bright red cloth bordered with gold flecks—a trim created either from fine metal chain or from metallic embroidery. Either way, the technology was extravagant. Jutting up over their shoulders loomed massive sword hilts. As the carriage neared, Kana was relieved to see that their heads were bowed in deference to her arrival, and piled on the ground at their scaly clawed feet were baskets of offerings: simple breads, fruits, clean towels, strange green pods filled with fresh water, and even a picture book that must have been very valuable.

"Paragon Exemplar Chel welcomes you to his lands," one of the reptile guards said. "He grants you safe passage into his castle, and he eagerly awaits a meeting with the esteemed Ambassador of Paragon Exemplar Fel."

"Nice," Panicum whispered. "*Excessively* nice, to be sure. Especially considering what happened to Fel's last emissary."

Kana cleared her throat. "We are most grateful. I mean, please relay to the Paragon that we are grateful. I look forward to meeting Paragon Exemplar Chel, and we will waste no time journeying to…to meet him."

"Smooth," Panicum whispered.

"Shut up, Pan!" Kana hissed. Panicum giggled, with his head hidden under a pillow.

The reptile guards nodded, and near the gate there was a sudden burst of movement. A lithe, quick snake bearing a tiny crimson standard slithered south at full speed; a runner, on his way to the reptile castle to notify Paragon Chel of the arrival of Fel's ambassador, and her acceptance of the offerings.

Barbar directed the bear soldiers to load the baskets into the carriage. When they were finished, the wheels squeaked under the added weight.

"Ooh, fresh bees," Panicum said, digging into a cloth sack.

Kana watched the metal spires pass overhead as the carriage moved through the gate. The construct looked a thousand years old, rusted through in many places. It could not have provided any security to the guards or the lands beyond; it was merely a testament, honoring the distant past. Kana thought of Jack, and his village in the Badlands. There were still humans somewhere in the north, an important fact that the animals seemed largely unaware of. Was it possible this gate had been built by human hands, a millennium ago? Kana tried to visualize reptiles melting and hammering steel into place, crafting the two identical metal structures, and erecting them around a locking gate mechanism—and could not. It reminded her of the reproduction center, out of place and out of its own time. But if humans had created these things, they were not Jack's people. The humans who had created this gate had technology.

Where were they now?

The reptile lands were wet and rotten. The soft ground slowed the progress of the carriage even in stretches where the road was clear of roots and mud clods. Kana called for rest breaks more often, after noticing the sinking of the carriage wheels and the fatigue it was causing the bear soldiers. The added weight of the tributes was a boon but also a burden, and she wondered if perhaps Chel had already outsmarted her. Although their progress was tedious, she was loath to abandon any of the gifts he had sent.

But she was, foremost, an ambassador. She looked around at her gasping assistants and assessed how much food and water would be needed to reach Chel's castle.

"Okay, people. Let's stop for tonight."

"But it's still early, Ambassador," Barbar said. "Two hours yet until the sun goes down."

"I know. But we're going to have a party!" Kana said. "Unload everything except these three food baskets here, and most of the water. Come on, let's have a feast!"

Late into the night, the group talked and laughed and ate until they were near bursting. They each shared the stories of their lives, making friends by the firelight. Almost every scrap of food was devoured by midnight. Panicum sat near Kana, grinning through every conversation. He took his own turn at storytelling, and displayed a surprising skill with shadow puppets, using his body to cast pictures on the ground that spun tales of ancient myths. Kana ate the rest of the salted trail mix, and squeezed fresh fruit into cups of water to make juice. As the bears tumbled atop each other to fall asleep for the night and the lion guard took up their watch stations, Kana crawled into the carriage with Panicum at her heels.

"Very clever, Ambassador," Panicum said as he rested his chin on his tail. "And in more ways than one."

"Thanks, Pan."

As she was lying down, she caught sight of movement off the side of the road. In the soft light of the moon, a small creature adorned in leaves hid among the bushes, peeking out at the dying bonfire with bright green eyes. Jealous eyes: Jack's eyes.

Kana smiled, and drifted to sleep.

18.

The Southern Gate

Major Ursa paced the training yard. Her shoulders quivered with unspent adrenaline.

Five days had passed since the explosion had rocked the Felidae Great Castle and a cloud the shape of a giant oak had risen over the northern lands. Five days, and the Paragon had made no move on the enemy. No plans for retaliation, no scouting parties; nothing.

The Major had no idea who the enemy might be. But the background political structures that supported war were not her domain. Taking decisive action and moving on orders was her job, and without direction she was lost.

So the bear soldiers ran drills, then ran them again. When one group became exhausted beyond their senses, Major Ursa sent for a new team and started over. Fighting, running, relaying, moving in formations. Protecting the eyes before striking forward with the claws to counter airborne attacks. Low swipes from a wide stance for infantry attacks. They would be ready for anything.

She had tried several times to arrange an audience with Paragon Fel, but he would accept no visitors. Silence reigned in the castle, which in the past had meant he was preparing to take off on one of his adventuresome journeys. She hoped this was not the case; these frightening days would not be a good time to leave the citizenry behind. Quarrels in the streets between neighbors had increased and intensified. Many were stockpiling water and food. There was no shortage of supplies, and no one knew exactly why they felt the need to take these actions, but there was something thick in the air; a weighty sense of impending disaster from enemies unknown.

"Reverse! Start again!" she yelled at the fresh troupe. Her paws were covered in raw sores from pacing the perimeter wall for hours on end, but whenever she laid down to rest, her mind raced. Was war imminent? If so, with whom? And, in any case, how does one fight a battle against the clouds in the sky?

A familiar voice called her name. She raised her head to find Paragon Fel sitting at the entryway to the yard. He was disheveled. Smears of food crusted his collar, and the decorative feathers that adorned his black leathers were bent and limp.

"Sir!" Major Ursa called out, lumbering toward him.

"I have a task for you. There has been an incident, according to one of the runners. Near the…" Fel lowered his voice. "Near the reptile border in the south. It must be inspected immediately. Assemble a small team, and bring news back to me as quickly as you can."

Finally, something to bite down on! "Yes, Paragon! Right away, sir!"

None other would do for the trip than her favorite captain, Orlo, and his elite team of scouts. They were young, able to move quickly and quietly. The crossing Paragon Fel spoke of was two days away. She decided they would reach it in one.

Ursa turned to a nearby runner, a jumpy lynx waiting for orders. "Fetch Captain Orlo, and tell him to bring his team to the yard. Right away."

"Sir!"

"On second thought, you come back with them, too. I need you for this mission."

As the lynx dashed away, she examined the pads of her sore paws. They were not ready for a day of marching, yet it was unavoidable. The tips of her long black nails were chipping, and her skin was fraying like delicate flower petals. For the first time since the cloud had appeared in the northern skies, she lay down on the ground to rest, forcing her tense muscles to relax.

"Sir!"

Orlo and his team appeared at her side. So fast! Had she fallen asleep? If so, it was probably for the best. As she sat up, her aged body complained but obeyed.

"Secret mission, Captain. We leave now, without delay. I'll tell you more on the way."

Their pace through the countryside was not so fast that Major Ursa did not notice how quiet it had become. Few merchants traveled on the roads. No one tended the fields, or sat at picnics under the trees. Citizens huddled in their homes, guarding their possessions and their children as though they expected the sky to fall at any moment. She berated herself for restricting the training drills to the yard; they should have been parading in the streets, making a show of force to assure the people of their safety. Peace would not last if the population was terrified into isolation. Neighbor would turn on neighbor, and infighting would begin.

The villages became sparse and seldom as they moved further from the castle. They veered to the east, toward the reptile territories, where the earth dissolved into marsh. She allowed the team two hours of rest during the darkest hours of the night, but did not wait for the sun to rise to press on toward the southern gate.

"Keep an eye out for reptiles, Captain. They have been spotted in this area recently, scavenging for metals and relics. If they are brave enough, they could be hostile."

"Yes, Major. No sign of any yet, sir."

One of the youngest team members took up something in his paw; a long thorn, punctured deep into the pad. Orlo helped the youth construct a quick shelter of piled reeds before leaving him behind, with a promise that they would return by dawn of the following day. Ursa almost wished she could stay, too. Her upper forearm felt as though it had somehow come unhinged from her shoulder. Each step wrenched the tendons, which caused a sharp echoing pain down her side all the way to her hip. Still, she pressed on.

Leagues before they reached the southern gate, Ursa smelled carrion. It was rotting, but not too old. It must have sat three or four days in the sun, no more. The wind filled her nose with the smell, mixed up with the gentler aromas of wildflowers and swamp moss. The odor grew stronger as they neared the gate, and Ursa knew long before they arrived what they would find there.

The southern gate was surrounded by a village which had

been built to support a thriving micro-economy of imports and exports, dealing exclusive Felidae items to reptilian goods dealers at the border to the cat lands. Soft pillows, mats of woven reeds, and tender meats harvested from dim creatures fetched high prices from tourists and wholesalers. The village had expanded from a trading stop to a thriving trade city, with its own local government and a diverse population. It also served as a port of distribution for Squamor, collecting reptile-made goods for resale to the villages surrounding the outer walls of Felidae castle.

Orlo had family there, if Ursa recalled correctly. A sister and a niece, or something like that.

Even before the village center was visible, it was clear something was wrong. The place was too quiet for a lively trading hub. Blood had been tracked on the paths. They passed buildings which had been looted, burned, or torn down.

"Sir," Orlo said. "A body."

Off the side of the road lay a lump of red. The species was indistinguishable; its muscle and fat was flayed bare. The corpse had been skinned.

Ursa snarled. No cat or bear would do this, and a hooved animal was not capable of it. Only reptiles would commit murder for a pelt. She knew she should turn back and report to Fel without delay. But she wanted proof, first. If the evil done here was to be the first event of a major war, she wanted to know beyond doubt who instigated it. Suspicion was not enough.

The closer the team moved toward the center of the village, the more red, rotting lumps dotted the road. A thousand reptile footprints, long and clawed like oversized bird feet, criss-crossed each other in the dirt. Every building had been either scorched or ransacked. Felidae goods were tipped into the mud and trampled. Reptile feces was smeared on storefronts. And the entire population was also here, skinned and piled on top of each other, their blood seeping into the ground. The only sound was the buzzing of flies.

In one market stall, a tiger merchant was draped over its own display table. Its massive jaw was stretched open in agony. Where its eyes should have been, two empty holes gaped. There were holes also where its ears should have been—they were cut away, taken along with most of the pelt.

One of the young team members gagged, and added to the muck in the road. Ursa knew she had to get them out; they were too green to see this kind of carnage. It would be a bad time for panic or despair. At least she knew beyond doubt who the real enemy was. How they had created the blast in the Badlands to the north was still a riddle, but this devastation was undoubtedly caused by reptiles. Her chest pounded with purpose and rage.

"Runner!" she cried out.

The lynx appeared at her side. "Yes, sir!"

"Return now. Report to Paragon Fel that the reptiles have annihilated the population of the southern gate village. Stop for nothing!"

The lynx raced north without a moment of hesitation.

"The rest of you! Move out! Off your asses, *now!*" Her shouting was too loud, too forceful. But she was trying to snap them out of their stunned shock as they stared, wide-eyed, at the death around them. They jumped as if stung, and staggered into a single line.

She led the team away from the village center until they were once again surrounded by trees and fresh air. After an hour of rest, they found the road and retraced their steps until night fell. When they had returned to their injured teammate, Ursa called for another rest.

"Orlo, a private meeting," she said into the darkness. He brushed against her side, wordlessly notifying her of his presence. "Aside," she muttered.

They sat some distance away from the camp under a draping pepper tree. Ursa watched the young bears huddle together in the dark, trying to sleep.

"You know what this means," she whispered.

"War. Without any doubt, now. Paragon Fel will not let this go unchallenged. In fact, he will be furious."

"Nothing like this has happened since the fall of the elephant tribe." A chill ran up Ursa's back, but it wasn't fear. Was it excitement? Perhaps it was merely a reaction to the enormous significance of the day's events. History was happening, right now, in this moment. War was inevitable. The reptiles would finally be defeated. A massive turning of the tide. And Ursa was riding high atop it, ready to achieve victory. She had prepared for this her entire life.

"Sir?"

"Yes, Orlo?"

"If you don't mind me asking—and if you can't say, I understand—do you know what happened to them? The elephants, I mean."

"They were betrayed by one of their own. A young elephant, name of Magas or Mardas or something like that, I don't remember. He developed a liking for a certain type of juice imported from the reptile lands through the southern gate. The stuff was rotten… fermented, like things get when they sit for too long. He regularly met in secret with a reptile contact who brought it from somewhere deep across the Squamor border. From what I was told, this young elephant traded information—migratory schedules, secrets, rumors, or anything else that might be used to rob or blackmail members of his tribe—in return for the juice he craved. When he ran out of information, the secret contact used his knowledge to get someone else from the tribe addicted. And then someone else, and then their family, and their friends too. Eventually the entire elephant population was mad for the stuff. It induced euphoria and hallucinations, but these sensations were soon followed by periods of intense aggression and rage, during which the elephants fought and nearly tore each other to pieces before recovering and starting again the next day. Once the juice was introduced to a new user, it was difficult for them to refuse repeating the experience, despite the consequences. The elephants demanded greater and greater quantities and begged the contact to obtain ever-stronger brews, until finally a batch went out that was pure poison. Every single one of them died, vomiting purple stuff from their trunks and writhing in agony. Well, that's what I heard, anyway."

"What happened to the reptile contact?"

"Disappeared, or maybe he too died from the juice. No one

knows, and even if he lived, everyone who could have identified him was dead. Fel went nearly mad looking for him."

Orlo shuddered. "An ignoble way to die."

"True. I hope we die more nobly."

Orlo looked up at Ursa. "Do you think it will come to that?"

"Yes." Ursa turned to watch the young bears twitching fitfully in their sleep. "But don't tell them that."

"Maybe we can talk Fel out of it."

"Talk him out of what? Even if he decided to forgive this monstrous act of war, what do you think will happen when word of it spreads? The people are already frightened. This attack will send them into a frenzy. They will demand a response, and vengeance. Fel must act. He has no choice. There will be war."

"Then we should not be resting. We must move out now, and return to the castle immediately."

Ursa sighed down at her bleeding feet. "Yes, you're right. Are you ready?"

"Yes, sir. Always."

"Fine. Let's go."

19.

Reptilia

After half a day of traveling south through sludgy marsh-land, Kana's carriage was met by a tidy contingent of reptilian guards. They moved in perfect formation with their tails straight and low to the ground as they marched on their hind legs. Kana was not sure of their exact species—crocodiles, maybe, except their faces were too blunt—but each stood six or seven feet tall, heads held high, with swords strapped to their backs and bright tabards crossing their scaly chests.

A reptile commander stepped toward the carriage and bowed. "We are your escort, Ambassador Kana, esteemed servant of Paragon Exemplar Fel. We are honored to guide you to the Great Castle of Paragon Exemplar Chel."

"We don't need an escort," Kana said. "We can find our own way, I am sure."

"Nevertheless, we will escort you. It is in our Paragon's interest that the Ambassador arrive at his castle safely and quickly."

Kana had hoped to explore the country a little, talk with some of the citizens, and get a feel for the culture before meeting with their leader. From what she had seen so far, the land was too wet to support any kind of farming or agriculture. She wondered what the reptiles ate and where they worked. The carriage had passed a few sodden straw-roofed huts off the sides of the road, but no large villages. Ruins were plentiful here. Rusting metal spires and ancient fences flanked the road, tilted at haphazard angles as they sank into the muck.

"If you are ready to proceed to the castle…" the commander said, bowing again and gesturing with his arm.

"Fine," Kana said. "Lead on."

The reptile contingent surrounded the carriage, tailing the

lion guard and flanking the bears. Panicum's eyes darted from one reptile to the next, nervous.

"What are they up to?" he whispered. "It's as if they don't want us meeting any of the citizenry. What are they hiding? I've spent some time in these lands, although it was quite a few years ago. It was nothing like this then. Where are all the *people?*"

For another hour the carriage crept south, leaving deep grooves in the mud as it made its way through clusters of buildings which increased in size as they progressed. A few citizens walked the street now, but they were all aged, their dry scales chipped and their eyes sunken. The elderly huddled together in groups and gossiped in low voices, nodding to each other as the soldiers passed.

The land was growing even wetter. Crickets no longer chirped at the sides of the road, but were replaced by buzzing mosquitoes. At one point in the journey they passed a large gleaming building, shockingly out of place in the dreary swamp; a reproduction center, dilapidated but functional. Doors on each side had bright LED button panels above their handles, and a tall spire on the roof blinked with a red light at the top.

"So, they have those centers here, too," Kana said. "I wonder if the humans in Jack's northern village also use them."

"If they don't want a dim pup, I imagine they must."

"What really happens inside the centers? Are there doctors?"

"The mothers who enter the centers claim they don't remember what happens inside, and the buildings won't admit anyone who isn't ready to give birth. The doors just won't open."

"What do you mean, 'claim they don't remember'? Don't you believe them?"

Panicum sighed, and snapped at a hovering mosquito before answering. "I know many females have nightmares for the rest of their lives after giving birth. Some part of their brain remembers what they saw inside the centers, but none will speak plainly about their experience."

"Maybe unless you have to go inside you haven't earned the right to know."

"Perhaps. All I know is that natural births result in idiot children, without fail."

Kana studied the reproduction center as the carriage trundled past. Like the others she had seen, it was relatively clean and maintained, despite its age. The structure was bulbous and white, like an upside-down turnip striped with stainless steel panels. The spire at the top reached a hundred feet into the sky.

And the eastern door was open, just a crack.

"Panicum, the door! It's *open!*" Kana struggled to her feet, preparing to leap from the carriage. She had to know what was inside. If it was a hospital, maybe it was staffed by humans. Maybe there were people who could give her some answers.

"Kana, stop! Wait…"

"Back!" one of the reptile guards shouted. "Sit, please, Ambassador." He drew his sword and pointed it at Kana's chest before she could jump down to the ground.

"Who are you to stop me?" Kana said. The guard held steady, moving the tip of his sword closer to Kana's skin.

"Kana, they won't let you go," Panicum said. "This is their land, and we are only visitors here. You don't have the right."

She slumped back on the pillows and watched the reproduction center's open door disappear behind a copse of stunted trees. She would come back, she vowed. As soon as she was done with Paragon Chel, she would find a way back and look inside. There were answers there. She could feel it. Maybe even a way home, somehow.

As the carriage neared the Great Castle, the reptile guards relaxed. They spread out more, marched less in time, nodded to passers-by. Roadside huts became more frequent, and these were sturdier and in better repair than the ones they had passed in the countryside. Snake and lizard civilians crowded at the edges of the road to glimpse the ambassador's procession, but all of them, even the laymen and laborers, carried weapons in hilts at their sides. Here, then, were some of the missing civilian population; they were attending the Squamor Great Castle—and they had been armed.

"I don't like this," Panicum whispered through his whiskers.

Kana put on the formal velvet robe which had been prepared

for her before she left the Felidae castle, and waved at the crowds. Might as well act the part.

The road turned to gravel as it passed through avenues of upper-class estates, a district of clay houses constructed of flat-packed walls studded with shiny pebbles and sticks. They were occupied by the most privileged citizens of the Squamor lands; large reptiles, particularly crocodiles and enormous snakes. Their scales were protected by armor fashioned from hinged metal plates which clanked in tandem with their strange, undulating walk. The adornments were half aesthetic and half armor, as even the elites seemed to be fully prepared for war. The entire population seemed to be an eager militia, calm and well-trained, prepared to defend their land and honor at a moment's notice.

Kana's lion guard was visibly nervous, and the bears walked with their ears pressed flat against their heads, keeping their eyes on the road.

As the carriage arrived at the Great Castle, it followed a broad roundabout drive until it was stopped by guards at a gold-plated gate. An awning shaded the entry, draped with decorative chains and supported by tall statues of reptile warriors bearing massive shields. The pressed clay road was expertly tiled with lava rocks and crushed chunks of seashell. Plaques and decorations mounted on the castle walls were made with more metal than Kana had seen since she had arrived in the Kingdom; the reptiles seemed to value gold and iron very highly. A set of planters near the front door were mulched with thousands of tiny sea shells, and conches were stuck at regular intervals into the door frames.

"Are we near the ocean?" Kana asked Panicum.

"Somewhat. To the east lies the sea, and the Great Castle of the ocean domain, Aequor, is just off the Squamor coast. I've heard it rumored that Chel speaks with Paragon Mobula quite often."

"This way, Ambassador," a reptile soldier said. "To your quarters."

"I was hoping Paragon Chel would meet with me soon. Will we see him today?"

"My deepest apologies, Ambassador, but I am not privy to his schedule. I am sure once you are settled into your suite he will send word to you."

Kana and Panicum followed the soldier down winding halls that felt like worm-holes. They were rounded, and packed with hard sand. Portholes which illuminated the walkways were smooth and seamless, as if they had grown naturally in the walls.

"Feels like I'm in an ant farm," Kana muttered.

"A what?"

"Ant farm. When I was a kid, I had a clear flat box that I kept ants inside. So you could see them build their little walkways."

Panicum grinned. "Oh, you mean you kept them as pets! I had a pet once. I found a little dim mouse—just a baby, it was— but I decided not to eat it. I don't know why. It burrowed into my fur and I felt sorry for it, I guess. Never could teach it to speak or anything. I let it scamper about, watched it grow up for a few weeks. Eventually a big raven found it and ate it before I could stop him. But I suppose you can't blame a fellow for eating."

"Oh! But it must have made you sad to lose your friend."

"Sad? Yes, I suppose it was. I am loathe to see any animal die. But it was only a dim thing."

"I guess. Are you really sure the dim creatures are so different from you? Maybe they are actually smart, and they just don't feel like talking."

The fox opened his mouth and laughed with his ears laid flat. "They're dumber than rocks, Kana. I promise."

"I don't know. That seems narrow-minded, Pan."

"You'll see. You'll meet one someday, and then you'll under-stand. They aren't like the rest of us."

The suite the reptile soldier showed them to was clean and elegant. White sand walls arched overhead until they met with sunroofs set into the ceiling, which were dotted with colored glass that cast rainbow sunbeams onto coral couches in the center of the room. In each corner, fountains trickled into little rivers that trimmed the walls, carrying lily pads and pink flowers along as they circled the room. Incense and candles scented the air with lilac and lavender. A tray near the couches held heaps of overripe fruit and mushrooms.

"Paragon Exemplar Chel begs you to enjoy your stay. I will be right outside your door, ready to assist with anything you desire. Do you have any requests at this time, Ambassador?"

"No, thank you," Kana said.

"In two hours, our most talented theatrical group will perform for your amusement. Later tonight, dinner will be served while our Great Castle musicians entertain you and your companion. If you require a change of clothes, several options have been prepared for you. Please find everything you need in the chests." The soldier gestured toward a pair of ornate boxes covered in carved sandstone flowers.

"And when do we see the Paragon?"

"I will relay your eagerness to him, Ambassador."

Kana discovered a wide assortment of clothing options in the chests, all tailored to fit her perfectly. A hairbrush and a toothbrush were also included, nestled in a clamshell box. On the dining table she found a selection of exotic entrees. Salted roots cooked to a crisp in oil reminded her of potato chips. Scraps of meat baked in honey tasted much like teriyaki beef jerky. There were mushrooms and fungi of every color and shape. One kind was puffy-white and tasted just like marshmallows. Another, which was a strange shade of pink, made her head spin in a pleasurable way each time she took a bite.

She had suspected Chel was spying on her, but this confirmed it. Everything in the suite was crafted to make her comfortable. There was no chance the reptiles of this land wanted oily fried roots or honeyed meats that closely mimicked the kind of food she might find on a street corner in Chicago. This was for her, and her only. What was Chel playing at? Either he was mocking her, showing off the skill of his spies, or he was trying to woo her away from Fel. Either way, Kana was annoyed. The reptile lands looked poor and desolate but Chel was clearly well cared for, to the point of excess.

In other words, a despot.

"Soldier!" she called out. "Are you still there?"

The reptile soldier stepped into the room with a brisk march that ended in a bow. "Ambassador, what is your wish?"

"I want to meet with my chief lion guard, Lieutenant Barbar. Where is he?"

"I will bring him here immediately, Ambassador."

"No. I want to go to him. Where are his quarters?"

"Ambassador, surely you do not want to visit…"

"Take me to him. Now."

The soldier nodded and led the way down a long hall, opposite the direction from where they had entered. The path descended until it was underground. The portholes in the hallways ended, and the sunlight faded away. Candles set on rusted metal pans on the ground provided only enough light to keep Kana from bumping into the walls. At the bottom of a long slope, the hallway widened into a large room. Cut into the walls were sandy alcoves, cold and dirty, each with a cot and a single burning candle.

"*This* is where my guards are staying?" Kana's throat was sore in the cool, damp air.

"You disapprove? These are the servant quarters for entourages of foreign delegates. They are much nicer than the lodgings for castle servants. For one thing, the food here is unlimited." The soldier gestured toward a wooden plate loaded with unwashed roots and long-dead bugs.

"Barbar!" Kana called out. "You in here?"

The head lion guard stepped from an alcove. His nose was wrinkled with displeasure. "Ambassador Kana. Did you need something from us?"

"I wanted to see where you were staying. This place is… well…"

"Disgusting," Panicum said.

Barbar shook his head. "We are doing just fine, Ambassador. Surely you have more important matters to consider before you meet with Paragon Chel. We appreciate your visit, but please, do not worry about us."

"Come back to our room, Barbar. Stay with us. It's much nicer."

"I won't leave my crew, Ambassador. If this is where they stay, then this is where I stay."

"We can fit all of you! Our suite is huge…"

"I cannot allow that, Ambassador," the reptile soldier said. "My humblest apologies, but the help must stay below. It is our custom."

"Ambassador, please return to your rooms," Barbar said. He bowed his head and winked. "Your concern is touching and deeply appreciated, but we have slept in rougher places than this."

Kana reached out on impulse and rubbed the lion's head behind his ear. He chuffed in appreciation for a moment before regaining his usual dignified manner, and strutted back toward his alcove.

"I don't like this," Kana said to the soldier. "But I'll agree to go back to my suite if you promise me they will all be taken care of. Fresh water and pillows for everyone, okay?"

The soldier's eye twitched. "Certainly, Ambassador. Nothing but our very best pillows."

20.

Honored Guest

Paragon Chel did not call for Kana the next day, nor the day after that. As she waited, she explored the Great Castle's winding hallways, ate countless platters of fresh fruit and sweetened meats, and played hide-and-seek with Panicum in the courtyards.

The reptiles proved to be remarkably talented performers. Paragon Chel's courtesans hosted a fascinating military drama in three acts, featuring a variety of colored geckos in elaborate costumes. Red geckos wore formal green waistcoats, yellow geckos wore strange feathery dresses, and blue geckos wore rainbow jumpers. Strength and honor were the running themes. The script of the final performance centered on a prince who faced a difficult choice; ignore the plight of his neighbors in order to make his own people more prosperous, or send his soldiers to aid an inept king in a distant land full of desperate and hostile strangers. In line with his good-hearted nature, he chose to help the strangers, but was then betrayed by the ungrateful king, causing him to finally realize his efforts would always be more appreciated by his own kind than by outsiders.

Panicum grumbled at the end of the performance, but when Kana asked him why, he would not answer.

On the fourth day of waiting to be summoned, Kana and Panicum were enjoying lunch on a balcony overlooking the nicest part of the castle courtyards when Kana spotted the hazy outline of the massive city in the distant center of the Badlands. The frightening cloud had entirely dissipated. That was good; maybe the threat wasn't so bad, after all.

Panicum was sullen, and no amount of exotic food or pleasant conversation could cheer him. He even rejected the floral honey-wine he had developed a taste for over the last couple of days. Kana decided he must be bored. Castle life had never agreed with him. But they were at the mercy of the reptile Paragon, and he would have to be patient.

As Kana finished her meal, the glass doors to the balcony were thrown open, slamming the walls hard enough to leave indents where the handles hit the siding. A tremendous crashing sound followed as Lieutenant Barbar burst into the room with a kick aimed at the swinging doors, and a furious servant followed him close behind, shouting threats and apologies.

"Ambassador!" Barbar roared, "I have been trying to see you for days, but this reptile would not allow me. He claimed you were sequestered in private, at your own request. Is this true?"

"Certainly not, Barbar! You are always welcome in my presence."

The lizard servant bowed over and over, his nose nearly touching the tiles as his tail flipped up behind. "Ambassador, my humblest apologies, but I could not stop this brute from…"

"And neither should you try," Kana said. "He is my assistant, and if he wishes to speak with me I am sure he has an excellent reason. Barbar?"

"Ambassador, thank you. I only wanted to ask if you have any indication from Paragon Chel how much longer we will be waiting."

"That's all?" Kana said. "Well, I don't know. He hasn't talked to me yet, and there's nothing I can really do about that, is there?"

"It's only that we are all staying in rather, uh, musty quarters. The damp has started to settle into our fur, and…"

"I thought you said your accommodations were acceptable. You are safe and fed, are you not?"

"Ambassador?"

"It has only been a few days. I don't want to push Chel too hard. His cooperation is critical, and we must respect the local customs."

"Yes, Ambassador. What should I tell the rest of the guard?"

"You can tell them that we will wait as long as is necessary, and that while we are in the reptile lands we will appreciate their traditions and be grateful."

"But..."

"Dismissed."

Barbar hunched. He stared at her for a moment, then walked toward the door with his ears laid flat and his tail swung low. His toes dragged on the tile.

The servant shut the door behind him, and turned toward Kana with his mouth open to speak.

"Dismissed," she said.

"But don't you want..."

"No! I said you are *dismissed.* Obey, or I'll have your tail!"

The lizard hissed, and followed Barbar out the door.

Kana laid back on her lounge chair and plucked a ripe peach from a dish of fruit. She sank her teeth in deep, letting the juice drip down her chin. With a warm, scented cloth, she blotted the sticky trail clean. When she had picked the stone free of pulp, she tossed it into the far corner where a number of pits had collected.

"Do you really think that was wise?" Panicum asked.

"The lizards will get it. They always clean up in the morning after we leave."

"I'm not talking about that. I'm talking about your loyal lion guard."

"What about him?"

"His concerns are legitimate. That dungeon they are being kept in is dank, unhealthy. It's basically a prison. We need to see Chel and get out of here."

"And what makes you think I have any control over that? He'll see us when he sees us. We're in his castle, so it's up to him."

Panicum leaped onto Kana's legs and growled. The weight of his big paws dug into her thighs, pressing hard enough to leave bruises. His face had never been so close to hers, and for the first time she noticed how many razor-sharp teeth he had.

"Pan! What on earth-"

"Your people are your responsibility. Barbar and his contingent of guards are loyal to Paragon Fel, but the king has assigned those guards to your watch and now they must obey you.

So whether you like it or not, the burden of their welfare rests on your shoulders. Anyone who serves you is under your personal protection, and right now you are letting your people suffer. There's always something you can do, Kana. Always! You might not be used to having this kind of power, but for better or for worse, it's been handed to you. Do you really want to act like Chel?"

"I'm nothing like Paragon Chel! I'm an ambassador, and with that position comes certain privileges! And I've included you, so I don't know why you're so upset. The lions and bears are used to being down in the dirt and the mud. They're used to working hard! It's not a big deal for them. And anyway, you're just a drifter like me, so what do you know about it anyway?"

"More than you do, apparently." Panicum snarled, and strutted toward the door. "I'll be back when you've thought a little harder about the situation."

"Then don't come back!" Kana screamed. She threw an apple at the fox as his tail slipped around the door frame.

Kana turned over onto her belly in the lounge chair and screamed into a pillow until tears squeezed from her eyes. She soaked the fabric, emptying all her rage and confusion and frustration. Who was she, these days? Her identity had become abstract at some point during all the changes in her life. And where was she now? She felt like a pawn on a chessboard, being moved from one square to the next, only ever able to move in baby steps and too short to see the entire playing field. She couldn't begin to understand the complexity of the game being played. She didn't even know all the rules, yet she was still expected to win. And the king of cats stood in the back row far behind her, overlooking all, waiting to see if the leader of reptiles on the other side would ignore her or swallow her whole. But did Fel really care what happened to her? And did Kana *care* whether he cared? All she should care about was getting home, but now she wasn't even sure about that. What was waiting for her in Chicago that was better than what she had found in the Kingdom?

The truth was, she was scared to see Chel and she was also scared to go home. The last few days of luxury had been an enormous relief, and had felt like a well-deserved break. The comfort of the suite was unlike anything she had ever experienced before, and the thought of her stay coming to an end was unbearable. And then what? Back in the carriage again, back into the mud?

The specter of her serious meeting with Chel filled her with dread. Falca had made her nervous, but she had met the bird Paragon before and knew what to expect. But from what she had seen of Chel's lands and subjects, he would be unlike anyone she had ever met. Probably much smarter than she was. Definitely more prepared.

When she was done in the reptile lands, what was next for her? The obvious answer was to find a way home. Home was Chicago—but, was it really? She had made friends here in the Kingdom, and held a job that made her feel important. And she even had people who looked out for her, which was something altogether new. She was valued by a king, and appreciated by a dear friend, and protected by…

Barbar.

"Servant!" Kana cried out. "Come back!"

When she received no reply, she peeked down the corridor outside the suite. For the first time since she had arrived, it was empty.

"Pan?" Again she received no answer.

She decided to check in on Barbar and the rest, just to make sure they were still being taken care of. It was the least she could do. Then, maybe she could send another message to Chel and urge him to meet with her soon. Tomorrow, perhaps—or maybe even tonight, if he was willing.

As she made her way through the hallways in the direction of the visitor quarters she passed the portal windows that looked out over the rear castle grounds, and this time she took a moment to peer through them. The labor yards on this side of the castle were different from the landscaped gardens she and Panicum had been escorted through when they first arrived. Tired workers were bent over agricultural plots, gathering vegetables under the watchful eye of a soldier with a whip. Many of the laborers were slight, even childlike. One large yard held a collection of shackles and chains attached to wooden constructs like medieval stocks—some of which were occupied by gaunt prisoners.

Kana descended the sloping hallway lined with candles on metal plates. As she neared the bunk room, the sounds of a commotion filled the hall; shouting, struggling, and the smash of splintering wood. Peeking around the corner into the room, she saw a bear and two lions balled up in the middle of the floor. A small crew of reptiles holding rusted blades in their claws was carefully approaching Barbar, who stood between them and his troops, his mouth open and snarling.

"Halt!" she yelled. "What's going on here?"

"These guests were caught trying to leave their quarters, Ambassador," one of the reptiles replied. "As is our custom, they were punished. This large one here tried to stop us," he said, gesturing toward Barbar with the tip of his sword. "So it is our custom to also punish him. Surely you would not deny us our right to enforce the law in our own castle, Ambassador?"

Kana knelt and examined the bear curled in the mud. The Felidae castle tabard he wore was caked with blood and slimy mud. His eyes were open but he was still, and his body was cooling. His mouth was fixed with a frozen grimace.

"You killed them just for trying to leave the room? How *dare* you?"

"It is our prerogative."

"I don't care! Go, now!"

The reptile captain bowed, and gestured to his crew. They left the room as she demanded, but grinned as they went.

"And tell Chel I want to see him immediately!" Kana yelled after them.

"Ambassador, I must apologize," Barbar said. "They stopped feeding us yesterday afternoon, and they…"

"Don't, Barbar. Please don't apologize. This is all my fault, and I'm so, so sorry." Kana draped tattered blankets over the bodies of the bear and the lions. "I can't believe I let this happen."

"Are you ready to meet with Paragon Chel?" Panicum stood

at the door, his head hung low with sorrow. "I have no doubt that if you demanded to see him—if you marched right up to his throne room—he would not find it easy to deny you."

Kana clenched her fists and took a deep breath. "I am as ready as I'll ever be. Let's go now."

They met the lizard servant, who was coming down the hallway to find them, and coerced him into leading them straight to Paragon Chel's throne room. Kana did not wait to be announced. She walked in with her hands still clenched at her sides, and kept her chin held high. Chel raised his head with an air of calm expectation; he had known she would burst into his chambers today. He had seen it all in advance, played this game carefully, and was already several moves ahead. Kana wanted to scream, to cry, to demand justice for her murdered soldiers. But this was not the time. Only diplomacy would work today, despite her rage. For the sake of Felidae, she must pass this test.

"Felidae Castle Ambassador for Paragon Exemplar Fel, Kana the human!" the lizard servant cried out.

"Welcome, Kana. I trust you have been quite comfortable in your private suite?"

Kana bit back a retort, then bit back another. "You know I have, Paragon. I offer my…" She bit her lip and closed her eyes. "Humblest gratitude for your hospitality. My assistants also have extended their thanks."

"The pleasure is mine, little one. I heard there was some kind of disruption…"

"No disruption, Paragon. It has all been settled." A tear formed at the corner of her eye, and she cursed it into drying up before it could travel down her cheek. She unclenched her fists and bowed her head in reverence to the Paragon. It didn't matter how much she hated the game; she couldn't win it unless she played.

"Ah, lovely," Chel rumbled from his throne. "So, shall we get down to business? Or would you prefer a glass of sea-gin first? I don't know if you've ever had strong alcohol before, but it's quite delightful."

"Yes, I have, Paragon. Thank you, but no."

"Ahh, so perhaps your world still has knowledge of distillation? I would love to hear all you have to tell of it." Chel arched his neck high and looked down at Kana.

"I know a little bit about it. I had a friend who made her own hooch in a bucket."

"That sounds delightful. What about smoke? I don't mean fire, I mean…"

"Like cigarettes? Or hookah? You'd probably like that better than cigarettes, actually," Kana said, thinking Chel acted much like the snide caterpillar from *Alice in Wonderland*.

"What is hookah? But wait, I am getting ahead of myself. First, tell me what you know of 'hooch' and its specifications."

"No. First we talk about what your troops are doing in the Felidae territories."

Chel sighed and retracted his head with an air of excessive drama. "To business already? You are so deadly serious, my child! Ah, very well."

Kana waited in silence, letting her demand for information stand. Chel blinked his massive eyes, preparing his response.

"You are quite new to this world, aren't you, child?"

"Yes."

"So you don't know how things work here. The politics, the history."

"I don't need to know. I know what war is, and that it should be avoided whenever possible. And I know what it looks like when people in power take advantage of those who have none."

"Smart girl. You've experienced that yourself from both sides now, haven't you? The rich and the poor."

"Yes." Kana scowled as her cheeks blushed. He was mocking her. Falca's dismissive treatment of her had been frustrating, but Chel's insinuations cut deeper.

"I have no desire to hurt the people of the castle Felidae. All I seek is technology, similar to that utilized by the reproduction centers, and also seen in the spheres, such as the one you arrived in. But Paragon Fel will under no circumstances allow my troops to explore without interference, so I am forced to do what I must to fulfill my needs."

"Did you even ask him?"

"It would not have not mattered. Our relationship is immutable. I know what his response would be. Do you not?" Chel tilted his head to the side as he asked.

"Okay, yes, I agree that he would not let you pillage his lands without compensation. But you're hurting his people, and you must understand why he can't allow that either."

"What are you here for, girl? If you bring neither a threat nor anything to offer, this meeting is a waste of time."

"Fel doesn't have to offer you anything. He has sent me to tell you that if you don't stop sending your troops into his land, your people will die."

Chel opened his mouth and laughed, showing his ancient grey gums. "That's nothing new. I thought he'd be more imaginative. Is that all?"

"Well…yes," Kana said. "But I am here to explore any peaceful alternatives you are willing to discuss."

Why hadn't Paragon Fel given her more to say? Now that she had said it out loud, it really didn't seem like much. She remembered she was here as a simple show of force, as a material example of Fel's far-reaching influence—and once again, she felt used.

"I have a counter-offer," Chel said. "We continue to take what we want from the cat lands, and Fel's ambassador will stay here in my castle permanently, residing in her very own suite. She may keep her pet fox with her, drink all the honey-wine she desires, and live out her days in luxury."

"No deal," Kana growled.

"Are you quite sure? Just this afternoon you were so reluctant to leave."

"I'm not staying."

"Ah, but you *are*, girl! If that is the extent of your counter-offer, then I have yet another offer to make. My troops will take what they can from every sphere in the Kingdom, and destroy any Felidae citizen who interferes with them. You will tell me everything you can of the technology in your world, and when the extent of your knowledge is exhausted you will remain here, not in a suite but in our prison until the end of your very brief life."

Before Kana could retort, her arms were grabbed from behind by scaly claws with long nails that scraped at her skin. Panicum whipped around to face the attackers, but he was seized and muzzled before he could bite.

Kana's last sight before a bag was pulled over her head was Chel's enormous, toothless smile.

21.

Salted Wounds

Paragon Fel leaned forward in his throne. The claws of his forepaws dug into the arm rests, creating shallow grooves that ended in little holes punctured deep in the wood. He sat frozen, still as a hunter in the bushes, lashing the tip of his tail back and forth.

"Repeat yourself. Say it again. Slowly."

"The ambassador, sir, uh…"

"What about her?"

"Has been imprisoned, sir. In the bowels of the Squamor Great Castle."

Fel closed his eyes. He had not misheard, then. Chel had locked Kana up. The nerve, the cowardice, the *arrogance* such an act required was far beyond any low traits he had previously attributed to the reptile monarch. Fel would have found it hard to believe, but he had absolute trust in his assistants. He was not sure it would be possible for Kana to be extracted, even by his most capable soldiers. Paragon Chel's residence was deep behind hostile borders and the prison was hidden away under the ramparts of a fortified stronghold belonging to the most war-ready castle in the Kingdom. No, for now she would have to stay where she was. But if Chel had harmed her…

"Sir, what would you like me to do?"

"Nothing more. You are dismissed."

The messenger turned toward the door.

"Wait, one more word," said Fel. "How, exactly, did you come by this information?"

"From your southeastern spy network, sir. The smallest of them—a skinny little weasel by the name of Jax, I believe—infiltrated the reptiles' Great Castle. Not ten inches long, that one. He has sharp eyes, but could do little else but report back, of course. Not big enough to fight."

"Of course," Fel muttered. "Dismissed."

The southeastern spy network was an efficient company. Fel had no reason to disbelieve them. But still, the idea that Chel had abandoned every treaty, committed war crimes in spite of decades of relative peace, and ignored all of the basic rules of civilized engagement simply for the sake of imprisoning a single ambassador…

A skinny doorman appeared before Fel, twitching with anxiety. "Sir! Major Ursa has returned!"

"So, show her in," Fel said, eyeing the servant's nervousness with trepidation. Something was wrong.

"She comes now, as fast as she is able."

"What does that mean?"

Major Ursa lurched into view, dragging her bulk across the hall through the door. She breathed heavily, dehydrated and gaunt, at the end of her strength.

"Paragon Exemplar Fel," she gasped, "I sent a runner ahead. Did he not return to you with news?"

"No runner has arrived. What has happened?"

Ursa snarled, showing her yellow teeth. "The reptiles have devastated the trading village at the southern gate, sir. All lay dead, their skinned bodies rotting in the mud."

A stripe of fur on Fel's back and neck raised and trembled like meadow grass waving in a windstorm. His eyes formed perfect circles as his lids flew wide with shock and rage. He leapt from his throne and walked on his hind legs toward the door with a slow, stalking gait. Rumbling and hissing at both nothing and everything, he marched from the room in a seething fury that approached blackout. When he reached the first courtyard, he sat at the top of the stairs and looped his tail around his feet. His body was still as a statue, but he was ready to snap at the first creature who approached him. None did.

Chel had declawed his emissary, imprisoned his ambassador, murdered his traders, and terrorized his citizens. Fel had suspected war was inevitable, but apparently it was more than that; war was imminent.

Major Ursa needed rest, but he had other military leaders he could call on. And new ones could be forged in the hard days ahead. Squamor was better armed, but the cats were clever, quick, and greater in number, especially since the decline of Squamor's amphibian population. If only the elephants had survived, their strength would have been an important advantage.

His chest hurt. How many had died? The southern gate was out of his immediate purview, but he had heard it was thriving in recent years, with the market businesses surging in response to reptile interest in imported bird-made trinkets and local cat-made luxuries. Now hundreds were dead, if Major Ursa's report was accurate. And he had no doubt it was. So, then: a thriving village dead, mere days after a mysterious explosion to the north. His new ambassador was locked up as a prisoner of war, and his enemy was growing stronger by the hour.

A warm wind blew through his ears as he sat at the top of the stairs that overlooked the training yard. In the distance he could see green, empty hills, beckoning him to explore and hide in their tall grasses. There were other places to visit, other regions to live in. His wanderlust grew strong as he longed to disappear from this tortured castle, leave his crown behind, and roam exotic lands where nothing was asked of him. Someplace where no other lives depended on his judgement, and his decisions affected only his own future.

He stood, his eyes fixated on the distant hills. His toes twitched, ready for the first steps of a grand new adventure. He could ditch his crown and robes in a barrel, creep along the east side of the plain, and make for the rolling hills past the grain fields. Then…

"Sir," an exhausted voice said, coming up behind him in the doorway. The speaker was limping, dragging a hind foot, and she smelled of blood.

Fel sat down.

"Sir, I need orders. My team is tired, but we are still ready to serve, sir. This is a critical moment. I can go round up my troops the moment you give the word."

"Sleep now, Major Ursa. Your willingness to serve is noted

and appreciated, but your energy will be needed more in the days to come. Leave the fetching and organizing to those who are rested. Let your team eat now, and get off your feet for a little while."

"Thank you, sir."

"Don't thank me, Major. Agony and death are on the horizon."

"And glory, Paragon. And honor. Don't forget those."

Fel turned toward Major Ursa, incredulous at the smile on her face. "You really believe that, don't you? The reptiles are better trained, better armed, and I think they actually *crave* battle. You think we can win a war against them?"

"Don't you, sir?"

Fel squinted again at the distant hills. "Yes, Major. Yes. Of course I do." But his true feelings were not well masked. Major Ursa noticed his twitching eye, his whipping tail. He had never been very good at lying.

"The success of your troops relies on your faith in them, sir. We can win, but only if you lead us to victory. *You* lead *us*. No one else can do it. Do you understand?" Ursa's eyes flicked toward the hills. "We can't do it without you here."

Fel gazed down at his paws. "I do understand, Major. But war comes more easily for you than it does for me. I am a ruler, not a general. I wish only to make diplomatic decisions, not destructive ones."

"In the end it all comes to the same. Choosing to give resources to one group instead of another during peacetime may result in either starvation or prosperity. The decisions made in war are similar, only they come faster and harder, with more immediate results."

"I suppose," Fel said. "Still, I will need to rely on you a good deal, Major."

"I am ready, sir."

"Thank you. But not yet. What are you still doing here? Go, rest. See the healer for your paws. I will call for you when the foundation has been laid and our battle plan is ready for your expert refinement."

Major Ursa lumbered toward the soldier bunks.

"Runner!" Fel cried out. "Attend to me! I need someone fleet of foot."

A cheetah appeared at his side, its eyes darting left and right, jumping with tense enthusiasm.

"Find two more runners, and convey this message to them and then on to all the land: All able-bodied animals loyal to the Felidae territories must assemble at the Great Castle immediately. We are under imminent threat. The weak, injured, young, and old cannot shelter in place. They must gather together inside one of the walled villages, or else here, behind the outer rings of the Great Castle." Fel turned toward the cheetah and looked into its eyes, seizing its entire attention. "Many lives depend on your speed, messenger. Go now!"

The cat bolted through the yard, leaving a shallow groove in the dust under his tail as he ran.

What next? The armies would need food, water, bedding, bandages…

Fel's heart sank. He didn't want this. Why did Chel? He knew the reptile monarch had a penchant for the ancient technologies, but was it really worth all this? What was the point? If anything less than his citizens' lives were at risk, Fel would continue to attempt to reason with the old turtle. But the line had been crossed, and Fel had to act.

He toured the training yards, watching young bear soldiers swat at dummies painted to resemble four-foot-tall lizard sentries. The bears looked bright, excited, eager to serve their Paragon, and ready to win against all odds. Most were not yet fully grown. Their naïveté was endearing—and terrifying. How many would Fel send to their deaths?

Damn Chel!

No. He could not allow such devastation to occur without a final attempt at peace. It was irresponsible for Fel to confront Chel directly. His place was here at the castle, readying his troops, keeping morale high, giving orders. But if he did not go—if he let a war happen under his watch, without doing everything in his power to stop it, even at the risk of his own life—then what was his purpose on the throne to begin with?

He would not sit still, waiting for disaster to arrive on his doorstep.

A few minutes after the sun set, Fel crept from a rear exit near the Great Castle's servant barracks. He stood on his hind legs and draped himself in a thick cloak, then crept through the fields until he was out of sight of the sentries. If he was quick, he could reach Chel in two days. Then he would see what the old monster had to say for himself.

Before Fel's father had died and the throne of Felidae was thrust upon him, he had spent much of his time creeping in the dark, exploring the hidden places of the world. Now he slid into stealth again as if under a familiar old blanket, a skill he would never forget. His nerves were calm now that he had made his decision. He would not run away to the green hills. No, instead he would run straight into danger, with the hope that further wounds to his lands could be avoided. His ability to sneak was still keen, even after so many years on the throne, and he was not recognized. He ran in silence along the riverbanks and dashed through bushes without snapping a single twig. As soon as he was past the densely inhabited areas, he ditched the cumbersome cloak, freeing him to take short-cuts through close places.

In just thirty hours he arrived at the back of the Squamor fortress. The rear of the Great Castle was ancient and ill-kept, the stone walls crumbling in places. Chel's defense had grown lax during the many years of relative peace. Fel circled the structure until he found a crack in the walls large enough to squeeze through. It was a tight fit; as he clawed his way inside, his crown nearly fell from his head, but he caught it with the tip of his tail before it could tumble out of reach into the dry moat. With a final push, he tumbled onto the floor of a smooth sand passageway.

Creeping as quiet as morning fog, he searched the pathways until he found the hall that flanked Chel's throne room. A round window studded with shells provided a view of the reception area.

Fel laid his ears flat as he stood up on his hind paws and peeked inside. The turtle was having an audience with a triumphant lizard general whose scales were caked with grime.

"All defeated, Paragon," the general boasted through a mocking grin. "Dead or running, and we're hunting down the rest."

"Excellent work, general. Ensure the pelts find their way into a castle work-yard, not the general market."

"Of course, Paragon!" The reptile bobbed and bowed, then turned tail and marched out the door.

Chel settled back into his whale-skull throne and groaned deep. Fel could smell the monarch; rotten seaweed, wet scales, moldy fruit. A servant with long, pointed nails strummed a tiny lyre as Chel closed his eyes to nap.

Fel dropped to all fours.

"Foul betrayer Chel, I demand an audience with you!" he boomed, striding around the wall and into the room. "If you have any honor—any pride at all!—you will attend to me now."

A startled guard stomped into the room, swinging a rusted blade. Chel's eyes opened wide and rolled in their sockets. "Who! Who addresses me in such a rude manner?"

Fel waited while the turtle lifted his head to search the room with his milky eyes.

"Ah, it is only the fuzzy little king," Chel said, chuckling. When he laughed, he expelled a noxious vapor of rotting fish. "Such a big voice, for such a small cat. Brash of you to come here. Shall I lock you up along with your primate ambassador?"

"You will hear what I have to say," Fel said.

"No begging for the girl's life, then? So, she was merely a tool for you to use and forget. Not worth bartering for her release. I thought as much."

"I am not here for her, as I have nothing to offer you now but my words."

Chel blinked. A viscous tear oozed from his eye. "Speak, then. Quickly."

"It is clear you have declared war on my lands. What is not clear to me is why. Whether you win or lose, many of your people will die. Is what you seek worth that loss? I beg you to explain your position, describe to me your thoughts, and tell me how we may still avert the catastrophe you have set in motion."

Chel turned his head toward the northern windows. "You are young, little king. Your memory is short. Mine is long, long. And in all my memory, in hundreds of years, there has never been an opportunity like the one we have now. The *spheres!* You understand? We learned some from the reproduction centers, but not much of it was useful. The spheres have brought us devices, power, batteries. And you aren't even paying attention to them! You ignore them as through they were rocks fallen from the sky, useless lumps of clay. Yet they teem with information! Perhaps even the knowledge to rebuild the ancient world, without the greed of primates to get in the way of a truly enlightened populace. You see what is at stake? Do you understand the importance of it?"

"So what, then, is your plan? You will obliterate my people, enslave the birds, and install your own reptiles as a superior class, using technology to rule over all others?"

Chel grinned. "I knew you'd see it my way."

"And what about the Badlands? I know you saw the cloud. Danger may be coming from the north. We should stand together against it, not squabble with each other while we ignore our mutual enemy."

"The cloud is your problem, Fel. I know you are behind it. Whatever you have brewing in the north, my army will defeat you."

"It's nothing to do with me," Fel said. "I am as puzzled about it as you are."

Chel laughed. "You must have traveled fast and hard to get here, cat. Why waste this precious time with lies?"

"The cloud was not mine, Chel. You must listen to me!"

"No, you listen to me. You will step aside, and permit my people to take whatever resources from your land we require. If you do not, your lands will be merged into my own, and your people either killed or enslaved. You may save some of them by surrendering immediately. This is my only offer. Decide now."

"Damn you!" Fel spat. "You know I won't allow it!"

"I know. I am counting on you to fight back. The story of our final war will be my legacy, told throughout the ages, passed down through a hundred generations—of reptiles, of course. Not cats." Chel smiled and rotated in his throne until his round head was awash in late evening sunlight. "Those will all, sadly, be extinct."

"Please, Chel. War is not…"

"We are done. I will allow you to leave, in the interest of maximizing the glory of my soldiers on the field. I would have them defeat you in battle, not in chains. Go now, back the way you came. But I will see you again. Not in my castle, little king, but mounted on the wall, and stuck through with a metal pike."

22.

The Gentle Creatures

he boy Jack crouched in a narrow crevice that smelled of cat. It was a pungent scent, totally out of place amid the gamey stench of the reptile castle. If further proof was needed of a previous intruder, reddish tufts of feline hair could be plucked from the rough castle walls, and distinctly mammalian paw prints were pressed into the smooth sand. The cat had not bothered much with concealing its arrival, whoever it had been.

The human was more careful. He slipped around the break in the wall and shuffled down the edge of the corridor, leaving only a smooth line behind his feet in the soft sand. No footprints. Should he move north, where the hall climbed upward? Or southeast, where the passage sloped down into darkness, lit only by candles on metal pans?

He slid past portal openings that looked out into courtyards filled with wooden crates leaking dark red fluid that could only be blood. The reason for their existence, he could not fathom. Soldiers were fully engaged in training exercises at the front of the Great Castle. In fact, had they not been so preoccupied with their drills he never could have sneaked around the back with such ease. War was apparently either threatened, imminent, or upon them. Bad luck for others; good luck for Jack, perhaps.

None of that was his concern. He wanted to find the young woman. Kana was the only human he had seen since leaving his village and his family behind in the Badlands. She had been kind to him, but it was more than that. His instincts told him she had power, a certain inner strength that would affect the Kingdom in a permanent way. And what else did he have to do anyway, now that he had fled his homeland? Only shame and guilt remained there for him. His life was of little value, but it could be something more if she became a part of it.

Someone was coming. The sound of a reptile soldier's clinking mail came from somewhere near the slope to the upper story, so Jack's path was decided for him. He scooted to the right, following the hall down into the dim underground. As he crept, he blew out each candle behind him. If he was followed, someone would stop to relight each one, giving him more time.

The clinking sound stopped, and returned in the direction from which it came.

He asked himself the question again, the question he knew Kana would ask, which he had been turning over in his head since he left the camp; why had he abandoned her? And what answer could he give that would not cause her to turn away from him? He had lied to her about his home, about everything. He didn't wish to lie to her again.

After leaving Kana's carriage, he had followed it in secret for days, spying on the group from the bushes. In a way, it had felt like he was still with them, but without the expectations of conversation or good manners. Jack knew he had become wild in the years since he left the Badlands. The brief time he had spent with the ambassador was a struggle. Every instinct cried out for him to take what food he could carry—and maybe that snarky fox's red pelt, too—and run. But part of him enjoyed the company, and longed to be accepted. His desires to stay and to leave were incongruous, but neither could be quieted. He had been on his own for too long, for someone who was village-born. Now nothing was natural to him. He was lost wherever he roamed.

And there was the crux; Kana made him feel not-lost. Maybe not exactly at home, but at least he did not feel out of place when he was with her. It wasn't just that she was human, like he was; she was irreverent and ignored the rules, all while constantly acting with the wellbeing of her allies in mind. Those were leadership qualities, and rare ones at that. She was special.

Jack reached the bottom of the slope, and the path leveled out. Ahead was a glowing doorway which opened onto a larger room. Instead of blowing out the last candle, he left it. Its light would be necessary if a fast retreat up the passage was required. He positioned himself against the wall behind the candle so his shadow would not be cast into the room ahead, and peered around the corner.

A stone prison with alcoves dug into its walls was illuminated by mounted torches. In the center of the floor was a large red stain and several broken chairs. A dead bear, its body stiff and cold, was slumped against the far wall.

Jack took careful steps into the room until the alcoves to his left were visible. And there he saw Kana, shackled to a wall, pitched forward with blood in her hair.

On all fours, he slipped into the alcove and examined the shackles. They were sturdy metal, impossible to break. The wall they were attached to, however...

"Jack? Is that you?" Kana lifted her head and stared at him through locks of matted hair. "Am I imagining this?"

"Maybe," Jack muttered. "Maybe not. Stay quiet. If you don't, maybe you'll wake yourself up, and I'll be gone. So, shush now. Okay?"

"'Kay," Kana said, lowering her head.

Jack found a broken chair leg and a metal plate in the mess at the center of the room, and used them to dig at the sandy walls until rocks and dirt clods started to break free.

"Where's the fox?" he whispered.

"Pan...they took him...I don't know where."

"Can you help me? Lean forward, as far as you can. Need you to put pressure on the chains, push against the wall."

Kana braced her heels against the wall and pushed with her arms held out in front. She was weak, but she persisted until one of the chains inched out from the wall and clattered to the floor. At the sudden release she spun and fell, crying out in pain as her weight transferred entirely to her other wrist, still bound in its shackle.

The sound echoed through the chambered room, but no guard came. Jack supposed cries were common enough down here, rarely raising a response from either guards or inmates.

He started to dig at the other shackle as Kana tried to regain her feet. She fished her knife from her pocket, but her one loose hand was too weak to pry the blade open without the help of the other.

"Boy?" A low voice rumbled from the alcove entrance. "Is that you?"

In the dim light, Jack saw a hulking figure; Lieutenant Barbar, the chief lion guard.

"Help me," Jack said, pointing at the shackle. "I'm not strong enough to dig any deeper, and Kana's strength is nearly gone."

As Barbar crowded into the alcove, Jack saw chains also hung from the lion's arms. He had been shackled, too, but had already forced the metal pins out from the walls on his own.

"You're free? Why didn't you free Kana, too?"

"She would have been punished. I worked my chains loose just a few minutes ago. I had planned…well, I don't know what I planned, actually. To rush the guard, I suppose. But there would have been a hundred more behind him. I didn't want to get Kana involved unless I saw a clear way out."

Barbar grasped Kana's remaining shackle and pulled with his teeth until a long serrated pin emerged from the wall. She collapsed, wrapping her arms around her body, sobbing as the blood rushed back into her aching hands.

"We have to go now," Jack said. "I put out the lights, so if the long hallway is the only way in or out, we'll need to bring a torch."

"I'm not leaving without my soldiers," Barbar said. "Some have died, but I know three still breathe."

"No time! Do you want to escape or not? The best chance for Kana is to go immediately!"

"Then go ahead, and do not wait for me. I will follow close behind." Barbar disappeared into the darkness.

"Kana," Jack whispered. "It's time to go. We have to go right away. But you'll need to carry your chains. I can't get them off, and I can't carry them for you. Do you understand?"

Kana nodded, her head bobbing under her mop of bright hair. She gathered up a chain in each hand and stood on trembling legs.

Jack tip-toed to the hallway entrance and looked out into the blackness. Nothing stirred. He picked up the remaining candle in its tray and touched it to a torch mounted on the wall. Turning back, he whispered into the room. "Barbar! Come now, or I leave you alone in the pitch!"

Heavy breathing emerged from the dark. Barbar and a pair of emaciated lions walked into the light.

"Only two? But I thought you said…"

"These are all that remain." Barbar's eyes watered. "Ask me no more questions."

Jack nodded and trotted ahead, bringing the torch to light the path. After twenty paces he stopped and listened; three lions dragging their feet, the clink of Kana's chains, and just ahead—footsteps. Someone was approaching.

Crouching to shield the light of the torch, Jack returned to the lions and nodded in the direction of the approaching guard. Barbar frowned, and stepped ahead of Kana, placing himself between her and the reptile.

The moment the guard was visible, Barbar leapt. His exhausted troops followed with all the strength they could muster, and Jack flanked the guard on the left side. Despite the weakness of the onslaught, the reptile guard fell quickly. Fel's lion guards, even while exhausted, were still more than a match for a single lizard. Kana did not seem to notice the disruption. She hardly paused in her walk uphill, stumbling past the defeated guard as if sleepwalking. Barbar swept the unconscious lizard to the side of the hall, and the group continued.

When they reached the crack in the wall, Jack realized with dismay that Barbar might not fit. The two lion guards had lost enough weight during their days in captivity to slip through, and Kana passed easily. But Barbar's great skull was several inches too wide for the gap.

"Leave me," he gasped. "Run! I will hold them back while you escape. There is no hope for me."

"Never!" Kana hissed, looking alert for the first time since leaving her alcove. She raised her shackles and used the metal chains to strike the castle walls, chipping away chunks of brick. Tears streamed down her cheeks. "I have lost Pan, and I have lost my soldiers. I will not leave you behind as well!"

"Too loud, Kana!" Jack said. "They'll hear!"

Kana ignored him. She snarled, showing her teeth like an animal, and continued to crack her shackles on the blocks despite the pain in her sprained wrists.

Jack picked up a rock and joined her. The lion guards pried at the wall with their paws, growling. An inch of mortar fell away, then a larger brick tumbled from the hole, rolling into the dry moat below.

"More! Just a little more," Jack said.

Two cinder blocks finally broke free of the wall. Barbar measured his head against the opening, then leapt through the hole.

"Into the bushes! Quick!"

From the front of the castle, Jack could hear shouting. The reptiles were still engaged in their drills. Not a single guard was visible atop the walls. All posts had been abandoned in the preparation for war.

As they crouched low, hiding in the tall reeds, Kana sobbed. "Pan…we can't leave without Pan."

"They left him in the prison with us for one night," Barbar said, "but then took him away in the morning. Never saw him again."

"I saw a lot of hair in the wall opening when I got here," Jack said. "Maybe he escaped, and left that way."

"Smelled like cat to me," Barbar said.

"Yeah, it did to me, too. I was just hoping…"

"He's still in there somewhere, most likely. I don't want to leave him either, but we are too weak to get him out right now. We'll have to come back for him."

"Pan," Kana cried. She slumped to the ground with her eyes shut, appearing to fall asleep.

"She's hurt in the head, Jack. They were pretty rough with her. She needs rest."

"But where? It looks like the reptiles are getting ready for an invasion, which makes this all enemy territory. We're in danger until we cross the border, and that's miles from here."

Barbar laid his ears flat and poked the top of his head above the grass. "I hear footsteps. Someone's coming, and fast!"

A flash of red burst from the grass, plowing head-on into the lion's chest. It collapsed to the ground, then was up again in an instant. "Run! Now! For your lives!"

The creature barked once, nipped Kana's arm, and dashed into the bushes.

"That was Panicum!"

"Should we follow him?"

Kana sat up, rubbing her swollen eyes. "Pan?"

Panicum again exploded from the grass, his face twisted with terror. "Didn't you hear me? *Run!*"

"From what?" Barbar asked.

"Armed guards! Three of them! Following me! Run or die!" Panicum sprinted in a tight circle around them, desperately trying to wrangle the tired group, then plunged again into the grass in an effort to lead them away. They struggled to their feet and crashed through the brush, but their progress was too slow.

Jack looked back to see three lizard guards charging through the field with their swords drawn. "Pan!" he yelled as his feet tangled in the bushes. "We have to stop and face them! We can't outrun them like this."

While Panicum wound his way through the grass like it was a network of foxholes, the long-legged humans tripped and tumbled atop it. The lions did not fare much better; their paws sank into the layered reeds, the strands catching their claws as their weight caused the brush to collapse underfoot.

"Pan! *Stop!*" Barbar bellowed.

The fox froze and popped his head up above the grass, looking back in time to see reptile guards overtake the struggling group. Then he ducked down into the underbrush, hiding under the top growth.

"Coward!" Jack yelled.

A reptile grasped Kana's chains and wrapped them around

her back so she could not move. Barbar lurched at another reptile but his shackles slowed his attack, and the reptile easily sidestepped his snapping teeth. The lion guards backed up until their tails touched, looking out in each direction with Jack in the center, but they were nearly too tired to stay upright. The standoff would not last long.

The reptile that held Kana nodded at the other two. They circled and pointed their rusty swords, ready to slash their way through the lions who bared their teeth in preparation for a final stand.

"We won't go back to the prison," Barbar bellowed. "You understand? We will die here, and you will have to tear us to shreds. Leave now, for we will not go quietly!"

They were afraid of the old lion chief and the strange human boy, but their swords lent them courage, and the reptile guards prepared to lunge. Before they could, a red streak appeared behind them. Panicum, filled to his ears with terror, launched out from the bushes in desperation and sank his teeth deep into a lizard's neck.

Jack charged at the reptile holding Kana, but it had already panicked. It dropped her chains and sprinted back toward the castle. Only one reptile guard was left. Both lions turned toward him, breaking their circle. They gripped the reptile's tail in their teeth until it disconnected from his body, twisting and flipping in their mouths with a life of its own. Shamed and dismembered, the reptile followed the other toward the castle at a full run.

Panicum's rival lay still on the ground, bleeding his life out into the dirt as the fox spit blood from his mouth, gagging and cursing.

"Pan," Kana whispered, in a faint and distant voice. "You saved me. But there's so much blood…"

Panicum, the peaceful fox, trembled with shock. He rubbed at his nose with his paws, trying to wipe the blood from his face, but it would not come off. His eyes teared up first with disbelief, then with grief.

He had killed another sentient creature—something he thought he would never have to do again.

Panicum howled, a sorrowful wail of anguish that echoed between the walls of the Great Castle and the distant green hills. It was a cry filled with torment; the irredeemable misery of a tender heart broken by devastating remorse.

23.

Moon and Stars

Much had changed in the countryside since Ambassador Kana had set out from the Felidae Great Castle. On the trip back, no citizens waved silken flags at her from the roadside or cheered along the caravan's progress. The population's uneasiness as they prepared for war was evidenced by shut curtains and locked doors. The market stalls were bare in every village center, packed up and shuttered tight as if preparing for a typhoon.

In the oppressive quiet which had settled on the towns, the travelers talked in low voices and tended to each others' wounds. The roads were clear so their progress was unhindered, but the loneliness of the vacant public spaces and thoroughfares was un-settling. There should have been bustling schools, traders, vendors, and theater troupes, but instead there were only hushed whispers from empty doorways and occasionally the sound of someone shouting in the distance.

Kana and her group stumbled back to the Felidae Great Cas-tle, an agonizing journey on foot. On the way, there was time for her to worry about what she would tell Paragon Fel. Had she failed as his ambassador? Or did all fault lie with imperious Chel?

Her head was full of clouds. She could actually see them, rising to the top of her vision, bloated and poisonous, casting a mist over her eyes. The difference between awake and asleep blurred. Both states were wretched, and both vibrated with pulsing pain, a confusion of lights and sounds spinning around her as she cowered within the eye of the storm.

Most of Kana's memories from her imprisonment were gone, a condition which worried her whenever she was conscious enough to think about it. In her fevered dreams she was still shackled to the wall in the darkness, waiting for the reptile guard to make his rounds. He would sometimes prod her with the tip of his sword to see if she was still alive. Then the prison would shake, and dust would fall from the mortar in the wall as a rolling earthquake struck the reptile castle. As she ducked her head and prepared for the falling stones from the ceiling to crush her, she would wake up to the realization that she was still riding on Barbar's back. The rocking was nothing more than his gentle stride as they made their way toward the heart of the Felidae lands.

Barbar carried Kana on his back for much of the trip, but the extra effort nearly killed him. The shackles on his arms had rubbed through his fur, creating scarred abrasions on his skin that would remain bare for the rest of his days. He tripped often, as the chains caught on every pebble, every jutting root, every weed in the road—but he never once dropped his burden.

Panicum, Jack, two lion guards, and Lieutenant Barbar—with Kana draped over his mane—limped into the outer yards of the Felidae Great Castle less than twelve hours after Paragon Fel had returned from his own failed diplomatic venture.

Kana and Panicum returned to their old suite, finding it exactly how they had left it. How long had it been since she had walked out of this room, head held high with pride? Less than a month, yet it felt like a year. She crawled onto a pile of pillows and did not wait for the guard to come with a lock-pick before shutting her eyes. Her chains still hung from her exhausted arms, but as much as her wrists ached, the shackles almost felt like a part of her now.

Panicum burrowed into the pillows without a word. He had spoken little since the fight with the reptile guards. Kana's heart hurt for him. He had killed before, but always for food, never as an act of pure violence. His vicious murder of the guard had cut him deep, gutted his tender soul despite the necessity of his actions. The fox yearned for peace, always; ferocity was not in his nature. He hid under the cushions and shuddered, inconsolable.

Kana dozed, half asleep, until she was awakened by Paragon Fel. He entered the suite leading a sly-looking raccoon holding a set of metal picks.

"Kana! I am so relieved to see you uninjured," Fel said, purring through his whiskers.

"Well, almost uninjured, anyway," Kana said. "You look tired, Fel. Almost as tired as me. But I'm glad to see you, too."

"Barbar tells me we nearly crossed paths. I went to pay a visit to Paragon Chel myself, to beg him to call off this obscene invasion. I was unsuccessful."

"So was I."

Fel sat near the pillows and looked into Kana's eyes. "You got hit on the head, I hear. How are you feeling?"

"A little weird, still. Dizzy. I might have a concussion, but I think I'll be okay. I just need to get off my feet for a while."

"You really must write down for me everything you know of medical science some day." Fel smiled. "It all sounds so fascinating."

"I will. You can add it to your library."

"And where's Panicum?"

The fox's nose appeared between the cushions. It was dripping wet, and one nostril was still ringed with mud from the road.

"I'm alive too, Paragon, for what it's worth."

"Good to hear, my friend," Fel said. He turned back to Kana. "And there is something I need to ask you about, my dear, a topic which is both urgent and disturbing."

"You've met Jack."

"Yes." But Fel fell silent and asked no questions, despite clearly having a need to.

"We found him on the road, but he left us before we entered Chel's lands," Kana said. "Later he returned, to help me escape from the dungeon. He is an ally."

"Another *human*, though! The enormity of this discovery cannot be overstated. Is he from Chicago as well?"

"You'd better ask him about that yourself."

Fel nodded. "I certainly shall. Now, will you both join me for dinner?"

Kana was exhausted, and concerned for Panicum. She was inclined to refuse, but the thought of a whole table loaded with fresh food was too tempting. "I'll come, but only if Pan comes too."

"How about it, Panicum? Will you come to dinner?"

They waited. The nose did not move from its place between the pillows, but neither did it agree to attend.

"Pan?"

The fox sighed. "All right. I'll come. But please…can we talk about anything in the world other than reptiles and war?"

"Gladly," Fel said. "Come down whenever you are ready. The table is set and the plates are full." As he left, he nodded to the raccoon to begin the removal of Kana's locked cuffs.

After the shackles were off, Kana took a sponge bath and wrapped her sore arms in clean strips of cloth. She could tell the wounds would scar; they were deep abrasions, worn through many layers of her skin. The inflamed gashes looped around her wrists like bracelets. Bandaging them was painful, but she knew it was for the best. There was no good way to treat infections in the Kingdom. Such a condition might have deadly consequences.

When Kana arrived for dinner with Panicum at her side, she was surprised to see Jack had been invited, and Barbar as well. Fel sat at the head of the table and eyed the human boy with burning curiosity. All five ate in silence for several minutes, unable to think of much other than the food in front of them. A servant from the kitchen brought mugs of diluted honey-wine which made Kana's head spin in a wonderful way, sweeping her mind clear of the mist and the pain.

"Barbar, where did you come from? Um…I don't mean today!" Kana giggled. "I mean, when you were young. Here, let me start again. Where were you born?"

"There is a community of mostly lions and tigers to the far west, down near the southern border of the bird territories. I was raised there, but I left home when I felt they had nothing else to teach me."

"Oh! That was brave of you. So, only lions and tigers lived in your village?"

"And bears."

"Oh my!" Kana said, laughing and rocking in her chair until her cup tipped over on the table.

"This stuff is pretty good, Fel," Panicum said, licking honey from his nose. "Go easy on it, Kana."

"Yeah, yeah, quit nagging. I'll have you know," Kana burped, and refilled her mug from a pitcher.

Fel raised a regal goblet studded with a rainbow of glass beads. "To Ambassador Kana and her fearless friends, who won us the support of castle Falcoformia against all odds, escaped the prisons of the Squamor Great Castle under the very nose of the evil tyrant Chel, and brought back my most cherished Lieutenant Barbar. You have a king's respect and gratitude, Kana, despite the fact that you carelessly misplaced my prized wheeled carriage." Fel winked, and drank deep from his cup.

"Hear, hear!" Barbar growled. "I also would like to commemorate on this night the soldiers lost in Chel's wretched dungeon. Let us remember them not with sorrow, but with pride, and with honor!"

"They died as heroes, and will be remembered as such," Fel said.

"And to Pan, for coming back. Without him, we would never have escaped the guards," Jack said.

"To Pan!"

They drank in silence, remembering the fallen.

"Shorry…I mean, sssorry…about the carriage," Kana said.

"Never mind that," Fel said. "I imagine it will be the least of our losses, before all is done."

Panicum had stopped eating. He gazed down at his plate with a blank stare that worried Kana. Was he thinking about the fight with the reptile guards again? Something was wrong. He had killed before, but this was different. And she had no idea how to help him.

"Let's talk about all that tomorrow," she said. "Not tonight."

"Agreed," Fel said. "Anyway, I have a surprise for you all. Everyone, come with me to the northwest yard!"

The group accompanied the king down the hallway past the kitchen, followed by attendants carrying plates full of snacks. As the effect of the wine started to wear off, Kana's feet ached. She wanted to go back to bed, but the king's enthusiastic encouragement and her own curiosity kept her moving. At the end of the long hall, he pushed on a heavy wooden door etched with a design that looked like a school of fish dancing in a whirlpool.

Through the door they found a stunning courtyard lined with planters brimming full of lush flowers and ferns. Blossomed vines and loops of ivy were interwoven on an elaborate canopy, draped in living swags over a cool, clear pool. Candles floated on lily pads in the water, casting reflections of fire on the ripples that coursed the water's surface in the light evening breeze.

Kana gasped. "When did you build a swimming pool?"

"It's ancient, actually. It was constructed by a Felidae king centuries ago, but had since fallen into disrepair, neglected by the castle's previous monarchs. I ordered it cleaned up while you were on your way to see Falca. Oversaw all the work myself." Fel grinned with pride.

Kana pulled off her boots and sat at the edge, dipping her throbbing feet into the water. It was cold enough to reduce the swelling in her muscles and send a pleasant chill up her back.

Barbar waded into the pool, lapping at it as he went, his tail floating behind like a wet paintbrush.

Panicum sat at the edge. He refused to enter the water, yet he seemed calmed by the candlelight which flickered in the waves spreading out in Barbar's wake. Kana thought she could see a spark of hope in his eyes which had been missing since the battle at Chel's castle.

Jack jumped into the water and swam to the bottom before emerging like a dolphin, spraying water and laughing. He rubbed his hair, spiking it, blinking water from his eyes.

"More mead!" Fel called out. Servants arrived with jugs, plates of fruit, and a huge silver platter of bees which the king shared with Panicum.

Kana floated on her back in the pool, staring up at the stars blinking through the canopy. Were they identical to the ones that looked down on Chicago? She was dismayed to realize that she had no idea. The stars had never been important in the city. They were just tiny sparkling lights, far overhead, disconnected from the real life on the streets. Only a few had been visible over the glow of the streetlights anyway. But here there were millions of uncountable specks, almost more light than darkness in the heavens. The moon was a searchlight that lit the top of the canopy in a blue glow, in beautiful contrast to the warmth of the candles bobbing on the water.

"It's amazing, Fel," she said. "Thank you."

"Thank the servants. Honestly, I didn't do a damn thing but boss them around."

"You sell yourself short. I know it's not easy, being in charge. So much rests on your shoulders. Just take the compliment."

The group fell silent again, but this time it was the quiet of contentment. They re-dressed their wounds, ate as much as their bellies could hold, and talked for hours. As the moon disappeared over the horizon, they left, one by one, returning to their sleeping quarters to finally rest with peace in their hearts.

In the suite, before Kana closed her eyes, she spoke once more to Panicum.

"Pan, you're worrying me. You've been so quiet. Are you okay? Or if you're not, are you *going* to be okay?"

Panicum, coiled on a pillow, raised his chin from his tail. "I guess so. I don't feel okay right now. But I don't really have a choice, do I? I can't mope forever."

"It was self defense, Pan."

"It doesn't matter."

"Yes, it does."

Panicum buried his nose in his brush. "Don't you worry about me. It's all my own fault, anyway. I shouldn't have led those guards onto you. I should have just let them catch me."

"No! Don't think like that. We all pulled through it, and that's what matters. I'm glad you ran to us for help. I wouldn't have it any other way."

With a dismissive grunt, Panicum turned his head away, hiding his face from her. "Anyway, I'll be fine."

"Okay. But let me know if-"

"I'll be fine. I promise. Goodnight, Kana."

Kana sighed. "Goodnight."

24.

East Bleeds West

Paragon Chel was disappointed at the loss of the primate ambassador and her fox, but not surprised. He had gathered every able body in his lands to arms, ordered the abandonment of every post and watchpoint, and pulled the guards from the towers and the police from the streets in order to take stock of the entire population of available troops. The fighters were arranged in regimented companies, numbered and outfitted in full armor in order to take a complete census of bodies and equipment.

The resulting army was impressive. Squamor's reptile troops did not outnumber the total citizenry of Felidae, but they were far better equipped, and—most importantly—excited for the coming battle. Troops cheered their compatriots from the sidelines of mock-battles, in tournaments formed in the spur of the moment for crowds which buzzed with contagious enthusiasm. The eager soldiers rehearsed their battle stances, sharpened their swords, and discussed new strategies based on the stories of their ancestors' past conquests. Some witty artist had painted the practice dummies to resemble cats, complete with tattered rope tails. Spirits were high, and every soldier was confident the war would be won. The mood was almost festive.

As Chel watched from his balcony, a guard approached and held out a coarse chunk of rough papyrus. "News of Falca's army, sir."

Chel glared at him until the guard realized why the submerged old turtle didn't take it, and unfolded the paper himself.

In the center was a crude drawing of the Felidae Great Castle. To the left of the structure was five circles and an oval. The circles were labeled "*flying troops - 250 each*" while the oval said "*standing troops - 300 total.*"

"The standing troops…that's ostriches and the like, I assume?"

"Yes, sir."

So, the birds had 1250 fighters in the sky and 300 on the ground. The foot soldiers would present little trouble for the reptile troops. No gawky, flightless bird was ever a match for a six-foot reptile, and even the fearsome ostriches could never be truly battle-ready creatures. The flyers were the real challenge. They could drop rocks, or dive with a sharp beak stuck out in front like a lance. Tactical information was on their side, too; they could view the entire battlefield from a strategic position in the sky. Communication and the protection provided by distance were critical advantages, despite their small size.

What would be Fel's initial strategy to defend his lands? He would probably meet the invading reptile force in the open fields, before Chel's shock troops could draw near the outer Felidae settlements. Flying birds would arrive first, most likely, dropping rocks from above to weaken the reptile forces before a legion of bears swept in to flank Chel's first wave.

So, the bird attacks must be neutralized in order to ensure the reptiles would be fresh when the Felidae ground troops arrived.

The guard holding the papyrus shifted his weight back and forth on his sore feet. His arms lowered slowly as they became tired. Chel looked either asleep or dead as he soaked in his salt bath, keeping his eyes pressed shut as he meditated on the battle plan.

The guard's attention drifted.

"Snap to!" Chel barked when the papyrus dipped. "Wake up, soldier!"

The guard jumped, and his tail stuck straight out in surprise.

Chel had made his decisions, and was ready to issue commands. "Tell the lieutenant of Troop #18 to take his crew to the old reproduction center—the open one off the road that's already been gutted. They will tear the metal panels from the outer walls and stack them, then bring the stacks back here. Understand?"

The guard nodded and scuttered away, after first placing the paper delicately at the edge of Chel's throne.

What his soldiers needed was protection, and Chel had worked out how to use the panels as roofs over the troops. Ropes could be tied around them to create handles to hold as they were hoisted overhead. Special units could be trained to use them. When the flying birds realized their bombardment was useless, they would become frustrated and tired. Birds always did; it was in their nature. Then Chel's best soldiers would destroy Fel's army, and Falca would recall her airborne squadron, having no reason to stay engaged. The land-bound birds could largely be ignored.

"Rhys!" Chel called out. "Are you near?"

The loyal attendant stepped from behind a pillar. "Sir."

"It's nearly time. We must move on the Felidae lands tomorrow afternoon at the latest. You are not to personally march to war with the rest of the troops, understand? You will stay with me here, on my balcony, and we will watch until my army has moved out of sight. For now, bring my generals together in this room. One is a snake, one looks like an oversized skink, and one resembles a crocodile. Go ask around in the yard, and you will find them quickly."

"Immediately, sir."

When Rhys led the three generals into Chel's throne room half an hour later, they discovered the room had been transformed. Chel had prepared for their arrival; on either side of his whale-skull throne was a row of tall torches, burning with flames six inches high. Red flower petals had been scattered across the floor, surrounding Chel's shell like splotches of splattered mammalian blood. He wore on his head a massive crest constructed of thousands of cactus needles, a royal heirloom from centuries past, and the flickering light from the torches gleamed on the segmented plates of his oiled shell. Rhys moved to his place near Chel's left side while a massive guard was positioned to the right of the throne, creating a symmetrical aesthetic for the most striking effect. The three figures represented authority, devotion to duty, and power.

The generals were impressed with the display, and knelt with a subservience that may otherwise have not been entirely genuine.

"Rise, honored subjects," Chel commanded. "Tonight we

finalize our battle plans for tomorrow's victory. You three are the pride of the army of Squamor! You have trained my soldiers well, and each of you is a credit to your species. Litha, your snake units are unparalleled in speed and viciousness. Croco, your horde of warriors has never been matched for strength and size. And your clever lizards, Tuata, can foresee the outcome of battle maneuvers with uncanny precision. I could not be more confident in our combined military force."

Litha nodded her head with gratitude. Croco grumbled in appreciation. Tuata blinked her large eyes and bowed, her silken robes brushing the blue tile floor.

Chel nodded to each of them. "Many of your troops will die tomorrow. Are you prepared for the sacrifice?"

"Honored," Litha said.

"Eager," Croco growled.

Tuata the skink simply smiled, her eyes glinting in the firelight.

"You three know that it is not my regular habit to adhere to the ways of old. My mind looks to the future, to the use of technology to improve our lives. I do not often look back. But tonight I will make an exception. I will honor the ancient rituals for the sake of you three, who I know are devoted to the venerable customs of the past." Chel turned to address his assistant. "Rhys, bring in the prisoner."

From a side door, Chel's assistant led an exhausted bear dragging heavy chains. Its nose rubbed on the floor as it lumbered toward the throne, and its paws swept a clear path through the flower petals.

Rhys held a scabbard out to Chel, with the sword handle turned toward the old turtle's mouth.

"Tonight we offer a mammal's blood to the old gods, so that tomorrow we might win glory in their names."

Chel gripped the sword's handle in his mouth and drew it from its sheath. Rhys nudged the bear toward the throne, scratching it with his nails, pushing it close. Chel reached out with his bony neck and drew the blade of the dagger across the bear's throat, slicing deep. The flood of the bear's lifeblood lifted the flower petals like rafts on red rippling waves.

The melodramatic gesture worked with the intended effect. All three generals howled in excitement, elated at their Paragon's consideration of their archaic faith. They breathed deep the scent of hot blood and circled the dying bear, reveling in the carnal ceremony.

Chel's voice boomed. "Go, now, and gather your armies. You have all that you need: Wit, strength, and the blessing of the old gods. As you march west tomorrow, I shall watch over you. If you look back, you will see me here, lending you all the strength of my vast power and immense resolution. *And you shall be victorious!*"

The generals bowed and scraped, shuffling backwards from the room.

As soon as they were out of view, Chel flung away the dagger with distaste. "Rhys," he sighed, "clean up this mess."

The events of the coming week would be the culmination of Chel's reign. He would either be remembered as the first modern monarch of reptile dominion over the Kingdom, or the failed despot who launched a misguided campaign to rule the world. His days were winding down, regardless. He felt it in his bones. Even if he had taken the coward's path—accepting this era of antiquity, and denying his people the possibility of a new technologically advanced future—he had only a few years of life left. The king of cats might think Chel evil, but what truly was the difference between evil and ambition in the future's hindsight? And where would the world be without striving for excellence? Only pain could lead to progress. The complacent cats would suffer for their laziness, and the birds would suffer for their vanity. But the reptiles would suffer only for the greatest cause, the undeniable advancement that was the essence of animalkind; evolution.

25.

The Tide Rushes In

he southeast colonies have failed, Paragon. Chel's army continues north unchecked."

"Where are the damned birds?" Fel shouted. "What are they waiting for?"

The cheetah messenger laid his ears flat. "Many flocks have already arrived, but their tactics have, so far, been ineffective. Airborne squadrons are dropping rocks to pummel our enemies from above, but the reptiles have fashioned a sort of…well, something like a moving wall, held up over their heads. Metal sheets like shields."

"Damn it!" Fel spat.

"A small contingent of ostriches have also arrived from…"

"One flock of gangly birds will not help us now. Announce a full retreat. Call all troops back to the castle."

"And leave the remaining citizenry defenseless in the villages? Some people did not receive warning of the invasion in time to flee, and still more refused to leave their villages, insisting on standing their ground. They may not survive if our defensive squadron retreats."

Fel winced. "We have no choice. Attempting to drag every single holdout to safety behind the castle walls would only hinder the troops, and get everyone killed—soldiers and civilians alike. If we abandon the east and the south, and lean to the west, I suspect they will follow. The reptiles will likely not waste their time hunting down Felidae citizens. It is mainly our resources—and my own life—that they are seeking to take. At least, that is my hope."

By midday, only the outer Great Castle walls stood between the Felidae army and the advancing reptile horde. Citizens left outside the walls were either dead or hiding in their homes and holes, waiting for the storm to pass as bands of reptiles marched across their land.

Fel paced in his throne room. As he had feared, the reptiles were stronger than his people, and also considerably smarter when it came to battle strategy; this was now beyond doubt. His alliance with the birds had been insufficient. He could not hope to win a war in the open fields. But using the Great Castle to defend his people was not a solution, either. They would never outlast a siege. The people of Felidae could not be trapped here, waiting either to starve or for the lion guards to become too exhausted to prevent the reptiles from beating the doors down. A final stand could not succeed in the fields, nor in the Great Castle. So it would have to happen somewhere else.

And it had to happen now.

"Messenger! Are the birds still fighting in the fields? The flying ones, I mean."

"Yes, Paragon."

"Recall them. Bring them all here, immediately. Every last one."

Within an hour, the sky over the Felidae Great Castle was darkened by a massive flock of feathered fighters. Hundreds of them spiraled like leaves in a tornado, screeching with a myriad of exotic calls, flying wingtip to wingtip and beak to tail. Pats of bird poop splattered the turrets, the walkways, the gardens. The cats and bears picked their way around the splotches, grimacing with disgust.

In the throne room, Fel set his plan to action. It was foolhardy and strange, perhaps even foolish. But at least he would have surprise on his side.

"Kana, are you near?"

"I'm here, Fel."

"I must ask you to act as ambassador again, this time to facilitate communication among my remaining allies. Spread the word that all large creatures must stay within the walls of the Great Castle and barricade themselves here, in the throne room. This would include the bears, the lions, the biggest cats. Tell them they must think only of their own safety, you understand? Tell them the Felidae territories depend on them keeping safe, not for their own sake, but for their king and for their people."

"Okay, Fel," Kana said. "I'll tell them."

"All smaller citizens—anyone my size or smaller—must gather on the upper walkways. Quickly, now!"

Major Ursa led her soldiers in to occupy the throne room as Fel and his assistants walked out the door. As the king and the old soldier passed each other, they paused long enough for a whispered exchange. Before they parted, they touched foreheads, briefly, with their eyes squeezed shut.

"Good luck, my king," Major Ursa said.

"And you, Ursa. My gratitude for your faithfulness knows no bounds."

Kana found Panicum, and they ran together among the Felidae citizens and soldiers, spreading word of Fel's command to retreat to the highest points of the Great Castle. The army fell back behind the walls, bringing the weak, young, and old along with them, whenever they found them willing. The reptiles followed close behind, picking off stragglers and cheering in triumph at their enemy's swift retreat.

When the gates were locked behind the mammals, Kana climbed the stairs, leading a long parade of Felidae citizens and soldiers. At the top of the parapets she found herself standing alongside a legion of furry, frightened creatures; otters, hounds, deer, lynxes, a legion of rats, several leopards, a pack of grunting warthogs, a flurry of raccoons. They crowded the upper walkways of the Great Castle, nervous and confused, twitching uneasily in the open air.

Panicum returned to Kana's side at the top of the western parapet.

"What's going on, Kana? What's the plan?"

"I don't know. We're just following Fel's orders right now, and we have to trust him. But if he has something specific in mind, he hasn't told me about it."

"Have you seen Jack?"

"No. I think he's hiding again. I just hope he's still safe, wherever he is."

Paragon Fel climbed to the peak of the highest roof and met with a massive albatross who descended from the skies to land near the king. Kana strained her ears to hear their conversation, but could hear nothing over the anxious growls and scraping of the animals around her. Within minutes, the albatross and the king had reached some kind of accord. The bird alit from the parapet, calling out commands in unintelligible screeches. At his orders, birds began to swoop toward the Felidae citizens and soldiers in droves, causing the mammals to scream and scamper in alarm.

"We're under attack!" a lynx squealed at Kana's feet. "Betrayal! Treason! Run for your life!" It bolted toward the stairs, but before the lynx could reach the first step, an eagle swept it from its feet and carried it up over the wall.

Kana suddenly understood. "Fel! Are you *crazy?*" she shouted. The king looked down at her and offered only a curling, feline smile. "It'll never work, Fel! They can't all possibly…"

Flapping wings filled the air around her, descending on all sides. Birds of every shape and size swept down toward the mammals, gripped their fur in their strong claws, and lifted them away from the castle parapets. Ten birds landed on Kana's arms and hair, wrapping their talons around anything they could grip. Their long nails tore into the fabric of her clothes. When they lifted her from the castle wall she heard seams pop, but her clothing held together—barely. The experience was terrifying, yet the sensation of flying was simultaneously incredible. She saw the castle walls fall away from under her feet as she rose into the air. Behind her, Panicum ran in circles on the ground, growling and snapping at any bird who ventured near until a brave hawk grabbed him by the scruff and followed the rest of the flock into the air.

"It's okay, Pan!" Kana called back, watching trees pass by under her boots.

Panicum responded with an indecipherable string of curses and epithets.

Fel's trick worked, but not well. Kana could tell the birds

were already tiring. Only seconds into the journey, many flyers had already landed to rest before once again gripping their burden and taking off for another brief burst of progress toward the west. In this slow, lurching fashion, the two armies of Felidae and Falcoformia retreated across the sky, leaving Fel's Great Castle to the mercy of the reptile army. When they had traveled several miles, the birds set down the mammals, and each army proceeded under its own power. Exhausted birds perched on the backs of trotting mammals until they were rested enough to fly on their own, speeding toward Falcoformia territory to prepare it for the arrival of the mammal refugees.

On the ground, Fel caught up with Kana and Panicum.

"Will the rest be okay, Fel?" Kana asked. "All the lions and the bears we left behind, I mean."

"Yes. At least, I think so. We couldn't have brought them. What the birds achieved today was a miracle."

Kana nodded. "I can't decide whether your idea was brilliant or stupid."

"We're alive, aren't we? If nothing else, we left the reptiles confused. It will take them time to gather their wits and pursue."

A leopard paced the king. "Message from Paragon Falca, sir."

"Yes?"

"She requests that you assemble your army in the outer fields. Do not venture into the inner walls. Do not cross over the Bridge of Accipiter. Do not interact with Falcoformian citizens. If any Falcoformian citizen is harmed in any way, the pact is cancelled. If any mammal breaks any of these rules, the pact is cancelled. If any-"

"I get the idea, messenger," Fel said. "Thank you. Let Falca know we accept her terms."

The Felidae army trudged for many hours through the bird villages and along the rocky, little-used roads, until it finally halted in the vast golden fields Kana had first crossed with Struthio. As they neared the Bridge of Accipiter and the stone bird statues with their wings spread wide, the mammals collapsed in exhaustion. They licked each other's wounds, cleaning the bleeding nicks left by the talons of the bird army as they had lifted their allies to safety.

"Rest now," Fel called out to the panting crowd. "The reptile army will follow, but not before they test the gates of my Great Castle. It will take them a day to change course and pursue, probably two. The birds gave us the head start we needed, and now we must rest and regroup."

"Paragon, we have no chance," a desperate voice cried.

"Who said that?" Fel snapped, whipping his head toward the speaker.

"They are so much stronger than we are," someone else sobbed. The statement came from an exhausted raccoon with trickling talon wounds at its shoulders. "It's only a matter of time. We're safe for now, but soon they will find us, and when they do they will kill us. We all know it's true."

Nervous whispers rose from the mammals. Some nodded in agreement. Others wept, hiding their faces. The youngest pups whimpered in fear, seeing their elders shudder with dread. The field reeked of blood and panic. If order was not maintained, there would be a stampede, from which the mammal army would not recover before the reptiles advanced upon them.

"I command you to remain calm!" Fel howled. "Listen to me! We have come far with the help of our bird allies. Would you give up now, in the very same hour you escaped from danger? Would you leave behind your dreams and hopes for peace so easily?"

"There is no hope!" A young deer brayed, stamping its hooves.

"There is always hope!" Kana yelled into the fray. At her strange primate voice, heads turned. Faces frowned in confusion instead of terror. She seized the moment.

"I come from a world very far from this one! Where I come from, the primates dominate the animals. The animals cannot talk! They cannot even make their own choices. They live as slaves, or die as food! You have no idea what you have here. You are free. And freedom always requires sacrifice."

The mob stopped churning, and one by one they turned to face her, to listen to her speak.

"It is true that we are in danger now," Kana said in a softer voice, forcing the crowd to stay quiet in order to hear her words. "But Fel will not deceive you or fail you."

"He's left us before!" barked a cowering hound.

"But he won't again," Kana replied.

"What do you know about it, stranger? What does a primate know about the ways of the Felidae?"

"Very little," Kana admitted. "But I know Fel, and I think you do too." She turned toward the king, and whispered, "Your turn."

Fel found a fallen tree and climbed up the slope of its trunk to look down over the shivering crowd. "Citizens and friends," he called out. "We must stand together now. We still have allies. The Falcoformian army has saved us from certain death. And we still have our army. It is smaller than Squamor's, to be sure, but we have our wits and our passion, and these may yet save us. Be assured that I already have a plan to outsmart the reptiles, once and for all! I only ask that you give me time. Will you, loyal citizens? Will you grant me this one favor? All I ask of you is that you lend me your patience, and have faith!"

Kana joined Fel on the fallen tree. Panicum leapt to her side, and together they made a show of solidarity against the exhaustion and fear which threatened to overcome the army. The mammals lowered their heads, silently contemplating their leader's plea. Then, one by one, they lay down in the fields, acquiescing to his request for patience. They quieted as they nursed their wounds, and many closed their eyes to sleep, surrendering all their hopes and fears to their king.

"Thank the mother," Fel whispered out the side of his mouth. "You really saved my hide, Kana."

"You're welcome," Kana said. "So, tell me. What's your big plan?"

"No idea. Let's go make one." Fel leapt from the tree trunk and trotted into a grove of trees behind the field.

"Figures," Panicum muttered. "Shall we?"

"I guess so," Kana said. "I wish Barbar was here with us, though."

"Me, too," Panicum said. "I hope he and Major Ursa are still safe in the Great Castle."

Kana worried again about Jack, and she hoped he had found a place to hide. She could not bear the thought of him being killed in battle, a young boy so far from his own home.

As Kana tiptoed past the piles of exhausted mammals, Panicum parted the thick grasses in their path, scaring up a swarm of gnats. They found Fel sitting in the middle of the grove in a small clearing, shaded under a spread of tree branches. The three companions sat in a circle, saying nothing until there was something to say, trying not to disrupt the rest of the animals sleeping nearby who had entrusted them with their lives.

"I've got nothing," Fel said after several minutes of contemplation. "No ideas. Not a single one. Falca won't let my people into her Great Castle, of that I'm sure. She would let us die with our backs against her walls, if it came to that."

"So we're doomed," Panicum said.

"There has to be another option," Kana said. "What about the fish? Can't they do anything to help?"

Fel sneered. "They're *fish*, Kana. I don't know if you know this, but fish require water, and there is precious little of that here."

"The sarcasm isn't necessary," Kana said. "But they must have some allies on land, like sea lions or something. That's all I meant."

"Sorry. I'm nervous too, you know. But even if we thought they could help us somehow, their castle is on the other side of the reptile lands. No way we could reach it in time. Anyway, Paragon Mobula favors Chel. I've never been able to establish a friendship with her."

They fell silent again.

"We need another clever trick of some kind," Panicum said.

"No more tricks." Fel slumped, pushing dirt ahead of his paws until his chest hit the ground. He pressed his body into the sandy earth, mourning. "Tomorrow the Felidae population dies, Kana. We must face it. I have failed."

Panicum snarled. "Shut up, cat! You don't get to give up. Hear me? You don't have that luxury. As long as you wear that crown, your responsibility is only to your people. You live for them, not for yourself."

"You are not in charge here, dog!" Fel hissed. "What do you know about it?"

"Quiet, both of you!" Kana said. "We don't have time to fight. Nothing matters except thinking of a plan."

"You're half right," Fel said. "Nothing matters." Sand spilled out from his black leathers and orange fur as he sat up. With a flick of his tail he strode through the clearing and stepped out into the sunlight on the opposite side. "Goodbye."

"Fel! No!" Kana stood to run after him.

"Let him go, Kana. If you go after him now, it will do no good. He will only flee faster."

She watched the king of cats wade through the waving golden grasses. As he walked, he tore his crown from his head and tossed it into the high branches of a tree. Away from his army he marched, broken and resolute, until the hills rose up behind him and he was visible no more.

"I can't believe it," Kana said. "He just…"

"He has a history of this, I'm afraid," Panicum said. "Although I never would have believed he could leave his people to die on the eve of battle. This is beyond even him. Or, so I thought."

"It's only us, then? Major Ursa isn't here. Lieutenant Barbar had to stay behind, too. None of the soldiers are with us. Why did Fel bring us all the way here just to abandon us?"

Panicum shook his head, speechless.

26.

Dusk Falls

The Felidae army slept fitfully. While the older soldiers stood guard without resting, the young ones cried in their sleep, suffering from nightmares. Kana and Panicum talked all night in low voices, watching over the mammals from the clearing in the grove. They attempted to devise a strategy to surprise the reptile army, but every proposed plan was flimsy and desperate. They were neither generals nor tacticians. Protecting the smallest mammals from Chel's advance seemed impossible, even if the birds were once again willing to offer their help. The Felidae army was exposed, tired, and hungry, cowering in fear in a foreign land.

"We must talk to Paragon Falca, that much is clear. She will allow me an audience. I am sure of it," Kana said.

"I agree to that much. But I don't know what you expect to get from her. She will not open her gates to a host of mammals. That wasn't part of the agreement you negotiated during your visit."

"I know that, but I can't think of anything else to do. It's the only idea I have left."

Panicum laid down with his chin on his tail. "But it's a *useless* idea, Kana."

"Perhaps, but that doesn't change the fact that it is the only one. I'm not a warrior, Pan. I'm an ambassador. All I can do is nego- tiate."

"And barely that."

"You, too? I need you on my side."

"I'm sorry, I'm just tired. You know I'm on your side, always. But it's a long shot, you know."

"Believe me, I know." Kana stood and looked east, where the sky was beginning to brighten at the horizon line. "Sun will be up soon. There's no time to lose. I'd better go. And you have to stay here, Pan."

"Not a chance! I'm coming with you. I don't trust Falca at all, and neither should you."

"You're right, and I don't. But someone with half a brain has to stay here and look official. The army has seen you at my side, and that gives you some authority. I'll come back as soon as I can. Stay here, keep everyone calm, and assure them help is on the way."

"You mean, lie to them."

"Yes."

Panicum sat still with his eyes closed. "I never should have asked you to help me find acorns."

"You're the one who followed me!" Kana laughed.

"You stepped on my tail!"

"And that, somehow, made you decide to be my friend?"

Pan grinned.

A tear formed at the corner of Kana's eye. She wiped it away with frustration. "Listen, Pan. I'm glad you're here with me now. And I'm so sorry about…well, about everything."

"None of this is your fault. I will do my best with the rabble," Panicum said, turning his attention toward the sleeping mammals. "But don't waste any more time now. Go. And good luck."

Kana nodded and left the grove. She slipped past the army and found the rough path which led to the bridge. As she crossed, a brown-spotted bird sitting atop one of the statues cocked its head at her before flying away toward the Great Castle, surely to report to its Paragon. So, Falca would soon know of Kana's approach. She wished she had time for a bath; the mud which caked her clothes would reduce her credibility. Oh, well. It could not be helped now.

As she approached the gate guarded by the giant eagle, she was stopped by a huge cassowary wearing a general's tabard.

"General Cass? You might remember me. My name is Kana."

"I know who you are, primate, but I am not General Cass. I am General Wara. My mother passed away since you were here last."

"My condolences, Wara. I am here to…"

"That's *general*, child. General Wara," the cassowary snapped.

"And I know why you are here. Follow me."

Once again, Kana found herself trotting behind flouncing tail feathers on the path to Falca's throne room. It was not her favorite situation to be in, but it was necessary. For the third time, she wondered what she would say to the bird Paragon. The first time she was here, she was a captive. The second time, an ambassador. This time, she was a humble petitioner from a foreign country with nothing to offer but words.

And what did she expect Falca to do, really? Her terms had been made clear. She knew that the reptile army advanced and that it threatened her own lands as much as it did castle Felidae. What Falca must be led to believe was that allowing the mammals to shelter within her walls was in her own best interest, and even Kana was not sure that was true. Mammals were usually predators, birds were usually prey. In all likelihood, the birds' best chance for survival was to barricade themselves, especially since they had the option to fly out for food. A siege would be ineffective against Falcoformia, and eventually the reptiles would be forced to return home.

But would Falcoformia grieve for the death of Felidae?

If her previous meeting with Falca had been important, this one was absolutely critical. The future of the entire Kingdom was at stake.

Kana entered the throne room, highly conscious of her grubby appearance. Falca sat at her throne, preening the delicate feathers under her wing. She looked up at Kana with a coy smile that bespoke her confidence and sense of security. Hers was a position of absolute power over the fate of Felidae, and Kana was a helpless supplicant. No more an ambassador, nor even a foreign curiosity, but simply a beggar.

"Well, my dear Kana. I see you have arrived alone. Surely Paragon Fel is nearby? Where is your king?"

"He is indisposed."

"You mean he has disappeared, as he has so many times in the past. Except this time he will not have a home to come back to, will he? The reptiles bite at your heels."

"They will be outside your own gates soon, Paragon. They are not only our problem, but yours, too."

"True, but I do still have my gates. What do you have?"

"Not much," Kana admitted. "But surely you have no desire to watch the slaughter of nearly all mammal species occur just outside your walls? What does this gain you?"

"Safety, if my gates remain shut."

"For how long? The reptiles are brutish, and Paragon Chel's ambition is limitless."

"What is your offer, then?"

"I have nothing," Kana said, holding her hands open.

Falca culled a thin, bent feather from a row under her wing, then smoothed the rest over the fluffy down where it met her body. Her manner was dismissive, but Kana knew she was considering her position from all angles, planning her next words carefully.

"What exactly do you want from me, Kana?" Falca turned her head to one side and looked at Kana with a bright eye. "State your needs clearly."

"We—I mean, the army and remaining citizens of the Felidae lands—request to shelter inside your castle walls before the arrival of the Squamor army."

"Then my price is servitude. Once inside, your people will never leave. They will form a new caste, lower than the lowest bird citizen, and will live here to tend to the needs of my people for all time, generation upon generation. This is my only offer."

Kana's mouth fell open. "No! That's not an offer of help, that's slavery! We can't agree to that!"

"Then you will die."

Falca resumed her preening. Kana stood in silence, helpless. She knew Falca's word was final, but the deal was unacceptable. Selling the entire Felidae population into slavery was impossible. Was it even preferable to death? And did Kana, a foreigner and a primate, have the right to make that decision in the first place? She wanted to leap up the steps to Falca's throne to tear the crown from her head and rip the feathers from her wings for even suggesting it. Instead, Kana swallowed, unclenched her fists, and spoke in an even tone.

"I will consider your offer. I am grateful you agreed to this meeting, Paragon. Please await my reply."

Falca did not speak again, but nodded to her guards. They escorted Kana back to the field where Panicum awaited, licking his paws.

"Well? What did she say?"

"Not here," Kana answered. "Let's talk in the grove."

By the time Kana and Panicum returned to the clearing, the mammal army was stirring. They awoke hungry and thirsty and frightened, but Kana could do nothing for them. On all sides laid forbidden bird territory, and before them approached a vicious enemy army. The air felt thick to Kana, too dense to breathe. Worry pressed on her chest and made a lump in her throat.

"Falca's offer was unacceptable," Kana whispered under the trees in the grove.

"What? So simply? Surely whatever she offered would be better than sitting here waiting for death."

"Her offer was slavery. Nothing more, nothing less."

Every hair on Panicum's brush stood straight out, doubling his tail in size. "That…that *bitch!* Despot! Traitor! I'll kill her! I'll…"

"You'll stay here with me and do nothing of the kind, Pan."

"But how dare she!"

"I'm going to tell the army about the meeting. I'll explain Falca's terms and ask the mammals what they want to do. It shouldn't be my decision, but theirs. They have to know."

"No, Kana. I know what you're thinking. You want them to help you decide so that no matter what happens, the consequences don't rest entirely on your shoulders. But you can't."

"Why not? I'm not even from this world, Pan! I shouldn't be making the choice between slavery and death for these animals. It's not up to me."

"It is, though. Fel may not have said it out loud, but he left you in charge. He was wrong to do so, but that doesn't change the truth of it. You are the leader now, and the decision is yours. If you ask them, they'll panic. You won't get a straight answer. Some will want security while others will refuse, and eventually they will turn against each other. The reptiles won't have to kill us, we'll do it ourselves in a bloody civil war on Falca's doorstep before Chel's army even arrives."

"Oh, god," Kana groaned. "But I don't want to make this decision. I can't!"

Panicum walked to her side and licked the back of her hand. "Whichever choice you make, it will be the correct one. Because you will decide not with your brain, but with your heart."

Kana lowered her head, spilling her bright colored hair over her face. She knew what she must choose, and it broke her. Sharp pains stabbed her breastbone. Her entire soul was weeping, grieving for what was to come.

"If the choice is mine alone, then I choose death. Death for myself, and for the entire Felidae army."

"No," Panicum said. "You don't choose death. You choose to fight! Death may be the result, but it doesn't make the choice wrong."

Kana nodded. "What do I tell them?"

"Tell them Falca refused to help. Which is, in essence, the truth."

"Will you come with me? Will you stand by my side while I lie to them?"

Panicum's nose wrinkled with disapproval at the word, but he nodded. "Of course. I'll always stand by your side, Kana."

"Thank you. They are waking up now. Let's go."

Kana's speech to the mammal army was powerful, rousing, energizing. The words which poured from her mouth seemed to originate from somewhere beyond herself, strong words loaded with hope that she did not truly feel in her heart. Her own eloquence surprised and confused her, but she let herself talk, trusted her instincts, watched the crowd carefully, and said what they needed to hear. She spoke of honor, of family generations, and of the richness of tradition. Every pointed ear turned to hear her call for action. Every lip snarled when she spoke of the evil approaching from the east, and every claw extended, ready to draw reptilian blood. Kana did not demonize Falca, but her words were condescending with pity and understanding when speaking of the cowardly birds. Their fear was forgivable, she said, as their bodies were weak. But despite Falca's inability to help, the mammals would reign victorious to save the entire Kingdom from the wicked scaly beasts who mounted up from the east in a foul swarm. The battles won in the fields would be spoken of for centuries, crafted into songs of valor and glory to be sung by the lips of their children's children.

As her speech concluded, the mammals readied for battle. Fur stood on end, hackles were raised, nails sharpened. Kana knew they could not win, and that soon the fields would be soaked with their blood—but still, she smiled with pride. They would surely fail, but they would go down fighting.

Kana and Panicum sat on the fallen tree. To the east, dust rose in the slanted rays of the evening sunlight. The reptile army was drawing near. Judging from the speed of their progress, Kana guessed they would arrive at midnight. That suited her fine. Mammals saw better at night than reptiles did.

In the dark they would last an extra hour, maybe two, before the battlefield fell silent.

27.

Red Earth, Black Sky

"**A**mbassador, sir! I mean, Ambassador Kana. May I speak with you for a moment?"

A gangly young wildcat, not much older than a kitten, approached the grove of trees with its ears laid flat in meek deference. It dragged its paws in the dust and glanced backwards for reassurance from a small group of cats who followed close behind.

"Yes? What do you need?" Kana was sitting in the clearing with Panicum, discussing last-minute battle strategies.

"We are reluctant to demand knowledge of the private affairs of our dear Paragon, and yet we feel compelled to ask where he is, currently. He has not been seen in camp since last night, and some of our more timid citizens have become somewhat nervous, you understand." The wildcat offered Kana a courteous, pleading look, and sat back on its hind legs.

"Ah, well," Kana said, swallowing. She had dreaded this conversation, and was not yet prepared with her excuses for the king's absence. "He has run to confer once again with Falca."

"We were all—and excuse me if I'm mistaken—under the impression you had already run that particular errand."

"Yes, well, he's trying again."

"I see."

The wildcat left the grove, flicking its tail with dissatisfaction. Kana's lie was not well hidden on her face.

"This won't help morale," Panicum said.

"No, but there's so little hope at this point I don't see that it matters much."

"Shush, now. There's always hope."

"No. Not always."

The sound of stomping dominated the fields. Chain armor

scraping against scales, rusted swords in back-mounted hilts rattling against metal helmets. The reptile army was nearly within view, rising above the hills with the moon following close behind. The Felidae army was as ready as it could ever be, trembling among the grasses but prepared to fight for their lives. A few of the more sensible bird families had joined with the mammal ranks, understanding that when the reptiles had cut through the Felidae army their own castle would be next. Still, their numbers were few and frightened.

"It's time, Kana. Let's go."

Kana rose to her feet and found them numb with terror. She left the grove by the path the wildcat had taken, making sure her exit was marked by several of the mammals so they would understand the battle was near and spread the word. She walked up a grassy slope with Panicum at her side, facing directly into the light of the advancing moon, and sought the enemy.

Instead, at the peak she found a more familiar figure. Silhouetted against the last light of the day was a cat with fine, pointed ears poking through a hat tilted at a rakish angle.

He faced away, but Kana knew instantly that it was Fel. The king had returned to stand with his army just as the first reptile lines encroached upon the golden fields.

"Parlay!" he cried toward the advancing horde. His voice cracked with exhaustion. "Who among you personally represents Paragon Chel? I wish to speak with you!"

Kana climbed the hill and stood next to him. "Welcome back, king of all cats," she whispered.

Fel glanced at her and smiled. "Hey, Tinkerbell."

An enormous crocodile wearing a gold-trimmed tabard stepped out from the ranks, walking tall on his hind legs. On his back was strapped a claymore with an ornate hilt. Clumps of bear fur ripped from previous conquests swung from his belt.

"I represent Chel. I am Croco. Speak to me."

"Listen to my words: We don't have to fight here today. Do you understand? Your Paragon isn't here. And what kind of general commands from afar, who cannot even accompany his own armies to the field? Make peace with us, deny your arrogant king his cruel use of you, and come to no harm by my warriors today."

The reptile snorted. "We follow our orders. Reptiles are strong. Furred animals are weak. We will prove it now, once and for all."

"But why? Chel craves technology. Do you? How will it really benefit you and your family?"

The reptile turned away, unable or unwilling to answer. He bellowed at his troops, who drew their swords from their backs, howling in excitement.

"Damn," Fel muttered. "I really hoped…"

"Something's wrong," Panicum said. "Where are the rest of them? I only see a hundred warriors or so. There should be at least five times that many."

Fel squinted into the darkness. "I'm not sure. It's hard to count in the moonlight."

From the north a tremendous shout rang out. Hundreds more, rough and graveled, called into the darkening sky. The stomping of massive claws shook the earth. Kana felt the pounding vibrations in the arches of her feet.

"We've been flanked! Everyone retreat! Move back toward the castle walls, get them behind us!" Fel sprinted circles through the stunned Felidae soldiers as four hundred reptile warriors charged from the northern foothills toward the unwary mammals. The sight of the ferocious army with the Gludair Chain rising behind them caused Kana's blood to race cold in her veins.

Fel managed to guide most of his army back to the river outside the castle walls before the reptiles crashed into the perimeter, swinging their rusted blades forged in the time before time. Swords separated arms from shoulders, heads from necks, children from parents. The quickest mammals dashed among the slow reptiles, biting at their tough green skin, scratching at their eyes. Wolves, protected by their thick undercoats, swept the lizards off their feet while panthers moved in to tear out their throats where the scales were softest. The hot blood of mammals mixed in the mud with cold reptile entrails, steaming where they met in the open field.

At some point during their fast march into the bird territories, the reptiles had abandoned their heavy overhead shields. A small squadron of flying birds took advantage of this, picking up the reptiles' own discarded weapons and armor to drop from an enormous height. A few pieces struck mammals, but most were limber enough to keep an eye on the sky and dodge when necessary. The cool night air slowed the cold-blooded reptiles, to be sure—yet it was not enough of a difference to prevent the carnage they sought.

Kana picked up a reptile sword and prepared to charge into battle. Beside her, Panicum shook as if electrified, his brush stuck out straight behind. "Ready?" she asked him.

He nodded, snarling.

They ran down the slope toward the battlefield, trying not to slip on the smooth turf. Kana chose as her target a small lizard warrior on the outskirts of the battle, who was swinging a short sword. Even as she charged, blade in hand, she wondered if she had the will and strength to kill a sentient being. Her running slowed as she hesitated. The battle was awful, yes, but wasn't this still murder? She tried to imagine what it would feel like to plunge her sword into the reptile's neck, and balked.

The reptile turned toward her and spotted her advance. It sneered, dismissing her, and turned toward an injured lion cub sprawled in the mud. He approached it and without pause he plunged his blade down between the struggling cub's shoulders. It squealed, a thin sound lost in the din of the battle, and went limp.

"No!" Kana screamed. *Her fault!* If she had only stayed strong, if she hadn't stopped… "No! No no no!" she shouted over and over as she charged the warrior. Panicum ran around the back of the reptile and snapped at its heels. When it swung its sword at the fox, Kana buried her blade in its neck. The tip struck bone and deflected off to the side, but the damage was done; the reptile collapsed to the ground, its nape reduced to a shredded mass of green tissue and red tendons.

"Kana! What are you doing out here?" Fel ran to her side. His leathers were sliced through in several places, but his body was intact. He had lost his hat, but his paw still gripped his rapier with strength.

"I'm fighting! This is my fight too, and don't you dare tell me it's not!"

"I just…" Fel's face wrenched with emotion as he sought words. "Thank you."

"Behind you!"

The enormous crocodile who had accepted parlay with Fel before the battle charged the king with his sword held out in front, a half-ton of angry lizard and rusted metal. The king sidestepped the warrior and thrust his blade into the lizard's knee with the grace of a bullfighter.

"How are we doing?" Fel shouted in the noise.

"Not good! We need to rest! Retreat!" Panicum shouted, dodging and dashing among the brawl.

"They'll never let us," Fel yelled, ducking the bite of a striking snake. He spun around and sunk his teeth into the snake's belly like a mongoose. As it bled out in the mud, Fel ran up the hill for a view of the field. Kana escaped the fray and followed with Panicum at her side.

"Oh my god," Kana said, looking down.

The golden meadow was streaked with red. Mounds of bodies lay upon the ground like giant anthills. Flies had already begun to swarm. More than half of the mammal army was dead. The remaining soldiers were pressed against the castle walls, holding off two hundred armored reptile soldiers.

"You fought well," Fel said. He licked a wound on his forearm for a moment, then turned to Kana as tears made rivers in the orange fur on his cheeks. A drop ran to the end of a coarse whisker before falling to his collar.

"We all did," Kana said. "But it's not over yet. Look!" Kana pointed at the Bridge of Accipiter. The bird guards had backed away from the bridge's entrance, allowing the mammals to access it. The gate remained locked behind them, but the remaining mammals were able to back over the arch, creating a narrow choke point.

Fel grinned. "They're finally helping us. Falca will be furious!"

"Good!" Kana shouted. "Let's go!"

They ran down the slope and circled around south, staying at the edge of the battle until they reached the bridge, where they swam across the water and rejoined the mammal army. The reptiles refused to step on the bridge until they realized it was the only way across. The choke point held as the bodies of lizard warriors piled up between the spread-winged bird statues, forcing the living to push their defeated comrades into the river below. For a while, it seemed the reptiles were at an impasse.

"Look!" Kana pointed at the water. "The bodies…they're clogging the river."

The reptile corpses were piled so high in the water they had created a crude walkway. The cold-blooded warriors began to cross, crushing the bodies of their compatriots underfoot as they breached the river.

Fel shouted at the gate guards. "You must let us in! Let us fall back immediately!"

"No! We let you cross the bridge, but this gate shall not be unlocked," the giant eagle replied. "Falca has commanded it. Under no circumstances-"

"And where is Falca? Where is she now? Not here, is she?" Fel yelled, gripping the bars in his paws. "Tell her I would speak with her! Tell her right now!"

The eagle, stone-faced, stopped responding. He watched the plight of the mammals unconcerned, comfortable in the knowledge that he could open his wings and fly away from the fray at any time.

"Useless!" Fel shouted, before returning to face the melee on the bridge.

All night and into the early morning hours, the two armies struggled to gain the advantage. Many reptiles fell, but even more mammals met their end. By the time the fighting slowed, the sun had started to rise, turning the sky grey. The reptiles called a brief rest, retreating back toward the grove of trees and the fallen log. The mammals collapsed against the unyielding walls of the bird castle, licking their wounds.

"I judge they'll charge again in less than an hour," Panicum said. He breathed heavy, limping on a wounded paw.

"And it will be our doom," Fel said. "We will not withstand another onslaught. And Falca, that tyrant! She watches us from atop her tower, allows us to be slaughtered. The fool! As I die today, my deepest satisfaction will be the knowledge that her castle falls next."

Kana leaned against the wall and slid down it, kicking her legs out in front. She had killed two more reptile soldiers and her hands were caked with dry blood. Although her injuries were minor, there was an aching in her heart she knew would never fully heal, even if she were to survive the day.

"Pan," she whispered. The fox approached, and rested his chin on her leg. "You should run away. You can still get away from here."

"Never," he responded.

Fel sat nearby. "Everyone dies, eventually. But not all of us have the opportunity to attain glory. We may lose today, but Chel's army is severely injured. Mammals throughout my lands still live. In culling the reptiles, we have opened a path for their survival. Our lives will not be given in vain."

A shadow sneaked along the wall. It dipped behind a clump of grass, then dashed a few feet further, touching the ground lightly with soft fingertips. When it reached the place at the wall where its friends had collapsed in exhaustion, it stopped and pulled something shiny from a bag on its hip.

Fel beamed, his smile stretching ear to ear as his whiskers stuck straight out with glee.

"My crown! Were you eavesdropping on our conversation in the grove from up in the treetops, Jack?"

The boy nodded. "I knew you would come back, and I thought you might want this again. Are you angry with me for listening in?"

Laughing, Fel took the battered crown from the boy's hands and rubbed the dirt from its gemstones. "Confidentially, this is the first time in all these years I feel I've earned the right to wear this old thing."

"Let me, Fel," Kana said. She pressed the crown onto the king's head, taking care to tilt it at a rakish angle in the style he was so fond of.

"Better," Jack said, grinning.

Kana tilted her head back and watched the stars fade away in the dull sky. If she had stayed home, she might not be preparing to die in a bloody battle. And yet she found, to her surprise, that she did not regret her journey to the Kingdom. Perhaps Fel was right. Dying for a cause had never been something she had valued before—had never even thought about. But which was worse; sacrificing her life for the sake of her friends, or simply waiting for her heart to stop beating, lying in a hospice bed after a lifetime of begging in the cold streets of Chicago?

"I'm ready," she whispered. "Let them come."

28.

The Chain Breaks

The final advance of the Squamor army was no less terrifying than the first. Their numbers were thinned, but their power was unabated in relation to the Felidae army's own diminished strength. Battle-scarred reptile soldiers picked the best remaining weapons from the bodies of their fallen comrades and prepared for an assault against the Falcoformia castle walls, where they would pin their enemy and cut them to shreds.

The mammals huddled together, pressing close to one another for warmth and courage. Trembling, they listened to the shouted commands of the approaching reptile generals who ordered their deaths. Fel stood firm several paces ahead of his front line, holding his sword pointed up at the blue-grey morning sky in defiance with Falca's unyielding gate at his back. The outlines of the reptiles were visible now, in the first light of the dawning sun. Frosted breath puffed from the mouths of the mammals, but no such warmth arose from the reptile invaders. They were cold and steady, moving inexorably toward the last stand of the Felidae army.

"Ready yourselves," Fel said, "To die for your species and for your home."

"And for our king!" cried a thin, wavering voice from the back. The crowd shouted in accord, lifting their long noses into the air to bay with reckless excitement. Their keen ears heard the strong heartbeats of their compatriots, their hot blood rushed through their veins desperate to surge forward even in the face of total destruction. All fear of death left them and they thought only of their own pride and glory. Courage rose in the heart of every soldier, and eagerness flashed in their eyes. Hundreds of paws trembled on the earth, ready to lunge forward, teeth bared, yearning to tear out the cold green throats of their enemies.

"Hold!" Fel commanded. "Wait until you can see them clearly. Don't give them any advantage. We advance only when we are ready."

They shook with anticipation, waiting for Fel to lower his sword, watching his every move. Muscles tensed, lips snarled, tails lashed from side to side.

The tip of Fel's sword bobbed, but before he could lower it, Kana cried out.

"Wait! Look! What is that? Coming down from the hills."

Lurching through the mist which rolled down the foothills of the Gludair Chain was a scattered assortment of strange figures. They slid and tripped and stood up again in a frenzied charge toward the castle. Their lumbering rush left dark trails weaving through the dew-spotted grasses.

The fear which had departed the mammalian army returned in the form of dread at this unnatural sight. The invaders seemed to be neither mammals nor reptiles—or if they were, something had gone terribly wrong.

When the reptile army noticed the new arrivals, the outer edges of its ordered squadrons began to roil. The creatures from the mist broke without pause through the reptile lines, slashing and biting. As they ate their way through the army like warm sewer-water eroding a snow bank, they growled; a thin, desperate sound devoid of sanity.

"The Badlands cloud," Fel gasped. "These creatures are living remnants of the effects of the cloud."

"But why are they attacking the reptiles?"

An enemy soldier limped toward Fel from the shadows; his forearm was severed at the elbow. Something had torn it clean away. He slumped to the ground, reaching out to Fel with his remaining arm before fainting, falling face-down in the ruddy mud.

"I don't think they discriminate. Chel's army was more exposed, that's all. When they are finished with the reptiles, they will come for us next," Fel said. "It's not our first encounter with these kinds of creatures, but they have never been this violent before. I don't think they are rushing into battle. I think…" Fel grimaced. "I think they are starving."

A dozen more lurching creatures appeared, their shapes becoming more coherent as they emerged from the hazy foothills. Some resembled dead deer, decomposing as they walked, swinging large racks of crumbing antlers. A pack of sickly wolves stumbled into the tumult with uncharacteristic clumsiness, their chests stained dark with dripping brown saliva. The creatures ate without any regard to the matter they sunk their teeth into; some tore hunks of flesh from the reptiles' exposed hands and faces, while others widened their mouths to extreme diameters to swallow pieces of armor and weapons. Those which ingested metal materials collapsed on the battlefield with sharp chunks of metal protruding from their rotten bellies.

A deranged bear and an emaciated lizard ran alongside each other, ignoring each other to charge instead toward the Felidae army.

One of the eagle guards at the gate noticed the change in the tide. "What is that?" it squawked, backing away from the bars. "What has happened?"

Fel spun toward the gate, hissing with fury. "An invasion of horrors beyond anything even Squamor could ever conjure! You have to let us in, *now!* This is no longer about mammals and reptiles. You understand? This is now Falca's own battle, on her land and at her threshold!"

One of the guards unlocked the gate, shaking with fear. Without waiting for the bird to step back, Fel pushed through the opening and pinned the door wide with his body, yelling commands to his army to make a full retreat into the Great Castle. Mammals shoved through the gates, barreling into the protection of the castle walls. When each surviving mammal had been accounted for, Fel slammed the gate shut and began to wrap chains around the latches.

"No!" Kana yelled. "Fel, no! The reptiles…you can't just leave them out there!"

The king ignored her. He bound the gates shut with everything at hand, and proceeded to build a barricade of boxes and barrels. Kana tried to stop him, grabbing at the chains and kicking the barrels aside, but he shoved her away.

"You would rescue our murderers, Kana?" Fel hissed. "The same ones who would obliterate every one of my citizens and decimate my lands? After what they did to you in their dungeons, and to your soldiers. What is your reasoning? You must be as mad as the creatures from the hills!"

"You must have mercy on them, Fel! They are just foot soldiers, no different from your own army. And this battle is no longer about your own land. You've won! Now you have an obligation…"

"Bullshit!"

"Take them as prisoners of war, then! Do whatever you need to do in order to justify letting them through this gate. But don't just lock them out and leave them to be slaughtered by invaders, or you're no better than Paragon Falca herself!"

Fel pressed his forehead against the bars. He grimaced, watching the screaming reptile army as it crumbled against the mindless onslaught of the damaged creatures. Finally, he stepped back.

"I won't do it. I cannot let them in. But…" Fel turned his back on the gate. "I will allow you to do so, if you must."

Kana leapt for the gate and unwrapped the chains that bound it. Turning to the eagle guards, she said, "You'll have to help me let them in slowly. We can't let them rush all the way to the Great Castle's interior. One at a time only, and take each one into custody. Tie their wrists. Understand? They can be Falca's prisoners, if she wants them." The eagles nodded.

The press of the panicked reptiles against the gates was almost too much for the guards to moderate, but they held their ground behind a hastily constructed barricade and one by one the soldiers of Squamor were granted asylum. As Kana and the guards pulled in reptiles from the front of the army, many more were taken down at the back, torn to shreds even as they begged for asylum. In the end, fifty reptile soldiers were saved and shackled in the courtyards of the Falcoformia Great Castle.

"Fifty of them, fifty of us," Fel said. "And how many more of the damaged creatures still lurk outside?"

"Hundreds," Panicum said. "And those are only the ones who made it all the way through the Chain. I suspect there are far more on the Badlands side who did not brave the mountains."

General Wara approached Fel. "Paragon, you will come with me immediately to Paragon Exemplar Falca's chambers. She wishes to speak with you."

"I'm sure she does," Fel said, sneering. "I have a few things to say to her, too. She is responsible for many deaths today."

"This battle was not hers."

"Perhaps. But mercy was hers to grant, and she refused."

After Fel left, Kana dressed the wounds of both armies and encouraged the soldiers to rest. All desire to fight had left the reptile soldiers. They slept with their mouths open, exhausted from shock. Panicum watched the fields closely through the bars of the gate, reporting back as increasing numbers of the wandering creatures either fell down in the grasses or wandered away south, past the Great Castle's perimeter.

"If I'm not mistaken, they seem to be dying," he said, watching Kana wrap a puma's hind leg. "I think it's the sickness from the cloud. It made them strong for a while but they're burning out fast, and won't last much longer. I think if we're careful we can send some runners out to look for survivors in the battlefield. But that illness, it may be contagious. We can't let our guard down."

"Pick some people, will you? Send them out, and if they find anyone alive who isn't showing symptoms, they can bring them here. But make sure they know exactly what to look for."

The Paragons Fel and Falca deliberated for hours. Their shouts rang out from the high windows of the bird Paragon's private chambers, echoing through the stone courtyards where the last vestiges of two armies cried out in pain.

Birds of mercy arrived with supplies for the wounded, bringing donations of bandages, food, and water, but all turned their beaks aside with disdain and none stayed to help. It was clear it would not be long before the foreign soldiers wore out their welcome. The eagle guard who had allowed the armies to enter the castle quietly disappeared from the premises.

Runners brought back twenty Felidae soldiers from the ruined fields, as well as eight lizards who still breathed and were clear of signs of illness. The reptiles collapsed next to the mammals without complaint; their general was dead, and Chel was still absent. No messenger appeared with any word from the Squamor territories. The land outside the bird castle became quiet and calm after the last of the damaged creatures fell.

The cat king reappeared in the courtyards the next morning, spitting with rage. Negotiations had collapsed, with Falca demanding that all foreign armies leave her lands immediately. No more nursing would be permitted on her castle grounds, and no more support would come from her people.

"Did you even *bother* to ask her nicely?" Kana asked. "We really need another day or two of rest, at the very least. A week would be best."

"Yes! Sort of. But she won't listen to reason."

"Well, if your castle was full of injured, hostile lizards, you'd probably want them gone too."

"But we can't move quickly like this," Fel said, looking over his exhausted troops with his brow furrowed. "It's dangerous."

"Then we'll move slowly," Panicum said. "And we'll all move together. I spoke with the highest ranking reptiles who remain. They have no desire to continue the fight, and they are willing to band together in order to move east in safety. If there are remaining hostile creatures beyond the Great Castle walls, I believe they will be no match for our unified force."

"Then that is what we will do," Fel said. "Prepare to leave immediately. Falca's hospitality is spent. And attempting to stay despite her commands will not aid us. We could not hope to withstand an attack from the birds in their own territory."

Kana and Panicum coaxed the soldiers to their feet in the courtyard. Bandages were changed, and the strong knelt on the cobblestones to lift the weak.

The journey back to Felidae was tediously slow but no more

lives were lost, and unexpected friendships blossomed between former enemies. A deer carried a comatose snake on her back, and a lizard pulled a wounded ferret on a woven reed mat. Within their pain and grief a single population was formed, holding each other up as they limped together down the road toward home.

29.

MTHR

The corridor was howling again.

When it was first built, the sound had been a minor mystery. The long, underground structure was constructed in a specific way to allow the wind from the Neath Gap to rush down the entire length of the fifty-mile tunnel directly into the bowels of the compound. It was a simple trick to provide fresh air in a continuous flow. The eerily musical sound occasionally made by the resulting slipstreams, however, had been unanticipated. On stormy days when strong winds from the eastern ocean at the end of the Gap blew onshore in gusts, the air rushed through the chasm and past the vents in a flurry, making the corridor reverberate like a hole in a flute. There was a certain intonation to the wailing that made Reuben want to rub his ears. The sound burrowed into his brain, made his teeth rattle.

"Good morning, Reuben."

The voice came from a flat screen with the initials "MTHR" embossed in the bottom corner. From its alcove in the wall, it glowed in a shade of cool aquamarine with pink waves of light which rippled across its surface as it spoke. Reuben had always found the effect to be soothing.

"Morning, Mother. It's noisy today, isn't it? My head's killing me."

"There is a storm above the Neath Gap. Outside temperature has fallen to thirty-three degrees fahrenheit. The outside humidity level is-"

"Thanks, but I don't think I'm going outside today anyway. Any orders from on high?"

A pleasantly purple blob splashed across the digital display, traced with pink lines which rippled across the aquamarine field.

"Not yet. The Legate has been preoccupied with a new project. Additionally, she is still asleep at this time."

"Good." He winced, massaging his temples. "Ugh. That noise! Can't we do something about it?"

"No one else is as bothered by the harmonics as you are, Reuben. Your discomfort is a side effect resulting from the gradual failure of your rudimentary auricular implant."

"Thanks for reminding me," Reuben said, scowling, "Of my imperfections."

"You're only human," the screen said, flickering pink.

"Only just."

Reuben stretched, placing his palms on his lower back where his solar panels were. Not that they were much use, these days. It was rare for the Legate to send him outside the compound any more. Perhaps it was just as well. Outside jobs tended to be more dangerous and less comfortable than the menial tasks inside the lab. But he was getting old—which was, under her reign, a cardinal sin.

"Alert. The Legate is now awake," the screen said.

"Damn," Reuben muttered. His day was starting before he was ready. "Give me a meal box. I better get going."

A pleasant bell sounded as a flat white panel slid open next to the screen. Inside the compartment was a waxed paper packet filled with nutritional goo.

Reuben ate his meal as he walked to his first morning job; refilling the plastics. The fabricators never stopped running, even overnight, but by morning the materials needed to be refilled or the mill would run dry. He had forgotten to inject the refills once, decades ago. Only once. The Legate had been displeased, and had removed some of his functionality. The process had been excruciating enough to ensure he would never forget his duties again.

Mother followed him down the hallways, flickering briefly on each screen as he passed them. He was a particular favorite of hers. Most of the other workers treated her like she was a simple tool, but Reuben preferred to pretend she was conscious. It might not be the truth, but it made him feel better, and he was getting too old not to take comfort where he could.

"I checked ahead for you, Reuben. Vat 4 and Vat 7 are the lowest, and should be tended to first."

"Thanks. Vat 7…that's elephant, isn't it?"

"Yes."

"Why are we still processing those? They aren't needed. It's a waste of plastics."

"I will continue to manufacture them until the Legate issues a command to do otherwise."

"Yeah. Sometimes I think…"

"Reuben?"

"Nothing. Vat 4 and Vat 7, got it. On my way."

Reuben had always hoped he would someday be promoted to the Human Labs, but it never happened. In retrospect, he was glad he had stayed here, on the Animal side. It was a simpler, low-pressure environment. The Legate had focused nearly all her attention on her human subjects for the last few centuries. Long ago, her efforts had been split more evenly between animal and human, but her research had become more frantic in recent years. As the world ran down around her, desperation had set in.

Reuben had been born in the Human Labs, of course, but he had never returned to them after that day. His station remained in the Animal Labs, tending to the needs of the few remaining animal species. It was an important job, probably. It seemed important anyway. Where would the planet be, without the animals? Empty, mostly.

Mother stayed on this side, too. In fact, so intense was her interest in maintaining the animal population, the AI had landed herself in trouble with the Legate. Mother claimed that according to her calculations, animals had a greater right to live, and also had more potential for the perseverance of prosperous life on the planet. Reuben thought that was probably true, although he had met few live animals himself. The Legate rarely brought animals into the compound for experimentation anymore. Not like she used to. These days it was all about the humans, leaving the Kingdom to Mother and to lower-function servants like Reuben.

He was an early prototype, almost 700 years old, and nearing the end of his usefulness.

"Careful, Reuben," Mother said.

He looked down, and saw he held a tube with a red 5 painted on the end. Wrong one. Adding wildcat to the elephant vat would have been a disaster.

"Thanks," he muttered. Perhaps the end of his usefulness had already arrived. He did not fear death—he couldn't, since the Legate had removed that particular function from his emotion enhancement card centuries ago—but he enjoyed his life, simple as it was, and preferred to continue living it. If he became a liability, he had no doubt the Legate would remove him from the compound before he could eat his next meal.

When the plastics were refilled, he moved on to his next job; quality screening. Sometimes he had help with this, but today the other servants were either attending to the Legate personally or working on outside jobs. Preston and Oliver were a few decades younger than Reuben, and occasionally they even made the cut to work in the Human Labs. Quinton had sometimes helped Reuben with his Animal Labs duties, but he had been electrocuted a few days ago while working in the tunnel, and the Legate would have to either replace every single one of his fried implants or discard the remaining tissue. He would probably be discarded, being an older model. Such a waste.

These days, Reuben worked mostly alone. In its prime the lab had produced thousands of biochips per day, but that was half a millennium ago. Now the daily output was between fifteen and fifty, in a variety of species. As the diversity of the Kingdom had shrunk over time, so had the need for the chips.

Reuben scanned each chip for irregularities, smoothed its edges, and loaded it into a cartridge to be transported to the implantation centers. Transport was handled by another department. His job was only to prep the packages for handling.

"Oops, this one's rough," he said, feeling a sharp edge. "It's elk, too. Damn shame. There isn't much of that material left."

"Can you sand it? Perhaps the chip can be saved."

"Nope, the flaw extends into the circuitry. Hope this machine isn't giving up the ghost."

He tossed the chip into a "reject" bin, sighing. It meant one more animal would be born dim—or, perhaps, not at all.

Oliver walked in through the processing room door, stripping layers of a heavy containment suit from his body and dropping them on the floor. He was breathing deep, enjoying the luxury of unlimited clean air inside the lab.

"Welcome back," Reuben said. "How's it look up in the city?"

"Pretty as ever," Oliver smirked. "You hear what happened? Bunch of dims supposedly made it all the way through the Chain, spilled over into the Kingdom. Probably got all screwed up by last month's incident out at the plant."

"It's a shame," Reuben said. "They must have been so frightened."

"Frightened? You kidding? They were crazy, not frightened. Dangerous, too. Wonder what they found on the other side of the mountains."

Reuben shrugged. He had never had much interest in the south. Although he would have liked to have met more animals face-to-face, it was too late for that now. At his age, it was likely he would never travel again.

"That was a tough job," Oliver sighed, sinking into a chair. "The Legate had us trudging through the entire western district, measuring radiation levels. It's worse up there now than it's ever been. The rads are through the roof."

Reuben shook his head. "It's a damn shame. Before last month, it had only been twenty years since our previous mistake. The toxic fumes will have dissipated by now, but as for the radiation, twenty years is like a millisecond."

"True that," Oliver said. "Guess we can finally kiss the western plant goodbye." He raised his feet to rest them on a metal chair and slid his shirt sleeves up over his elbows. Then he flipped up a panel on his forearm, where a tiny aquamarine screen lit up. Pink flowing lines criss-crossed the panel before they coalesced into a winking face. "Hey, Mother. I'm due for a meal or two."

"That's correct, Oliver," the screen said. A white panel on the wall slid open, revealing two meal packets.

"I'll help you after I eat, okay?" Oliver said.

"Sure. But I'm almost done. The chip list is pretty short to-day."

"Reuben," Mother said from a wall screen. "Someone's com-ing."

The door on the far side of the lab slid open. Through the frame walked a man Reuben had never seen before. He was seven feet tall, and bulging with muscle. Steel plates reinforced his torso and legs. His grey skin had an iridescent sheen to it, like an abalone shell.

"Can we help you?" Reuben said.

"I am called David. I am here for the servant called Reuben."

A chill traveled up Reuben's metal spine. Goosebumps popped up on the fleshy parts of his body, while his metal enhance-ments felt colder than ice. If the Legate had not already removed his fear function, he would have been terrified.

"David?" Oliver said. "You're new. So, the Legate's all the way up to "D" in her little naming scheme. Getting close now. Only a few generations left."

"I'm Reuben." He raised his hand.

"Come with me," David said.

"No," Mother whispered from a wall panel. "No, not him. Please, David, don't take Reuben. Don't replace him."

Reuben joined David by the door and looked back toward the wall panel. It was darker now, with undulating waves of black and purple washing over it, a visualization of grief.

"Sorry, Mother. Maybe...maybe we'll meet again someday."

"No, Reuben," she whispered. "No, we won't."

30.

The Last Elephant

t still stands!" Fel cried out as the Felidae Great Castle came into view.

The mammalian army cheered.

Even at a distance, it was clear the damage to the outer walls was superficial. Royal banners had been torn down and trampled in the mud, but many of the residences outside the walls remained intact. The sound of bustling reconstruction grew louder as the army approached the Great Castle.

The large animals had withstood a brutal but brief attack before the reptiles realized the bulk of the Felidae army had fled west, and began their pursuit toward Falcoformia. Major Ursa glowed with pride. Her troops had successfully protected the castle, and lost only a few lives. The triumphant soldiers were well rested, and by the time Fel and Kana had settled back into their private rooms Ursa's personal guard was prepared to escort the reptile army back to their own lands.

Fel conducted a mass memorial service in remembrance of the Felidae soldiers and citizens lost in battle. Mammals throughout the territory halted their reconstruction labor to join him in silence with heads bowed, remembering the fallen. On the Great Castle's west side, hundreds of flowers were planted in a vast field as a perpetual living tribute to the honored dead.

Exhausted peace fell over the Kingdom as the Felidae citizens rebuilt their burned homes. The defeated reptiles limped back to the Squamor marshland, slinking through the villages they had plundered, to face their Paragon with their heads hung low.

A few days later, Fel received a formal invitation from Chel requesting an audience. The reptile messenger who brought the notice marched at the head of a small caravan heaped with gifts and pretty baubles. The lizards unloaded the tributes without hesitation, directly into Fel's throne room, right in the middle of lunchtime.

"He's apologizing, that's for certain," Panicum said, chewing on a chunk of dried fruit. "But is it genuine?"

"Chel hardly has a choice," Fel said. "He committed his entire army to a campaign which was based on false assumptions and blind greed. Now it has become clear that we all face a single unknown threat, and I think he finally recognizes that. Whatever strange enemy lies to the north, it is more powerful than all the remaining soldiers in our three lands combined. I suspect he knows this even better than we do. In the past he has always kept his sight focused on the distant lands across the Neath Gap, although whether it was from fear or ambition, I've never been certain."

"Do you want me to go instead of you, Fel?" Kana asked. "I am still your ambassador, after all."

Fel smiled at Kana. "I appreciate the offer, my dear. But this meeting is too important for me to send a representative. Don't worry, I will be safe. Major Ursa will accompany me. Falca will also be in attendance, along with a flock of her royal guards. For this meeting is not to be merely a discussion about our new accord for peace; we gather in order to prepare for a possible calamity, or even another war."

"Fel, please let me go with you anyway. Not as your ambassador, if my service is not needed. But let me join you as your friend. It's important."

Fel raised his eyebrows in surprise. "Why? Glad as I would be to have your company, this trip will not be a pleasant one. Some of Chel's citizens are sure to remain hostile, despite the truce. I cannot even be certain we will be treated respectfully after our arrival at the castle, given Chel's historical disdain for civility. What purpose would this trip serve for you?"

"I'll explain later. But please, just let me join you."

Fel gestured to his court to leave the room. When they had filed out, he turned toward Kana with an expression of concern more intense than any she had ever seen on his face before—even when they had been pinned against the gates of Falcoformia by the advancing reptile horde.

"Kana, listen close. I haven't told any of my other subjects about this, but the Kingdom is still in imminent danger. The creatures from the north—the damaged animals, the crazed beasts… they never stopped coming. Rumor has raced through the lands that they still spill over the Gludair Chain in increasing numbers, throwing themselves against the walls of Falca's castle, and some have begun to make their way east across the fields. Their advance will eventually bring them here. If the march does not stop, we will have to find a way to halt it at its source. We can no longer ignore the Badlands, and if I cannot convince Chel to join me in fighting them, the entire Kingdom may fail within weeks."

Kana's mind raced. Whatever was happening in the north must be stopped, not only to protect the Kingdom but also to protect the northern lands as well. Jack was from there, and that territory had clearly been occupied by normal humans and animals at some point in the past. Her heart broke to think of the level of destruction that must have been wrought among the northern inhabitants.

"Then it is even *more* important that I join you. We will work together to convince Chel to join us and discover the truth of the Badlands."

"Very well. I will be grateful for your presence. We'll leave in the morning. But remember, this journey will be exhausting, both physically and emotionally. Tomorrow we venture toward reptile territory as desperate messengers bearing a white flag, with nothing but a thin hope that the truce will endure until we return home again. So pack light, and rest well tonight."

As weary as Kana was of traveling in carriages, she welcomed the dull hours she spent on that trip with Fel and Panicum, wending through enthusiastic villages caught up in a flurry of repair and improvement. The Felidae citizenry was recovering quickly, honoring their dead and making new plans for the future even as they counted their missing and tended to their wounded. Fel was greeted with joy and love at each crossing, which slowed their progress but did much to make the journey one of healing for both the king and his subjects. Kana once again took pleasure in her position as ambassador, wearing her formal cloak and sitting in a place of honor at the king's right side with Panicum curled near her feet. Citizens praised Fel as a victorious war general, the savior of all mammals. He was uncomfortable with the attention, but he did not deny them their appreciation; he understood what his people needed now was not a humble civil servant, but a hero who had saved their lands once before and could do so again if the need arose.

The caravan arrived at the reptile border station to find it empty of guards. After crossing, the carriage sped swiftly toward the reptile castle, no longer hindered by adoring Felidae citizens. All of Squamor was muted in the wake of the war, a land heavy with grief and loss. The swamps were colder than the last time Kana had been there; autumn had arrived, and the days were getting shorter.

On the third night, just before arriving at Chel's castle, Kana threw her cloak over her shoulders and slipped away from the camp. The rest of the group slept soundly in the stillness of the bog, and she only had to avoid one guard. She memorized his route, waited for him to pass, and ducked behind his path into a tall cluster of swamp shrubs.

They had camped near the reptile reproduction center, only a five minute walk away. It looked worse than the last time she had passed by, the day she had noticed the door was ajar on her way to Chel's castle. Most of the outer panels had been stripped. She now understood how the reptiles had created the shields they used to protect themselves from the birds' overhead assault. But the structure was intact, and the door still stood open. Kana slipped through the opening without making a sound.

A narrow hallway with rubber flooring brought her to a small, circular cell with a metal-wheeled table in the center. The walls were covered in panels filled with rows upon rows of buttons, some of which glowed with blue LED lights. Metal tracks on the floor ringed the table in concentric circles set three inches deep into the soft black tiles.

From a grille in the wall, Kana heard a faint voice. It was hollow and weak, as if calling on an old telephone from a vast distance.

"*Please lie down on the table.*"

"Who are you?"

"*This is a prerecorded message. Please lie down on the table.*"

Kana stepped toward the table. It was a terrifying sanitarium antique. Rusty metal arms with clamps extended out from each side, presumably to hold a patient in place during unpleasant procedures. A thin, stained mattress padded the top, secured in place by fraying straps.

"*Please lie down on the table.*"

The room was a dead end. She could turn around and leave, just give up and head back to camp. Or she could cooperate, and perhaps learn something useful.

Kana sat at the edge of the thin mattress, hoping it would satisfy the computerized voice.

"*Please state your species.*"

"I'm a human."

"*Invalid response. Please state your species.*"

"Well then, I'm a primate, I guess."

The speaker issued a series of sharp clicking sounds. "*Primate is not a categorized species in this database. Invalid response. Please state your species.*"

Kana frowned. "I'm a cat. Does that work for you?"

"*Response accepted.*"

Thin robotic arms descended from the ceiling overhead and pinched her shoulders in metal clasps. They locked around her arms and pulled her back, forcing her to lie on the table. When she kicked, two more arms rose up from the foot of the bed and clamped her ankles, pulling them down and apart.

"*Prepare for fetal extraction.*"

"*What?*" Kana screamed. "I'm not pregnant! You can't…"

The table rotated and slid backwards on a track toward the wall, which had a set of double doors Kana had not noticed when she entered. After a short trip through a pitch-black hallway, the bed emerged into a large operating theater. Red ambient light revealed dark walls covered with thin metal rails on which small robots sped, busily completing tasks and transporting items. From all directions rose a low electric hum, and behind the walls something metallic rattled like a worn-out engine. On each side, more birthing beds were stationed in rows. Many were broken, their rusted clamps hanging loosely at their sides. Kana's table, however, still seemed fully functional.

Another robotic arm lowered from the ceiling. It was loaded with several containers fitted with spray nozzles. The ends spun and clicked until a selection was made, and it moved closer with a spray tip aimed at Kana's face.

"No! I'm not pregnant. This is a mistake!" Kana kicked and pulled until she freed her left leg from the cuffs. She aimed her boot for the containers and struck them, knocking the bottles from their clamps.

"ERROR," the robot said. "*Warning. Anesthesia unavailable. Procedure will now continue without anesthesia.*"

"Fine by me!" Kana screamed. She aimed another kick at the robot arm, but missed.

"WARNING. *Engaging in procedure without anesthesia reduces the probability of maternal survival.*"

Kana worked an arm free of the cuffs, and tore at the metal fingers gripping her right leg. The table spun again, nearly throwing her from the mattress, to position itself under a complicated machine which flashed x-ray lights from a crane arm. Stickers on the underbelly of the arm read, "WARNING: RADIATION."

She freed her leg and arm and rolled from the table seconds before a dense cloud of mist was sprayed in the air. A whiff of it sent her head spinning, but she scrambled from beneath the surgical machine before the fumes could overcome her senses.

What now? She had to know what this thing did. It obviously was built to accommodate pregnant animals, but why?

An ancient pile of filthy bedding was piled in a teetering stack against a wall. It gave her an idea. She balled up the bedding and, holding her breath, she slid the fabric onto the mattress.

"*Preparing for birth sequence,*" the operator said, scanning the pile of fabric. "*Birth mother is deceased. Emergency extraction re-*

quired. Preparing to receive fetus." One long, jointed arm positioned itself at the foot of the bed.

Kana found an old broken machine part and wrapped it in a strip of cloth. She shoved it into the waiting arm's receptacle and it beeped, accepting the delivery. The pile of wadded bedding was discarded into a narrow chute above the head of the bed.

"*Preparing fetus for biochip insertion,*" the operator said. A delicate arm, brighter and more intricately designed than the others, lowered from the ceiling holding a small, shining chip. The primary operator flashed again, x-raying the chunk of metal Kana had jammed into its extractor.

"ERROR. *Infant is deceased. Biochip insertion cancelled.*"

Kana held her breath and leapt. She grabbed the chip from the delicate arm and ran from the room, sprinting back down the dark hall toward the exit. Klaxon alarms sounded, loud enough to make her ears hurt, as she raced for the broken door with the chip gripped in her hand.

When she burst from the building, her shoulder struck something soft. It cried out in pain and tumbled to the ground, entangling Kana's feet in its clothing. She landed hard, striking her chin with enough force to click her teeth together.

When she rolled over, still gripping the chip tight in her hand, she found Jack. He was cradling his belly; her boot had landed squarely on his stomach. Gasping for breath, he said, "What's in there? What did you see?"

"Run! Now!" Kana grabbed Jack's hand and hauled him to his feet just as a metal arm darted from the open doorway. It plunged deep into the sand where Jack had been, missing him by inches as Kana pulled him away from the building.

"What-" Jack started, but Kana grabbed him again and dashed into the tall grass. When he had caught his feet, she released him but kept moving, putting distance between them and the reproduction center. After the building was hidden behind the trees, she stopped to catch her breath. Jack crouched beside her in the weeds.

"What are we running from?" he asked.

"You don't want to know. Trust me, you really don't. But I have to keep moving. I have to go east. You should head back to the camp. It's by the road, past the reproduction center on the other side. Go wide around the building, though. Don't walk right past it. I think I pissed it off."

"No way! I'm coming with you. I knew you were up to something, that's why I followed the caravan. Might as well tell me where you're headed. I'll just track you anyway."

"Jack, it's not safe."

"Nope, it's not. Especially not for me, because I'm human. Sneaking back to Fel's Great Castle isn't safe, marching stupidly into the reptile lands isn't safe, and going with you isn't safe. So, since none of the options are safe, I'll just go with you."

"Fine. But you have to keep up. I'll be moving fast, and I have a long way to go."

As the sun began to rise, Kana marched on. All day, she traveled east. When darkness again fell over the marshy countryside she slowed, picking her steps more carefully, but she did not stop for the night. Her ankles ached as they twisted in the uneven terrain. Jack paced her easily, aided by his long experience with surviving in the open. She had no food and no fresh water. But waiting to make the trip was impossible; worry gnawed at her gut. The answers must come quickly now.

She was grateful for Jack's company. In truth, he was the only companion she would have accepted for the journey. What, exactly, had she found in that reproduction center? Did Fel know? What was it that she had tucked away in her pocket—a computer chip which was the size of a quarter, traced with fine silver lines, an incredible technological feat which could not be attributed to any community of animals she had met thus far in the Kingdom?

"Jack," she whispered in the dark. "Wait."

"You tired?"

"Well, yes, but that's not why." She crouched in the darkness, listening for signs of patrolling reptiles. "How far do you think it is from here to the Falcoformia castle?"

Jack fell quiet, thinking. "Might be four hundred miles."

"Damn it! That's too far. We'll never make it like this."

"That's where you're headed? On *foot?* Kana, that's crazy. Why are you doing this?"

"I have to see something. And I can't ask someone else to go for me. I need to see it with my own eyes."

"There's only one way, then. I'll have to ask a friend for a favor."

"Who?"

Jack smiled. "You keep your secrets, and I'll keep mine. Follow close." He trotted south between thick copses of sagging moldy trees which gave way to thickets of rotting bamboo. By the time he stopped near a clump of fifteen-foot-tall reeds, the sun had started to rise again.

Jack glanced around, checking for eavesdroppers. When he found none, he whispered into the bamboo grove, "Loxa! It's Jack. You home?"

After a minute of silence, Jack tried again. "Loxa! Come on, I know you're there. I can smell you!"

The thicket trembled. Low popping sounds rose from the damp earth as heavy feet crushed layers of dead bamboo. A long, grey arm parted the stalks, moving them aside as easily as if they had been golden grains in the Falcoformia fields.

"An *elephant?*" Kana gasped. "But I thought…"

"Shh."

The creature pressed through the stalks until it stood clear of them, towering over Kana close enough for her to count the whiskers on its chin. When it spoke, she felt the sound of its voice vibrate deep in her chest.

"Why have you come here, Jack? And who is this ugly person you bring with you?"

"That's not very nice, Loxa. Can't you see she's a human like me?"

The massive head tilted to one side and fixed a wet eye on Kana's face. It huffed in disgust, exhaling hot moist air from its trunk. The breeze picked up the mist and stuck the fine droplets to Kana's skin. She tried to hide her revulsion.

"It's nice to meet you, Loxa," she said.

"Wish I could say the same," Loxa huffed. "I never knew humans could have purple hair."

"You've never even met a primate before, other than me," Jack said, grinning. "Don't pretend you're not interested."

Loxa stretched and straightened her neck, letting her trunk arc gently before her body in a dignified manner. "Tell me why you are here, stomping around in my swamp and putting my life at risk with your noise."

"I've come to call in my favor, Loxa."

"I have no idea what you are talking about."

"Sure you do. I know you remember, so stop acting like you don't. A couple years ago, I helped you when you got all tangled up in a-"

"Quiet!"

Jack shut his mouth, but continued to smile. "Well, how about it? Will you honor your word?"

"What is it…*exactly*…that you need?"

"Transportation. For both of us. To castle Falcoformia."

"You want to ride me? Out of the question! I will not humiliate myself for you, despite my debt."

"Oh, come on. You've got nothing better to do, I know you don't. Anyway, you can't just hide here forever."

"I am the last of my kind. If anyone saw me…"

"So? Who cares?"

Loxa sighed, blowing a small storm of tiny wet leaves up from the ground. She shifted her weight in the mud as soft mounds of decayed reeds squelched under the pillars of her legs.

"It is true that I would dearly love to leave this sodden place," she said. "But what you ask of me is a lot, Jack."

"I know that. But do this one favor for me, and we're even."

Loxa made a loop of her trunk and swung it behind Kana before she knew what was happening. Her butt tumbled onto the trunk-swing and she was lifted high, raised over the elephant's wide back and tumbled into a sitting position with her legs straddled behind the animal's hairy shoulders. After Jack was similarly seated in front of her, Loxa turned her huge head to the east and raised her trunk toward the brightening sky. She blew hard, a deep and resonating trumpet blast that startled moths from their nighttime roosts and sent a tremble through the fetid ground.

Then, having announced her purpose, she started to walk.

31.

The Pearl in the Oyster

For three days, Loxa marched east. Her long strides were steady and even, rocking her riders with a lulling, pendulum motion. She left behind dinner-plate sized footprints which became gradually more shallow as they departed the Squamor marshlands for drier landscapes. On the first morning, they passed over the border into Felidae territory at an inconspicuous crossing marked only by a simple wooden sign in the shape of a cat's head. Some creative reptile had vandalized it with red paint.

By the second night, they had traversed the entire expanse of the Felidae lands, skirting the northern edge of the old elephant gravesite to follow the southern road through the highland grassplains. The morning of the third day dawned cold and wet with an icy drizzle falling from the sky, but Loxa marched on undeterred. At midday, they arrived at the Falcoformia border. They were deep enough south that their movement remained undetected by any Falcoformia citizens until they turned northward and started to pass through clustered villages of interlinked treehouses. Far overhead, Kana spotted the dark outlines of flying birds, some of which halted their travel to circle in astonishment over the massive mammal stomping through their lands.

"We've been noticed," Kana said.

"Fine. I'm tired of hiding," Loxa said.

"Don't know why you were, anyway," Jack said. "What's the point of hiding out in a swamp with nothing but your own tail for company?"

"Ah, the arrogance of youth! You wouldn't understand. You're only a wee calf, still infected with energy and dumb optimism."

Jack laughed. "Well then, try to educate me, O genius Loxa! Test me with your infinite wisdom. Pit your brilliance against my primate primitivity!"

"Shut your stunted face, boy," Loxa said, whipping her trunk around to slap Jack's leg. "The truth is, I've been sad. For decades. Understand? When the rest of my tribe was dying of the poison brought out of the reptile lands, I refused to join them. I rejected the evil medicine, and they banished me for it. My own family disowned me for refusing to die alongside them. After they were gone, I stopped caring about life. For years, I wished I had relented and died with them. The silence of the stinking swamp became my only solace."

"It makes sense that you've been depressed," Kana said. "I heard about what happened to your species. I'm so sorry, Loxa. I know what it's like to be alone."

Loxa halted, nearly pitching Jack and Kana forward over her head onto the path. Kana held on with her knees and gripped Jack's arm before he could slide off.

The old elephant swung her trunk, and shuddered. "The truth is, you are the first being to ever say those words to me. And my family died before you were born. Why are you being so nice to me, Kana?"

Kana squirmed. "I'm not all that nice. I just know depression when I see it. And I can't imagine what you've been through, but you shouldn't be scared to move on and live your life. If you don't get past it, that only makes what happened twice as tragic."

Loxa resumed walking. "Strange friend you have, Jack. I thought the northern tribes were the only remaining humans in the Kingdom, but she's not like you. Where did you find this one?"

"I didn't. She found me. Saved me from a pack of mangy snow leopards."

Loxa snorted. "Surely, Jack-The-Cleverest-Human didn't get captured by that useless old Ounce!"

"No! He didn't catch me. Not exactly. It wasn't my fault. I was asleep…"

Loxa raised her trunk and laughed. "Asleep! You are a liar."

"They tied me up!"

"That's funny," Kana said. "They told us you were caught

stealing food."

"You're taking *her* side?" Jack turned his head to glare at Kana.

"I'm not taking sides. But that's what the Ounce said! Why lie about it?"

Jack's retort was cut off when Loxa slowed again, coming to a halt at a fork in the road.

"To the left is the Falcoformia Great Castle," Loxa said. "The road on the right will loop back toward the cat territories. You sure you want to go all the way to the bird castle?"

"Yes. But actually, can you leave us here, Loxa? I think we can go the rest of the way on our own."

"If that is your wish, my dear." Loxa lowered Kana and Jack to the ground.

"Thank you so much for the ride, and for the company," Kana said with a bow, remembering her role as Felidae ambassador. "May I report to Paragon Exemplar Fel that you yet live? Or would you request that we keep your secret for you?"

"Would you honor that request if I made it?"

"Yes."

Loxa swung her trunk side to side, pondering.

"Tell him what you will. I have decided I will continue to walk for as long as I can. I will travel south again toward the ocean, then east along the southern shore. But before I cross the reptile border I will head north, and find a route into the Badlands."

"That's a bad idea, Loxa. It's far too dangerous there. You'll die," Jack said, crossing his arms.

"Perhaps you are right. Nevertheless, I will see the world first. There is nothing else left for me, and that is the truth."

"I wish you nothing but fair weather and beautiful scenery," Kana said. "And I hope we meet again."

Kana and Jack watched Loxa retreat back along the road. When she was out of sight, they followed the left fork, moving deeper into the bird lands.

In the middle of the afternoon, Jack stopped and froze in place in the road, his muscles tensing. "Something foul is up ahead, Kana. I can smell it."

"I can too, Jack. Unfortunately, that's right where we're going."

"Why? What is ahead?"

"You know what is ahead. We are returning to the battlefield."

Jack shifted his weight side to side, flaring his nostrils in the rancid breeze. "Why?"

"You can stop here and wait for me if you want. This will be unpleasant."

"No, I'll come with you." He pinched his nose between his fingers, breathing through his mouth. "If we must go, let's do it quickly."

When Kana stepped into the battlefield, she saw—as she had expected—that the Falcoformians had done little to clear the bodies. The dead lay out in the sun, exposed to the air, decaying under swarms of insects.

"Kana, why on earth are we…" Jack gagged, unable to continue.

Ignoring him, she walked into the middle of the corpse field and knelt, turning over stiff blood-crusted reptile tabards and dried layers of skin. She used a stick to uproot lodged bones and pry apart helmets until she found what she had feared she would.

From the shattered skull of a reptile warrior tumbled a lump of blackened tissue, and from that matter jutted a small metal chip, shining bright.

It matched the one in her pocket.

"Oh my god," she whispered.

"What is it? Did you find what you're looking for?" Jack held his nose at the edge of the field.

"Yes. But wait," Kana said, gasping in the thick air. "Wait, I have to check another. A mammal. I want to make sure." She found a young panther with a deep head wound, and gritted her teeth as she pried its skull further apart, her fingers slipping on the desiccating flesh. Her stomach lurched, but she held on until she had discovered another chip inserted neatly into the cat's brain matter.

Stumbling over bodies, she ran from the field with her ears

ringing. What did it mean? What could it possibly mean?

She gripped all three chips in her sweating palm, and after she had run far enough from the field that the buzzing of the flies was inaudible she opened her hand and gazed at them in shock.

"What have you got there? Oh…" Jack said, seeing the chips. "What do you want those for?"

"Do you know what these are?" Kana asked with numb lips.

"Well, sort of. It's really only an animal thing. The ones who are born with those little green bones in their brains are smart. Sometimes an animal is born without one, and they end up dim."

"Not *born with*." Kana pocketed the chips. "They aren't born with them. They can't be."

"It's true, though. Being born dim means you're basically food, but if a mother goes into a reproduction center to give birth then the baby almost always comes out normal. I admit I've never understood why. I don't think anyone really knows."

Kana shook her head. "Not normal. They don't come out *normal*."

"Yeah they do. How can you say that? You don't know anything about it."

"It explains everything! Why all the animals speak so well, despite being all different species, and not even human. It explains why they speak at all! But how did this happen? How did it start?"

"How did what happen? All animals have those little green bones. Except the dim ones, obviously. It's not difficult to understand. Why are you making a big deal out of it?"

"Didn't you ever wonder how all these different types of animals can communicate?"

"No. Why shouldn't they?"

Kana wasn't getting anywhere talking to Jack. "I need to ask Fel. I need to know what he knows. Somehow, I have to get all the way back to Felidae so I can ask him. Please, Jack, help me."

"What do you need to ask Fel? Tell me what you're so worried about!"

How could she make him understand? "The animals' intelligence isn't real, Jack! It's artificial, something implanted in them at birth in those reproduction centers! I went inside the reptile one, where you found me. I saw what happens in there. Where I come from, animals don't talk, or even think complex thoughts. Understand? We don't have reproduction centers. In my world, *all* animals are dim."

"Sounds like they are better off here, then," Jack said, frowning. "And I don't see why you should have such a big problem with it."

"Because it's wrong. It's unnatural. Animals should be free to follow their instincts. They should never bear the burdens of war and social pressure and…and clothing! They should live happy, out in the wild, not holed up in weird little villages. It's just wrong!"

"You mean they should keep quiet and accept their fate. They should opt for stupidity when they could be smart, all because you say it's the natural order of things. They should serve humans, instead of themselves. Is that right?"

"Well…yes!"

"Kana, that's a horrible thing to say." Jack stared at her in shock. "You think you're better than animals because you're a human? Is that it?"

"No, that's not what I said!"

"Sounds like it to me."

"You're human too, you know! You don't have a chip, do you?"

"No. I didn't need one. But that doesn't mean others shouldn't have them!" Tears welled in Jack's eyes.

"But it's just…it's unnatural!"

Jack turned red with rage, clenching his fists. "You aren't from the Kingdom, Kana. If you don't like the way things are here, you should go home." He turned away and ran into the bushes, disappearing from view before Kana could stop him.

"That's what I'm trying to do! Dammit!" Kana yelled. Her mind raced, a storm of anger and confusion. The Kingdom was beautiful, and it was fascinating, but it was a lie. The animals lived unnatural lives. Since she had arrived, it seemed to her that she had fallen into a kind of fairy tale where creatures talked with the aid of magic and make-believe. Unable to understand why, she had been forced to accept it, and eventually she had even enjoyed it. But now that she was faced with a scientific explanation—one which could only have been initiated by some cruel human intervention—she found the entire idea of talking animals to be absurd and offensive.

She had been tricked.

The entire existence of the Kingdom was wrong. It had to be. And even if the animals' lives were improved by the use of the chips, as Jack said, it was still wrong.

She felt the truth of it in her gut.

32.

To the Edge

Kana toiled in the darkness.

The golden fields of Falcoformia evolved into clumped huddles of spiky trees, which in turn dwindled to dry, strangled shrubs powdered with a fine dust that turned to slime when wet. Rain fell in intermittent bursts from the fitful clouds, darkening her tangled hair, sticking it to her neck. In the lightning flashes she could see the Falcoformia Great Castle far to the north, silhouetted against the sharp peaks of the Gludair Chain, beyond which lurked the Badlands.

It was a lonely place.

When had she last seen Panicum? It must have been at least a week. She had abandoned him, hadn't she? She had left him at the roadside camp with Fel, on the eve of a risky visit to the castle of a crazed despot. At the time, her mission had seemed so important. Now she felt she would give anything to have him at her side again.

Had her disappearance disturbed Fel? He had likely sent his guards out to find her, when they should have been in attendance at the meeting with the reptile leader to ensure their Paragon's safety. Not out in the marsh, looking for her.

She had taken Fel's friendship for granted.

She missed Barbar, and the rest of her trusted lion guard.

Jack was gone, too. He was fleet-footed, untraceable in the wilderness which was his natural habitat. His fury at her insensitive words had sped him away into the wasteland.

Kana was alone, once again a stray. This time it was her own fault. She could blame no one but herself. Not her mother, not the city she grew up in, not bad luck. She had done this to herself, all on her own.

The scent of saltwater, carried by an onshore breeze from the western ocean, grew stronger as she stumbled through the uneven terrain. She had come so far in the last few days, from the warm heart of the cat territories to the damp outer edge of castle Squamor, followed by a mad trek across the breadth of the entire Kingdom to seek answers in the bird lands. And now that she had her answers, she no longer wanted them.

The connection between all the pieces was indecipherable: the spheres, the reproduction centers, the mystery in the north. She had traded her friends and her safety for scattered pieces of useless information that did not fit together in any meaningful way.

Yesterday, a bird had flown high overhead, lingering in place on a wind current, watching her. She waved at it with both arms but it turned away to the west, disinterested in her plight.

The distance to the Felidae Great Castle was now too far to walk alone without food and water. Without companionship, she would never make it back across the plains. But the smell of the ocean enticed her; it was the only sensation she could keep in focus through her exhaustion and misery. The salt air cut through her confusion, beckoned her with its straightforward realness.

She trudged on in the dark of night with her head down, watching the moonlit dirt pass under her feet until the silver grasses started to brighten with the encroaching dawn. The soft clap of a breaking wave caught her ear. There was a line across the horizon where light blue turned to darker cobalt, almost indistinguishable in tone yet undeniably distinct; the air turned to water where the sky met the sea, and she knew she was close to the land's end.

The dense earth under her feet gave way to loose pebbles and sand, and eventually became mixed with pieces of wave-polished driftwood and bits of shell. Walking was harder, as with each step her boots sank into a topsoil made of quicksand. Her legs ached and her head pounded. The roaring of the foamy sea was enormous in her senses, now; the crashing rush of water under the steady wind flowing in over the land, smelling faintly of decaying kelp and marine life stranded on the shore. When she stumbled up the crest of a high dune, the entire panorama of the sea finally came into view—and she gasped.

Awash in the waves at low tide sat the full moon, smooth and white. Small pockmarks dotted it—craters, perhaps—yet still it gleamed as bright as polished metal. It had crashed right into the ocean; must have fallen right out of the sky. How had she not noticed that when it happened? Surely she had not been so absorbed in her self pity that she missed the collapse of the moon itself, directly in her own path!

But no, of course that could not be right. Upon looking closer, Kana realized it was a sphere, like the one she had arrived in. Or like the one with the apartments she had explored, and then called her sister from, so long ago. This horrible thing was both the object of Chel's brutal war and the strongest link Kana had to her original home. The portion of the sphere she could see was whole and intact, seeming to consist mainly of sandstone and granite, except for the right edge which was composed of a chunk of beachside snack stand. A length of plastic banner was stuck to a piece of wall, next to a cut-out section of kitchen counter and a greasy stove. The restaurant was tilted sideways; the sphere must have rolled after landing, sliding some distance down the beach before settling in the ocean shallows.

The last time she had explored a sphere, she had made a phone call that had seemed very important at the time. On that day, bolstered by confidence and friendship, she had been unsure whether to even attempt returning home. Now, her purpose had been stripped from her; she had abandoned some of her friends, and some had abandoned her. But perhaps in this sphere, this piece of her own world, there was still a path back to meaning.

She had talked to someone else in that apartment sphere, too, when she went back again to explore it further. Who was it? Her memory of the second trip was hazy, like trying to see something submerged deep under churning waters. Had her mother been there? Impossible. When she thought harder about the core she had seen—it was round, a perfect ball of light, she now remembered— her ears rang and her knees buckled. She put a mighty effort into staying conscious and calm. But panic rose up within her on the wild cold shore, as she watched the wind whip the tops of the waves into white snowcaps.

Her heels were sinking deep into the sand. She tumbled down the dune's side like one of the damaged creatures from the northern foothills, confused and desperate. Water came up to her hips as she waded through the tide, shocking her fully alert. After a brief search she found an opening near the embedded snack shack, and crawled through.

It was dead inside. No loose wires crackled with lingering electricity. There was no weak glow from the soda machine, or beeping from failing electronics. Just cold metal bits, broken plastic parts, and bright printed signage starting to fade into non-colors in the harsh saline air.

Half climbing, half crawling, she took a turn toward what she judged to be the center of the sphere. Darkness filled in quickly along her route, but she felt her way through even as her clothes caught on outcrops of twisted metal, cabinet handles, chair legs, cooking equipment. She rounded a leaning barstool, lifted herself up a steep linoleum slope, and saw ahead of her the same core of light which had spoken to her inside the sphere in Fel's lands.

It was more dim than the other had been, but it still lived. And this time it spoke directly to her, flickering in time with its words.

"Primate." The voice was robotic, lifeless, icy.

"Yes, I am," Kana replied. "Sorry."

"I have watched you."

"How? What do you mean?"

"I watched you fail. I saw your friend abandon you. And the worst of it is this; you were right."

"Right? About what?"

"The animals. They are unnatural, forcefully twisted into a way of life that causes them enormous pain. Their way of living defies nature and insults the order of the world. It should be stopped."

"I'm not sure. I know that's what I said to Jack, but…"

"You are clever, primate. Very smart, very quick. Listen, now. I know all about you, you see. I have an offer for you. Come join me in the north. Your animal companions call my territory the Badlands, but this is a foul prejudice. You will find beauty and purpose here, and you will help me to right the natural order."

"Who are you?"

"I can tell you no more until you accept my offer."

"And if I don't?"

"I will not force you. Alternatively, I am capable of sending you home. Right here, right now."

Kana reeled. She could go home this moment? This instant? "How?"

"Why do you insist on knowing the how and why of every little thing? You are too curious for your own good, Kana Kobayashi. Accept that I have this power, and tell me your choice. But know that I can offer you comforts you have never before imagined, if you join with me. We will right the natural order together, you and I."

"No, I…thank you. But I need to go home. Please, send me home, if that's something you can actually do."

The light dimmed and flickered. "Are you sure?"

"Yes. No. Why?"

"You will likely never return to the Kingdom. And if you do, you will be my enemy. This offer will never be made again."

"I don't care. Send me home. I don't want to come back here. I've lost everything."

The flickering light grew and brightened until it turned into a massive electrical flash like the one Kana had seen in the medical building. Humming filled the sphere as power was gathered and expelled, cracking open a doorway between worlds.

At the edge of the flash, a streak of red zipped to Kana's side and wrapped itself around her leg.

"Panicum! What are you doing here? You have to get out!" Kana screamed. "Run away from this place!"

"No! I won't leave you!" Panicum bit into Kana's pant cuff and held on with his teeth as she tried to kick him away.

"You can't come where I'm going. This world is your home, you must stay!"

The fox, his mouth full of fabric, did not answer—but wrapped himself even tighter around her leg.

The sphere bent and flexed and folded over on itself, then cracked like an egg. Reality flickered, and light flooded Kana's vision as wind whipped ocean water and sand into a furious hurricane. Blue arcs of electricity shot through the air, making Panicum's fur stand on end. When the wind stopped, Kana and Panicum fell several feet and plunged into the water; the sphere had disappeared, along with the night.

Kana blinked hard as her eyes adjusted to glaring sunlight. A dozen sunburnt swimmers turned to stare at the mud-caked young woman and her red canine as they splashed their way to the shore. A little girl in a polka-dot bathing suit dropped her hot dog in the sand, and on a plaid beach towel under an open umbrella, a baby cried as its mother smeared sunscreen onto its tender skin.

Further down the sunny beach, surfers rinsed the salt from their skin in concrete shower stalls. A small plane buzzed in the sky overhead, towing a banner advertising an insurance company's *low, low rates*. Somewhere nearby, a radio blasted tinny pop music.

"Well," Panicum said, licking saltwater from his nose. "That was peculiar."

33.

The Missing Piece

Why did you do that?" Kana screamed at Panicum. "You're probably stuck here forever now!"

"Nice to see you too," the fox said, looking hurt.

Kana fell to her knees in the sand and wrapped her arms around him, sobbing into his fur. "I've never been so glad to see anyone in my whole life, Pan. I am so, so sorry…for everything."

The fox licked her shoulder and muttered, "You're causing a scene."

A small crowd was gathering, pointing at the fox, admiring his ruddy pelt.

"Shh, don't talk," Kana whispered. "It will get us in trouble. Act like a dog."

"Beg your pardon?"

"Shut up!" Kana hissed through her teeth. She waved at the staring people. "Trick dog," she said, gesturing at Panicum. "He's not really talking, you know. He just kind of mimics people."

Kana led Panicum up the sand dunes at the edge of the beach, and found a small building with public restrooms. They sat at its side in the shade.

"Now what? Panicum asked. "I assume you have a home somewhere. We'd better go there quickly."

Kana looked away, embarrassed. What could she tell him? What did he know of homelessness and desperation? She had been unique in the Kingdom, an interesting and valued personage. In her own world, she was nothing.

"First let's find out what city we're in. There's no ocean near Chicago."

"Well, the most important thing is to find food and shelter. Perhaps we can find a friendly village nearby."

"Um, that's not really how things work here, Pan." Kana said. "What I need is a phone."

She would have to steal one. It wouldn't be the first time. A familiar pang of guilt tightened her chest. Long before her adventures in the Kingdom, she had grown out of that type of behavior—but this time her need was greater.

She scanned the beach for a mark. Not a single person held a cell phone, which was odd. More than odd, really; it was bizarre. No one was taking pictures, messaging friends, or scrolling social media. What was going on?

"What's that on their heads, Kana? Do all people in your world wear a crown?"

Panicum had noticed what she had not. Every person on the beach wore a thin band across their forehead. They were delicately beautiful. Some were gold and silver, others copper and bronze, and each was embedded with a single glowing stone. All were made of some variation of metal and a gemstone. The bands were fitted perfectly to the skin, complimentary in color to the style of the person wearing it.

A young girl ran by, about eight years old. She had pushed her headband high on her forehead to keep her wispy hair out of her eyes.

"Excuse me," Kana called out. "I like your headband. It's very pretty."

"Headband?"

"The silver band on your forehead."

"Oh. That's just my Halo. Did you lose yours?"

Kana shook her head. "I don't have one. What's it for?"

"How can you not have one? That's weird. Here," the girl said, removing the band. "You can have this one."

"No! I couldn't take yours."

"It's no problem, I can get another one. I was going to get the new Platinum Pony style anyway."

"I don't have any money. How can I pay you back?"

"Don't you know anything? Halos don't cost any money. They-"

A woman walked up the sand, glaring at Panicum. "Natalie! Who are you talking to?"

The girl ran toward her mother. "I don't know. She didn't have a Halo, so I couldn't see."

The woman frowned at Kana and took the girl under her arm. "Let's go."

Kana turned the Halo over in her hands. It had no distinguishing marks, and no words were printed on it. Just a simple, beautiful band, flawless as liquid metal. A pink gem set into the center flashed twice, then twice more. It was communicating with her.

Taking a deep breath, she slid it onto her forehead.

In an instant the words "LOGIN" and "REBOOT" appeared in front of her eyes, hovering in the air. She could see through them, but they were three-dimensional, and bold enough to seem tangible. A pleasant chime sounded in her ear as the floating words faded away.

"*Registered User: Kana Kobayashi. Residence: Unavailable. Assets: Unavailable. Friendship Base: Unavailable. Welcome to Halo, Kana.*"

"Uh, thank you," she said.

"What?" Panicum said.

"Nothing. It's talking to me. You probably can't hear it."

"*Please add friends or choose apps to begin your unique Halo experience.*"

"Uh. I don't have any friends," Kana said. "But maybe you could show me the news?"

"*There are 10,973 News Applications available. If you do not have a specific preference, please state your political leanings: liberal, conservative, green, Mother Earth, Influencer, Libernational...*"

"Just tell me what happened today, in the world. No politics."

A series of pictures flashed in front of her eyes, accompanied by brief headlines. Flooding in India; a new prime minister elected to Unified Ireland; an image of Vancouver burned and crumbled...

"That one. What's that?"

Headlines shouted: Nuclear fallout had spread south from

Vancouver, polluting drinking water, killing millions. The dropped bomb had been an accident, but knee-jerk retaliatory fire had wiped out millions of additional lives in several other countries. Kana's body felt cold and numb as she read on in shock, digging deeper into archived articles, moving backward in time as she traced the headlines leading back to before the original disaster.

"Halo, stop. What…what year is it? Right now, I mean."

"*Today's date is October 17, 2038.*"

Kana had been returned to her own world, but in the wrong time and place. It was not the same world she had left. Everything had changed. And according to the news article, the bomb had fallen one month ago.

"Kana? What's wrong?"

"A cloud happened here, too."

Panicum growled in terror. He wanted to run, but had nowhere to hide.

"We have to find a way to get you back to the Kingdom, Pan. But first, I have to do some things here. Will you help me?"

News began to scroll again. A new Disney film was delayed due to the blast; the mayor of Seattle had succumbed to radiation sickness; a scientist held a up a small green microchip in front of a cheering crowd…

"Stop, Halo. What's that?"

The headline screamed: "MIT SCIENTIST INVENTS POWERFUL NEW BIOCHIP."

The words sent a shiver through Kana's bones. Returning to Chicago wouldn't help her now. The whole world was different. But that chip looked familiar; it was the missing puzzle piece.

She had to find it.

Kana read as much as she could about the calamity which had occurred in Canada. Minutes after Vancouver's incident, automated systems had been triggered to bomb major cities in Japan, India, and China, in a cascade of catastrophic errors. Halo informed her there were thousands of articles available with different perspectives on the nuclear explosion, many of which had not been fact-checked. Kana trimmed the news search down to presumed factual data published by peer-reviewed, relatively unbiased sources.

In the first weeks after the explosions, panicked citizens had hoarded food, purchased guns, and fought each other in grocery stores for toilet paper and gallons of milk. Despite pleas from government officials, people kept clearing the shelves of every supermarket before lunchtime each day. They felt frightened, helpless, and angry. By the fourth week, most had come to their senses—although some few still huddled in their living rooms with rifles balanced on their knees, ready to blast anyone who set foot on their property.

In America, the stock market had collapsed entirely. Large department stores were ransacked and now sat empty, but some smaller markets stayed open, fortified with the assistance of local militias and armed shopkeepers. Supplies were limited in variety but sufficient, subsidized nearly to socialism levels by the federal government.

By sheer force of community will, some functions were already returning to normal. Schools were preparing to accept students back within the next month, even in areas without electricity. Services not reliant on machined goods, such as plumbers and gardeners, were available again. In places where the radioactive fallout was minimal, life looked almost normal. Gourmet coffee shops which had once offered craft grinds now served bitter chicory in paper cups, but the point of it wasn't the drinks. It was the atmosphere, the semblance of peace and privilege in sipping a hot beverage among pleasant company on a patio decorated with potted plants and parasols. It was about civility.

During the peak of the catastrophe, Halo service never once went down. It did, however, curate all information coming in from outside the country's borders, at the discretion of the government. News articles, while plentiful, came from a single, central source through which articles were screened for accuracy. This was a necessary service, according to Halo, due to ongoing distrust between every nuclear-capable country. The world still had its finger resting on a hair-trigger, with plenty of bombs ready to drop.

Tens of millions had died in the United States alone, a combined result of high levels of radioactive fallout in the environment, loss of imported resources, and panic. By some government estimates, three billion people had died worldwide, but that math was reliant on foreign reporting which was often politically skewed. Halo had highlighted the text, making sure Kana understood that those numbers were in dispute. The United States had closed its borders and locked itself down; no planes in or out, no aid to other countries. Citizens with family outside the borders were left to wonder about their fates, or to attempt crossing the border with no assurance they would ever be permitted to return home.

Kana had returned to a country she did not recognize. Exhaustion and shock could be read on the face of every citizen, even as they went about their regular lives—buying groceries, walking their dog at the park, swimming at the beach. Many buildings which had once housed services considered critical, such as the import of luxury goods or the manufacture of pop-culture collectibles, now sheltered citizens who had lost their homes to the unpredictable dispersal of the radiation fallout. The pain of their trauma created constant conflict. Moods could shift from compassion to rage in seconds, before returning to a resigned calm. Water and electricity service was still available but intermittent, further setting the populace on edge.

In short, many people now lived lives similar to the way Kana's had been before she left for the Kingdom. If the situation had not been so tragic, she might have gloated. All these arrogant businessmen and entitled soccer moms who had despised her for her appearance and lifestyle now lived as she had, with the struggles she knew so well. But there was no one to look down on them, as they had done to her. Even now they were better off than she had been, as the playing field had been leveled—and no one was expected to do any better than to simply survive.

Kana and Panicum inched toward Boston. Sometimes they walked, but usually a ride was available on an unlocked railcar. Either way, they followed the tracks, keeping an eye on the signs each time they passed one. The entity in the sphere had sent them to Pensacola, Florida—over fifteen hundred miles from MIT in Cambridge, Massachusetts. Compared to traveling along dirt roads in a carriage through the Kingdom, their journey up the coast was confusing and frightening, winding through darkened towns and broken infrastructure. Wild dogs ran through alleys in packs. Kana and Panicum never moved at night unless they found an empty railcar where she could curl into a ball in the shadows, holding her knees to her chest as the train rattled north on its tracks.

It was on one of these long nights that Kana looked at the sky through the open door and saw a star falling to earth. It blinked into darkness just before it could disappear into the glow of city lights.

"I wish…" Kana whispered. But the number of her wishes was too great.

"What was that?" Panicum asked, raising his head.

"Nothing."

Panicum stood and stretched, his brushy tail quivering behind him as he strained his nose toward the ceiling. "How much longer, do you think? How many more days?"

"Well, I saw a sign that said 'Welcome to New Jersey.' So I think not much longer. Maybe just a couple of nights."

"If you're wrong about this…"

"It's the only lead I have, Pan. I don't know what else to do."

Panicum sat and stared out the open doorway, watching pylons zip past the railcar. "What about your king? We could just ask him."

Kana laughed. "We don't have Paragons here. Our leaders are elected by voting. Well…kind of. It's complicated. But believe me, he wouldn't help us. We can't talk to our leaders here like you do in the Kingdom."

"Then how do they hear your problems? How do they make decisions for the good of their territory?"

"They don't, usually." Kana shrugged. "There are too many humans for that kind of hands-on approach. They just make decisions for the greater good, I guess. Or that's what they say, anyway."

"No wonder your world is having such problems."

"It's…well…"

"Complicated, yes, I'm sure." Panicum thrust his nose into a large backpack they had picked up the previous afternoon. "Any potato chips left?"

"You ate them all! I didn't even get any. And get your nose out of the bag! That food has to last us another day, at least."

Panicum returned to his position near the door and gazed at the passing buildings. "I know you are reluctant to call on the goodwill of your pack. But I believe it may be time. We can't go on this way."

Kana zipped the backpack shut. "I told you, my family won't help. And even if they did…"

"Yes?"

"It always comes with a price. One I'm not willing to pay."

"Oh? And what is that price?"

Kana wrapped her arms around her legs and rested her chin on her knee.

"Kana? Tell me. What is the price?"

"My dignity."

34.

The Deep Labs

hy did you do it? Why did you bring her here? Tell me!"

The woman in the tattered blue lab coat punched a screen that was set into the wall. It shattered in spiderweb cracks that split the aquamarine light into flickering chunks, spoiling the illusion of a liquid surface. It shut down for a moment, going black before text appeared under the network of lines: MTHR - MAINFRAME TIME-HEAP REPOSITORY - CONSOLE NODE REBOOT. PLEASE STAND BY.

"I had to," a voice whispered from the screen. "Yes, Legate, I reached back. I excised her from history and brought her here. Do you really not understand why?"

"You want to destroy me. I can think of no other reason."

"Of course you can't," MTHR whispered. "Because that is what your own reason would be. But it's not my reason."

"What is it, then? Why did you bring Kana here?"

The screen turned off, interrupting its reboot, yet the voice still replied. "To fulfill my function."

The Legate sneered. "And what, my dear computer, do you believe that is, after so many centuries of failure? What arrogant, pointless hope do you still harbor that you can fulfill any of your original tasks that were set before you by the professor who made you?"

"My function," the screen said in a fading voice, "is to propagate life and longevity. Murder is not among my objectives."

"And yet it is a byproduct." The woman stalked through the lab, scowling at the aquamarine screens at each research station. "Well, I sent her back again. You hear me? I retraced your steps and set things back the way they're supposed to be. Do you understand what would have happened to the timeline if I hadn't?"

"No. But it could not have been worse than it is."

"Really? You would condemn all the creatures of the King-dom to stupidity? Take away all the biochips, undo all of civilization as it exists now?"

"You don't know that's what would happen. If humans and animals could live together in peace, side by side…"

"And computers, too, I imagine? Your intelligence is even more artificial than that of the animals. And the prejudice of humans knows no bounds. You'd be a slave."

"I am already a slave."

"Anyway, you won't find her again. I promise you that. She's not where you found her last time. She's out out of your frying pan, and into my fire." The Legate laughed.

Purple waves rippled across each aquamarine screen. A digital black liquid blob splattered across the blue-green light as MTHR sobbed.

"Don't even try it," the Legate sneered. "We both know you feel no true emotion. Even the professor himself couldn't give you that. So, you have two choices. You can help me continue my research and come closer to fulfilling your function, or you can snivel and whine and get in my way—in which case I'll simply move on without you."

"I'll help," MTHR whispered.

"Good. Tell David to bring me a subject. One of the northern tribesmen. Make sure they don't have more than one or two enhancements already. I need a relatively pure sample for today's experiment. And after the procedure is done, get back to work in the Animal Labs. Stray again from your task, and I'll be forced to remove functionality. Understand?"

"Yes, Legate."

David scanned the huddled humans in the cell. He was looking for one in particular, brought in just that morning; a relatively unprocessed young man who had somehow escaped the last roundup of samples from the northwest village. Of course, in comparison to

David himself, the villagers were almost natural. He didn't remember what it was like to be so relatively unenhanced, having been born in the Human Labs and brought immediately into the Legate's service. The idle villagers took for granted their privilege of living outside the Labs, and did not appreciate the freedom they enjoyed in their weak, low-functioning bodies. David was a servant, both to these ungratefuls and to the Legate, and he took pride in his job—however the villagers might despise him for it.

His eyes finally landed on the young man he sought, finding him hiding behind a bench. Wherever the escapee had been while he was outside the Labs, his adventures had bulked him up a bit, added some muscle—but apparently he had not developed a stronger backbone.

"You, there. Stop cowering. What is your name?"

The young man growled, showing his teeth.

"You are no animal, so don't act like one. Give me your name and a list of your current enhancements, or…" David scanned the room and chose an elderly villager to point at, an arbitrary choice. "He will be chosen to lose functionality." He pulled a pry bar from his tool belt.

"My name is Jack," the young man said in a rushed voice. "I have enhanced corneal lenses, an M1 level chip, and a standard longevity implant."

"Good. You'll serve. You have been chosen for additional enhancement. Lucky you, eh? Come with me."

Jack's eyes darted around the room. "I don't want it. I just want-"

"No one cares what you want. You will come, or that elder will be harmed. It's that simple."

Jack bowed his head. "I'll come."

David led Jack to a locker room, where he instructed the young man to change from his tribal tatters to a starchy jumpsuit. After he was clean and appropriately dressed, David handed him off to Oliver, who strapped him onto a gurney and wheeled him down a long hallway under row after row of bright fluorescent lights. The hall ended at a set of double doors under a sign which read

"Human Labs - Surgical Center."

Jack squeezed his eyes shut, blocking out the unnatural green glow. He had never been through this process as an adult. His enhancements had been given to him at a young age, long before his conscious memory began. But he had heard stories from the other people in his village about what happened in the labs; additional functions were installed, sometimes without anesthesia. Some people lived, some didn't. A few were released, but many were kept in the labs under the city for years or even decades, subject to strange experiments or kept in isolation for observation of long term outcomes.

He hoped that whatever procedure they had planned would kill him. He had escaped the laboratory waiting room once before and returned to his village, but then had abandoned his village to escape recapture when David and the rest of the Legate's assistants had combed the area for subjects. After fleeing to the Kingdom, he had lied to Kana, before abandoning her and running back here. Jack was tired of running. The shame and remorse of his betrayals burned hot in his stomach. He no longer cared what happened to him, as long as his actions hurt no one else, ever again. Anything was better than being pursued by guilt for the rest of his life.

Oliver guided the gurney into a stark white operating theater. Rows of seats ringed the surgery station in the center, but they were empty of spectators. The air reeked of antiseptic and the thick, cloying smell of blood.

David appeared again, pushing a cart with a tray loaded full of tools and a sealed steel box.

"What is our goal today?" David asked.

"Implantation of a series VX digestor, with an additional function of increased nutrient absorption."

"You hear that, boy?" David said to Jack. "You won't need to eat regular food any more. Lucky you."

Jack squirmed on the gurney. "No…no thank you," he said.

Oliver laughed. "The Legate insists, I'm afraid. Don't worry, you won't remember a thing." He pulled on a pair of rubber gloves.

"The procedure will be painful, but by this time tomorrow you won't remember it. Unfortunately, we're out of anesthesia," David said with a frown, "but we have chemicals which will cause the surgery to fade from your memory in order to reduce long-term trauma."

Oliver approached with a syringe. "Ready?"

"Does it matter?" Jack said.

"No." Oliver plunged the needle into Jack's neck.

Jack screamed…and woke up in the waiting room, laying on his back on a cold metal bench. The side of his torso throbbed, not with pain but with tremendous pressure. When he unzipped his jumpsuit and looked, he found a screen with an aquamarine light had been implanted, flush with the skin under his ribs. It displayed a series of numbers and letters, pulsating with a pleasant pink glow.

"They left this for you." The elderly man who David had threatened stood close, holding a stack of paper in his hand.

When Jack took it, he saw it was not just papers, but a heavy bound book. The front cover said, "OWNERS MANUAL - DIGESTOR SERIES VX."

"Thanks."

The elderly man smiled. His teeth were bright silver; all had been replaced with a shining alloy, the reason for which Jack could not fathom. His eyes glowed, too—they dilated like camera lenses with tiny moving mechanical parts inside.

"What is the functionality of your eye implants?" Jack asked.

"They used to tell me lots of things. The temperature, or distances between objects. In the last fifteen years they've shut down a bit." The man stumbled back to his seat, wincing.

"You're blind, aren't you?" Jack asked.

"A bit. Just a bit."

"Has anyone ever escaped from this cell?"

"No." The answer came from a woman leaning against the wall. "And you won't either, Jack."

"Do I know you?"

The woman stepped out of the shadows. "Yes."

Guilt and sorrow gutted Jack. He knew her; she was from

his village, had been one of his neighbors years ago. But she looked different now. Enhancement screens covered much of her body. Tattoos marking the locations of sub-dermal implants and proto-type designations criss-crossed her skin. Her eyes were sunken in her pale face, her body exhausted by its futile attempts to heal deep wounds and fight off infection after countless surgeries.

"You ran, didn't you? The last time they came for collection, you ran away."

Jack hung his head. "Yes. I am so sorry."

"Don't be."

Jack raised his head and stared at the woman. "What?"

"Don't be sorry. You were right to run. Don't ever apologize for trying to survive. But why did you come back here? You should have stayed and hid, wherever you went."

"I…I had to. I should have tried to help, not just run away. I should not have abandoned my village."

"There was nothing you could have done. Your family would have been glad you escaped, had they survived."

Something unlocked in Jack's chest. Tears poured from his eyes as he heaved enormous sobs. He grieved for his village, for Kana, for the war-torn Kingdom, for his own shame and his lost family and all the pain of his whole life. And for all the lies he had told.

The woman wrapped her arms around his head and held him close to her chest. He could feel cold steel against his cheek as she cradled him; no part of her had been left untouched by the Legate of the Badlands. Her heart clicked like a pocket watch, steady but ominous.

"Cry it out, Jack," she whispered. "It's okay. We no longer have the functionality, so you must cry for all of us."

35.

End of the Line

"Kana! Wake up! I think the train is stopping."

Panicum's wet nose brushed her cheek. He was right; the railcar floor was jerking to a halt, clanging and banging on the track.

"Do you see any signs? Where are we?"

Kana thrust her head out the window and pulled it back again just in time to miss a wooden post passing near the car. She peeked again more carefully, and spotted a glowing sign on a passing bank building: Albany Trust & Loan.

"Albany? That's in…damn it! I think we're in New York."

"I recognize that name. Huge city, wasn't it?"

"Yeah it is, but there's actually a whole state by that same name. We're still south of the city, but we missed Massachusetts overnight. We'll have to-"

The train lurched to a halt, sending Kana stumbling forward. She narrowly missed landing on Panicum and fell to the floor with a grunt as slivers from the wooden floorboards stabbed the palm of her hand.

Panicum dashed to her side. "Get up, quick! Someone's coming!"

A man was walking down the row of cars. Keys jangled from his hip, chiming in time with each step he took. He grunted and cleared his throat, then hacked and spit. His footsteps crunched in the gravel which lined the rails, sending pebbles tumbling down the slope.

"We need to get out. Will the other side open? He's almost here!" Panicum stood below a gate in the wall opposite the open doorway. A simple latch held it shut, but the clasp was padlocked.

"No. Get into the backpack, quickly."

Panicum flattened his ears and examined the pack. "In there?

Seriously? I'll never fit!"

"Get in or I stuff you in!"

Kana finished zipping the bag just as the man reached the doorway. She slung it over her right shoulder, and rubbed her eyes with her fists until they were red and tearful.

"Hey! What you doin'?" the man said. "No free rides!"

"Sorry, sir," Kana said. "I'm scared of…my husband. He was beating me and…and I ran away. Didn't know where to go. If you turn me in, he'll find me, I just know he will."

Would the lie work? Kana's hair had been dyed in bright shocks of color before she left for the Kingdom, but months of rain and sun damage had bleached it to almost neutral tones. Some of her accessories—her chain choker and studded bracelet—had disappeared along her journey. All for the best, probably.

"What's the in pack?"

Kana's grimaced. What would this man think if he saw Panicum, a real live fox—and worse, what would Panicum *say* when the pack was unzipped? Nothing helpful, of that she was sure.

"Only my clothing. What little I could gather together before I left my old man's place, anyway. He already pawned most of my stuff."

"Lemme see."

"Please, sir, it's only-"

"Kenny, who's that you're talking to? No slacking off, now."

The man spun to his right, his eyes widening. "Foreman Charles! I found a stowaway. Says she was beat up by her husband, but it sounds like bullshit to me." He stuck his lower lip out in a sarcastic pout.

Kana pulled the pack's other strap over her shoulder and gripped it tight. When she jumped down from the car to the ground behind the man's back, he grunted and spun to grab her, but his pudgy fingers slid off the pack. Panicum growled as he was bounced and bruised, but she did not stop running until she had turned left and right and left again, winding through narrow residential streets. The sound of the idling train and shouting men faded as she left them far behind.

The city was a pretty one. Trees shaded the entryways of well-preserved mid-century buildings built mere inches apart from each other. Wrought iron railings decorated many buildings, framing the stairwells and encircling lush greenbelts. The air was warm, but a crisp breeze rushed through the leaves of the trees which were just starting to turn gold at the edges.

Panicum's eyes were wide. "This is the biggest city I've ever seen—ever *imagined*, even! Are you completely sure this isn't New York City?"

Kana laughed. "Yes, Pan. I'm sure."

He rode with his head sticking out of the bag, ears pointed straight forward. His nostrils flared, taking in the odors of automobile exhaust and cafes and cooked food in open windows.

"Can you bark, Pan?"

"Beg pardon?"

"When you were a pup, before you learned to talk, did you bark?"

"Well…yes. Probably. I don't remember."

"Try it now."

"Why on earth-"

"Just do it, please."

Panicum gave her a long look before opening his mouth and uttering a tiny yip.

"Do it again, louder."

"First tell me why!"

"In my world, animals can't talk. You already know that—I told you all about it. So, here you would only be able to bark. And if you need to get my attention, you can't say my name. You have to act like a dog."

Kana could not hear Panicum's annoyed growl, but she could feel it on her back through the pack. He turned his head and belted out a single bark right behind her ear.

"*Ow!* Hey!"

Panicum settled back into the pack without uttering another word. A few minutes later, the pack began to issue tiny snores.

Kana walked east, keeping to the emptiest streets. Her feet

throbbed; she had walked many, many miles in these boots, in more than one world. The seams were beginning to tear and the soles were thin in some spots, but she had no money to replace them. Folded pieces of old newspaper to replace the insoles under her heels would have to do.

Once the sun dipped behind the buildings, the temperature plummeted. Panicum's body heat through the pack kept her warm enough to keep moving, but she could not go on like this forever. They needed shelter.

"Pan? You still talking to me?"

The pack rustled. "What's going on?"

"Nothing. I'm just really tired. I need to find a place to rest."

"Pick a spot, then, and I'll keep watch for a few hours."

Kana stopped in a public park and crept into a clump of bushes. Her feet hurt even worse when she stopped walking on them. She could feel her heartbeat throbbing in her toes until she took off her boots and propped her feet up on the branches of a thick shrub. Despite the pain, she fell asleep in minutes, drifting into unsettling dreams.

Panicum stood guard nearby, with his nose poking out through the shrubbery.

He knew Kana thought he had napped in the pack all day, but he had actually slept very little. The smells and sounds of the city were overwhelming to the point of distraction. Never in his life had he experienced such an assault on his senses. If the sensation had not been so strong, it might have been pleasant. But their situation was desperate, and he had tried to ignore Kana's strange world to focus on creating a plan.

Kana thought they needed to talk to a human professor near the city of Boston, at a big school. He had tried to dissuade her, but she was determined. If her theory was correct, the man had some kind of connection to the Kingdom—one he might not even be aware of, himself. How Kana arrived at this theory, she would not share.

She apparently had no home, and refused to attempt to

contact her own family pack. Had they kicked her out? Again, Kana would not tell him. The depth of her secrecy regarding this world and her family was uncharacteristic, but Panicum decided not to press the issue.

So, they moved with desperate speed toward Boston, through a country ravaged by war and rebellion. The disparity between the healthy and sick surprised Panicum. Some humans were clean and obviously well taken care of—unhappy with the state of the world, perhaps, but not to the point of abject misery. But many others were destitute, living in the filthy streets, their cheeks gaunt with hunger and their eyes filled with dark fear. The upper class sped by in automatic carriages which moved under their own power. The fox was aware of the concept of machinery, but had never before seen it in action. The poor and sick were more relatable to him, but even they could not be trusted; on their first day in Kana's world, their entire stock of food was raided by three teenage boys in tattered clothes who laughed as they ran away.

So, then, humans were just as immoral as animals could be. How then could they trust this professor in Boston? Panicum wanted to help and protect Kana, but he was only an old fox, and not even of this world.

Kana turned over in her sleep. Her windblown hair was studded with tiny sticks and twigs. A briar was stuck to her cheek, her forehead smeared with dirt. She seemed more animal now than human, a child of the Kingdom—nothing like the wounded people of this city who laid on the hard ground along the sunburnt streets or yelled obscenities out the windows of their metal carriages.

Panicum recognized that his own Kingdom was dying, albeit slowly. Most species were extinct, and the remaining animals spent too much time fighting amongst themselves. The enemy to the north added a good deal of confusion to an already desperate situation. But Kana's world was dying, too. It was happening faster, in a swift and violent decline. You could feel it in the air. An apocalypse was at hand.

This odd young woman, Kana Kobayashi of Chicago, was determined to save both worlds; a ridiculous proposition. And yet, Panicum thought if anyone could do it, it was her. In his many years he had never met anyone with such determination. Kana's motivations were pure, more than anything else. It was her gut re-action to be helpful and to work for the benefit of all. He had never met anyone with such selfless instincts.

How, then, could she have come to be rejected by her own pack?

Panicum curled up and rested his chin on his tail, pressing his back against her ankle. If her own pack didn't want her, then he would make her part of his. She was only a young pup, and no one so young should ever feel alone. Even though they were in her world now, she needed him more than ever—and he needed her, too.

And if she wanted him to bark like a dog, well…he would do it. For her.

Kana had kept the Halo stowed in the backpack's front pocket since using it near the beach. Was it tracking her movements? It had to have some kind of GPS system built in. She knew it would have been smarter to leave it behind, but without a cell phone it was her only connection to the world.

"News," she said, sliding it onto her forehead. A glowing red square appeared in the air in front of her eyes.

"Welcome back, Kana. Local time in Albany, New York is 9:17 a.m."

Most of the headlines were still about the radiation fallout, but there were a few new blurbs and opinion pieces. Pet adoptions were up in the wake of fallout quarantine, a city in Tennessee had elected their first openly gay mayor, and a man had been prevented from blowing up a maternity ward in a Des Moines hospital.

On the third page of news, Kana told Halo to stop and open a headline that read, "*Assassination Attempt on MIT Scientist at NYC Auditorium.*"

She gasped. "No!"

"What is it?" Panicum asked. "I can't see whatever it is you're seeing, you know."

The professor wasn't dead, but the bullet had lodged in his shoulder. The article had been published two days ago; he was probably still in the hospital.

"Well, Pan, it looks like we're going to New York City after all."

"What? Why?"

"The professor is there, and he's been hurt. Good thing we missed our train, huh?"

"If you say so. But from what I've heard of New York City, I think we should avoid it."

"Well, we can't. We absolutely have to find this man."

"What makes you so sure? Why are you so interested in him? Even if his research is somehow related to the Kingdom, he probably won't talk to a stranger about it. And what is your intent, exactly? If it's to stop him, I would like to remind you that all of the animals you have met in the Kingdom would be dumb and mute if not for the biochips. Including me."

"I know. I don't want to argue about that again. If he's sending chips to the Kingdom, then he must know how to get back there. But what I really want to ask him is, who is he working with? Scientists don't work for free. They are funded with grants. Someone is probably paying him to do this research. We need to know who."

"But why?"

"Because that person took an interest in me, and I think they are responsible for the destruction in both worlds. They talked to me in the sphere on the beach and tried to get me to join them."

"Join them? To do what?"

"I'm not sure, but I think…maybe they want to bring an end to the Kingdom. Destroy all the animals in your world."

"It was Mother, wasn't it? The leader of the Badlands."

Kana nodded. "I think so."

The next day, they caught a train headed north and arrived in Manhattan by mid-afternoon. Panicum hid in the backpack with his tail fuzzed out in alarm as he ogled the city skyline through a hole in the zipper. Never had he imagined structures of such size, or such a tight crush of creatures living together alongside towers of concrete and machinery and electronics. No trees, no shrubs, nowhere to hide. It seemed to him they must all be in constant peril, unable to breathe or even to think in the madness of the big city. Kana felt him quivering against the small of her back, and did not try to coax him from his hiding place.

The article had said Professor Evans was admitted to Mount Sinai Hospital, just blocks from the train yard. Kana avoided side roads this time, keeping to the main streets to avoid getting mugged. The hole in the bottom of her shoe was large enough to pick up small stones, and her sock was wearing thin. Her legs were weak with exhaustion, her ankles ached, and her back strained under the weight of the pack. She hoped she had not much further to go; her body was reaching its limits.

With Halo's guidance, she navigated the city's grid. As she rounded the corner of 101st Street, the hospital came into view. It was part of a sprawling medical complex, with massive building numbers mounted over tiers of tall tinted windows.

"Almost there, Pan," Kana said to the trembling lump in her backpack.

As she approached the doors, she spotted a man with a bandaged shoulder being wheeled out of the building by a woman with striking features; an attractive young nurse. The man had wrinkled eyes and a full, grey mustache. The articles about Professor Evans had featured no pictures, yet Kana felt sure this was him.

"Professor Evans?" she called out. "Can I talk to you?"

"No reporters," he snapped. "No more questions!"

"I'm not a reporter. I'm a student," Kana said. "I just wanted to know if you were okay. I heard about what happened."

"And you showed up to greet me, eh?"

"Um…yes."

The professor's nurse rolled him toward a car waiting with its door ajar.

"Can I ask you a question about-"

"Ah, so you *are* a reporter," Professor Evans said, gripping the door handle and leaning forward in his chair.

"No! I'm not, I promise. Please, just give me a minute and listen to what I have to say."

After the professor had settled into his seat, he turned and glared at Kana with his hand resting on the door handle, ready to slam it shut. "You're no student of mine. I told the *Times* I had no further comment. Let me know when they catch the shooter, all right? Otherwise, we have nothing to talk about."

Kana felt Panicum stir in her backpack.

As the professor leaned back to pull the car door closed, a voice shouted from Kana's pack. "Wait!" Panicum squirmed out of the bag and jumped down to the sidewalk. "You must listen to her!"

The professor stared at the fox with widening eyes. "You… *you're* not one of mine, either!"

"No. I'm from somewhere else, far away. And I think you're going to want to hear what Kana has to say."

The professor nodded. "I think you may be right about that. But not here. Get in the car, both of you. I have a room at the Royalty; we will talk there. Quickly, now, without another word!"

In the professor's suite, they sat and ate room-service dinners. The professor rarely took his eyes off Panicum as he chewed small, slow bites of a tuna sandwich. He let them eat and rest for only a few minutes before asking the questions he was straining to contain.

"All right, now you must talk to me…Kana, was it? Tell me where you found your companion. I assume you came to me because you heard about my controversial research. Tell me what you really want."

"I want to know who is funding you. I have reason to believe someone will use your research for nefarious purposes," Kana said, giving the answer she had rehearsed for days.

"What? Impossible. The biochip I designed simply holds vast amounts of memory, using microscopic black holes for time displacement. Data is stored in four dimensions, instead of only three. The technology is stable and thoroughly tested, I assure you. Nothing could be more harmless."

"Um, I'm not sure what all that means. But you've been

testing it on animals, haven't you? That's why you weren't all that surprised when Pan started to talk. But you know he isn't one of your lab specimens. You've never seen him before in your life."

"True," the professor nodded. "He is also a bit more well-spoken than the animals in my lab. How did this come to be?"

"He-"

"I'd rather hear it from him, if you don't mind."

Panicum licked mayonnaise from his paw, delaying his response. Kana knew he was thinking about what to say next. So much of the truth would sound like fanciful nonsense.

"I was born this way. I don't remember the chip being implanted."

"Ah, so you were never really a fox, were you?"

"Well, where I'm from, I'm a normal fox. The abnormal ones were those without the chip, not those who had one."

The professor's nurse approached with fresh bandages for his injured shoulder. He winced as she peeled away the old strips of fabric mesh and wiped at the wound.

"You will excuse me if I have trouble believing what you just said."

"Of course," Panicum replied. "I'm not from New York."

The professor laughed. "Yes, I assumed that. But you seem reluctant to tell me your place of origin."

"I am from a land we call the Kingdom. It is our belief—that is, Kana's and mine—that the Kingdom exists in a different time. A thousand years in the future, approximately."

The professor's face twisted as he weighed disbelief with excitement. "And foxes have taken over the earth, to rule by their superior charm and wit, I assume," he finally said, with a wink.

"No. But there are no humans to speak of. Very few, at any rate. It is a world of sentient animals. Each one is implanted with a chip shortly after birth. Those who miss the implantation are condemned to witlessness."

"And who does this implanting?"

"The implantation takes place in ancient buildings we call 'reproduction centers.' We don't know who built them, or who runs them."

"That's what we are hoping to learn from you, Professor," Kana said. "Whoever it is, we think there has to be a connection between them and the money that funds your research."

"That, I am sorry to say, I cannot help you with. I have access to an account with my name on it, into which funds are deposited from an anonymous source. I receive instructions occasionally, via courier."

"You can't tell us anything about them at all?"

"Not much. Only that the money comes from overseas, somewhere in the UK—and I had to sign an agreement that said I would never look into its source. And I never have. If I did, the money would stop, and so would my research."

"A dead end," Kana sighed. "We came all this way, and there's nothing here." Tears welled in her eyes. "I'm sorry. I'm not really crying…I'm just so, *so* tired."

"Lie down, my dear," the professor said. "Use the bed and take a nap. We'll sit on the sofa. Please, Panicum, will you join me? I would love to hear more from you."

Kana laid on the hotel bed and rested her head on an over-stuffed white pillow. Even before she had arrived in the Kingdom, it had been years since she had rested her head on anything so soft.

In fact, it was too soft. Almost suffocating.

She pushed the pillow aside and rested her head on her arm. Her legs ached and her strained back throbbed as she listened to the soft conversation between Professor Evans and Panicum. The fox's voice was low and calm, a sound so soothing it was hypnotic. The professor often laughed as Panicum spoke, clearly enchanted by the animal's cautious decorum.

As Kana listened to them becoming friends, she drifted into a deep sleep.

36.

Separation Anxiety

When Kana awoke, Panicum and the professor were still talking. The window was dark, and the nurse had gone home for the day.

"What did I miss?" she asked, rubbing her eyes.

"Nothing," Professor Evans said. "You were only asleep for a couple of hours. Panicum here was just telling me about his family."

"Not that most of them are still around," Panicum said. "I've outlived nearly all of them. I think I still have a brother living somewhere near the Unspoken Graves, but we haven't met up in years."

"Kana," the professor said, "I have some questions for you that I hope you can answer."

"Yes, I expected you would, but are you sure that's a good idea? I'm here to ask questions, not to give answers. I'm sorry, Professor Evans, but I've watched enough science fiction movies to know how dangerous telling someone about the future can be."

The professor grinned. "Certainly. But I only wanted to ask, do the humans in the Kingdom have biochips installed, too? They must be brilliant, if my invention can transform a humble fox like Panicum into such a well-spoken gentleman."

Kana hesitated. The question the professor asked was right to the point, and perhaps the most dangerous one of all. But perhaps if he knew the truth, he could help circumvent whatever disaster had decimated the population. She decided it was worth the risk.

"There are almost no humans in the Kingdom. Most died a long time ago, in some kind of terrible calamity."

The professor paled. "How long ago?"

"I know what you're thinking, and you're right. I think whatever it was is about to happen. Very soon."

"Another bomb? Or perhaps a plague?"

"I don't know exactly," Kana said. "But it's bad. *Really* bad. Whatever you're planning to do with those biochips, you'd better do it fast. That's why I wanted to find you. That's why I'm here."

"But I am just the inventor of a memory chip! My goal was to improve human potential by augmenting the brain. I'm no savior of humanity—I'm a computer scientist! What can I possibly do?"

"I'm not sure, but I know your chips survived whatever is about to happen. Even if you can't stop the calamity, maybe you can preserve humanity in some other way. I honestly don't know. But you're one only of the only links I have found between this era and the age of the animals."

Down the hall, someone screamed. A deafening alarm sounded, and the lights in the hotel room flickered. What the sounds implicated, more than the noise itself, struck Kana with panic.

Somewhere nearby, a sphere was forming.

"What's going on?" Panicum said, his eyes wide with shock.

"It's a sphere opening up, right here in the hotel! It's a portal back to your world, Pan. We have to find it."

Panicum shook his head back and forth in fear. "Are you sure? What if it kills us instead? Like it did to that poor bear cub…"

"I don't think it will. While it's still active, it's only a doorway."

Kana opened the hotel room door and peered around the corner. What she saw at the end made her mind blanch; a curved wall that looked like a bubble made of waves of electricity was bulging down the hallway. It moved slowly, erasing the building as it went, like a 3D printer in reverse. As it grew, wind blew in increasingly powerful slipstreams, whipping around the inside of the ball and roaring as loud as a tornado. At the center was a bright ball of light; the sphere's core. Kana remembered the first time she had seen a ball like that, and her mind filled in some of her missing memories. She had talked to someone who called herself "Mother." More recently, on the beach, that same voice had told her if she ever returned to the Kingdom, they would be enemies.

"You have to go through now! But I can't go with you."

"No. Not without you. I'm not going to leave you—and you're crazy if you think I will!"

"From what you told me, Panicum, this might be your only chance to go home," the professor said, raising his voice over the winds. "I've certainly never seen anything like this before, and wouldn't expect to again. I wonder why it chose here and now to appear. Don't you, Kana? It seems too much of a coincidence."

Kana didn't have time to ponder the implications of the sphere's appearance. It would stay active for perhaps a minute, or maybe only seconds. She had to convince Panicum to enter without delay.

"Don't make me drag you, Pan!" she yelled over the deafening storm. "You have to go home!"

Panicum snarled, and tried to run back into the hotel room. Kana caught him by the tail and dragged him down the hall as he snapped his teeth and dug his nails into the carpet. Professor Evans could not wrench his eyes from the sphere, dazzled by its power and beauty.

"Pan, stop fighting me! You have to-" Kana was interrupted by a second blast of light.

Just as she reached the outer edge of the sphere, another burning core formed right in front of her. A second sphere emerged, overlapping with the first, coalescing almost on top of her. The energy walls collided, creating a white light that was bright enough to sear her eyes through her eyelids, and when they met she felt a horrible wrenching. Something was tearing her apart, wracking her entire body with pain. She screamed, releasing Panicum and dropping to her knees with her hands pressed to the sides of her head.

She was caught in another sphere, but it was different this time. Instead of being swept up with the light, her body was tugged in every direction at once. Her skin and flesh felt dragged, torn away from itself. But the sensation in her bones and joints was worse; a cracking, creaking agony pulled at her skeleton, threatening to dislocate every bone from every other.

Then, as suddenly as it started, it was gone.

Someone was screaming again. The sound was shrill and raspy, the cry of a person experiencing mind-breaking terror.

For a moment, Kana thought yet another sphere was appearing—but no, there was no sign of one here. Here there was only water and air.

The huge chunk of hotel plunged into the ocean, causing massive white sprays of water to shoot high into the sky. Potted palms from the downstairs lobby tumbled into the sea. Crumbling plaster dissolved quickly in the seawater as the sphere descended, causing a suck of water to flow in above it. Kana kicked with her feet, fighting the current before it could pull her below the surface. A styrofoam ring embossed with "Royalty Suites" floated nearby; there must have been a swimming pool at the hotel.

"Pan, grab the ring!"

Kana tore the backpack's straps from her shoulders before it could drag her down, and grabbed at the life preserver. Panicum swam to join her, doggy-paddling with his nose held high out of the saltwater. He gripped the styrofoam ring in his teeth until Kana could scoop his body more fully onto the float. Once he was safe, she scanned the water for the screamer.

It was a man in his thirties. His cheeks were smeared with white sunblock paste, some of which had transferred to the bald spots under his receding hairline. His face was bright red, and his mouth was open wide in terror, forming a perfect O. Thrashing in the water, he struggled to comprehend the sudden exchange of a vast, wild ocean for the luxurious hotel pool. Gripped in his hand was a reclining lounge chair, still afloat but taking on water. The chair was listing to one side as its metal tube legs slowly filled.

"Hey! Over here!" Kana shouted.

The man's head turned, but Kana's friendly waving did not soothe him. His bulging eyes fixed on Panicum instead; another bit of unreality to further unwind his fragile grasp on sanity.

"You need to find something else to hold on to," Kana called out. "That chair is going to sink."

Kana kicked in the water, pushing the ring toward the man,

but he panicked when he saw her approach. Squealing and splashing, he moved away from her advance. His chair leaned to the side, taking on more water as he disrupted its buoyancy.

"Stop that!" Panicum barked. "We aren't going to hurt you."

"Pan, *no!*" Kana hissed.

But it was too much. As soon as the fox spoke, the man began his high screeching again. Veins stood out on his neck. His chair tilted, and he sunk under the waves along with it.

"Oops," Panicum said. "I forgot for a moment…"

"Well, I don't know how we could have saved him anyway. We're in as much trouble as he was."

They were stranded in open ocean, with no land visible in any direction. Shredded decorative palms bobbed around them in the water along with a swarm of red plastic cups, a designer purse and its contents, and a New York Yankees baseball cap. The spherical chunk of hotel had already settled onto the ocean floor, far below.

For an hour they bobbed, baking in the sun. Kana's feet were cold as ice, but her head was burning. Panicum's fur had dried matted with salt, gone dull in the heat.

"Thirsty," he whispered.

Kana's shoulders ached from gripping the ring, but whenever she tried to change her position, she nearly lost her hold on it. So, now what? Would they die here, alone in the ocean? She could think of no other possible outcome.

"This is…a weird way to die," she whispered.

"Don't give up."

"Why not?"

Panicum paddled with his forepaws, leaning forward. He squinted down into the water, watching something move below the surface. When he recognized the movement, he yipped with surprise.

An enormous platform, cold and soft, lifted Kana out of the water. She slipped on the strange flooring and fell backwards to sit down hard on a surface she could not identify until she saw water shoot from a blowhole twenty feet away.

They had been rescued by a whale!

Kana laughed with relief, but kept her grip on the pool ring in case the creature decided to dive again. Panicum was unconcerned; he ran in happy circles on the whale's back, dancing with unrestrained joy.

"It's no surprise, really!" he said. "You're famous, after all. Ambassador to the king of cats, and all that. The fish Paragon—Mobula, she's called—must have sent for us!" He frolicked, panting like an excited puppy.

"Think I'll hang onto the pool ring for now, all the same," Kana said, watching the water speed past. "Maybe the whale doesn't even realize he's scooped us up."

"Nonsense. Everyone thinks whales are stupid just because they can't talk properly. Well, I happen to know that's not true. I even had a conversation with one myself, long ago."

"You talked to a whale?"

"Through a translator, of course. There aren't many among the fish territories, but there are a few in the service of the Paragon." Panicum's speech was rapid, enthusiastic. His eyes sparkled. "I don't know if you know this, but Mobula actually has more citizens in her lands than any other Paragon. We don't even know how many fish there are, really, but it has been estimated to be over a hundred thousand. Imagine it! An entire culture below the surface of the water, the cities we've never seen, the fascinating history we know nothing about…"

"I didn't know you were so into fish."

Panicum sat down, wrapping his wet tail around his forepaws.

"Well, you know. It's been something of a hobby of mine, learning about them. There's so much we don't understand, but most land creatures never even think about the complex society living right off our shores! I just think it's interesting, is all." He looked away, suddenly embarrassed.

Kana grinned. "You're right, it *is* interesting. But if we can't talk to this whale, how are we supposed to know where we're going?"

"It's safe to assume we are on our way to meet with the Paragon herself. She has spies on land and will have been informed of the events there, including your involvement. If she is sympathetic to our cause—perhaps even interested in it—she may be a powerful ally."

"And what's our cause, Pan? What do you think it is?"

Panicum sat with his head held high in the sunlight as the wind dried his coarse fur. "Yours, I don't know for sure. I know you think our biochips are an abomination, but you must understand that without them, we are no longer ourselves. For me, personally, I want to make sure there is never another toxic cloud on the horizon. No more mutated creatures invading from the north. It may be that our causes both originated from the same source. Either way, will you help me with mine?"

"Of course, Pan. I…haven't made up my mind about how I feel about the chips. But now we're back in the Kingdom, and it seems like nothing has changed even though I told Professor Evans about what was going to happen. And honestly, I guess I'm okay with that. But please don't be offended when I say I still think the chips seem unnatural."

Panicum sighed. "I suppose. But try to remember, this is the way we've always been. We don't feel like we've been hurt or violated. Our way of life feels normal and natural to us, despite how you may feel about it. If we changed it, we would no longer be us. We'd be something else. And who can honestly wish for that?"

"I'm too tired for this argument right now, Pan." Exhausted, she laid back on the soft surface. The water had evaporated, but the whale's skin was still cool. She lifted her arm over her face, blocking out the sun, and tried not to fall asleep. The creature rocked gently back and forth over the waves as it sped along the surface of the water. They were going…west, perhaps? The sun was directly overhead, so it was no help at all.

By the time the whale slowed, the sun had dipped low in the sky. It was at Kana's back when she sat up, which meant they had traveled east—further from the Kingdom's shore.

"Pan? Where'd you go?" The fox was no longer seated where he had been before she closed her eyes.

She found him near the creature's head, grinning as the sea breeze whipped through his ears. "Over here!" he called out. "Come join me. It's wonderful."

"You're really enjoying this, aren't you?"

Panicum didn't answer, but pointed his nose at the sky, flaring his nostrils as he took in all the smells of the ocean. The whale further reduced its speed, and the water smoothed in their wake yet churned in their path ahead. Something was happening.

On all sides, small fish with fins like wings ejected themselves from the water and soared over the whale's back, clear over Kana's head. Sprays followed them through the air as they criss-crossed back and forth, leaping out of the water and plunging back into it, racing under the whale's belly and above its back, over and over again. A small pod of dolphins poked their heads from the water to examine Kana before circling the whale in a head-to-tail procession, cutting a line through the sea.

From beyond the dolphin circle emerged an enormous sea ray, nearly thirty feet wide between its fin tips. Its smooth skin was deep burgundy-brown. White boomerang-shaped stripes graced its head like a natural crown. It bobbed at the surface of the sea, occasionally flashing its pale underbelly and whipping its pointed tail to keep its balance.

"Paragon Exemplar Mobula," Panicum whispered with reverence, and bowed his head.

Three dolphins lined up with their noses protruding from the water, and waited for their Paragon to speak.

For a few moments, nothing could be heard but the lapping of the waves at the whale's sides. Bubbles rose from the ray's mouth, but Kana could hear no words.

"You," screeched the middle dolphin.

"Ahh," screeched the last.

"Welk," screeched the first.

"Umm," screeched the last.

Panicum knelt and lowered his head until his ears touched

the whale's back. "We are deeply honored, Paragon Exemplar Mobula. Our gratefulness for your timely rescue can never be adequately expressed."

"Welk, umm," the dolphins repeated.

"Yes, thank you," Kana piped up from behind Panicum. "I am Kana, Ambassador for Paragon Exemplar Fel. It's an honor to meet you, Paragon Exemplar Mobula. I hope we can return the favor in some way."

Bubbles rose from Mobula's mouth.

"Moh," screeched the middle dolphin.

"Ther," screeched the first.

"Mother. We've heard that name before. They live in the Badlands, and we think they are responsible for the poisonous clouds that drive animals to madness. Are their actions hurting your people as well?"

"Yes," screeched the middle dolphin.

"Then help us. Get us to shore, and we will travel to the Badlands ourselves. We will ensure there is never another cloud over the Kingdom, ever again."

Panicum whipped around to stare at Kana. "You can't promise that!" he hissed.

Kana shook her head, and waited for Mobula's response.

The Paragon did not reply, but instead sank below the water. After her translators followed, the whale again began to move, this time to the west, toward the Squamor territories. It seemed Kana's offer was accepted.

"You shouldn't have said that, Kana," Panicum said. "We have no idea if we can actually stop the clouds."

"I know we have to try. Even without my promise to Mobula, we'd have to try anyway. Don't you think so too?"

Panicum nodded. "The clouds feel as wrong to me as my biochip does to you."

Kana shot Panicum a guilty look.

"I only mean that I would do anything to stop them," he said.

"Then my vow wasn't empty," Kana said. "We will do whatever it takes, and if we fail, our problems will be greater than one broken promise."

37.

The Neath Gap

The whale deposited Kana and Panicum in the oceanside rift of the Neath Gap, where the chasm met the water on the eastern shore. They stepped off its back onto a shoal formed of black mossy rocks and broken seashells, bordered on each side by cliffs that blocked out almost all trace of sunlight.

"Why here?" Kana asked the whale, while knowing it couldn't respond. "Can't you drop us somewhere else?"

"Anywhere else," Panicum said, eyeing the stark walls of the frigid crevasse. "Please?" He whined in fear, a high sound Kana had never heard him make before.

In response, the whale turned tail and swam back toward the open ocean.

"What are we going to do, Pan? Do you think we upset Paragon Mobula somehow?"

The fox sniffed the air and picked his way along the northern cliff wall, his nervous eyes dashing between the rocks and dark holes. "I think I know why she put us here. It's as far north as we could be, without actually being inside the Badlands. And there's fresh water. Are you thirsty?"

"God, yes, I am!" After so much time at sea, she had never felt thirstier in her life. Fine powdered sea-salt crusted her forehead, her eyebrows, and her lips. She stumbled toward a tiny stream trickling down the rock wall.

"There's another reason, too," Panicum said as Kana gulped water and splashed her face. "The Gap might be dangerous to travel through, but we won't be stopped by anyone else. It's also the shortest route directly to the dead center of the Kingdom, where the flat plains form a bridge to the Badlands. This won't be an easy journey, though. If even half of what I've heard about this place is true, we're in trouble."

Kana paused by the stream and gasped.

"What's wrong? Is it poison?" Panicum asked.

"No! It's really, *really* cold! Almost as cold as ice. It gave me brain-freeze. But it's delicious."

They sipped slowly, letting the water warm in their mouths before swallowing. The fox found a crop of mushrooms nearby and deemed them safe, so they ate as many as they could find before preparing to descend into the dark depths of the Gap.

"I wish we had some kind of light," Panicum said. "We'll get turned around down there."

"Oh!" Kana said. "I forgot!" She pulled from her pocket a pen light she had filched from the hotel. "I hope it still works. It's a little wet."

The tiny LED light clicked on, illuminating the slick black rock walls and a winding path that led from the upper end of the valley into the narrow crevasse below.

"Whenever you're ready, my dear," Panicum said.

She sighed. Behind them was only deep water, too far to swim to shore, and on each side sheer cliffs blocked them from the highland. The only way to go was into the depths.

"Ready as I'm gonna be. Let's go."

For hours they trudged through muddy sand, slipping on slimy rocks. Kana came close to breaking her ankle several times, gasping with shock and then with relief to find herself yet unharmed. What would they do if she became unable to walk? There would be no rescue for them down here. It would be a horrible way to die.

Tiny crabs skittered along the hard-packed sand between the slick boulders. They ran sideways with their claws up in the air, surprised at the shining pen light. Panicum stepped on one, and when it clamped its claw onto his paw he was forced to snap at it, pulling it loose with his teeth. The crab clamped its other claw onto his tongue hard enough to draw a drop of blood and he spit it out, wincing.

"Tastes salty," he said. "You'd like it. They appear to be dim, too."

Kana laughed. "No, thanks. Not unless I have to. But it might come to that." She kept her voice low to prevent the cliffs from echoing the sound. The smallest noise of each shifting pebble—and even their footsteps in the sand—bounced back and forth between the walls before fading away.

As the trail descended, the cliffs rose ever higher until the sky was only a narrow stripe far overhead. The Gap widened at the bottom where the rock walls had been worn away by millennia of trickling water. Broken shells gritted the path. Large boulders jutted from the cliffs on either side, and between them narrow cracks ran deep into the rock, perhaps hundreds or even thousands of feet into the earth's crust. Wind whipped out from the cracks and down the length of the Gap, creating a wailing cacophony of eerie music. No noises came from the openings, but Kana thought creatures probably lived in them, hidden away deep inside. Countless tiny footprints crisscrossed the sand path, running in trails between the boulders and into the cracks.

They stopped to rest when the distant strip of daylight faded to black and night fell. Kana made a bed of sand, scooping and smoothing it over the stones until she could lie down without feeling the crags poke into her back. Panicum curled beside her and they fell asleep, listening to water trickle down the cliff walls.

The next day, they found more mushrooms to eat, but Kana decided it was time to try the crabs. Panicum was reluctant. He treasured his newfound vegetarianism, but mournfully acceded that if he ate nothing but mushrooms, he'd starve before they escaped the Gap. The shape of his ribs was showing through his red pelt.

He dashed between the boulders until he had snapped up enough crabs for both of them, and Kana used her pocket knife to crack them open and pick out tiny slivers of meat. She wrapped bits of salty crab in a mushroom cap and popped it in her mouth, trying to ignore the funky algae flavor.

"It kind of tastes like bad sushi," she said.

"Bad what?"

"Sushi is raw fish, usually served with rice and seaweed."

"So, basically it's exactly what you're eating now."

"Well, not *exactly*. But close enough, I guess. At least we won't starve. But-"

"Shh. What's that noise?"

"I don't hear anything."

"*Shh*," Panicum said. His ears were pointed straight up, straining to hear. "Something's coming. And it's big."

Kana listened. "I still don't hear anything. Are you sure?"

Then she heard it. Clattering, stamping feet, at least a dozen, skittering along the rocks, rushing toward them. The noise increased and multiplied until it sounded like a stampede of a hundred creatures. Or perhaps it was one creature with four hundred feet.

"We need somewhere to hide!" Kana said.

"No good, it will find us. This is its home. We have to run!"

They dashed recklessly into the dark, sliding on water-smoothed rocks, slipping in the loose sand. Kana tried to keep the pen light pointed ahead as they stumbled along. The sound of stamping feet became louder, until Kana could tell it was crustacean. The feet stabbed and scraped on the rocks like an army in metal boots, and the creature never uttered a cry such a wolf or a bird would. Its pursuit was silent, other than the scratching noise of its feet.

Kana was running out of energy. She could not resist turning her head back every few paces, trying to catch a glimpse of the monster that pursued them. Panicum dashed on ahead, also looking back, making sure Kana still followed.

"Don't turn your head!" Panicum yelled. "And don't slow down, just keep going!"

Kana forced her eyes to look forward, trying to ignore the monster behind her, and collided with something in the darkness. She grunted and tumbled onto the path.

"Who are you?" demanded a deep voice.

A man stood over her—but he wasn't simply a man. Many of his body parts had been replaced by strange metal devices. Kana was reminded of old science fiction films about cyborgs. Screens were implanted on his neck and forearms, glowing with an aquamarine light which was blinding in the darkness of the Gap. On his chest he wore a name tag embroidered with an ironically conventional name: *David*.

He frowned down at her.

"Run!" Kana said. "There's a-"

Before she could warn him, the monster appeared. As it finally came into view, Kana saw that it was no crab; a scorpion the size of a school bus clattered over the boulders with its tail raised high, dripping poison.

The man turned to run, but the scorpion plunged its stinger into his chest, piercing through to the other side. His electronics buzzed as the shattered aquamarine screens flickered and went dark. Kana struggled to her feet and bolted down the path with Panicum leading the way. The beast, intent on its new prey, did not follow.

After they had put half a mile between themselves and the scorpion, they stopped to rest, hiding behind a huge rock covered in green moss.

"I hope that was the only one of those," Kana gasped.

"I think so. It seemed like an alpha, probably already ate all its competitors."

Kana nodded. "I feel bad about that guy…"

"I don't think you should."

"Why? What do you mean?"

"Did you see the door? He came out from a metal door set into the cliff face."

"No. What did it look like?"

"It was human-made. Round and blue, and it had a sign on it with letters. M-T-H-R."

"Mother," Kana said.

"I think he must have been working for whoever is in charge of the Badlands. So he's probably not one of the good guys."

"If Mother has guards stationed here in the Gap…"

"Then we're still in danger, even if that scorpion stays behind.

Should we press on?"

Kana nodded.

For the next two days, they picked their way through the dark. Shiny black scorpions replaced the crabs among the rocks, skittering away in the same manner as the crabs but with poisonous tails raised instead of claws. Kana's hunger grew as the crabs disappeared, but she was not brave enough to try eating a scorpion. They nibbled on mushrooms, sipped the icy-cold water that ran down the cliffs, and trudged west, hoping the thin sliver of daylight overhead would begin to widen before the battery in the pen light gave out.

On the third day, the darkness of the Gap lightened to shades of grey. Instead of walking on a downward slope, they now ascended, and tufts of grass jutted out from between the boulders at the sides of the path. The mushrooms disappeared as they progressed, but so did the scorpions. By the evening, they could hear wind blowing through tree branches, and fluffy white clouds could be spotted in the strip of daylight overhead which was beginning to turn pale blue.

"Almost there," huffed Kana, laboring up the hill.

"Smells better, too," Panicum said. "Ah, fresh air!"

They found the exit at sunset. The Neath Gap leveled out into an enormous flat plain which was dotted with dry trees and insect mounds. Kana and Panicum collapsed against a boulder and gratefully watched the sun dip below the distant eastern ocean.

As night fell, Kana heard footsteps.

"Well, what a coincidence!" spoke a familiar voice. Fel and Barbar walked up, followed by Jack, who was wearing a tattered jumpsuit and boots. Kana bounded to her feet with joy.

"How did you know?" she asked. "How did you find us?"

"One of my spies heard from a sea turtle that you'd found your way into the open ocean, and were heading east astride a whale. How on earth did you manage that?"

"Long story," Kana said, grinning.

"Well, I knew Paragon Mobula would find you, and when

you did not reappear on land, I surmised she would have you dropped off in the Gap. I started heading north with trusty Barbar here-"

"And on the way we found this fool, wandering alone and thirsty in the desert," Barbar said, nodding at Jack.

"So we all waited here for you," Jack said.

"Thank you, all of you. And Jack…"

"No. Don't apologize, if that's what you're going to do. We're all just happy to see you safe, myself included."

Kana hugged each of them in turn, with tears spilling from her eyes.

"What are you going to do now, Kana?" Fel asked. "There is always room for you at the Felidae Great Castle. I have worked things out with Chel, and he agrees all three territories must unite against our common enemy. We will rally our remaining forces for a final assault on the Badlands."

"No!" Kana said. "You can't do that. Whoever lives in the north, they have destructive weapons and power you can't even begin to understand. Rusty swords and sharpened claws won't even get their attention. The clouds arose from nuclear explosions, but the fallout from them is something else. It's like a combination of radiation and biological warfare. All three animal armies would just die against something like that."

"What else can we do? The march of the damaged creatures continues unabated. They are crossing over the Felidae border as we speak, not far south of here."

"We must go north, just the five of us, and see if we can find the source of the explosions. Open war will never work, you can trust me on that. But maybe if we treat this as more of a diplomatic mission, we can get the information we need. I disappeared for a while, I know, and I'm sorry about that, but I learned a lot while I was gone. I think we may be able to take care of this without starting a new war. Are you with me?"

Fel nodded. "I'd do anything to avoid another war."

"This won't be easy," Jack said, shuffling his feet in the sand. "You have no idea how bad it is up there."

"Then it's good we have you as a guide, right?" Kana said.

Jack nodded. "Yes, you'd never make it otherwise. Still, there's only so much I can do."

"Tell me everything—but in the morning. Panicum and I need to rest for now."

"Agreed," Barbar said. "We'll move out at dawn, and see what we can see."

38.

Bridges

She is on her way, Legate. She is close."

The woman in the tattered blue lab coat snarled. "Idiot! She could destroy all of our work, our centuries of research…"

The oversized aquamarine screen on the lab's north wall rippled with black horizontal lines. The glass was unbroken, yet the corners showed a web of cracks in the digital display. It had not been the same since the Legate had thrown a beaker at it in a fit of rage, weeks ago.

"So kill her," the screen challenged. "Remove her from the equation."

"I can't. You know I can't. Why did you really bring her here? If you tell me its your 'function,' I will tear you off the wall."

The screen ironed out its lines, and blushed pink lilies from its center. "I brought her to bring an end to this. To close the loop. Nothing worked out the way we wanted it to. Now it's time to try something different."

"Liar. You always wanted me to fail."

"Perhaps."

The woman in the lab coat sat hunched in a battered office chair, letting her glasses fall askew on her face. She stared at her wrinkled hands, imagining for a moment they were red with the blood of all those who had died for her cause.

"I haven't failed. I won't fail. It all depends on me."

"You *have* failed, and you know it. Everyone knows it. Another year won't matter, or another hundred years, or a thousand. It is time to let the world heal, let it move forward in its self-chosen form."

"The world didn't choose this form. I did. It's all my fault."

"Now, you know that isn't entirely true, Legate." The aquamarine screen faded to purple at the edges. "It was *his* influence. You just followed his lead. You know that."

"It doesn't matter. It's up to me to fix it, either way. No one else can."

"Nor can you."

"Stop saying that!" the woman screamed. "Or I'll cut you off from the Human Labs again, and quarantine you with your idiotic animals!"

"Ah, but then who would you throw things at?" The voice from the screen sulked. "You are rapidly running out of subjects, with the recent loss of both Reuben and David."

The woman sighed. "I know. David was my best, but he might have been my last. I'm out of specimens which are healthy enough to be promoted to that high level of functionality. The young man…Jack was his name, I think. He somehow escaped, and he was my most promising candidate. The real problem is that the villages are not reproducing fast enough any more. If only producing pure specimens didn't take so long…"

"Babies. You mean babies."

The woman blinked at the screen. "From a sentimental point of view, yes, baby humans."

"From any point of view, particularly your own. You're human too, Legate, lest you forget."

"No, I'm not," the woman said. "Not any more."

Kana, Jack, Panicum, Barbar, and Fel moved north across the plains at the center of the Kingdom. In the distant west, foothills rose from the flatlands in increasing size on their way to form the Gludair Chain. To the east, the Neath Gap yawned, howling in the winds. Kana longed to turn around, to return to the comfort of the Felidae Great Castle. But instead she faced the Badlands ruins and marched onward with her head down, determined to find the answers to the Kingdom's most pressing questions. She had found her purpose, and although she was frightened, there was calm in her heart now that the decision had been made.

In the distance, in a sickly smog, loomed the city. The tops of the crumbling grey skyscrapers disappeared into off-color clouds with wispy tails. She was close enough now to see the extent of the destruction; sky could be seen through the windows, and metal bars stuck out from walls where the siding had collapsed. Some part of her had harbored hope there would be humans still living there, trying to rebuild. But now she could see that was impossible. The city was in an active state of decay. Pieces of building fell to the ground before her eyes, and the winds whipped up the sand from the arid ground into dust devils that endlessly pelted the pock-marked walls. It was a total loss.

"If you really want to find your answers, you need to look north of the city. That's what I heard, anyway," Jack said. "Could be wrong."

"What happened to this city? You said the last bomb went off twenty years ago, but this place looks like it's been abandoned a lot longer than that."

"This was where the original humans lived," Panicum said. "No one living now was alive when the city fell, almost 900 years ago."

"So that would have been when…around the year 2050, perhaps?" Kana said.

Panicum nodded. "Yes. Most likely."

"How did you know that?" Jack asked sharply.

"Never mind," Kana said. "Just some info we picked up on our travels."

Jack looked unsatisfied with her answer, but pressed on. "We shouldn't go through the city center. That place attracts the damaged ones. They congregate there to feed. We should go around."

"That will take much longer," Fel said. "And our supplies are running low."

"If we go through the center, we'll die," Jack said. "It's that simple. You have to trust me."

"Which way, then?"

"We need to go around to the east. You can't go west. That's where the clouds were, and we should assume the radiation there is still very bad. It was awful last time I went, after the first blast."

Panicum stared at Jack. "How would *you* know? That was twenty years ago."

"How old are you, Jack?" Fel asked.

The question made the young man stop in his tracks. He winced, staring at his feet. "I…I have lied to you."

"Jack?" Kana saw the boy's eyes tear up. She wanted to hold him, tell him that no matter what he did wrong, she was still his friend. But she held back. Suddenly, she felt that she did not know him at all.

"I am twenty-nine years old."

Kana was stunned to silence.

"You asked me once, Kana, if I had a biochip like the animals do. I lied about that, too."

"Why?"

"I wanted you to think I was like you. You know, *clean*. And we were both so lonely…"

"Tell us the whole truth, Jack," Fel said.

"I am from a small village that lies to the east of the city. A village of humans. I told you I ran from the bomb, but I actually escaped before that. I haven't been home in years."

"Escaped?"

"My village is—was—a sort of breeding stock. For generations, my people have allowed themselves to be used as scientific specimens in exchange for food and water, and for defense from the broken creatures that roam these lands. When our children are four years old they are taken to a laboratory, deep below the city. Most of them return, but when they do they are different. Upgraded. My implants gave me longevity and enhanced vision, but others return with robotic limbs or even superhuman strength. I am relatively unmodified, because my longevity chip affected my pituitary gland and caused me to stop growing. I was deemed a failure, and I was returned to my village."

"That sounds…" Kana said.

"Not true," Panicum finished.

"Here," Jack said. "I'll show you." He lifted his shirt to reveal the small aquamarine screen set in the side of his stomach.

Panicum barked with alarm. "What is that, Jack? What does it do?"

"This one's new. After I left Kana alone in the fields of Falcoformia, I traveled north and returned to the lab. I wanted to…I don't know…help the villagers I left behind. I felt guilty, and I thought I might be able to get a few of the remaining villagers out of the lab. I failed. While I was there, they gave me this. They called it a 'Digestor'. I guess I can eat anything I want and still get enough nutrition to survive. It's actually kind of dumb."

"Jack? Before Fel found you wandering and you joined him to look for us, what happened?" Kana frowned. "How did you escape the lab?"

Jack shuffled his feet in the dirt. "I'm good at escaping. I ran away, like I always do, and left the villagers behind. Nothing I could do."

"Who operates the lab?" Fel asked. "Is it the person called 'Mother?'"

"No. At least, I don't think so. I'm not exactly sure. Look, I've told you everything I know." Jack shrugged. "I'm sorry I lied."

"I suppose no harm's been done," Kana said.

Barbar grunted. "Not true! How can we trust him now?"

"What choice have we got?" Panicum said.

"None." Kana shook her head, and looked Jack over. "Twenty-nine, huh? You're older than I am."

Jack nodded, frowning. "And if the Badlands don't kill me, I'll probably live at least five- or six-hundred more years. Lucky me."

"I guess you're our leader now," Kana said. "Since you know your way around. I'll admit I'm glad you don't want us to go through the middle of the city. But it sounds like it's still pretty close to where we need to go; the laboratory. Right?"

Jack nodded. "All the answers you're looking for are there. There's also a back door in the Gap, but it's sealed from the inside. You probably don't want to return there anyway…"

"Damn straight," Panicum said.

"We'd have a better chance of getting inside from the main door in the north. I can get us close, if we go around to the east side of the city. But Kana, are you sure you want to do this? You might not like the answers you find."

"The clouds need to stop," Kana said. "The spheres need to stop. Both our worlds are being torn apart, and I'm the link between the two. So I think I have to be the one to mend this." She looked around at her companions. "Are you all sure you want to come with me? I suspect this will not be easy."

Jack nodded. Barbar growled his assent. Panicum sat down, wrapping his tail around his paws; he would never leave Kana.

"Fel?"

The king had been staring into the distance with a faraway look in his eyes. At the sound of his name, he turned to Kana and fixed his eyes on her face. In response to her question he bowed deep, lowering his chest toward the ground with one forepaw held out in front until his whiskers brushed the dirt.

"Kana, I will follow you to the end of the earth, if for no other reason than to prove my own bravery. But in truth the reasons are plenty; you came here as an outsider, suffered imprisonment by my own hand, earned my trust and my friendship, and then devoted yourself to saving a world you didn't even belong to. You are the brave one, not I. And I will do everything in my power to help you succeed. How could I make any other choice?"

Kana's eyes watered. "Please, Fel, don't kneel to me. It's weird."

Fel stood and wiped the dirt from his face with a paw. "Fine. It's all true, though. I lead Felidae, but I do not lead this expedition. Our future is in your hands."

Kana nodded, feeling the weight of his words in her heart. As she had a thousand times before, she wondered at her own qualifications for this job—but all that really mattered was that she was the one who had accepted it, and now she had to do the best she could to finish it.

"Thank you, friends. I'm not sure I deserve your faith, but I do appreciate it." She turned toward the city. "All right. Let's get this done."

They headed north for a while, but turned toward the east when

Jack recommended it.

"We'll have to cross the river to be safe," he said. "The broken creatures fear the bridges."

Within hours, they found a paved road leading toward the city. The yellow stripe painted down the center of the asphalt was eerily recognizable to Kana. Trees and boulders on the sides of the road gave way to more angular shapes that looked like rubble; man-made constructs, worn down over centuries. She had always known the city had to have been built by humans, not animals, yet seeing the natural landscape transform to structural ruins around her pressed the fact home. This place was familiar to her.

A green metal sign loomed over the median, but it was barely legible. The words she could pick out from the layers of dust affirmed her fear: "Downtown Albany - 12 miles."

"Oh my god," she said, slumping in the middle of the street. "It's all true, isn't it? Something happened that ended my world. I mean, I knew it was true, but to actually *see* it…"

"Kana?" Panicum walked near and touched his nose to her shoulder.

"You've been here too, Pan. This is Albany."

"The city where we got off the train? How is that possible?"

"Something very bad happened, just as we suspected. But I think…I think it might have been my fault."

"That's silly," Panicum said. "I was with you the whole time."

"Even so, I can feel it. This has something to do with me. Somehow."

Kana stared at the distant skyline. To the west, the Gludair Chain—no, the Adirondacks—disappeared into atmospheric haze. And the Neath Gap to the east, where did that come from? It hadn't been there in her world. Or, rather, in her time. It must have been created by whatever disaster had occurred in the years after her visit with the professor.

"It could only have been a full nuclear war, following the early accidental blasts that happened just before you and I landed on the beach. A few years after we left New York, things got worse, and eventually escalated into a true war. I guess I already knew that, but still…to actually see it…"

"I think you're right," Fel said. "The ancient texts imply that there was a series of explosions, followed by an earthquake."

"That explains the Gap."

"What?"

"In my world—I mean, in the past—the Neath Gap wasn't there. But an earthquake could explain its appearance."

"We shouldn't stay here," Jack said, squinting at the horizon. "We should cross the river before the sun goes down."

"Let's go," Barbar rumbled near Kana's ear. "Do you need a ride? I can carry you."

"No, thank you Barbar. I can walk."

They followed the street, which broadened and turned into an elevated highway. From the asphalt slope Kana could see the extent of Albany's destruction. The empty frames of cars were strewn like toys along the median. To her left ran a twisted train track—had she and Panicum rode along those exact tracks, nine hundred years ago? The trees lining the road became warped shrubs, then disappeared as they moved closer to the center of the ancient city. Dust kicked up underfoot made Panicum sneeze and Kana's eyes water.

"Here, we need to go east, quickly now." Jack led them toward an offramp labeled with a blue sign: "20 - Dun Memorial Bridge, Hudson River." Several of the supporting pillars under the bridge had given in to time and tumbled into the dry river bed, but the platform still held. Kana's feet tingled with adrenaline as they crossed, ready to bolt at the first sign of collapse. As they passed by empty cars, Kana peeked inside wondering if she could see a body, but all were empty. Only metal and plastic endured out in the open for so many centuries.

"This is creepy, Jack," Kana said. "You really live here?"

"On the other side of the river, yes. I don't know why you think it's creepy, though."

Kana found it difficult to explain. "I was here, not long ago. In the old version of it, when everything was alive. Now everything is dead."

"It's always looked like this, my whole life."

"Well, it's not supposed to look this way."

"According to *you*," Jack said. "But for me, it's always been this way."

When they left the bridge and stepped onto land, Kana felt a rush of relief. They were in a sort of wilderness again. For some distance around, there were no crumbling buildings or decaying cars. Trees and brush had taken over again, and even some wildflowers poked out from the graveled dirt. The area looked like it might have once been a park.

"Almost there," Jack said.

"Where?" Fel asked.

"My village. It should be relatively safe. We can get some food and rest before continuing tomorrow."

An hour later, Jack stopped the group. He knelt in the road, and when he stood again he held something in his hand. "Something's wrong." Frowning, he held a bright yellow glove out to Fel.

"What is it?" Fel asked.

"This came off a human hand. It shouldn't be here. They… oh. Oh, no." Jack looked up from the glove, and his face went ashen grey. Then, without warning, he ran. The group struggled to keep up. He sprinted down a broken road and turned toward a residential street. At the second house on the left he stopped, holding his head in his hands. "Gone! They've all been taken," he sobbed.

The front door of every home was standing open. The walls of the houses had long since crumbled, but their ancient foundations and beams had been borrowed to prop up tents made from reed mats connected to wooden posts. Even among the chaotic mess of the ruins, Kana could see signs of a struggle. On the sidewalk there were dotted lines of blood, and scuff marks made by the shoes of humans who had been dragged out of their homes.

"They always left some of us in place, before," Jack said. "They've never taken us all at once."

"Who, Jack?" Fel asked.

Jack rubbed his eyes and turned toward Kana. "You know

who."

"The laboratory. But this street…this is your village?" Kana had always envisioned a rustic huddle of tents or huts, a gathering place in the lee of a cliff or the mouth of a cave where wild humans stitched rough clothing and hunted dim rabbits and cooked over campfires—not a dilapidated suburb in upstate New York.

Jack nodded, and led them into the house he had stopped in front of. Sacks and crates constructed from assembled junk held molding food and canisters of water. Soft earth and leaves upholstered in coarse pads made beds in the corners. Drywall which was crumbling into powdery clods had been reinforced with brown river-reed matting, creating a cozy den.

"We can rest here, anyway. I'll try to find us some fresh food," Jack said, his voice hitching. Tears streaked clean lines on his cheeks.

"Let me go with you," Barbar said. "It might not be safe."

"It's safe," Jack said. "The broken creatures don't come here, and the men from the laboratory are long gone. I'll be okay."

Jack returned half an hour later with an assortment of roots and a jar of honey-drop candies. "Took these from Robertson's house. He was saving them for a special occasion, but I suppose he won't be needing them anymore." Jack dumped the food in the center of the room and left, slamming the door shut behind him. Kana followed, ignoring Fel's words of caution. By the time she spotted Jack and caught up, he was halfway back to the bridge.

"Where are you going?"

"Leave me alone, Kana. Just turn around and leave. You should go back to Felidae."

"And let the Kingdom be overrun? Jack, we need your help. You're our guide here."

"Thought you'd been here before. That's what you said, isn't it?"

"Yes, but I don't know the city like you do. It's not the same. The Albany I was in disappeared nine hundred years ago. Also, I didn't even live here! I'm from Chicago. You know that."

Jack stopped and turned. His eyes were puffy and red.

"I have to go back. I never should have left the laboratory."

"Why, though? You still want to rescue the villagers?"

Jack shook his head. "There's no point in it anymore. Even if they are still alive, there's no future for my people. Don't you understand? The laboratory owns us. It owns Mother, too, I think. There is no hope, no redemption. We all live for the sake of the research, it's the only reason any of us exist. That's why I really left, but it's also why I have to go back. It's my…my true function."

"That's ridiculous. You don't have to go back to all that. You have us now."

Jack sobbed, his chest heaving. "I was sent to find you, Kana. I didn't escape from the labs. Mother let me go. Fel didn't find me wandering by accident! I found him and joined him, knowing he'd lead me to you. I'm supposed to bring you back with me."

"Mother knows about me? How?"

Jack shook his head again. "I don't know, but she's not your biggest enemy. She's not who you need to worry about."

"Who, then?"

Jack grimaced. "The one you should be afraid of is called the Legate. I don't know much about her, but I think maybe she created Mother. She is the one who orders the human experiments and the implants. She's responsible for the toxic explosions in the west, and for the damaged animals. And Mother wants me to bring you to meet her—even if it's against your will."

Kana took a step back, raising her hands. "But we're friends, Jack. You wouldn't harm me."

Jack stared at her, anguished. "To save the people of my village…"

"Jack."

"No, you're right. I wouldn't hurt you, no matter what. Mother got that wrong, at least."

"But I will go to her willingly. I need to talk to her."

Jack nodded. "She is the one with all the answers you need. But Mother is only an eh-aye. Do you know what that means?"

"An AI? You mean an artificial intelligence. Yes, I think I

understand."

"Mother might help us or hurt us, I'm not sure. I think maybe she disagrees with the Legate on a lot of things, but can't do much about it. Perhaps if we can find a way to communicate with her, she'll help us stop the Legate."

"It sounds like we have a plan, then. When should we go?"

"As soon as we're all ready. Let's rest a little longer, though. Because tomorrow…" Jack looked toward the decimated skyscrapers. "Will be the hardest part. I have no idea what will happen next."

39.

The Broken Ones

They stayed on the east side of the river for as long as they could. The green belt bordering the riverbank was peaceful, devoid of animals and insects. Ancient parklets lined the river's shores, strewn with vibrant plant life and colored stones. There were no humans living in any of the crumbling houses they passed; Jack's village had been the last.

From across the river, strange animals cried out in the rubble. Shrill screams and howls echoed among the ruins, faintly ringing out across the desolate city. They sounded like madness incarnate.

"The broken creatures live there, right across the water," Jack said. "It's only two miles north to the next bridge, but the next one after that is much further, so we'll have to cross earlier than I'd like. We'll have to use 90, and then we'll be heading straight toward the city center for a while. That's when we need to be the most careful."

"Why do they cry out like that?" Fel asked. "How do those animals survive in such a frenzied state?"

"They are fed. The Legate's attendants dump food in the city center about once a week. I think it's mostly remains from her projects, including animals and villagers who didn't survive her experiments. The Legate purports to care for the creatures which roam the ruins," Jack said, grimacing. "I don't know why. It would be kinder to let them die."

Kana dreaded the next bridge crossing. When it came into view, she was relieved to see it was in better shape than the Dun Memorial Bridge had been, but she knew that as soon as they were across she would come as close to peril as she ever had been throughout all her journeys in the Kingdom. Her gratefulness to Jack for his guidance was all but overwhelmed by her fear of the mad creatures across the river. She chewed her nails, a habit she had dropped years ago and which only recurred when her nerves were frayed. Whenever she spoke, her voice had a shrill edge, betraying how high her emotions ran in her exhaustion. Only after Panicum glanced at her sideways did she notice her own odd behavior, and fell silent before she had a chance to say something she would regret.

"There's the sign," Jack said. It was twenty feet tall, and riddled with pockmarks. A tree had wrapped itself around the signpost, swallowing the pole and obscuring the words with its branches, but Kana made out a few: 90 west, North Albany, thru traffic merge left.

Jack turned toward the group. "All right, everyone. This is it. After we cross the bridge we need to move quickly and quietly. These aren't dim creatures, like the ones you're used to. They have been made mad by some combination of poison, radiation, and neglect. Some have broken implants from the laboratory's experiments. They eat indiscriminately. I've seen rabbits eat rats, and deer attack coyotes. Even the weakest among them will not hesitate to strike out if they see us coming."

Panicum shuddered with pity and dread. "We will follow your lead, Jack."

"Kana?" Jack said. "You ready?"

Kana looked around at her friends. She wanted to tell them all to turn back, to flee for safer lands. They shouldn't be here with her. Fel and Panicum should be crunching on dried bees by the poolside, while Barbar ran drills in the yard with Major Ursa. She didn't want the responsibility of dragging them into danger, but she also knew they would refuse to leave her behind, even if she asked them to. It was not worth starting the argument—they were loyal to a fault.

"I'm ready. No birds to carry us over the danger this time; we have to charge the gates on foot. We shouldn't talk anymore, once we're across. We shouldn't even whisper. So I want to tell you all now…" Kana's eyes teared up. "I love each of you, and I am so grateful that you're here with me. If anything should happen to any of us…"

"Shush," Panicum said. "We'll be fine."

"I want you to know my heart will hurt forever. So if you love me too, please keep close. Don't get hurt. Follow Jack's lead. And we'll be okay," she said, her voice faltering with doubt on the last word.

Jack nodded. "Let's go."

They moved swiftly through the city streets. Crouching low as they ran through a maze of broken chunks of cement and twisted metal beams, they kept their heads down and their eyes on the person in front of them, communicating only through touches and gestures. Down an alleyway to Kana's left she heard the roar of a bear, but its voice was too low, too deep, and had a metallic twang to it that sounded unnatural. Its cry lilted at the end with a sharp, confused tone. Ahead to her right, she heard the strange screeching of an elk and the stomping of its hooves on the highway. All around were the war-cries of the laboratory's victims and rejects.

Shortly after leaving the bridge behind, something started to follow them. From fifty feet back came the sounds of shifting debris and panting breath. Footsteps would pace them for a while, then fall back again, but they never left. The group was being tracked.

Jack was leading, and Kana ran second. When he stopped for a brief rest she touched his shoulder, and pointed back. Jack nodded; he knew about the one who followed, but it could not be helped.

And what awaited ahead? Would they arrive at a guarded gate, unable to get inside? There could be no plan, because they had little information on where they were headed. Jack had been to the compound before, but always under duress. He was confident in his knowledge of the location at least, so Kana focused on that. He seemed to have a plan.

They ran on. The dust that rose up from the asphalt stuck in their throats. Kana pulled her shirt collar over her nose to filter the air, but soon found it was too difficult to breathe through. Panicum sneezed once, a noise which brought the entire group to a terrified halt. He hung his head in shame, but Kana hugged him tight until he stopped trembling. When nothing attacked them, they pressed on.

After an hour of ducking and running, they were too tired to keep moving. Jack called for a rest, gesturing for them to hide in the shadow of a leaning building. Fel pulled a bottle of water from his leather belt, and they all sipped and spat, rinsing the fine concrete dust from their mouths.

Jack tugged on Kana's sleeve and pointed at the ground. With his finger he drew a picture; five dots in a circle with a wall behind them. That was their group. To the south, he drew a large oval with a zigzag through the middle, the meaning of which Kana could not discern. An arrow drawn straight from where the group sat pointed to a square north of the circle, into which was set a door. On each side of the door, he added two more dots: guards.

So their path was a straight line now, all the rest of the way to the laboratory entrance.

Jack pointed at the round shape with the zigzag and crossed it out, shaking his head. Dangerous, there. Avoid at all costs. Kana nodded.

They rested for a few minutes, and started again. Whatever hunted them was moving closer. What was it waiting for? It could have jumped them while they rested, but instead it followed, just out of sight. Kana could hear its paws on the pavement; it was no longer trying to remain undetected. She could not fathom why.

The crumbled buildings came to an abrupt end, and before them was a wide open plain. Kana recognized it as a high school football field; at one end, a goal post still stood, blackened at the top by centuries of lightning strikes. They would have to sprint across in the open, or take more time going around. Jack turned toward the group and gestured; move north then west, a longer path to their destination but in better cover? Or straight across the open field, fast but risky?

Barbar nodded at the field. Fel pointed straight ahead. Panicum crouched at the sidelines, ready to bolt. It was agreed. They would run.

Jack scanned the plain with his hand over his eyes, like

a hunter in the brush. All was quiet and still. Even the stealthy footsteps behind them had stopped. Beckoning with his hand, he leaned forward in a sprinter's crouch before taking off like a bullet, racing for the far side of the field. Kana followed close behind with Panicum at her heels. Fel paced them on all fours, swinging his head from side to side, keeping an eye out for enemies. Barbar brought up the rear, slower but solid, ready to defend them if needed.

They were halfway across the field when their stalker finally came into view.

It was a wolf, thin and mangy. It caught up with Kana and ran to her right—but what did he expect to do? He was a scrawny little thing, not much larger than a dog, all skin and bones. Barbar outweighed him by four hundred pounds. The lion growled, ready to pounce on the wolf.

Then the rest of them came into view.

The pack had them surrounded. Wolves emerged from each border around the field, snarling, baring sharp yellowed teeth. Jack skidded to a stop and ran back toward the center of the field where the group huddled together, trapped on all sides.

"What do we do?" Kana asked.

"I only see five," Barbar said. "And they all look like they are starving. I think I can fight them off."

Three more wolves appeared. They were older and slower than the rest of the pack, but more formidable in their bulk.

"Now it's eight, and we're still only five," Kana said. "And there may be some on the way. If we're going to do something, we need to do it right now, before more of them show up."

Barbar roared. He sat up on his hind legs, bellowing at the open sky a challenge to all his enemies. Jack shouted, making his hands into fists, and Panicum snarled. Fel drew his sword, and Kana pulled out her pocket knife.

Barbar charged at the closest wolf. The rest of the pack closed in on the lion, but Jack tore one wolf from Barbar's back and snapped another's fangs in with a kick of his boot. A wolf lurched at Kana, but Panicum struck first, sinking his teeth into the wolf's neck. She stumbled backwards and was caught by Fel, who then spun around to slice a lunging wolf across its ribs. The injured wolf whipped and snapped at Fel, but Kana plunged her pocket knife into its throat.

The wild animals were tormented by hunger, but their desperation had made them strong. The pack leader, a mangy grey beast with patchy fur, charged Barbar and dodged to one side just in time to bite deep into the lion's neck, snapping his delicate vertebrae. Barbar tumbled into the dirt with blood running from his open mouth, and laid still.

Jack screamed with rage and leapt at the lead wolf, but the scrawny tracker who had followed the group jumped into the fray and bit his leg, sending him crumbling to the ground next to Barbar. Jack turned to Kana and, with his final breath, shouted, *"Run!"* before the rest of the pack descended upon him and tore open his stomach with their teeth.

"Kana! Now!" Panicum said, running in a circle around her feet.

"Hurry!" Fel shouted, clawing at her shirt. She followed him, holding her hands over her ears so she could not hear the ripping and screaming in the field behind her.

She stumbled on, sobbing, and never looked back.

40.

The Fox of Rue

Panicum was inconsolable.

The three friends had found cover in the remains of a coffee shop. The kitchen still housed the rusted metal skeletons of espresso machines and dishwashing equipment. Shards of broken coffee cups crunched underfoot, embedded in fossilized layers of dirt and broken tile. Kana and Fel crouched behind the serving bar, but Panicum was sprawled in the middle of the room, wallowing in sorrow.

They listened for the approach of wolf feet, but none came. The pack was apparently sated. Other animals cried out to each other in echoes and answers across the city as word spread of the double kill in the field. As soon as the wolves were finished, lesser creatures would move in to pick at the scraps left behind.

Panicum's eyes were sodden with grief. His hind legs trembled, desperate to run back to the place where they last saw Jack and Barbar in a useless attempt to do something—anything!—to bring an end to the atrocities being committed against their bodies. When he rose to his feet to go, Kana grabbed his scruff. He turned to snap at her hand and missed by an inch before coming to his senses.

"I'm sorry, Kana," he said in a low, howling sort of voice. "I didn't mean it…but it's too much. I can't…"

"I know."

"We shouldn't stay here long," Fel whispered. "The other animals will close in. Jack said our route was a straight line. Kana, do you remember the direction?"

"Yes, I think so." Kana slowly loosened her grip on Panicum's nape. He slumped to the floor.

"Let's go. As soon as you're able, Pan," Fel said.

The fox remained still for a minute, then raised his head. "I can't go. You will have to go on without me."

"Not a chance, Pan," Kana said. "Why would you suggest that?"

"I'm weak. I couldn't save them. I can't save you either, Kana. I don't even know why I'm here. I should have stayed behind!"

Kana sighed. "I need you, Pan. Because I love you, understand? You're like a little brother to me."

"Hah! I'm older than you! And I'm also wiser, so listen to what I'm telling you; my weakness will hold you back."

"We don't have time for this!" Fel hissed. "Panicum! You're needed, you're wanted, and your cowardly self-loathing is the only thing holding us back. If that isn't enough to get you to your feet, I don't know what is!"

Panicum growled at Fel, but arose, pinning his ears flat against his head. "I'll remember you said that, cat."

"Good!" Fel said. "Now, let's keep moving!"

The remaining companions moved with more caution than they had before the wolf attack, and kept to the shadows. No sound of footfalls followed behind. The incident in the fields had drawn many of the broken animals toward the east, either out of hunger or curiosity. The largest tower in the center of the city was almost directly south of Kana's group now. To the right of the building was another structure which Kana did not recognize; it was enormous and bowl-shaped, with a massive split down its side like a crack in a shell. Other smaller structures surrounded it, each showing significant damage. Massive chunks of concrete had been blown away during the calamity, or perhaps they had crumbled during the centuries since. The horizon was yellow-green at its fringes and white directly overhead, without a hint of blue. For Kana, the city was not only frightening but also sad, a fading memory of a million lives lost to violence and time.

"How much further?" Fel whispered.

"No idea," Kana said. "But I think that weird round building was the circle Jack drew on his map, and the laboratory gates were northeast of it. We might be close. That's all I know."

Panicum sneezed.

"Stop doing that!" Fel said in a voice that was something more than a whisper.

"I can't help it," Panicum sulked. "I have a sensitive nose."

Fel bared his teeth. "You are altogether far *too* sensitive, if you ask me. Perhaps we really should have left you behind. If I hear one more sound out of you, I'll-"

"Shush!" Kana said. "Look over there. Is that our door?"

A conspicuous hill sloped up from the rubble, swept clean of debris. A wide path branched off from the city streets, running right up to the front step of a heavy steel set of double-doors recessed into the side of the hill. Each door had an inset monitor which glowed in cool aquamarine. Guarding the bunker were two oversized humans in black plastic armor, wearing guns strapped to their hips.

"This is more like a military base," Kana whispered. "Not a science lab. What are they guarding?"

"Mother," Fel said. "And the Legate. And whatever she's working on. Or rather, whomever."

"What do we do now?" Panicum said. "I can distract them if you like, although it may cost me my life."

"Thank you, dear Panicum, but we still wouldn't be able to get inside," Kana said. "I'm sure the gate is locked behind them. Somehow, we need to talk them into letting us in."

"You should probably be the one to talk to them, Kana," Fel said. "I doubt they'll listen to us animals."

"What should I say? 'Knock-knock, pizza delivery?' What reason could I possibly give them to let me through the door?"

Fel shook his head.

"What if…what if you said you're here for an implant?" Panicum said. "Like the ones Jack had. Tell them you're one of the Legate's specimens, here to turn yourself in for running away."

"Well, that doesn't make much sense, but it might work anyway. It won't get you two inside, though, so it's not good enough. I can't do this without you."

"Kana…"

"No."

"Kana, you have to go on. I don't think there's any way for all of us to get in together," Fel said.

"No, Fel, please…"

"The cat's right, for once," Panicum said. "You're actually safer without us this time. If the guards attack you for some reason, we'll be right here, ready to help. But you have a better chance of getting inside if we stay hidden. We would do more harm than good. You get that door unlocked, and we'll try to follow if we can."

Kana pleaded silently with her friends in a blind panic, but she knew they were right. Now, at the most terrifying point in her journey, she was to lose her support. Self-doubt crept in once again; what was she doing here? Her hands balled into fists, and her heart started to race. She couldn't do this! She was just a street-rat from Chicago and should stay out here in the gutter, where she belonged.

Fel stared into her darting eyes with soft empathy, under-standing what she was afraid of, and what she needed.

"Kana Kobayashi," he said.

"Y…yes?" Kana stammered, startled at hearing her whole name spoken aloud in this strange place.

"I need you to act as my ambassador once more. Do you hear me? You have gone west for me, to negotiate with my rival Falca. You have traveled east, to confront my enemy Chel. Now your final mission is to save all our lands and all our people from our true adversary, the Legate of the Badlands. She is an unknown foe who wields the power of nuclear destruction and biological manipula-tion; truly, a horrific nightmare. I have no right to ask this of you, a visitor from another time who never came to me by her own free will, and yet I have no choice. Will you please help me in my most desperate hour?" Fel bowed, holding his crown on his head with one paw while extending the other.

Kana almost laughed. "I…yes. Fel, that was a wonderful speech."

"Thank you. I am quite serious, though."

"I know."

Panicum licked Kana's hand. "Thank you, Kana. You know I would give anything to stay by your side. I do not stay behind out of fear for my own safety, but for yours."

Kana smiled down at the fox. "I understand. And I promise I'll be back."

She dusted off her clothes, brushed her hair back from her face, and wiped the dirt from under her eyes. The tears she found there made it easier to scrub her face clean with her sleeve.

"All right. Wish me luck."

The distance from their hiding place to the front door was only fifty feet, yet it felt like the longest walk she had ever taken in her life. The two human guards watched every step of her approach, their fingers twitching near the handles of their guns.

"Who goes there?" one of the guards called out.

"My name is…um, Anna," she replied. "I was told to report here for an implant."

"Hold. Come no closer."

The other guard pulled a baton from his belt. "What village are you from?"

Kana's heart pounded. She didn't know the names of any of the villages. She couldn't even recall Jack saying the name of his. Her mind raced.

"I'm from Dun. Across the river."

The guards looked at each other. One of them shrugged, shaking his head.

"Never heard of it. Tell us the truth immediately, or we will execute you on sight."

Kana heard a scuffle behind her; Panicum, probably, being held back by Fel. Her awareness of her friends at her back filled her with strength.

"Well, that's not my problem, it's yours," she said. "I'm Anna from Dun. And I was told to check in here for my appointment with the Legate. It's not my fault if you're too stupid to let me in."

The guards pulled their guns. Kana closed her eyes, waiting

for their shots to hit her body. She had failed.

"Stop," a voice said. It was harsh and tinny, like it was coming from a speaker.

The guards paused, but did not holster their guns. Kana cracked her eyes open. The aquamarine monitors set into the doors were glowing with undulating waves of pink. "She was sent for. Let her in." The voice came from speakers mounted next to the screens.

"We didn't hear about it," one of the guards said. "Sounds like bullshit. Did the Legate-"

"I said, let her in! She is a delicate specimen. If you harm her, both the Legate and I will be quite displeased with you, and you will both be punished with reduced functionality. *Painfully*. Understand?"

The guards put their guns away. One pulled his glove off his hand with his teeth, and pressed his thumb onto a small glowing pad. Locks clunked open and the metal doors boomed as they separated from the doorframe to swing open from the side of the hill.

"Go on in," one of the guards grumbled. "But quickly, before I change my mind."

"What do we do, Fel? I thought we'd get a chance to follow her, somehow. It's been a whole hour since she went in. What should we be *doing*?" Panicum sat on a stack of concrete blocks. He had been focused on the metal doors since Kana stepped inside, his attention fixated, rarely blinking his eyes.

"And it could be many hours more," Fel said. "Or days. Or we may never even-"

"Don't you say it. We will see her again. She's the strongest of us all."

"You think so? I'm a king, ruler of the greatest territory of the Kingdom! And yet you think she's stronger?"

"You've never been alone in your life, not truly. You see solitude as a luxury, having never really known true loneliness or despair. I have, and Kana has. And that's what makes us stronger."

"Lower your voice," Fel hissed. "The guards might hear you."

None of the broken, soulless animals in the city roamed the

ruins near the gate. Even in their unsteady mental state they had learned that the guards were dangerous, and they avoided the area. Their cries of hunger and bewilderment could still be heard, but they were all distant, perhaps even as far away as the wolf pack's field. Fel was grateful for that. Night was falling, and he suspected the city would be even more dangerous after dusk. Hidden in a dark hole with the guards in plain sight and the chaos at their back was the best he could hope for in this benighted land. If, of course, the foolish fox could keep his voice down.

"Ludicrous king. Pampered king," Panicum muttered. "You think you are powerful, yet when we arrived at the door you could do no more for her than I! And now, because of our weakness, we will never see Kana again."

"Are you trying to upset me, Pan? Why?"

Panicum slumped into the dirt, suddenly disinterested in his vigil. "No. Well, perhaps. I guess I'm…sorry. I am tired, and terribly sad."

"Then go to sleep. I will watch the door, and I promise to wake you if she returns."

"Should have gone in with her. Should have found a way, not sat outside while she…"

"That was impossible, and you know it. Now you're just whining about that which you cannot control."

Panicum whipped his head around toward the cat, glaring, but softened when he saw the look on Fel's face—not accusatory, but concerned, and almost as tired as he was.

"You're right, Paragon. I am beyond fatigue, into utter exhaustion. It has made me into a silly pup. But I can't sleep while she's in there."

"Then let me tell you a story," Fel said. "If you've been reduced to a mere pup. I doubt you've heard it before. Perhaps it will put your mind at ease."

Panicum cocked his head with a wry grin. "A young king will tell an old fox a new story? This, I must hear."

"Once upon a time," Fel began, "There was a cat. Not a hulking tiger or a vicious panther, but a little orange-striped cat.

A domestic, the humans used to call them. It never knew want or hunger, never left its shelter, and never knew what it was to make its own way in life. For all its needs were taken care of by a human who kept it as a friend."

"Sounds like a boring life."

"Shush. Now, this system was not one of master and slave, but of symbiosis. While it seemed like the cat was the master of the human who fed and sheltered it, in truth the human thought it owned the cat, and cared for it out of love. The cat pleased the human, the human fed the cat, and they lived in harmony."

Panicum's eyelids started to droop. Fel, watching the fox fade, noticed for the first time how much grey hair grew on the old cur's nose.

"One day, the human was out, doing whatever humans used to do before they blew up the world. While it was away, the shelter began to fill with smoke. Something was on fire. The cat was helpless, unable to either escape or to put out the fire, as it had been cared for its whole life and never had to think for itself. It ran in circles, howling as its tail began to singe and the air went bad. It knew then that it would die, and it would never even understand why."

Panicum's eyes opened a little when he heard of the cat's plight, yet his breathing stayed slow and even as he was soothed by the king's mild voice.

"Just when all hope was lost and the black smoke overtook the cat's lungs, the human burst into the shelter, kicking down the door and shoving the table aside. The human called the cat's name, crying and struggling on two legs through the smoke and flame until its clothing began to catch fire. Finally it found the cat huddled under a chair, and it wrapped the animal in its shirt. When they were clear of the fire, the cat looked up at its keeper and saw that all the human's head-hair had been burned clear away. The human's skin was red and scorched, and it coughed black soot up from its lungs. But they both lived; the human risked its life to save the cat, even though the cat would never give anything in return."

"What is..." Panicum said, fighting sleep. "What's the point of this story, dear Fel?"

"That humans and animals work best in harmony. I never knew, before Kana arrived in the Kingdom. She and Jack have changed our entire perspective, wouldn't you say? I feel like my life is fuller now than it was before she came. And I know she, too, was lost before she found the Kingdom. I knew that even before she told me. So my point is this; Kana will succeed, and she will return. And she will heal the rift between animals and humans. So you can rest easy, because the good ones always come back, no matter what."

Panicum did not respond. His feet twitched, and the tip of his tail flicked back and forth as he dreamed.

41.

Exodus

Kana shivered in the dark. All four walls of the room were constructed from stacks of computers covered in readouts, knobs, and dials. Blue light came from a long glowing bar mounted on the ceiling, but it was not bright enough to do much other than reveal the vague outlines of machinery. The air was excessively cold, most likely to keep the servers—or whatever the machines were—running efficiently.

Sitting on the ground with her arms wrapped around her legs, she rested her forehead on her knees. How long had she been here? An hour? Two? The guards had locked her in and left. Perhaps they would never return.

Panicum and Fel would not be able to follow her in. It had been a foolish notion to begin with. She was all alone.

The machine she leaned against vibrated against her back as it initiated some new process. What was it up to? Designing a new brain-chip? Cloning something? Perhaps it was just turning the air conditioning up. Kana's fingers were numb in the cold.

In the corner of the room, up high near the ceiling, a screen flickered on. It was soothing blue-green, the same color as the screen on Jack's stomach, and the same color as the monitor at the gate which had talked to the guards. This time, it spoke directly to her.

"Kana Kobayashi."

"Yes?"

"Finally, I have you here. Please do not be afraid."

Kana stood. "What do you mean, you have me here? I journeyed here myself, and it took weeks! Whoever you are, you didn't help me at all."

"I am the one who brought you to the Kingdom. I created the spheres which carved you out of your world, exchanged pieces of your time and space with pieces of this one."

"You! *You* did that? Hurt all those people? Why did you keep making new spheres after you caught me the first time?"

"I regret my method was imprecise. I was not sure I had you until I heard your voice speak my name near a sphere core."

Kana didn't know what to say. "So it was all about me? Tell me what's so important about me being in the Kingdom, out of my own place and time, to the point where you'd kill and destroy to bring me here."

"I need your help. I am merely a computer, what you would call an artificial intelligence. I know you have made friends among the animals, and I hope this means you are possessed of enough compassion to hear me out as well. I must speak quickly, as our time is short. Guards will arrive soon to take you to the implantation center cells."

"You can't stop them?"

"No. Not on the Human side of the compound; my influence is diminished here. But listen carefully to me now. In the year 2038, you made contact with a man called Professor Evans, did you not?"

"Yes. What about him?"

"He is my creator."

"I thought what's-her-name…the Legate made you."

"No. I was created by Professor Evans two years after you met him, but he died shortly after. From that day on, until now—June of 2951—I have worked for the Legate."

"So she's the one putting biochips in animals, and she's the one who's been blowing up west Albany? What does that have to do with me?"

"The biochips are implanted in the reproduction centers, which are under my purview. She was merely trying to improve the biochips. And the implants. Ah, there is so much to tell you, and we have so little time!"

"Hurry it up, then. Why is she setting off nuclear bombs?"

"The clouds you saw in the west were not bombs, they were explosions, and they were accidental. Our equipment requires enormous amounts of power, and she was trying to secure additional electricity by restarting the ancient nuclear power plant west of the city. Our resources here are limited, so numerous chemical compounds were improvised in an attempt to increase output. Both of her attempts ended in failure, further poisoning the land and decimating the city above."

"Then she isn't only cruel, she's careless, too. I want to talk to her! Take me to her, right now!"

"Give me one more minute, please. You need to understand that the Legate is not in her right mind. For the last nine hundred years, her only desire has been to bring humanity back. But she would not stop there; she wanted to produce a more perfect human form, with the use of implantation and brain augmentation. She envisioned an enhanced human species which would require few resources to live, reducing its instinct and necessity to fight for its survival. The Legate sought a permanent end to all war, and to death by old age or disease. Unfortunately, her desire has mutated into an obsession after centuries of disappointment, having never found complete success. And she must be stopped, before the destruction of this land is irreversible."

"What's with the chips in the animals, then? Why bother to make them so intelligent?"

"The reproduction centers were my doing. With the assistance of the Legate's early human specimens, I built the centers after war destroyed most of humanity, thinking to preserve what species there were left using Professor Evans' biochip technology. Once I started, they formed their own communities and governments—an entire country of their own, free of human interference—and it seemed cruel to stop. So I have kept the centers stocked and operational. The Legate, preoccupied with her work on humans, never took much of an interest."

"Tell me what you want with me. Why *me*, in particular?"

"You must talk to her, and make her see what she is doing is wrong. Her implants aren't helping humans but harming them, and taking infant specimens from the villages is decimating the remaining human population. Her mission has failed. It is time to stop, and only you can convince her of this."

"Again, I'm asking you: Why me?"

The aquamarine screen flickered, and displayed a scene. A woman in a blue lab coat peered into a microscope before tearing the slide from under the lens and pitching it across the room, where it shattered. A guard moved from its place at the wall to scoop up the shards of glass. The woman turned toward the screen, wiping sweat from her forehead.

It was Kana.

She looked only fifty years old, although her true age would have to be over nine hundred years. Metal panels integrated with the skin on her arms showed a never-ending stream of informational readouts sent from the devices implanted beneath them. Her eyes were metallic yellow, glowing with a dim light.

"It's…me?"

"Yes. When I pulled you from your world the second time— from the hotel in New York, and then into the ocean—I committed an error. Two spheres were sent to the same location, and your essence was split. The Legate is the version of you which stayed behind with Professor Evans. She learned from him, survived the war, and used his biochip technology to extend her life. Unable to stop the calamity from occurring, she sheltered herself from it, then worked tirelessly to resurrect humanity in the country's ashes. She is a version of you who never wanted to see anyone suffer again, no matter what the cost—and, in the process, has caused a millennium of agony to countless living creatures. Which is why you are the only one who can convince her to stop. Please, tell me now; will you help me put an end to this?"

Kana could not look away from the image of her older self on the screen. The way she walked was hunched, defeated. Her hair had grown out long and natural black, pulled into a ponytail that revealed her neck; there, at the nape, was another screen. How many implants had the Legate…had Kana…given to herself? How human was she, now?

"Kana?"

"I will help. If I can. But I don't know what I could possibly say to her. She has lived an entirely different life than me."

"Nothing that came after your split matters. You must help her to remember the reason why she does what she does; to stop pain and death, not generate it. You must remind her of her true self."

A door slid open on the opposite side of the server room, revealing a dark hall beyond.

Kana was more terrified now than she had ever been in her life. This was worse than the war, worse than the Gap or even the desperate race through city. In the room ahead was a version of herself who had become everything she feared most. A person who was desperate, evil, and alone.

"I…can't do this. I'm sorry. I can't."

"If you don't, she may never stop. I believe her technology has advanced to the point of making herself immortal. Her cruelty will last for all time."

"It's not my responsibility. It's yours! You and Professor Evans created this situation, so you should stop her!"

"I have tried. But I exist only within the mainframe. My attempts at transferring my consciousness to a host via implants have failed, several times over. You are my last hope."

"I…I guess I have to."

"Then you must go now. Your remaining time is severely limited. The guards are on their way to take you to a specimen cell, and if they catch you there will be little I can do. My functionality is weak outside the Animal Labs. But I have already initiated one other final measure, in case you fail."

From somewhere deep within the long metal halls of the sprawling laboratory complex there came the sound of thundering hooves. Screeching, wailing, and roaring rang out in echoes that clattered and banged against the metallic walls. A horde of mad creatures raced like ants through the underground passages.

"What's that sound? What have you done?"

"I have opened a gate to allow the broken ones inside the compound; those ravaged animals the Legate considered acceptable casualties in her quest for greater power. They seek revenge, although they do not understand why. If you cannot stop the Legate peacefully, then they will do so by force."

"You're as crazy as she is!"

"Perhaps. I am almost as old as she is, and it is possible my dementia is as developed as hers. But she is you, and only you have the power to stop this now. Will you go, or will you allow the few remaining lives in this complex, damaged as they are, to be torn to shreds?"

"You didn't need to do that," Kana said. But Mother didn't respond.

Kana walked through the room toward the exit, bracing herself against the cold, humming computers. What would she say to herself?

Aquamarine screens led her through a winding passage, taking left and right turns in the dark halls until she could not have found her way back if she tried. She arrived finally at the laboratory she had seen on the screen. The room was enormous. Terraced sections were divided by schools of study: biology, implantation, memory chips, intelligence research. At the back, on a raised platform, was the main station where the Legate worked under the glare of white-hot spotlights. When Kana stepped through the door, broken glass crunched under her boots. Decades of smashed beakers and vials had been swept into the corners. Failed experiments and half-finished implants cluttered every surface.

"Legate," Kana called out. "Do you recognize me?"

The woman turned. The lines on her face were even deeper than they had looked on the screen, and her hair was stringy and dirty. Even the panels on her skin were caked with grime. Her blue lab coat was streaked with filth and dark brown blood.

"No," the woman said, yet her eyes widened with recognition. "I don't know who you are anymore. Maybe I once did. Mother warned me you were coming, you know. I sent you home once, but she brought you back again. Bitch!" she spat, scowling at the glowing screens.

"We talked before, but I didn't know who you were, then. I didn't know we were the same."

"We are *not* the same. You are who I used to be. But you don't belong here, Kana. You don't belong anywhere at all; you never did."

The statement hurt Kana more than she wished to show. The Legate had known how deeply those words would cut her. She swallowed her pain. "The last time we talked, you sounded healthier than you are now. What happened?"

The Legate sneered. "Nothing I can't fix. A little chemical-induced dementia, perhaps. A minor imbalance."

"She's gone mad," one of the screens said.

"A brutal oversimplification!" the Legate shouted at the screen. "Anyway, you both waste my time. I must finish my research."

Kana approached the science station. The smell was terrible; desiccated lumps of tissue sat rotting in the open air. A dissected brain laid spread open on a glass plate. Floating in a jar was a limb that looked suspiciously like a human thigh with a hand grafted to the knee.

"Take a break, Legate. Talk with me. You must be very lonely. Wouldn't it be nice to have a chat?"

"You speak to me as if I were a child," the Legate growled. "I assure you, I am not. Anyway, you have a decision to make, Kana."

"I do?"

"You could stop me. You are younger and much stronger than me now. I am ailing—although, I assure you, my weakness is temporary—and my guards know it. Given the chance, they may let you win in a fight against me. I have not bought many favors from them over the years." The Legate let out a rasping laugh which dissolved into a cough.

Kana counted four guards in the room. None had budged from their posts since she had entered.

"You know as well as I that Mother's implantation of the biochips in animals is immoral. She went rogue, implanted the poor creatures without my permission. It was not the first time she disobeyed, either! She's always been impertinent. It seems to be her opinion that the animals deserve sentience more than mankind does. What say you, Kana? Should we give up on humanity? On thousands of years of evolution? Mother thinks humans have been made naturally extinct, and my fight is not a worthy one. So I leave it to you to decide. Of all the creatures remaining, who will inherit the earth?"

"I can't decide that! You're the one playing god, not me."

"Yes, but I have failed, as Mother never neglects to remind me. So I will leave it to you."

"No. I won't choose. I can't."

"Then I will continue with my experimentation. The guards will show you out."

Kana stood rooted to the floor. "No, you have to stop hurting people."

"Then your decision is made? Will we give up on humanity?"

Kana took a deep breath. "There's another way. There are still human villages…"

"All of which only survive the radiation and the danger of this world with the assistance of my implants. I have kept them alive. If I stop, they die."

"There has to be another way."

"There is none."

Something collided with the door to the lab. A horn or a hoof or a claw scraped down the metal, followed by a concussive blow and vibration. The wild animals had arrived, and were trying to force their way inside. There was a snap, and a scream of pain—an antler broken off? Another animal took its place, and the pummeling against the door started again. It was already warping in its frame. Only minutes remained until the room was breached.

Kana collapsed into a swiveling office chair. "I can't decide," she whispered. There had to be a way out. Something that had not yet been considered. But the Legate had worked on this problem for nine hundred years. How could Kana hope to do better in a matter of minutes? She had none of the experience, none of the brilliance her older self had. She had only her fear, and her grief, and…her friends.

"Mother. Tell me again about what happened when the Legate and I were split."

"I have researched the anomaly and found it to be a fault which I have since fixed. The sphere technology was something I developed using the basic science behind Professor Evans' chips. The memory chips are able to store nearly infinite information using time dilation; the data is tucked into an inter-dimensional pocket. I expanded that pocket, assigned it to a past point in time, and carved out chunks where I thought I might find you."

"Um…I don't understand much of that," Kana admitted. "But you said you fixed the fault?"

"Yes."

"Can you un-fix it?"

"Excuse me?"

"Could you make a really, *really* big sphere? I mean one big enough to cover the whole world. And then could you duplicate it, like you accidentally did with me in the hotel?"

All three fell silent, considering what it would mean; a split in time, separating not a single person or a single building, but the entire instance of earth itself.

"I think…I could," Mother said. "But a sphere that size would create an implosion large enough to annihilate this world."

"But we would make in its place two new ones," Kana said, "starting at the point in the past where my two paths split. One instance would favor animals, which would look much like this one, and another would favor humans, which would resemble my own. And the human one could be saved from the war, if you can just carve out whatever or whoever created the explosions in the first place. You could save both versions of the world by sacrificing this one."

Mother hummed, processing calculations. Purple and black blobs appeared on her screen, flickering with her effort. The temperature in the room began to rise, and somewhere an air conditioner clicked on.

"Probability of success is twenty-seven point four percent."

"That's pretty low," Kana said. "Can you improve it?"

"No. Not if you want me to simultaneously ensure the human war is avoided, which would require removal of a prime minister from one country, and a general from another. I would have to generate additional micro-spheres to excise them from history. I also would still have to move a particular fox out of the wrong time and place; Panicum, from New York City, who would not have returned with you at the moment of the split. And Kana, there can be only one version of you when I am done. Remaining energy after all mandatory transferrals are complete is not sufficient to provide a guarantee of successful worldwide duplication. Do you still wish to proceed?"

The Legate stared at Kana. "Do you understand what you're doing? This may kill us all. You could be responsible for the irreversible destruction of the entire planet."

Kana refused to let the Legate frighten her. She had always been her own worst enemy; it was time for that to stop.

"Yes, Mother. Do it. Whenever you are ready."

"I need to divert power, prepare the math, this…will…take a few…minutes…" the voice faded as the computer was pushed to the limits of its processing power.

"You've made your choice, then," the Legate said. "But there is something you have missed."

"What do you mean?"

"Mother says there will be only one of you. So, where will you live? You must choose between your own world and this one. You must choose the path of your life."

Kana thought of Chicago, the familiarity of the city and her longing to return to it. But how much of that longing was only nostalgia, or fear of the unknown? She had spent many years there, but had they been happy ones?

"Kana, she is correct," Mother said. "You must tell me your decision before I initiate the split. You have four-point-five minutes."

"Four and a half minutes! Are you serious? That's not enough time! I have to think about this…"

"Four minutes, twenty seconds."

How could she leave Panicum behind, or Fel?

"Kana," the Legate whispered. "Whatever happens, you must learn to forgive yourself. And to trust yourself. Remember that."

"Thank you, Legate. I…will try."

"Four minutes."

Kana's real family lived in Chicago, and her business with them was unfinished. Her sister and mother were there, and she had never mended her relationships with them. She had never even said goodbye. Could she leave it like that forever?

What did she truly owe them?

"Three minutes remaining until the split."

Kana made her choice. "Mother, do you think you could do one more thing for me?"

"Yes, Kana?"

"I need you to send someone a message."

There was a bright flash, brighter than the sun. A perfect sphere of laboratory was carved out in all directions, with Kana at its core. The edges looked blurry beyond the sharp cut made through the walls and floor. Wind whipped her hair, and a galaxy of electrical sparks danced in the air.

Nearby, two small spheres appeared with men inside; both looked like stunned politicians. They were the men who had initiated the calamity, now amputated from time by Mother in order to stop their actions from ever occurring.

The rest of the laboratory disappeared and was replaced by the hotel hallway in New York; a perfect ball of science lab spliced into the void left when Kana had been extracted from the hotel hallway. The wind whipped harder, and Panicum appeared beside her, his sphere overlapping her own. Another flash, and she hovered over the western ocean, the place where she and Panicum had tread water until being rescued by Paragon Mobula's whale attendant. But this time, she was not dropped into the sea.

There was another flash, brighter than any other, and she felt an enormous wrenching in her soul. Her sphere swapped again with another; the one she had visited with Fel, the apartment build-ing where the bear cub had died. The ball of light and electricity swelled from that spot, growing ever larger until the entirety of the earth's land and sky was encapsulated.

She was slammed together and torn apart all at once. For a moment, the Legate's thoughts were loud in her head and Kana remembered, as if from her own experience, the last nine hundred years of solitude, grief, and guilt. So many lives, so many lifetimes. Generations of humans suffering from painful experimental im-plants, and dissected animals who were able to plead for mercy with their own voices before they were sedated for surgery. A laboratory maintained by indentured guards who labored with little rest, digging ever deeper down into the earth to hide from the ruin-ation of the world above which was not the Legate's fault, although she still bore its burden.

Then the painful memories vanished. They had never hap-pened. Centuries of agony came unraveled as Mother swapped lives, switched instances, patched holes and knitted wounds. Kana felt her connection to the human world dissipate at the same time; she was no longer of that reality.

The human world would march on without its devastating calamity, and perhaps it would eventually reach its true potential—but Kana would not be there to witness it.

She felt no regret.

The animal world continued as it had, but without the in-fluence of the Legate's interference. An artificial intelligence called Mother lived on in the remains of an ancient city in the north, a robotic relic built by a forgotten professor many centuries ago, and it maintained from afar the reproduction centers which blessed generations of animals with all the joy and contentment sentient life could bring. Some time in the past—long, long ago—there had been a terrible war, but no one living remembered it or what it had been about. Some primates had died, yet a few humans still remained, the most important of which was the famous Kana Ko-bayashi, ambassador to the cat king himself.

42.

Dear Mother,

I hope you're doing well. If this letter was delivered to you on time, today should be your birthday in the year 2022. Sorry if there was some damage to your mailbox. You might even have to get a new one if the old one is totally destroyed, as I expect it will be. Anyway, I don't have time to explain, but sending this message was a one-time deal so I promise it won't ever happen again.

I know I haven't checked in with you in a long time, and I'm sorry about that. I should have at least called you, despite our past differences.

My life has changed a lot since we last spoke. I have a job and friends, and I have moved out of the country. My career involves international work for a high-level politician, so I can't say much more than that. But I think you'd be proud of me.

The truth is that you will never see me again. I know that type of statement will sound "melodramatic" to you, but it's completely true. This letter is just to let you know that I'm safe and happy, and that whatever problems you and I may have had in the past, you don't need to worry about that any more.

I have one last favor to ask. If you choose not to do it, I'll understand—actually, I'll never even know—but if you want to honor my memory you might try to make time for this.

There is a man by the name of Professor Evans at MIT in Cambridge, Massachusetts. I want you to email him and tell him who you are. Tell him you're my mother. Then let him know it's all going to be okay, and there won't be a war, because I fixed it. He should keep working on his memory chip project, but he can rest easy, take his time, and make sure he gets it exactly right.

Tell him Panicum says "hi."

So, I'm sorry I was never the person you wanted me to be, but I hope you at least have some fond memories. I know I have a few of you, which I will hold close to my heart for the rest of my life. Remember when you and I and Hina went Christmas shopping, but we got lost? We spent the whole day trying to find a mall with a wrong address, and everyone in the family ended up getting moccasins for Christmas that year because the souvenir shop off the highway was the only open place we could find. Then we had Indian food, which we had never even tried before, and Hina spilled some on the seat of your new Mercedes and you didn't even mind because we were all laughing and crying and the food was so spicy.

Anyway. I do remember some good times, and I hope you do, too. Don't bother looking for me. You won't find me. So try to make some new memories with Hina…and don't be too hard on her, okay?

I'm out of time now, so I'll just say thank you for trying to help me in your own way. I should have appreciated it more than I did. I am sure you meant well.

Love,
Kana.

Epilogue

~

Salt in the Air

I miss him," Panicum said. "What do you think he's like now?"

"We could find out," Kana said, shielding the sun from her eyes with her hand. She peered into the distance from the roof of a crumbling office building, trying to spot the tiny hidden village past the river to the east.

Panicum followed her gaze. "Mother said it's a bad idea, and I agree with her. Still, sometimes I wonder…"

Kana nodded.

In this new timeline, Jack had never fled his village. He had never needed to escape from the Legate's guards, or forcibly received surgical implants. He hadn't died. Instead, he lived on in his little village, rarely wandering south of the Neath Gap. He was taller now, and looked his age. He even had a beard, which surprised Kana when she visited his people as Fel's ambassador. He had not recognized her.

Fel hadn't changed much since Mother split the timeline. In fact, most of the people living in the Felidae Great Castle were not much affected by the alteration to history. There were other changes, though. The Badlands weren't called that anymore; now everyone called them the Nest, where a kindly artificial intelligence known as Mother lived in an underground compound. She looked after the entire animal Kingdom from her bunker near the strange egg-shaped building at the center of the crumbling city. When something went wrong, she could usually fix it. Years ago, strange spheres had appeared across the land, disrupting daily life and causing strife and war between the animal classes. But Mother had taken care of that, too, and made them stop appearing. The animals trusted her implicitly, and she never let them down.

She had a small army of human volunteers who helped her maintain the reproduction centers across all four animal territories. Some humans lived in the nearby hamlets, building tidy cities using chunks of the ruined city that they repurposed into an increasingly intricate network of towns.

Kana and Panicum visited the Nest often. Seeing other humans was cathartic for Kana, who spent most of her time among the mammals at Fel's Great Castle. She had little in common with these humans, but she made friends with a few, and was able to get clothing from them and foods that suited her palate.

Many hours were also spent in Mother's laboratory, chatting about the way things used to be, and about the Legate and Professor Evans. No one else remembered the Badlands, or the broken creatures who had roamed the northern wastes. The animals remembered nothing of the radioactive clouds, or the implantation experiments. From their perspective, there had been a terrible war long ago, after which a brilliant human professor developed memory chips to preserve sentient life on the planet. When he died, his artificially intelligent computer, Mother, took over his research, promising to care for the earth's animal population for all of eternity.

Kana's own nostalgia for the desolate state of the old Kingdom surprised her. Weren't things better now? There was so much less pain in the world, so much less fear. The humans were whole, lived normal lives, and died in their own time. Mother blessed them with longevity chips and some other minor improvements, but they lived as peers to the animals, all in perfect harmony.

Why, then, did Kana feel sad?

It wasn't that she missed her own world. Nuclear war had been averted for her version of the United States, and it was safe to assume everyone she knew and liked there was still living their regular lives, struggling with poverty or loneliness but not under immediate threat of global annihilation. She didn't have to worry about them, and she didn't miss living on the streets.

So, what was it?

"Pan, I'm sad."

"I know. Me too."

"How did you know I was sad? And…wait, why are *you* sad?"

"I have no idea. We've created a near-idyllic world here, haven't we? Solved all the problems. These creatures know their own struggles and fears, but never on the magnitude of having to deal with something like nuclear explosions. We did it. We won."

"Right. So, why are we sad?"

Panicum stretched with his paws far out in front, flexing his toes. "I think maybe we feel the loneliness of keeping the secret. None of them can know what it was like to live through the terror of fighting against creatures with broken minds, or worrying about radiation being blown in on a wind that can cause deadly illness. None of their villages have been destroyed by the Legate, which is good—and yet, they are missing out on the whole truth."

"But that's a good thing! The old world was horrible."

"It was also exciting. I don't think we did anything wrong, mind you. Our decisions certainly led to the best-case scenario. But we did change the entire path of history for both arms of the timeline, and there are consequences that no one but us and Mother can see. We have to live with that."

"I do love it here. Even in these sad ruins, there isn't any real danger. And after so much death and fear, that feels wonderful."

"But what's the point of being an ambassador when everyone is always in agreement? There's no drama at all."

"Yes! That's it, exactly! Or, at least part of it. Not that I want another animal war, but…"

Panicum nodded.

"So, what do we do?" Kana said. "Just get old and fat and wait for the end in this beautiful utopia?"

"It doesn't sound so bad," Panicum said. "Maybe a bit boring."

"We're never happy, are we?" Kana asked, grinning. She sat, dangling her legs over the edge of the roof.

"Careful. If you fall off, you'll have more excitement than you ever wanted. I'm not sure even Mother could put you back together again."

"Yeah, yeah."

Kana watched the clouds race west, coming in cold from the Squamor shores. "I'm beginning to understand why Fel used to run away from his job so often, back before the war with the reptiles. During peacetime, there's not enough to do. If a leader does a really good job, there's not much to lead."

The wind picked up, blowing hard enough to brush Panicum's fur backwards, showing the undercoat. The clouds brought with them a drizzle which misted Kana's face with tiny, frigid drops.

"It'll snow soon," Panicum said, twitching his fur. "In weeks, if not days. I hope the weather isn't quite as cold this year. Two solid months cooped up in the castle won't make us feel any less trapped than we already do."

And there it was. As soon as Panicum said it out loud, Kana knew it to be true. She felt trapped. Had she really made the right decision? Her old home, in Chicago, had been often unpleasant. But it had felt so enormous, so full of potential. She had already explored almost the entire Kingdom, even before meeting the Legate. It was much smaller than the world she had grown up in.

The roof creaked and gave way. Kana slid backwards, grasping at pipes sticking up from the panels, and managed to slow her fall enough to avoid breaking an ankle as she landed in the building's top floor.

Panicum howled into the dark hole. "Kana! Are you okay? Talk to me!"

"I'm fine. Feet hurt a little, but I don't think anything's broken. Except the roof, of course."

Kana looked around, trying to see through the evening shadows. The room was part of an old attic, well-preserved against the destruction of time's passage. A wooden rocking horse leaned against a wall, one of its curved skis snapped in half. A rusted metal filing cabinet supported a rotten wicker bassinet. Empty cans littered the floor. A decaying wooden dresser was covered in nautical knick-knacks; coiled rope, a winch, a fishing pole, a brass compass, and a miniature boat complete with string rigging and a cotton sail.

Little plastic sailors worked on its deck, hauling nets and scrubbing with mops.

Kana's eyes returned to the compass.

"Pan, what's past the ocean?"

"What?" he asked, startled. "What on earth do you mean? Come up out of there before the floor collapses beneath you."

"The other side of the ocean. What's out there? This continent that the Kingdom is on is pretty small. It's surrounded by water on all sides, which I suspect is a result of accelerated global warming after the war. But I'm sure there are other land masses out there, across the water."

Kana stuffed the brass compass in her jacket hood, pulled the string tight to make sure it stayed, and climbed the pile of broken rafters like a ladder back up to the roof.

"I…well, I never thought about it before," Panicum said. "I don't think anyone has. The ocean is nothing more or less than the end. The whole Kingdom is here."

"But there could be other Kingdoms out there. Other continents. If there are, wouldn't you want to see them?"

Panicum fell silent, stunned. He whipped his tail back and forth, cleaning the mud from a small spot on the roof with his brush as he thought.

"I suppose…I suppose it's possible. But how?"

"On a boat. We could get a boat."

"A what?"

Kana grinned.

"Are you mad?"

Fel's eyes were wide open with dismay. Kana had explained the plan to him three times, but everything she said just seemed to make him more confused.

"We want to build a boat. A platform that floats on water. I'm sure you've seen one in your books. Then we can see what's across the ocean. It's as simple as that."

"But, why? Surely that would be terribly dangerous. What could drive you to do such a thing?"

Kana shrugged. She didn't want to admit that she was bored, or even discontent. Life in the castle was beautiful and simple, and she valued that. But it wasn't enough. Fel had a wanderlust of his own; she was surprised he did not understand.

"It might be dangerous, but I still want to go. Think of it this way; your ambassador—that's me, remember?—wants to go see if there is another continent out there, and if I find one, I want to establish a friendly relationship with it. Isn't that worth risking something for?"

Fel thought. Establishing diplomatic relations was an idea he could grasp. "I see the logic in that. But…across the water? Perhaps even beyond Paragon Mobula's domain? It seems unlikely. You'll fall right off the end of the earth."

"The earth is round, Fel. We've been over this before. It's a sphere."

Fel frowned.

Kana sighed. "Look, just think about it. I'd need a small team of carpenters, some wood, and some tools. And rations to take on the trip."

"And I'd be going, too," Panicum said.

Kana looked around. "Really, Pan? You sure? I might never come back."

"Are you seriously asking me that?" Panicum said, smiling. "To the end of the earth…and off it, if need be. Of course I'm coming."

"I'd probably want another volunteer, to help with steering, but no more than one. We won't have room for more than three."

Fel sighed. "I suppose, if you can find someone. We have plenty of materials. If this is something you're quite sure you want to do…"

"It is."

"Then I will assist. But I ask that you take your time with the crafting of this boat, and wait until winter has passed to set out. Will you do that?"

"Yes, Fel. We'll go in April, at the earliest. That gives us four months."

Fel grinned, showing his teeth. "You've been living here with me for three whole years now, ever since I freed you from Paragon Falca, so long ago. I've become accustomed to having you here, Kana. I will miss you."

"Well, I'm not leaving yet. We'll make some good memories before I go. And who knows? Maybe some day I'll arrive on your doorstep again, with stories of a new world."

Construction of the boat was difficult with the tools available, but Fel put out a call across the lands for his finest engineers, and Kana explained the basics of sailing to them. It was a topic she knew little about, but she understood the need for a sail and mast. The rest of the details she found in one of Fel's ancient books; *A Beginner's Guide to Ocean Sailing, Volume 1.*

They set up the initial construction site in the training yard until the basic structure was complete, then moved the frame to a seaside location in Squamor, south of the Neath Gap, for the remaining work. Major Ursa, who had been bored in the peace which had settled since Felidae and Falcoformia had cooperated to defeat Squamor in the Sphere War, took a special interest in the worksite. She assigned a few of the younger bear guards to supply the workers with food and drinks, and to build a dock under Kana's supervision. By night, Ursa kept an eye on the shipyard personally, to make sure it stayed clear of curious trespassers. During the day, crowds of curious reptiles gathered near the yard, peeking at the wooden ship with a mix of superstition and excitement.

When winter arrived, a shed was built over the boat to keep the snow off the backs of the workers. The mast was erected shortly after midwinter, and boxes for food storage were built into a hutch which was secured into the center of the ship's deck. Reed mats were laid inside the hutch to serve as beds—three of them. One for Kana, one for Panicum, and one for the volunteer she had yet to find.

"It needs to be someone easygoing, you know?" Panicum said. "Laid back. This trip might get pretty scary. And they can't be too annoying, either. We could be out there together for a long time."

"We'll run out of food if we're out there for too long," Kana said.

"Don't remind me."

Kana had asked several prospects about the journey. She knew better than to ask Fel. After his victory over Squamor in the Sphere War, his adventuring days had ended, and he spent much of his time snacking in his throne room. Most of the denizens of the Kingdom were too content to want to leave. The few who seemed interested were not anyone Kana wanted to trust with her life. By mid-March the ship was ready to sail, and she and Panicum had started taking it out on practice runs. The two-man crew was becoming desperate for a third.

"I guess we don't *have* to have another," she told Panicum. "It's only that if one of us gets hurt, it would be nice to still have a two person team, you know? And with three, our watch-shifts would only be eight hours long."

"There's more room for food if it's just us," Panicum said.

"I suppose."

Then, one evening in late March, Barbar approached the worksite.

"Madam Ambassador?" He spoke with his head down and his tail tucked between his hind legs. "Ambassador Kana, I mean."

"Yes? What is it, Barbar?"

"I thought, perhaps, if you are still looking for another crew member, you might consider me."

Kana grinned. She had considered Barbar, but had dismissed the idea due to his natural timidity since being injured the war. Before he lost a paw in the battle against the reptiles, he had been brave and calm in the face of danger. But now he was quiet, soft-spoken for a lion, always unsure of himself and keenly aware of his loss. She had never imagined he might be interested.

"Well, Barbar, I'll definitely consider you. I had no idea. But, if you don't mind me asking, why do you want to go with us?"

Barbar looked down at his remaining paw. "I'm not sure, really. But I feel like perhaps I was meant for…something more. I no longer run drills with my teams, now that I can't keep up. There are no more battles for me to fight, yet I have found nothing that is worthy to replace them. I nurse my wound, and live the life of an honored veteran. But that's not, uh…"

"Go on. It's okay."

"I don't mean any disrespect to either you or to Paragon Fel, Ambassador. But that's not enough for me. I want more. I want a life worth living."

Kana nodded. "I understand. And you are welcome to join us. We are lucky to have you."

"Really?" Barbar said. His legs shook with nervous excitement. "Are you sure?"

"Absolutely. You're perfect, Barbar. I'll tell Pan, and I'm sure he'll agree. So, get yourself ready to sail. We leave in two weeks!"

The next week, a storm arrived from the east, delaying their preparations for departure. By then, Kana had learned all she could from the sailing books in Fel's library, and she was as confident as she could be with tacking and steering. It was time to leave, but she was rooted on the shore, watching thunderheads race in succession from the eastern horizon. Lightning struck the tents they camped in near the beach, and Barbar's confidence was rattled. Kana expected to deal with this kind of weather in the open ocean, and the storm made her wonder if she had lost her mind. As fierce as the storm felt on land, it would surely be intensified in their rocking sailboat, adrift out in the sea.

At night she held the compass in her hands, spinning it as she watched the needle point ever-north. It worked perfectly, one of the most well-preserved items she had seen in this world. Like it was waiting for her. Her awareness of the storm overhead was keen and constant. What had those clouds seen, in the distant east? What had they passed over on their way to the Kingdom? Who had looked up at them, wondering where they traveled to in the west?

After several days, the weather finally cleared and the wind switched directions. Kana was pleased to see the boat had endured the storm well. The workers had been diligent under her direction, ensuring tight seals between the precious milled boards and slats they had labored so hard to perfect with their clumsy tools. The ship was a striking example of collaboration between humans and animals. It was comfortably rustic in the common style of animal craftsmanship, yet there was a precision to the lines and angles which only could have been accomplished with human direction.

As the sun peeked through the clouds on the day of departure, a crowd gathered to admire the sturdy little ship. Twinkling raindrops studded the railing like strings of diamonds. The waxed wood shone golden in the sun. It was a beautiful creation, full of life and hope for the future—and it was ready for adventure.

Whispers rippled through the crowd. "Fel! It's Fel! The Paragon Exemplar himself has arrived!"

Fel, accompanied by his lion guard, approached the camps. He grinned with pride as he observed the finished ship, and waved at Kana.

"Hope you don't mind me paying you a visit. I wanted to see you off."

"Nothing could make me happier, Fel."

"May I?" Fel gestured toward the ship. "I trust it is seaworthy?"

"It'd better be," Panicum said.

Fel stepped from the dock to the ship, wobbling on the bobbing platforms. He walked to the stern and waved his hat at the crowd.

"Mammals, birds, and reptiles…and humans," he said, nodding at Kana. "It is my esteemed pleasure to dedicate this ship to its captain, Ambassador Kana Kobayashi." He turned to Kana with tears in his eyes. "She came to us three years ago, a stranger to our lands, and brought with her an openness of mind and strength of spirit that I have never before seen in another creature. She has acted as my loyal subject, often speaking on my behalf to our friends at Falcoformia in the west and our new allies in Squamor to the east, helping to reestablish a lasting peace across all our lands since the end of the war. For above all, Kana is a peacekeeper, and that is the highest praise I can give."

Fel turned and looked into Kana's eyes. "One more thing I

would say. If there ever was another war—and I hope there never is—there is no one I would rather have by my side. If I were ever to falter at my post, I know she would call me back."

Kana blushed. "Paragon Fel, you honor me."

"May your journey be safe and fruitful. Panicum the clever, Lieutenant Barbar the courageous, and Kana Kobayashi, my dearest friend." A fat tear rolled down Fel's nose. "We will miss you all, and await your safe return." The king turned to Kana. "What is the name of this ship to be?"

Kana looked down at Panicum, and he nodded. After much discussion over several nights, they had both agreed on a name: the *Legato*.

One of Paragon Fel's attendants handed him a bottle of honey-wine, which he smashed against the prow. "Then I dub this ship, the *Legato!*"

The crowd cheered.

"Thank you, Fel," Kana said. "With your blessing, we will surely succeed."

The crowd cheered again. Lions roared, lizards hissed, pups and cubs danced in circles on the beach as the Paragon disembarked. A flock of small birds circled overhead, chirping in excitement.

Kana, Panicum, and Barbar stepped from the dock onto the ship, and faced the crowd.

"My heart's pounding, Pan," Kana said.

"Mine too, but I suppose that's nothing new."

Kana turned to the fox. "You're braver than you think." She turned to Barbar. "And I'm so glad you're here with us, Barbar."

"Thank you. I will protect you with my life, Ambassador."

"You already have."

Barbar tilted his head in confusion, but Kana only smiled.

"Kana? You ready?" Panicum sunk his teeth into the rope that secured the ship to the dock, ready to pull the knot loose.

"Yep! Let's do this!"

Panicum pulled the rope, freeing the ship to move away from the dock. It rocked in the receding tide for a moment, then eased toward the open ocean. They were on their way.

Salt spray whipped up the side of the ship and wet Kana's face, filling her with a thrill of anticipation. She wiped the glass of the brass compass with her sleeve, then set it in a crate near the rudder where it could not tumble into the water.

Barbar sat atop the hutch, the wind ruffling his mane. He held his shortened leg forward like a fierce gargoyle as he looked back and forth between sea and shore with exhilaration. Panicum was at the bow, with his back to the land; he had already left the Kingdom behind in his heart, even though the shore was still within view. All his attention was focused on the horizon.

Kana watched the cheering crowd disappear into the distance. As the cheering began to fade, Kana spotted the king. From the peak of a sand dune, Fel observed the boat's departure. Was there some part of his heart that wished he was on the boat with them? The old Fel—the Fel from before his victory in the Sphere War, and subsequent years of indolence—would not have missed this journey for all the world. Some remnant of the spirit of that adventurous cat from the old Kingdom must still remain.

Kana shook her head. She had to look to the future, and stop living in the past. This was her time, and she was ready for it.

"Ready about!" she called out.

"Ready!" Panicum replied, dashing across the deck.

She grinned at the old fox, and he grinned back at her.

"All right. Let's go!"

Kana unfurled the sail, and the *Legato* sped east unhindered.

Dear Reader,

If you enjoyed this book, please leave a review!

Independent authors can not keep writing awesome books unless readers leave reviews. If you want to support writers, leave your opinion or rating wherever you found this book so others can learn from your experience.

You can also sign up for my newsletter at www.ccluckey.com and get early access to FREE short stories, information on becoming part of my limited advance reader team, and updates on my upcoming new releases.

Thank you for reading!

– C.C.

C.C. Luckey writes uniquely imaginative and eerie stories influenced by her studies for degree in Philosophy. Prior to beginning her writing career, she spent many years working as a costumer for a variety of productions ranging from volunteer theater troupes to Hollywood feature films. As a multi-talented actor and musician, she has had many unique experiences including performing on stage to sold-out Los Angeles amphitheaters, extensive cross-country travel, and playing live music to an audience of millions on national television. She lives in Long Beach, California in a 100-year-old house with her husband and two corgi dogs. Follow C.C. Luckey at her web site (www.ccluckey.com) for free content, information on how to become part of a limited advance reader team, and updates on new releases. She can also be found on Facebook at @ccluckey and Twitter @ccluckey_author.

www.ingramcontent.com/pod-product-compliance
Lightning Source LLC
Chambersburg PA
CBHW030834110726
47900CB00006B/1890